THE WINGLESS KING

K.C WASSEM

Book Cover by David Garcias

Edited by Tabatha Chandler

Map by K.C Wassem using Map Effects

Scene breaks by Torie Beller

First edition 2024

For my family, for always believing in me.

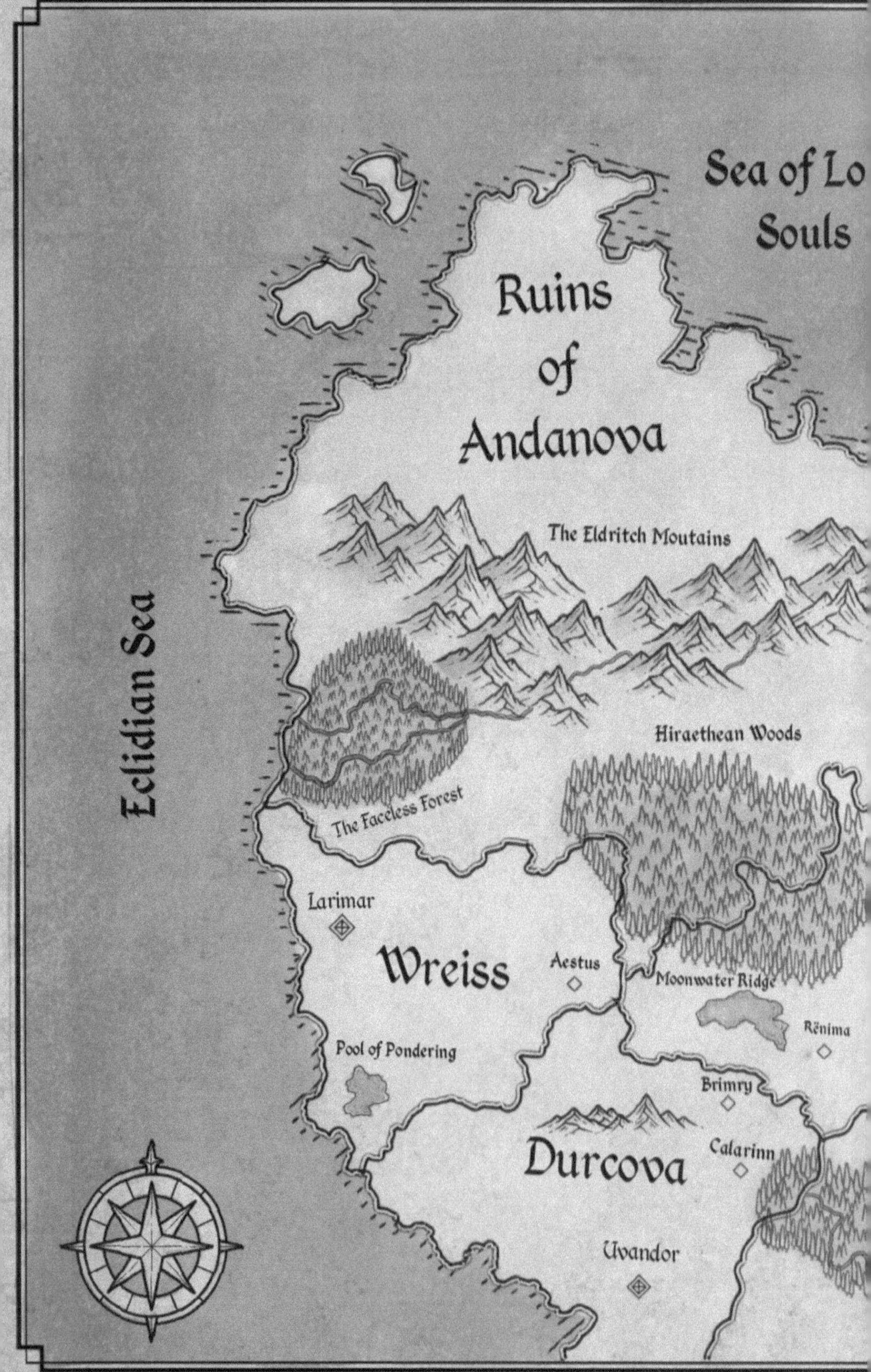

Sea of Lo
Souls
Ruins
of
Andanova
The Eldritch Moutains
Hiraethean Woods
Eclidian Sea
The Faceless Forest
Larimar
Wreiss
Aestus
Moonwater Ridge
Rĕnima
Pool of Pondering
Brimry
Calarinn
Durcova
Uvandor

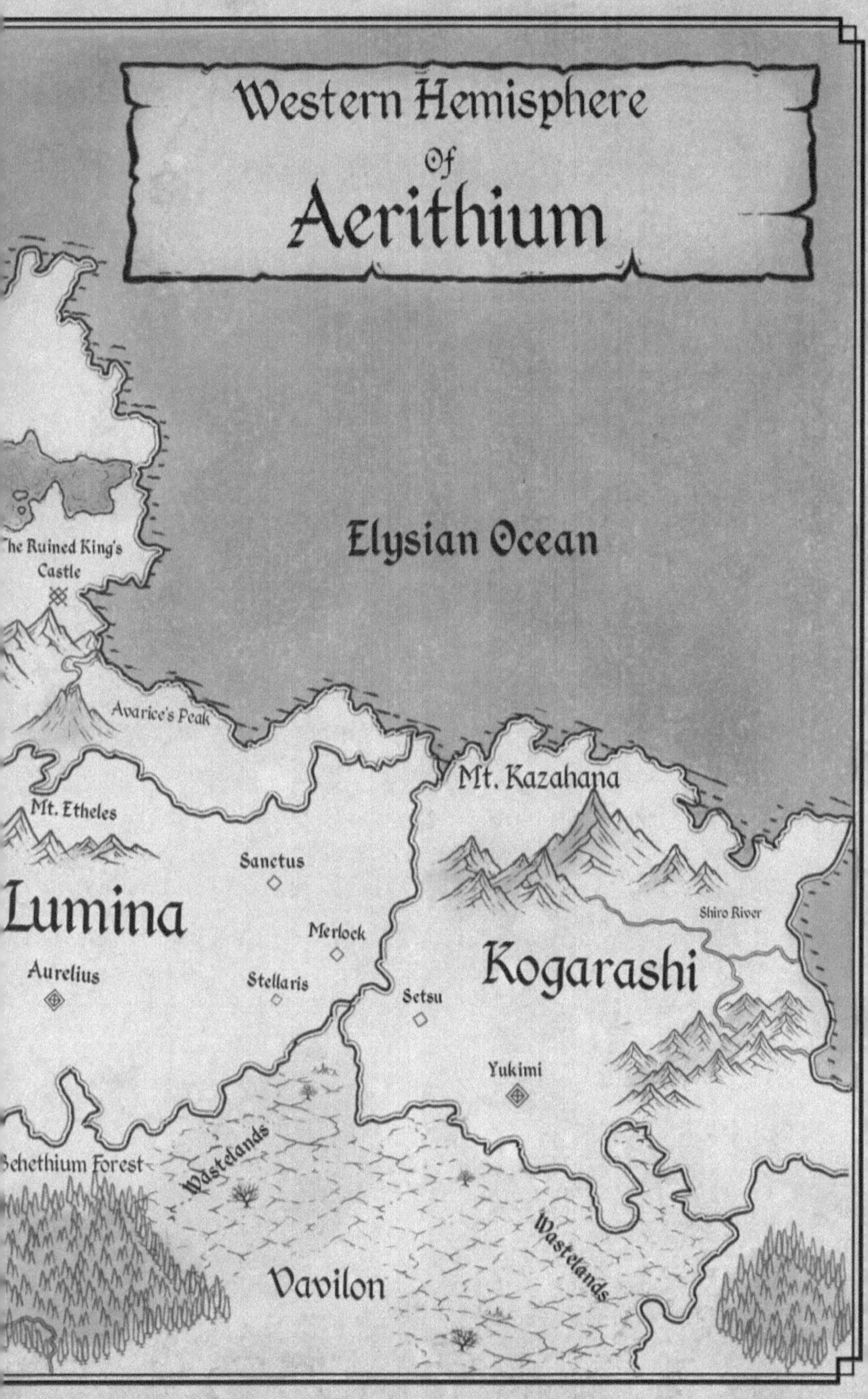

Western Hemisphere
Of
Aerithium
Elysian Ocean
The Ruined King's Castle
Avarice's Peak
Mt. Kazahana
Mt. Etheles
Sanctus
Lumina
Merlock
Shiro River
Aurelius
Stellaris
Kogarashi
Setsu
Yukimi
Wastelands
Behethium Forest
Wastelands
Vavilon

"Are humans the root of all evil?

Or was evil born from the otherlings?

A vile sickness that consumes human souls,

A disease borne from bygone sins.

Does He whisper in our ears?

Is the coercion of treachery too much to bear?

Are men born wicked?

Or does a man evolve into a monster?

That the Devil wishes him to be?

Or is this the delusion we feed ourselves?

Only to dim the fear in our hearts,

That dares to devour us bone by bone,

Splinter by splinter,

Until not even our soul has a home to remain."

The Personal Diary of Felix Amos

Prologue

1013 A.E.C.

It had been snowing for several days, bringing an endless winter. The cypress trees groaned, burdened by the weight of the ice and snow that clung to every branch. Seeking refuge from the sharp gusts of wind, Aiden leaned his aching body against the cracked walls of the church. The frigid air nearly shook him to his core, piercing his bones through his winter robes. Aiden shifted slightly against the wind, his ankles brushing against the burgundy hellebores that littered the icy grass. With a sigh, he looked into the dreary sky as if anticipating an answer from the heavens.

Positioned high up in towering buildings across the way, a young child sat perched upon a frosted windowsill. With one hand supporting his rounded chin and the other pressed gently against the azure-stained glass, his fingertips traced the paths of the falling snowflakes. As the powdery downfall intensified, the child's fascination seemed to be overcome with boredom, compelling him to withdraw his finger. At that moment, as their eyes unexpectedly met, an unfamiliar chill coursed through Aiden.

The waif had arrived weeks ago, clinging unrelentingly to his mother's side. Aiden found himself unable to shake the memory of that peculiar night, the events replaying in his mind. The boy's mother had arrived on the church's doorstep during twilight. Aiden was struck by the young woman's stunning beauty from the second he laid eyes on her, his breath catching in his throat. Without a word, he ushered her inside the church. She tentatively entered, clutching her son as if someone would rip him from her embrace.

It was difficult for Aiden to get a read on the pair, as neither the woman nor her son had uttered a single syllable throughout the first night. So, Aiden had summoned Enid, his handmaiden, to ensure their comfort. As the High Priest, Aiden's commands were law.

The Church of Caelestis served as a haven for prayer and a sanctuary for those seeking solace. The church welcomed all who entered without judgment or hesitation. Many people lived in the residential buildings lining the church's estate, and throughout their small community, curiosity brewed regarding the mysterious woman's arrival. Still, Aiden refrained from pressuring the woman into speaking and expected the same from everyone else.

After three days, she finally said her name, Emeryn. Her name was like honey on his lips.

"You can rest at ease here, Emeryn," Aiden assured her. "I may not know what you are seeking sanctuary from, but I promise that within these sacred walls, you are safe."

Her cheeks blossomed like a red rose. "What makes you think I am hiding from something?" she whispered. Emeryn's eyes instinctively shifted to her son. The small child, hardly even six years old, sat at her feet, playing with a small, ragged bear that Enid had kindly given him.

There was no doubt that there was something strange about Emeryn's son. When Aiden focused his Sight on him, he noticed a distorted Aura, as if a presence shielded the child. The Sight was a rare gift bestowed upon a select few. It allowed its bearers to perceive beyond the ordinary. However, it was only when the boy fell ill that Aiden could see beyond the strange Aura. Then, he noticed the violet hue plaguing the child's irises, an anomaly he had never encountered before.

Even so, Aiden couldn't discern any malevolence in the boy. Demons of great power could conceal themselves among humans with certain abilities, but the boy's nature seemed benign. As the child recovered from his illness, his Aura once again became distorted. Nevertheless, the High Priest couldn't shake the unsettling feeling that there was something truly extraordinary about him.

"Is it true?" Emeryn had asked. "True evil cannot enter the holy grounds of the church?"

Aiden vividly recalled the sensation of her touch on that fateful day. His eyes softened, and he grabbed Emeryn's hands without thinking. He held her soft palms against his as if they'd known each other for years.

"Yes. These walls were built with ancient materials and holy crystalline that I perform blessings on routinely. True evil cannot enter without extreme difficulty. And even if you cannot trust anyone else in the world, I hope someday—you can trust me." And this was true. Protective jewels and stones adorned the walls with murals depicting scriptures, including the tale of Adamus and Eden, the first two humans.

Aiden had often seen Emeryn strolling along the magnificent walls of the church, her fingers brushing past the embossed artwork. He couldn't help but be captivated by her, a compelling force drawing him closer. Aiden had developed a deep affection for this young woman, desperately hoping she would remain by his side indefinitely. Her beauty was unparalleled in Aiden's eyes, but it wasn't just her appearance that ensorcelled him. Tenderness emanated from her, a warmth that calmed his restless soul. Aiden was confident that her heart overflowed with goodness, devoid of malicious intentions.

Yet, Emeryn kept her son far from everyone, and Aiden couldn't help but wonder why. He would toss and turn at night, wondering how the child's eyes glistened like raw amethyst, as if stardust glimmered inside him. How much did his mother know? And would she tell him the truth if he asked? Aiden was drawn to the answers to the point of obsession.

Winter soon turned to spring; the snow melted, and flowers filled the land. Colors of sunset bloomed all around the rolling hills, and sweet scents carried on the afternoon breeze. Aiden's longing for Emeryn's presence had not been in vain, for she finally appeared before him on the day of the Spring Equinox celebration. She burst into his study, her cheeks full of color. Peonies and lilacs decorated her hair, carefully woven into a delicate braid that encircled her head like a crown.

"I know you see it," she said breathlessly. The smell of celebratory wine lingered on her breath. "I know you have the Sight. I have heard rumors about you."

Aiden tried to hide his surprise that she knew of his gift.

"Yes," he said calmly. "So, are you aware of your son?"

Emeryn's eyes welled up with tears, and she slumped into a chair.

"Yes," she sighed.

"Do you know what he is?"

"No."

A sour taste filled the inside of Aiden's mouth. She was lying. This lie appeared well-hidden and vital for her to keep. He could feel the heaviness in the room as her eyes bore into him.

She stood up, stumbling slightly in her drunken state. "Let's not speak of this ever again," she snapped. Her intensity surprised him, as he had not even witnessed this side of her before. Her eyes softened. "Please."

A realization struck Aiden, reminiscent of his countless hours immersed in his studies. What if the boy's presence within the church was not merely a coincidence? What if he held the key to everything Aiden had devoted his entire life preparing for? The notion dawned upon him that the boy could be the long-awaited missing piece, the answer to unraveling the mysteries that had consumed him for so long.

ONE

"When the wind underneath was stolen, the sound of the choir carried a noiseless blunder, the righteous sin. 'Tis the careless-ness of mankind, and brevity of human life."

—Book One of Metanoia

1025 A.E.C.

He was finally free. This was where he belonged and where he had always longed to be. His fingers grazed the clouds, and the wind kissed his face. The zephyrs gently ruffled his hair as he touched the heavens. He was laughing, and the stars were laughing with him. And there, in all its glory, he saw it radiating above him, the brightest star in the sky. He reached out to grab it and claim it as his own. He was so close, but the moment his fingers brushed across the light, his hand faltered. He was sent hurtling into the depths below. Deeper. Farther. Until he couldn't see the light anymore. Was this the last time he'd see the sky? Who was crying? Was it him? Who...was...he?

A cold voice pierced through his mind.

"Sedate him again."

No, he pleaded silently.

He didn't want to sleep.

A sharp, searing sensation shot through his arm, spreading its claws with a familiar grip. His body froze, immobile, as if all connections between his mind and muscles had been severed. The darkness called, pulling him toward its depths and threatening to consume him entirely. A fleeting moment of recognition flashed through his mind as if he had arrived exactly where he was supposed to be. It didn't take long for him to surrender to the darkness as it enveloped him like an old friend.

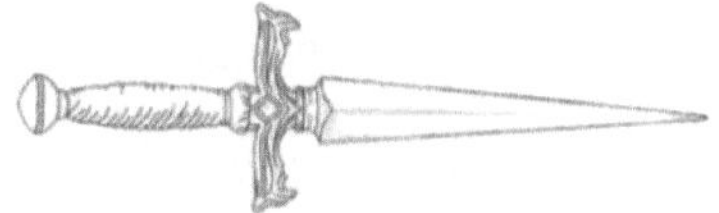

"*Wake up,*" a velvety voice spilled across the void. Whispers flooded the abyss from all directions. "*You must wake up. You are stronger than this.*"

But he didn't want to wake up. He longed to remain in the darkness, to let it consume his entire essence until nothing was left. What did it matter? He didn't even know his name, and the sky was gone. Nothing mattered.

"*Seren.*" The voice transformed, seething with anger, its tone sharp as glass. "*Seren, wake up!*"

That's right. Seren. That was his name.

The world transformed as light flooded in, blinding and overwhelming.

"Welcome back, Seren."

But this voice was different. There was nothing warm or comforting about it. It was condescending and cruel.

Through the murky haze of black spots, Seren fought to discern the slender figure looming above him. It took every ounce of effort to pierce through the shrouded veil of darkness. Then, like a fragile mirage, the man materialized before his eyes. Under the unforgiving glow of the lights, the man's sharp, angular features came into focus, resembling a cunning fox. His pale complexion contrasted starkly against the artificial illumination, and his piercing gaze met Seren's.

"Who are you?" Seren coughed. A dry rasp escaped his throat, each syllable cracking painfully.

"Interesting," the man mused. "This again."

A bout of rage surged within Seren's chest, like a feral creature awoken from a deep slumber. He instinctively jerked forward, only to be abruptly halted by the icy grip of steel bands. Pain radiated from his wrists and ankles as he fought against the restraints.

How long had he been struggling against them?

"What is this?" Seren asked, his voice quivering. He pulled against the restraints again, feeling the color drain from his face.

"Going somewhere?" the man sneered.

Seren's head whipped around as realization dawned on him. He and the strange man were not alone. White-coated figures, engrossed in their tasks, surrounded them. One woman caught his attention, her hand reaching for a beaker on the counter, causing its contents to surge and froth with vibrant, fiery hues. Scientists? Seren couldn't believe his eyes, nor did he want to.

These scientists moved with eerie indifference, their impassive expressions devoid of surprise or curiosity, as they occasionally cast glances in his direction. It was as if Seren's presence, bound and captive, was an inconsequential backdrop to their work.

The foxlike man muttered incomprehensible words under his breath while he focused on a glowing blue device in his hand—a Holographus. Seren shook his head as if trying to expel the thought. He shouldn't even know what the device was called, let alone be in the same room with these people.

"What is this place?" Seren managed.

Seren received brief, lazy glances from the crowd, but a young man with tousled, golden locks stood out. His perplexed expression, etching deep furrows on his forehead, betrayed an anxious energy that manifested in restless fidgeting. Their eyes briefly locked, but the young man's gaze darted away instantly as if evading Seren's stare like a criminal fleeing the scene.

"Where am I?" Seren repeated. Though he already knew the answer, he couldn't help but voice the question aloud. There was no mistaking it. He was in the Godless City. The evidence was sprawled before him.

Countertops lined the walls; each flooded with an assortment of test tubes and syringes, their contents varying from empty to some containing remnants of a bluish liquid. Somnia. A shiver traveled down his spine as he somehow recalled the madness the drug could induce. Was this what these crazed scientists had been subjecting him to? Was this even real?

Seren's eyes swiveled upwards, locking onto a security camera with its lenses fixated perfectly on him. How many unseen watchers sat on the other side? The absence of windows and the singular steel door further reinforced the notion that escape was impossible. This place was meant to confine him. His heart pounded in his chest frantically.

"Can someone answer me?" Seren demanded.

The strange man tore his gaze away from his Holographus, a glint of amusement dancing in his eyes as he shifted his attention to Seren. The screen's projection temporarily appeared, providing Seren with a glimpse of the glowing words.

Subject Zero: Male, 18 years old.

"Are you enjoying yourself?" the man snapped. "I don't have time for games."

"Enjoying myself?" Seren sputtered. And to think he was accusing him of playing games. Was this man insane?

The young man, who had been discreetly stealing additional glances in their direction, hesitantly sat up from his seat. "Uhm, Doctor Lumen?" he stammered. "Forgive me if I am overstepping, but wouldn't it make sense if he's having amnesic side effects? It's a miracle he's still alive. Nobody has ever survived this amount of Somnia before."

Seren tensed at the words. So, they had been pumping him full of drugs. Was that why his head felt so heavy?

The doctor remained fixed on Seren, not acknowledging that the young man had spoken to him. "Seren, we have known each other for quite some time. You're hurting my feelings," Lumen purred. "I am not in the mood for your silly little antics."

"I'm not playing games," Seren said through clenched teeth.

Lumen let out an exasperated sigh as if the conversation was boring him. He leaned forward, his platinum hair falling around his yellow-rimmed glasses. "You may have forgotten your sad, pathetic past," he said. "But I know you have not forgotten me."

Seren flexed his hand, clenching it tightly as if he could feel Lumen's skinny neck under his grip. The tension in the room thickened with every passing second.

"I guess you're not very memorable," Seren replied bitterly.

Lumen leaned forward, his face hovering inches from Seren's. His piercing gaze locked onto Seren, their breaths almost mingling. "Wouldn't that be convenient?" Lumen whispered. "To forget all your sins?" His fingers tapped on the metal surface of Seren's confinement. "I think we both know the truth. You and I aren't much different." A strand of Lumen's long hair brushed against Seren's bare shoulders. "Weren't you the one who called me a *monster*?"

Frustration boiled over within Seren, surging through his veins like an electric current. With a sudden, desperate lunge, he propelled his body forward. The gurney's entire frame shuddered violently under the force of his attack, the metal legs screeching in protest as it wobbled on the floor.

An unmoving pillar of calm, Lumen's eyes, cool and calculating, met Seren's with a faint, knowing glint. A subtle smile curled at the corners of his lips, revealing a confidence that seemed to say, "You can try, but you won't escape."

"I want to know why I'm in the Godless City," Seren spat. "I don't belong here."

Feigning a frown, Lumen's voice dripped with sarcasm. "Oh, do you think so?" The doctor took a step backward, casually tucking his hands into his pockets. "You're starting to sound like a sniffling child."

Once more, Seren lunged forward, demanding, "Tell me!"

The room seemed to freeze, scientists pausing at his outburst.

"Ah, there it is," Lumen remarked, his voice dripping with satisfaction. "There's the anger I was waiting for. I was starting to think you'd gone soft on me." Lumen paused, savoring the moment, and took a deliberate step toward Seren. "Tell me something, boy," he continued. "How does it feel? To be reduced to nothing more than a rat in my lab?"

Seren's struggle intensified, his muscles straining against the metal cuffs. Beads of sweat glistened on his forehead as he writhed against his restraints.

Lumen's grin widened. "Oh, you're quite the fighter, aren't you?" he taunted. "But those cuffs won't break, my dear Subject Zero."

"Get me out of here," Seren gasped. "I don't belong here."

"Is that all you can say?" Lumen asked. "Besides, you sure you don't belong here, Seren? I'd say you deserve to be here. This is your judgment."

Seren froze. He felt as if a knife had twisted into him. Judgment.

"I miss our talks, Seren," Lumen said softly. "But unfortunately, those will be coming to an end. You will soon be of no use to me." He turned to the young man who was, yet again, staring in their direction. "You, take the subject back to the Cerulean Room. I am done for the day."

"William," the young man said quietly.

Lumen raised his thin eyebrows. "Excuse me?"

"My name is William," he said louder than before.

"I don't recall asking for your name," the doctor growled. "Just get up and do what you've been told."

William nodded and rushed over, almost stumbling over his own feet. The soft curves of his heart-shaped face stood out next to Lumen, making it hard to believe he was a doctor or even a grown man. He couldn't be much older than Seren, who found it remarkable how young William appeared.

"By myself?" William asked nervously. "You're sure it's alright? Isn't he dangerous, sir?" He clenched his jaw, the veins in his throat bulging through his golden skin.

Lumen responded with an exasperated roll of his eyes. "You've been useless since you arrived here. Just do it." With a dismissive flick, he grumbled and tossed a set of keys into William's hands. "Unchain the gurney from the ground and wheel him. He isn't going anywhere, so there's no need to look so alarmed." Lumen waved him off, his impatience clear. "I have other business to attend to." The doctor quickly turned on his heels, heading for the door. He slipped his keycard inside a metallic box mounted on the wall. The small red light above the door glowed green.

"Wait," William blurted out. He approached Lumen, side-eying Seren as he discreetly leaned in to whisper in the doctor's ear. Lumen's patience was clearly worn thin, and he rolled his eyes once more. He responded in a hushed tone, too quiet for Seren to decipher. And without another word, Lumen vanished behind the closed door.

Silently, Seren watched as William approached him, fumbling with the keys. His uncertain blue eyes briefly met Seren's.

Seren squinted at him, his brow furrowed in confusion. "Why are you looking at me like that?" he muttered.

Without responding, William leaned down to unchain the gurney. Seren tried to raise his head, but the throbbing behind his eyes intensified. With a quiet groan, he squeezed them shut. As William leaned to unchain the gurney, he lowered his voice to hardly even a whisper. "I'm a friend."

The word sounded foreign when he spoke it. Friend? The corner of Seren's mouth twitched, almost forming a scoff, but his energy was drained. He clenched his teeth, the bitter taste of bile creeping up his throat as William wheeled the gurney across the room.

Forcing his eyes open, Seren heard the door swinging ajar. They had entered an elongated corridor, dimly lit by dreary blue overhead lights. Cameras were perched in every corner and crevice, their unblinking red eyes focused on them, tracking their every move. The gurney's wheels squealed against the cold tiles, its ominous echo ringing through the corridor. He inhaled shakily, trying to slow his pounding heart.

"Don't fall asleep, Seren. You need to stay alert for me. Okay?"

Seren's eyelids were too heavy; he could barely grasp the outline of William's face.

"I don't feel good," he managed. His mouth was dry, and every breath of air felt tiresome. "Just let me sleep."

Was he about to be denied even the simple pleasure of sleeping? Seren flexed his fingers in annoyance at the thought.

"Quiet. Listen to me. You don't belong here," William whispered hastily.

William kept his eyes forward, his pace quickening. "Please, do your best to keep awake and wait for me. You're in bad shape, Seren. I will get you out of here no matter what it takes."

The young doctor abruptly stopped wheeling Seren and inserted his keycard into a slot beside a foreboding entrance. A resonant click sounded as he forcefully swung the door open.

"Welcome back," William said bitterly. "To the Cerulean Room." As his voice filled the chamber, he leaned in, his face hovering over Seren's. "The cameras are watching, forgive me."

He positioned the gurney upright and released the shackles without another word. Seren lurched forward, descending several feet. His knees collided harshly with solid ground, echoing with a loud, agonizing thump.

The heavy door slammed shut behind him, plunging him into absolute darkness. Struggling, Seren pushed himself into a sitting position, emitting a groan of pain. The muscles between his shoulders burned with the effort. As he steadied himself, a metallic clang echoed through the room as his wrist contacted the floor. In the darkness, he felt the cold touch of a delicate bracelet encircling his wrist.

The room was too quiet. Seren's heart thumped against his ribcage, and blood roared in his ears. It was as though his fear could be heard, vibrating within the depths of his bones. He stepped back, colliding with the cold surface of the door.

The air suddenly filled with the sound of running water. It quickly pooled around Seren's ankles. He scrambled in the dark like a rat confined in a cage, searching blindly for an exit. But there was no escape. The water surged, rapidly filling the room and propelling him further into the chamber, sweeping him from the walls.

This is it, Seren thought. *This is how I die.*

Two

"When riches' reign meets its decline, royal blood shall cease to shine. Awake the Sea of Souls, so grand, as death tightens its withering hand."

—Book Two of Metanoia

1014 A.E.C.

The rain outside was deafening; it echoed through the entire church. Thunder rolled distantly in the hills, and the wind howled through the trees.

"I can't concentrate with the sound of that damn rain," Aiden cursed. Wondering if his failings were consequential, he watched the storm ravage the land. Aiden shook his head in frustration and curled his fingers in contempt. "Curse this downpour," he growled. "The rivers will flood at this rate."

The frigid, damp weather was something Aiden detested. It caused his joints to ache, and he had no energy to reserve for his pain. At thirty-five years old and burdened with numerous responsibilities as a High Priest, Aiden had more important matters to attend to. He couldn't be bothered by something as trivial as the rain.

Aiden paced relentlessly in his cramped study, mumbling like a madman. His hands trembled uncontrollably, and his blood pressure rose, but that didn't cease his manic behavior. Aiden's fingers skimmed into the chaotic stacks of paperwork on his desk, their crumpled edges grazing his skin as he sifted through them. With a sudden burst of frustration, Aiden struck the oaken table with a resounding thud. Papers took flight in all directions, floating to the ground like a flurry of autumn leaves.

"I don't understand!" Aiden shouted. "There must be something I'm missing." He rubbed the crease on his forehead.

Time was slipping away from Aiden, much like grains of sand through his fingers. The Veil—a once ethereal place that existed between the realm of the Gods and mortals—was weakening, and so too were its barriers. Over the centuries, they had thinned, and now the Veil was colliding with the human realm, two planes of existence that were never meant to meld.

In ancient times, mortals had used the Veil as a sacred bridge between the two realms, a conduit that allowed them to seek the counsel and blessings of the Gods. It was a cherished link between humanity and the divine, a source of hope and guidance that spanned the ages. But that golden age was now a distant memory, fading into the annals of history, for more than a millennium had passed since the Veil had held such a pure connection.

The Veil had fallen victim to malevolent forces, and a pervasive darkness had tainted its pure essence. However, not all of it had succumbed to this corruption; within its intricate fabric remained sanctified pockets of purity where the divine connection still thrived. The whispers of the Devil's influence echoed throughout the world, disrupting the once-harmonious balance between realms. Yet, small sacred passages endured, allowing Priests and Saints to maintain their connection with the Gods.

Aiden couldn't escape the icy grip of dread that clutched at his soul, a reminder of the imminent danger. The Veil was continuously colliding with their world, "opening" in small bursts across the land. And it was getting worse. It was only a matter of time before the worlds clashed completely, overlapping with each other indefinitely.

Aiden had gotten the news days ago—the Veil had completely overtaken the north. And for the first time in history, it had permanently merged with their world. An entire country now served as a gateway into the other realm. The Kingdom of Andanova had fallen, and no survivors, including the royal family, were left behind. The entire land had become hell on earth, and the demons had consumed the souls of every Andanovan.

Even the natural order of the cosmos had begun to unravel. The moon's cycles, a steady rhythm that guided their lives, had become erratic. The Veil's openings, once predictable passages, now fluctuated wildly, creating a maddening uncertainty that haunted Aiden's every thought. Even some of his followers of the Trinity had lost their faith and turned to the Godless City in fear. Aiden knew the truth. Even Vavilon's technological advances would fall short when the Sundering came to pass.

A faint knock echoed through the study, startling Aiden. He hastily began to load his arms with the scattered papers, trying to fix his mess. The door creaked open, an eye peering in curiously.

"May I come in, Aiden?"

Emeryn stepped through the door, her cream-colored nightgown brushing against her bare ankles.

"You're up late," Aiden said, trying to sound calm. "Still losing sleep?"

Rosy blush filled her cheeks, a feature she could never hide. She twirled her fingers nervously in her loose curls. "Yes. I was thinking about what you said the other day. Are you sure it's a good idea?"

Aiden's shoulders relaxed. He smiled gently, setting down the loose papers in his hands. He strode over to her, tenderly lifting her chin. "Oh, Emeryn, of course I am." Aiden ran his hand down the small of her back.

She leaned in slightly at his touch. "But what would they think of you?" she murmured. "My son is not yours, and I don't even know who his father is. It's...blasphemous."

He rested a finger on her full lips. "I don't care, Emeryn. We will be diligent to keep this to ourselves. And even if rumors are to spread, and judgment is cast upon me, I am bound to this church by blood. I am the High Priest. You have nothing to worry about."

Aiden lovingly pressed his lips against hers. Emeryn moaned in response as her mouth parted and her head tilted. The taste of cherries intertwined with her breath while the faint scent of roses cascaded from her. She pressed her supple body against Aiden. He pulled away, still cupping her chin. "And even if you lie to me, I'll always forgive you."

Emeryn's eyes widened, and she pushed him away. "What do you mean?" she demanded. "I have never lied to you."

Immediately regretting his words, Aiden set a hand on her slender shoulder. "Forget what I said, Emeryn. You should rest." Aiden turned his back to her, his heart heavy. He watched the relentless rain pelt against the yellow roses outside his window, the petals barely clinging on. "Forgive me. I'm under a lot of pressure right now."

She sighed softly. "There's nothing anyone could have done for Andanova, Aiden. None of us could have known that such a tragedy was coming."

"I know," Aiden murmured. "It was destined to happen. It was their fate. And if something is not done, and the prophecies are not fulfilled, then it is our fate as well." Aiden turned to Emeryn, his expression wild. "And what if the answer is here, right now? What if he is sleeping up in the church tower?"

With her back against the wall, she studied Aiden's face in the flickering candlelight. "Aiden, what are you implying?"

Aiden's trembling fingers seized a green leather-bound book from his desk in a frenzy. He fumbled with the golden clasp that held it shut, the metal jingling as it fell open. His eyes darted across the aged pages, scanning for the right words to show her.

"On the day of the Spring Equinox, Emeryn, you told me. You said you knew I could see it. And I can. His Aura is different, unlike anything I've ever witnessed. The Kingdom of Andanova, the relentless whispers of the Auguries, it's all here, right before our eyes. Don't you see? It aligns with the scriptures and the prophecies the Seers have upheld for centuries. The Sundering is fast approaching, closer with each passing day." Aiden's voice wavered as he spoke. He ran a frantic hand through his disheveled black hair. "I just want you to understand, Emeryn. I'm terrified that my words might scare you away, but I can't keep this truth to myself any longer."

He pointed to a section in the book. "Don't you see?"

Emeryn took a deep breath. "Is this the sole reason you let us stay? Because you believe he's connected to all of this?"

Startled, Aiden placed the book on the desk and gently held her hands. "No, that's not the only reason. I promise you."

Her expression remained unreadable, her hands lax in his grasp.

"Who else have you shared this with?" Emeryn asked with a dry tone, closing her eyes briefly. "We may have to leave."

Aiden looked at her, desperation in his voice. "Why? What's prompting you to leave?"

"I can't explain. You wouldn't understand. I'm sorry, Aiden."

"I care for you, Emeryn. And I care for your son as well. I have not told anyone of my suspicions. I know you feel as if you must keep secrets from me, but you can trust me. I want you to feel safe here. That's all that really matters to me. But..." he trailed off. "I believe he could be the key to the prophecy that the Caelestis have waited for centuries. And if he is, it cannot be ignored."

"He's just a boy," she choked.

"Yes," he agreed. "But one day, he will be a man."

He got down on his knee and wrapped his hands tighter around Emeryn's. "Please, Em, you can trust me."

Her green eyes met his, and she squeezed his hands.

"I've always known he was different," Emeryn whispered. "But where I am from, they do not take differences lightly. I'm sorry for the way I reacted." Her gaze met the ground. "I'm scared for him." Then, she faced Aiden with her eyes filled with tears. "I want him to grow up like any other child. I want him to be happy and have a place he can call home. I need him to be safe." Her expression was pleading. "And I need you to guide him and teach him. He will need a father to look up to."

"Of course," Aiden managed.

"You mustn't tell anyone else of this," Emeryn begged. "If they find out we're here, you'll never see me again."

Aiden wanted to ask who *they* were but held his tongue. His chest ached at her words; Aiden didn't want to lose her.

"You have my word."

Aiden hid his discontent and confusion. Did she believe he could live a normal life? If Aiden was correct, then the boy needed to know. It was Aiden's duty to ensure that the child's destiny was carried out exactly as the prophecies intended. Doubts nagged at him, but deep down, Aiden remained convinced that he held significance in shaping the future of humanity.

Yet, Aiden knew that Emeryn kept secrets from him, secrets that could potentially change the course of her son's fate. Despite that, he had no desire to push Emeryn. He trusted her. No, he *loved* her. She was changing something inside of him, giving him a newfound purpose. He never believed he could trust in something as completely as his faith until her.

"Why did you come here, Emeryn?" Aiden asked.

She said nothing and walked over to the window. Aiden stood behind her, the two of them quiet as the rain pelted the glass. The wind had uprooted the roses outside, leaving nothing but a mess in their wake.

"Because," Emeryn replied. "I had nowhere else to go."

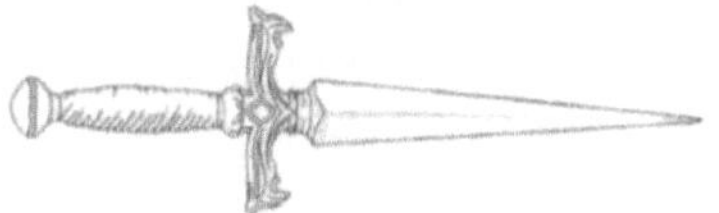

Kneeling in prayer, Aiden looked up at the painting of the Mother Goddess. Her white wings folded elegantly against her, and her snow-kissed hair flowed gracefully down her body.

"Mother Goddess, please hear me. In death, in life, and in light. I ask for you to guide me and show me the path. What can I do? Have you returned? Please... I must know."

Aiden's knees ached from the many hours he had spent here, praying repeatedly, only to be met with silence. It reminded him of his journey to Mount Etheles many years ago, when he had prayed for days on end until the Gods finally bestowed the gift of magic upon him. Except his magic waned, fading out like a flickering flame. Frustration welled up within him, and he couldn't contain it any longer. With a fierce cry, he slammed his fist into the unforgiving, cold stone floor, feeling his knees give way underneath him.

"I swear, your sacrifice will not be in vain, Alernaea," Aiden promised. He met the purple-painted eyes of the Goddess. "The Veil will be cleansed again. I will see to it. If it is the last thing I do."

THREE

*"The Mother Goddess sacrificed herself for our sins during the
Great War, hence the creation of the Veil. And what have we
done to repay Her? The sins of humanity still plague the land,
and because of this, the Godless City still stands."*

—High Priest of Aurelius

1025 A.E.C.

It could have been minutes or hours; the soundless abyss revealed no clues. Seren had no way to measure time while floating atop the water in the Cerulean Room.

The rushing of hot blood beneath his skin, the shallow, rattled pants of air, and even the persistent ache of his bones were a cacophony of sound in the otherwise silent void. Seren was alone, surrounded by emptiness, and he had felt this before. He was sure of it. All he had was the faint glimmer of hope that help would come, and the answers he sought would be within reach. William had called himself a friend, and Seren had chosen to believe that. What other choice did he have?

At least his name, Seren, sounded familiar. It comforted him to know he had something anchoring him. How long had he been here? Days?

Months? Years? He desperately wanted to remember. He willed his body to relax, attempting to release every ounce of tension that had knotted his muscles. The water around him suddenly felt warmer as he allowed himself to drift away. William's warning flooded his brain like a distress call: "Don't fall asleep, Seren."

He focused on the sound of his beating heart for several minutes.

Thump. Thump. Thump.

"I remember pain," he whispered, the words filling his mouth like sand.

And it was all he remembered—hot—searing, white pain.

Time continuously ticked by. Sleep was tempting—an escape from whatever this was. How much longer? Unless William had been lying. Seren thought of how William had stumbled on his words while talking to Lumen, resembling a scared child. Was he supposed to believe he was coming to his rescue? What a joke. And to think he'd almost believed him. Lumen and William were sure to be laughing about it. Nobody was coming.

Why was Seren even in the Godless City? The thought made his head spin as it echoed repeatedly. This place was forbidden, and those who resided here had turned their backs on the Gods forever. Who could do such a thing? And for what reason? A false sense of protection from the encroaching evil that threatened the world? Would he be denied the Gods' presence because he was here? Had they already abandoned him? A distant pang pierced his chest, prompting him to squeeze his eyes shut.

I'm sorry.

If only he could see the stars. If only they could hear him. Maybe they didn't listen to anyone in the Godless City. Perhaps Seren was so lost and alone that not even the Gods would listen to his prayers.

Please, help me. Forgive me for whatever I may have done.

A loud rumble echoed through the Cerulean Room. The water sloshed against his skin as the vibrations grew louder. He felt his body slowly sinking as the water level changed. Before long, his back connected with the hard, cold floor. In an instant, the dim illumination of blue lights flickered to life on the ceiling. He shielded himself against the sudden brightness, trying to ease the throbbing behind his eyes.

The room was much smaller than he had expected, not much larger than the lab he had been in before. A large drain sat in the middle of the tiled floor, clumps of salt clinging to its rim. Summoning all his strength, Seren staggered to his feet. His body protested, causing him to stumble into the nearby wall. Another horrible wave of nausea washed over him.

"Oh, Gods," Seren moaned. Leaning forward, he couldn't hold it any longer and retched for several minutes, although it was painfully clear that his stomach was empty. When it was finally over, he wiped his mouth and regained composure.

Squinting through the dimness, Seren's eyes locked onto a ladder that stretched upward, its rungs disappearing up to a distant platform. On that elevated platform, a sturdy metal door was the lone means of escape.

"You've got to be kidding me," he grumbled.

Carefully, he began his ascent, and with each agonizing step, groans of pain escaped past clenched teeth. Joints protested loudly, yet he pulled himself up, rung by rung, until he reached the top. Collapsing at last, he took deep, gasping breaths.

Did that jerk really have to throw me off the ledge? Seren thought.

Then, as if his thoughts had been much too loud, the door swung open on its hinges. William stood in the doorway with a silver pistol in his grip. Beads of sweat clung to his disheveled hair, and he gasped for breath. To Seren's astonishment, a broad smile spread across William's face.

"Good," he panted, his eyes traveling to Seren. "You're awake." In a casual motion, he tossed a medical gown in Seren's direction. Seren looked down at himself, realizing that he was half-dressed.

"You came back," Seren said in disbelief.

Had the Gods answered his prayers?

William reached his hand out, helping Seren on his feet. "That's one thing you should know about me," he laughed. "I *always* come back." He concealed the gun within the waistband of his lab coat. "Here, let me help."

Seren snatched the gown away as William reached for it. "I can do it myself," he muttered. He leaned against the wall for support and slid the gown over his head.

"Sorry," William said nervously.

Seren tried to stand up straight, grimacing at the ugly, multicolored gown.

"It's only temporary. Besides, I'd say you pull it off," William offered with a smile. He swung his arms over Seren's shoulders, grabbing both of his hands. Before Seren could question William's intentions, a pair of cuffs snapped around his wrists.

"Seriously?" Seren managed.

He was starting to dislike this guy.

"Trust me," William assured. "It's all a part of the plan."

"Does your plan involve throwing me six feet again?" Seren asked coldly.

"Not this time," William said with a smirk. With surprising strength, the young man interlocked his arms with Seren's, effectively sharing the burden of his weight. "Wouldn't you know? You're as light as a feather."

Seren blinked slowly. This wasn't the same timid young man he had encountered earlier.

"I'm not feeling so great," Seren admitted. "I don't know how far I'll be able to go."

William nodded emphatically. "I know. I'm going to help you."

He reached into his pocket and pulled out a syringe. Seren barely had time to react before the needle pierced his thigh, and a sharp yelp involuntarily escaped his lips. He instinctively lunged at William, slamming him against the wall. William raised his hands in a gesture of surrender.

"What the hell was that?" Seren panted. "What did you do to me?"

"I gave you adrenaline," William said calmly. "It will help you. You can trust me, Seren. Honestly."

Seren's shoulders slacked, hearing the sincerity in his voice. He reluctantly released his grip, his hands falling to his sides.

"Right," he said, his voice trembling. "Sorry."

"It's alright. Just follow me, okay?"

Seren stumbled alongside William as they made their way down the endless hallway. Each step felt unsteady and clumsy. The surveillance cameras no longer emitted their red glow, leaving them in a silence broken only by the faint shuffle of their feet against the featureless floor.

"The adrenaline should kick in any minute, Seren. Bear with me."

"Why are you doing this?" Seren huffed beside him.

"Just focus on walking. Small talk later."

And William had been right. Seren's heart began pounding in his chest as if determined to break free. Beads of sweat formed on his forehead. The weakness in his legs disappeared, replaced with a surge of vigor. His blood coursed through his veins, carrying torrents of pure energy throughout his body. Empowered by this newfound strength, he matched William's pace, no longer reliant on stumbling against him for support.

"There you go!" William shouted. "It won't be long until the security system is back on, so let's get the hell out of here!"

Seren's lungs burned, yet his body pulsed with enough energy to ignore it. The two of them pressed on, minutes blending together until they finally halted before a door marking the end of the hallway. William's hands quivered ever so slightly as he reached into his pocket, extracting a sleek keycard with the name *Lumen Yukimura*.

"How did you manage to get that?" Seren asked, gasping for breath. "Did you use the gun?"

William chuckled with a touch of nervousness and flashed Seren a mischievous grin. "I promise I didn't resort to violence. I'm just exceptionally lucky and skilled. I pickpocketed that creep and swapped my card for his."

"So, you're not a doctor, are you?" Seren asked, his words coming out slowly.

"No," William admitted. "And William isn't even my real name."

Seren's curiosity got the better of him. "Does Lumen make everyone call him by his first name?"

William's lips curved upwards. "Yeah, he's quite the character. But there's no time to delve into that now. Stay quiet, stick close, and follow my lead. I'll explain everything later."

Seren's mysterious rescuer clicked the keycard in the door, and it automatically swung open. Much to his dismay, their journey to freedom was far from complete. The newfound room before them was an expansive labyrinth of hallways, branching off in a myriad of directions. The walls and floors, composed of cold concrete, seemed to absorb every hint of warmth from the air. A chill crept over Seren's skin, causing goosebumps to prickle on his fair arms.

In the heart of the room stood a security guard cubicle, its glass windows reflecting the harsh, fluorescent lights. Seated nonchalantly, a solitary figure of stout stature reclined, engulfed in a plume of smoke from his cigarette.

"Hiya Will!" bellowed the guard. "There was a nasty storm above ground, and the security system seems to be down. I heard that the Novem thinks someone hijacked the weather simulator! Would ya believe that? Jackson and Castro are going to check out the surveillance room to try to fix the cameras. Just our luck, considering we're short-staffed today. What are you and..." He looked at Seren up and down. "That isn't *Subject Zero*, is it?" His hand slowly went to the gun on his side as his eyes narrowed. "What're you doing with him, Will? I thought Lumen made clear orders that he was never to be removed from the Cerulean Room?"

William laughed so confidently it almost seemed rehearsed. "Due to the outage, the security in the Cerulean Room is completely down. I'm on special orders. Lumen sent me to move him into a more secure facility. I am taking him to Floor Eleven. Their backup generators are up and running." Will flashed Lumen's keycard. "He gave me this earlier today in case this happened so I could access the area."

The man's face relaxed. He eyed the cuffs on Seren's wrists. "Oh, alright. He doesn't look like he'll put up much of a fight anyway."

William looked at Seren with a grimace. "Oh, he's been heavily sedated. I doubt he even knows where he is right now."

The guard took a drag off his cigarette. "Interesting. He looks like nothing more than a scrawny kid to me. Why is he so top secret?" he huffed.

William stiffened. "I guess that's why they call it a secret. I couldn't tell you. Anyway, I'll be on my way. Lumen won't be happy if I don't lock him up right away." He gripped Seren's shoulder tightly and took a sharp left.

William released a shaky breath. "Lucky for me, he isn't the brightest and believes almost anything I tell him. We probably only have a few minutes left," he whispered nervously. "Once we reach the elevator, we better pray that the guards don't realize that someone sabotaged everything in the surveillance room. It's been a miracle that I even got this far with how tight security is. Everything is going as planned so far." William gritted his teeth and rubbed the back of his neck. "If we don't get out of here fast... I'm dead or worse. I'm surprised my alias lasted this long."

"Dead?" Seren hissed. "You're risking your life for me?"

William grinned. "It's exciting, isn't it? You're my damsel in distress."

Seren hoped William noticed his annoyance at his choice of words.

They swiftly moved out of the security guard's sight, fleeing down another long hallway until they reached a set of large steel doors. Without hesitation, William swiped Lumen's keycard, and the doors opened, revealing the austere interior of the elevator. They rushed inside, and William frantically swiped Lumen's card across the keypad.

"Hey," Seren said nervously. "I'm not sure he bought your story."

"What?" William looked upwards, spotting the guard from earlier accompanied by two others heading their way. "Oh, shit." He swiped the keycard again, but red light beamed across the buttons.

"They're getting closer," Seren whispered hurriedly.

"Stop right there, William!" bellowed the guard.

William's hand went for his hip, revealing his weapon. He shoved the keycard into Seren's trembling hand. "Zero, seven, eight, five, two, zero," he said rapidly.

"What?" Seren asked, bewildered.

William stepped out of the elevator, his finger resting on the trigger of the gun. "Is there a problem?" he said politely. "I'm doing what Lumen asked of me."

One of the guards gripped his pistol firmly. Seren's heart raced.

Oh no.

But William moved faster than Seren ever imagined. He drew his weapon with lightning reflexes and aimed it at the approaching guard.

"Must we always resort to violence?" William chided.

The guard didn't hesitate. A gunshot rang out, and Seren instinctively pressed his back against the wall as the bullet lodged itself into the elevator's interior.

William was a blur, his legs moving beneath him with precision. His shot found its mark, hitting the guard's hand. With a scream, the man's gun clattered to the floor, crimson splattering around him.

"You little…!"

Seren had never seen someone dodge bullets before, let alone fire a gun. Either they were horrendous shots, or William was incredibly agile, or it was a combination of both. William surged toward them, his gun steady in his hand.

"The code, Seren!"

Fumbling with the keycard, Seren swiped it again and started to input the numbers. Zero. Seven…

"William, what're the numbers?" Seren shouted.

As he glanced up, he saw William expertly disarm the guard, spinning around him and delivering a knee to the jaw. William wasn't a doctor. And whatever he was, he surely knew how to fight. Seren winced as a guard's fist connected with William's jaw, leaving a red mark. Without flinching, the butt of his gun struck one guard's head while his foot connected with the other's abdomen. Seren gaped as he watched the two men crumple in unison. The remaining guard lay on the ground, as pale as a ghost, unconscious and clutching his bleeding hand.

William beamed at Seren. "Did you catch that?" he asked. "I'd say I am hero material, wouldn't you agree?" He strode over, gently taking the card from Seren's hands. "I guess it slipped my mind that you're a bit forgetful. I'll take it from here."

Seren watched William's fingers dance across the elevator keypad, each button press accompanied by a soft beep. Seren's nails dug into his palms, and his hands shook uncontrollably at his sides. His left foot tapped an impatient rhythm against the floor, a staccato beat echoing his racing heart. Each second felt like an eternity as they waited for the elevator to respond to William's coded command.

"That was impressive," Seren sputtered. His words came out faster than he intended.

William grinned. "It's normal," he said softly. "The adrenaline makes you jittery. Just remember to breathe."

"Yeah," Seren mumbled. "Okay." The elevator doors finally closed, and it started to ascend. "Where did you learn to fight like that?"

"One learns many things while trying to survive," he laughed. "Besides, I might've been showing off a little." He raised an eyebrow.

Seren couldn't help but trace over his features. Brilliant blue eyes, a smile that seemed to come naturally. Who exactly was this guy?

"So, what is your name?" Seren asked curiously. "If it's not William."

The young man's eyes twinkled with a hint of mischief. "I thought you'd never ask. It's Jude." He pulled out a key, unlocking the cuffs from Seren's wrists and allowing them to fall to the floor. Then, he retrieved a minuscule tool from his pocket. He held Seren's right wrist, observing the small metallic bracelet. He used the cylindrical tool to pierce a tiny slot on the bracelet. It clicked open, falling into Jude's open palm.

"This is a tracker," he told Seren. "Lumen tried to put one *in* you, but your body rejected all of them. If we're separated..." Jude sighed. "Find someone's pocket to slip it into. It should buy you some time."

The elevator finally came to an abrupt stop.

Jude raised his hand, signaling for Seren to remain in place. With deliberate steps, he exited the elevator, surveying the surroundings with caution. Ahead, the rich maroon walls were adorned with intricate golden filigree. Jude settled his eyes on the large potted plant that flanked the right side of the elevator.

"Good. It's still here."

With a deft movement, Jude extended his hand behind the plant, retrieving a leather suitcase carefully concealed in the lush foliage. Swiftly unlatching it, he grabbed two folded stacks of clothes, accompanied by a pair of masquerade masks.

"Trust me, you'll need this," Jude assured. He placed a pile of clothing in Seren's hands and then presented him with an onyx mask embellished with golden leaves. Seren stood dumbfounded, holding the apparel in his hands.

"Well, hurry up," Jude breathed. "There's no need to be modest. And I doubt we've seen the last of the guards."

Seren's cheeks grew hot, and he turned away. He removed his damp shorts and the ugly gown, pulling on the black pants. He gingerly draped the matching blazer over his slender shoulders, flinching in discomfort. Remarkably, every piece fit him flawlessly. With an exhale, he placed the mask over his face. The adrenaline was fading, an ebb of pain returning.

Jude slid the tracker into Seren's pocket. "Just as before. Stay close and follow my lead." As he ran his fingers through Seren's hair, smoothing out the saltwater tangles, Seren shot him a disapproving glare.

"Are you always this touchy-feely?" Seren grumbled.

"Don't mind me," Jude replied, offering a faint smile. "I just don't want to draw any attention to ourselves. Luckily, it's still a bit wet from your wonderful soak. Looking presentable is a bit important here."

Jude reached for his mask.

A vibrant light started pulsating above the elevator, capturing their attention.

"Damn it!"

In a sudden motion, Jude forcefully pushed Seren out of the elevator, causing him to stumble and fall. As Seren struggled to stand, his gaze met Jude's intense, sapphire-blue eyes. The world around them seemed to slow. The moment passed in a heartbeat, the elevator doors snapping shut before Seren could even catch his breath.

"Jude!"

Seren desperately tried to pry the unyielding doors open, his nails scraping the metal.

"Can you hear me?" Jude's voice remained surprisingly calm.

"Yes," Seren replied.

He held his breath.

"Listen, Seren—"

"How will I find you?" he interrupted, panic coursing through him.

"Just go! Look for a girl named Mila. She can help you. I'll find you. Go left down this hall and out the door. Use Lumen's keycard. It's in your pocket. Get the hell out of here!"

Seren stumbled against the wall, sweat pouring down his forehead. Leaving Jude felt like a betrayal, but there was no other choice.

His shoes hit the carpet before he could even process another thought. He raced down the hallway with all the energy he had remaining. Sure enough, a door was at the end of the short hallway, with an opening for a keycard. He fumbled, looking in his pockets, and found it neatly tucked into his jacket. Quickly swiping it, the green light appeared, and the door clicked open. He pushed the door open slowly.

Seren's eyes widened in awe at the sight before him. A large, glorious topaz chandelier shined above his head. Dazzling crystals dropped from the center of the room, igniting it with a warm ambiance. Beneath his feet, the floor boasted a stunning hue of burgundy.

"Wow," he whispered.

The room buzzed with life as a multitude of people filled the space, their voices mingling in a lively symphony. Laughter echoed alongside the clinking of glasses as patrons reveled in the pleasures of an open bar. The guests were adorned in resplendent attire, their identities concealed behind intricate masks. Opulent jewelry adorned the women's necks, a testament to their wealth. In every corner, obsidian tabletops displayed extravagant feasts featuring succulent meats, freshly baked bread, glistening red apples, and an array of cheeses that made Seren's mouth water.

A collective of musicians played unique instruments, strumming lively melodies throughout the entire building. Women danced provocatively amidst the tables, their bodies adorned solely by an array of encrusted jewels of various colors. Men laughed and bantered with the women as they swayed their hips to the music for sheer entertainment.

So, this was the Godless City.

"Are you lost?"

Seren spun around, almost colliding with the girl standing behind him. Her curious eyes, the color of warm caramel, peered at him from behind the mysterious dark green mask.

"No, excuse me," Seren said, the words rushing out.

He nonchalantly trailed behind a passing woman, hoping to blend in with the crowd. As she approached the bar, Seren kept a cautious distance. Shooting a glance over his shoulder, he could feel the girl's unwavering eyes on him. He nervously played with the bracelet tucked away in his pocket, knowing his time was limited. How was he going to get out of here?

A hand seized him from behind, and Seren spun around.

"You're a jumpy little thing, aren't you?"

A blonde woman gripped his arm, leaning in with a flirtatious smile beneath her ivory mask.

"No, will you—" Seren began but stopped abruptly.

"I've never seen you here before," the woman said, batting her hazel eyes. "You look like you're handsome under that mask." She leaned closer, her warm breath cascading across him. A rush of warmth flooded Seren's cheeks as she tugged at his shirt. "I'm curious to see your entire face. Do you want to get out of here?"

It could be his only chance. He straightened his posture, adopting a more charming demeanor. "That sounds quite tempting," he replied, his words flowing from his lips like honey. "It does appear that this place is missing the excitement one might hope for."

The woman swayed, a veracious smile spreading across her face. "First, one more drink." She held up a manicured hand to beckon the barkeep.

Seren put his hand over hers. "Why waste any more time?"

The woman giggled, clearly just as surprised with his confidence as he was. She stood up, and as she reached for her purse, he stumbled into her, knocking it to the floor.

"I'm so sorry. I must have had too much to drink. Let me grab that for you," he said.

He leaned down with the tracker tucked inside his palm. He exhaled a sigh of relief, seeing her unfastened purse, allowing him to let the bracelet fall inside.

"Thank you. My Obsidian name is Rema, by the way," she said as he handed her the purse.

The woman guided him through the throngs of people. They maneuvered their way past the rowdy kitchen, where the sound of sizzling meat and animated chatter in unfamiliar languages filled the air.

With Rema's hand clasped in his, she led him toward a back entrance. Stepping out into the dimly lit alleyway, Seren couldn't help but notice the teetering stack of boxes and piles of overflowing trash bags. The relentless downpour had transformed the alley into a murky pool.

"This weather is disgusting," Rema exclaimed. "I'd love to speak to whoever is in charge of the weather simulator." With a grin, she pressed her body against his, urging him toward the dampened wall. "No matter. I'll bet you have a gorgeous home that you could take me to."

Seren bit his cheek, desperately wishing the woman would get away from him. As her hands found their way around his neck, he couldn't take it anymore. Seren pushed her away from himself, breathing heavily. Rema's eyes widened as she stumbled slightly, dusting her dress off.

"You certainly *are* jumpy," she said through gritted teeth.

I need to get out of here.

Seren felt sweat drip down his back. "I—"

"He sure looks a little young, even for you."

Appearing from behind the stack of boxes, the girl from earlier stepped into view, her arms crossed over her chest.

Rema wrinkled her nose. "Kamilah, shouldn't you be working?" she scoffed.

As the young woman drew nearer, she stepped into a slender beam of light. With a thoughtful purse of her lips, she ran her fingers through the dark brown cascade of hair that flowed over her shoulders.

Seren recognized the green mask. She wore a black dress with long sleeves that covered every inch of her besides her long legs and the curves of her collarbones. Even in the dim glow of the streetlamps, her warm brown complexion seemed to emit a subtle radiance akin to the soft caress of the afternoon sun. Though her face remained veiled behind the mask, her breathtaking beauty was undeniable.

Rema cast Seren a withering glance like she had effortlessly plucked his thoughts from the air.

"No. My shift is over," Kamilah replied. She tilted her head. "Where is your husband, Rema?"

Rema's body went rigid. "I was about to meet him inside," she replied sourly, guiltily glancing in Seren's direction. "I'm sorry. I must go."

"No need to apologize," he assured her.

Thank the Gods, Seren thought.

He put a hand against the wall, trying to steady himself as a wave of nausea hit him. He blinked profusely, trying to shake off the sudden dizziness.

Seren watched Rema wave goodbye, her parting gesture less than polite. Kamilah, leaning against the wall, rolled her eyes.

"Sorry, lover boy. She's more trouble than she's worth. Her husband would kill you."

Seren collapsed onto his knees with a gasp. Kamilah peered at him, concern evident in her eyes.

"Are you alright?" she asked.

"I'm fine," Seren gruffly replied. "I just need to get out of here."

He attempted to stand up but fell back against the wall, utterly exhausted. Kamilah's eyes widened as she observed his condition.

"You didn't drink anything from that awful woman, did you?" she asked.

Seren shook his head. "I'm okay."

Kamilah extended a hand toward him.

"Let me walk with you. The storm died down, but it's still nasty out here. And it wouldn't be safe wandering the streets like that."

"I can walk," Seren protested. But his voice was shaky, and he felt as if his body would give way any moment.

Kamilah leaned down, setting her hand upon his arm.

"Don't touch me!" Seren's voice rang out, and the world seemed to still. Kamilah recoiled, shock on her face. It was as if the pouring of the rain seemed to intensify. Seren breathed heavily, digging his fingers through his dark hair. "I'm sorry..." Seren took a quivering breath. "Everyone just keeps...touching me."

Kamilah's voice was hushed. "I'm not sure you can walk on your own. Let me help you."

Seren was too exhausted to argue.

"I'm going to take your mask off, okay? Nobody needs to know we came from the Obsidian." She reached up and slid the mask off his face.

Seren's eyes traveled to the door. Had Jude gotten away safely?

"Thank you," Seren finally said. "Sorry."

Kamilah wrapped her arms around Seren, ensuring he remained steady as they walked down the alley. His head spun, and he closed his eyes, focusing on following the pace of Kamilah's footsteps.

"Where do you live?" she asked.

Seren's feet stopped beneath him. They stood in the middle of a quiet street, blue and purple lights appearing as blurry splotches in his vision. The wind howled, and the rain poured, making his clothes heavy as they clung to his skin.

"I don't know. I don't know where I'm going. I don't know where I am."

Seren doubled over, his fist pounding his chest in a desperate attempt to catch his breath. Each inhalation seemed to come harder than the last. Kamilah hesitated before she placed a gentle hand on his shoulder, offering silent comfort. His gaze locked onto hers, yet his vision remained unfocused.

"Jude told me to find Mila."

Kamilah's eyes widened, and she looked nervously behind her shoulder.

"Come quickly," she urged. "I'm staying down the street from here."

The rest of the walk blurred into a dreamlike haze. As they crossed the threshold into Kamilah's home, it felt as though reality and illusion intertwined. And when Seren's head finally met the embrace of a plush pillow, the world dissolved away.

FOUR

"A king will rise from the burdens of the past, roses will bloom at long last, and all that is cast in shadow shall find the light. An era of peace, for all that is right."

—Book One of Metanoia

1005 A.E.C.

The cherry blossoms were in full bloom. Pastel petals twirled and pirouetted on the soft breeze, covering the streets like a layer of pink snow. Birds sang cheerful tunes from the treetops as they bathed their wings in the sunlight.

The quaint town of Brimry hummed with an unprecedented vitality, energized by the splendid weather that had graced it after months of a harsh winter. Merchants lined the streets selling a myriad of items, including rare spices, weaponry, clothing, and medicinal herbs that were hard to come by unless one traveled to the nearest city.

Emeryn had no money of any means, and her stomach was rumbling terribly at the smell of food from the nearby vendors. She clutched her waist at the thought of a fresh meal, feeling the protrusion of her ribs under her hand.

With a sigh, Emeryn watched the children frolicking in the meadow. She wore a bittersweet smile as their laughter carried into the expanse of the sky. She twiddled her fingers, pressing her hands into the fabric of her powder blue dress that had gone unwashed for days.

How much longer would she have to run?

Emeryn looked upwards into the sky, a sorrowful feeling plaguing her once more. A piece of her believed that she did not deserve happiness. She'd always felt tormented, as if she was being punished by the Gods themselves.

She tenderly rubbed her aching thighs, wincing as she grazed over deep bruises that hid beneath the layers of her dress. They served as a painful reminder of her identity as the woman she had been and would always be.

"Mind if I sit here?"

His voice glided like velvet, sending a shiver down Emeryn's spine. Looking up, she found herself locking eyes with a strikingly handsome stranger. She couldn't help but suppress a gasp at his beauty. Not only that, but he was also impeccably dressed, donning a flawless midnight blue suit embroidered with silver thread.

"N-not at all," she stammered. "Go ahead and sit."

His eyes lingered on Emeryn for a moment, but he quickly tore his piercing gaze away.

Emeryn swallowed. She clasped onto the folds of her dress, bracing herself for a quick getaway as the man sat beside her. Her muscles tensed as she watched his hand slide into his pocket.

"I like to feed the doves," the man said softly. This time, his voice wrapped around Emeryn like a warm hug. "They seem to enjoy my company in return."

He smiled at her, sending her heart pounding.

Emeryn tried to recall seeing doves in the park, but she had only seen sparrows in the area. She had no interest in arguing with a stranger and gave him a slow nod of acknowledgment. Yet, in a matter of seconds, she watched as a dove descended from a nearby tree, coming to rest at the man's feet. Its deep brown eyes widened at him as he opened his outstretched hand, overflowing with birdseed. The bird ate from his palm without hesitation, cooing softly.

"Why is it that you come here?" the man asked suddenly. "I have seen you here for the last several days."

"Are you spying on me?" Emeryn found herself saying.

The man chuckled nervously. "Oh no, not at all," he assured. "I'm here on some business-related matters, and I was passing through when I noticed you here."

She mulled over his suit. It wasn't anything like the clothing she had seen the locals wearing. Surely, he wasn't from around here.

"You're not coming from Vavilon, are you?" she said slowly.

He raised his eyebrows. "Would it bother you if I was? I can leave if you're not comfortable."

Emeryn's heart continued pounding in her chest. She had never seen the man and wondered how she'd never noticed him before. He certainly would have been impossible to forget. He was the most beautiful man she had ever seen.

Perhaps he was harmless.

"No," Emeryn finally said. "I don't mind. And to answer your question, I'm enjoying the fresh air is all."

The man smiled, flashing his perfect teeth. "A partial lie," he replied matter-of-factly. He laughed at her vexed expression. "I do not expect you to tell a stranger the truth. It's all right."

Emeryn balled up her fists. "It really is none of your business," she declared. "If you must know, I come here for many reasons. I've just…" She clenched her stomach, glancing over at the playing children. "I have nowhere else to go right now."

The man eyed the hand wrapped around her waist. "Oh," he said. "I understand now."

Emeryn looked away, hoping to hide the reddening of her face.

"Would you like to feed her?" the man asked.

Emeryn turned back toward him, nodding stiffly before extending her hand. The stranger gently poured birdseed into her open palms. Doves erupted unexpectedly from behind her, their pearly wings unfurling around her. As they encircled her, their soft coos filled Emeryn's ears. She let out childish giggles as doves surrounded her, sitting on her arms and shoulders, fervently reaching for the birdseed in her hands.

"They like you," he murmured. "They are quite vain birds." He looked at a dove that was perched on his finger, stroking the top of its head with his tanned thumb. "They're drawn to beauty." He smiled again, looking almost sad. "I cannot say I blame them."

Emeryn sprinkled the remaining bits of birdseed on the ground. The birds leaped off her and proceeded to polish it off.

"My name is Emeryn," she told the man.

"Nice to meet you, dear Emeryn," he replied. "I have many names. But you may call me Samael."

She blushed.

"You don't have to be nervous around me," Samael said as if reading her mind. "And please, by all means, tell me to leave if I make you uncomfortable in any manner."

It didn't bother Emeryn that he had come from the Godless City; in fact, for some reason, it made her feel more at ease. She leaned back against the bench, sighing as her tense muscles finally relaxed.

"Oh well," Emeryn whispered. "I honestly do love the company."

Samael stood up, extending a hand. "Would you like to walk with me?" he asked.

She didn't hesitate, accepting his hand as he pulled her to her feet. She walked alongside him, exploring every aspect of his face. His features were chiseled to perfection. His eyes were a stunning amber color, almost golden in the sunlight that reflected from his olive skin. Despite his youthful appearance, a prominent streak of silver elegantly intertwined with his dark hair.

"Your eyes," she found herself saying. "They look like sunlight."

He rubbed his chin. "If I am not mistaken, I'd say you're fawning over me right now," Samael teased.

Emeryn opened her mouth in protest, but he spoke too quickly.

"Or perhaps I am projecting my own feelings. You're quite beautiful, Emeryn. I am sure you hear that often."

Emeryn couldn't help but laugh. "You think you're very cunning, don't you?"

He chuckled. "Well, don't you?"

She rolled her eyes playfully.

"Tell me something about yourself."

"Like what?"

"What do you love?"

Emeryn let out a laugh. "That's a rather intimate question to ask a stranger."

"I find you can learn a lot about a person," Samael answered. "When knowing what it is they have come to love."

Emeryn found herself sighing, defeated. "I don't know." She looked upwards, watching a dove fly across the afternoon sky. "A silly thing to say, I suppose, but I do love the stars."

Samael stiffened beside her. "Not silly at all," he mused quietly.

Suddenly, he stopped in his tracks, his shoes grinding to a halt on the cobblestone path.

"Were you aware you were being followed, Miss Emeryn?" Samael asked with his voice lowered.

She froze, gripping her dress.

"What—what do they look like?" she managed to whisper.

She didn't dare look.

Samael pressed himself close to Emeryn, his smell flooding her senses. He smelled like rain-kissed roses and a midnight's summer breath.

"Two men. They both appear to be dressed like acolytes of some sort."

She whimpered. "My husband probably sent them."

Samael glanced down at her hand, noticing the lack of a ring on her finger. He lowered his head, his hot breath on her neck.

"Is he a dangerous man?" he asked.

Emeryn trembled. "He's just—it's that he's–" she tripped over her words. "He is a Lord for the Disciples of Servius, and I ran from him."

Samael clenched his jaw. "The Gods have a funny sense of humor," he said wryly. He studied Emeryn's face, almost looking pained. "In more than one way, it seems."

Emeryn's breathing quickened. The Disciples of Servius did not forgive, nor did they look kindly upon those who did not adhere to the rigidity of their moral code. Servius was a God of Obedience, and Emeryn had been anything but obedient.

"I can't believe he's already found me," Emeryn choked.

"And you don't want to go back?" Samael asked.

"No," Emeryn uttered. "I don't. I never got to choose my husband. They picked me out of that orphanage like some sort of prize."

Young girls were expected to wed the husbands handpicked for them. Upon reaching maturity, they were dispatched to fulfill the traditional role expected of women: one of subservience to their spouses. Emeryn's beauty had swayed many, even as an orphan living of the Servius Sanctum.

Samael raised an eyebrow, looking genuinely curious. "It's not often a Lord hunts down a runaway wife across the continent."

"Lord Glyn is rich and powerful. I'm expected to be obedient and bear his heirs, and I...I can't." She placed her hand on her stomach. "My life is considered meaningless if I fail," she said. "And it seems men of power always get what they want."

"Not always," Samael murmured.

Emeryn recounted how Lord Glyn had chosen her quickly, his visits to the orphanage, and his declaration that she would be his wife, all while the other girls looked on in envy.

"It's okay," Emeryn said in defeat. "I will accept my death."

"No," growled Samael. "You might, but I will not."

She could not read his face as he stood stone-cold. Why did he bother? Emeryn was a stranger.

"Close your eyes," he whispered. "And I will take you far from here."

So, Emeryn obeyed. His strong arm wrapped around her tiny waist, and a flurry of doves cascaded around them.

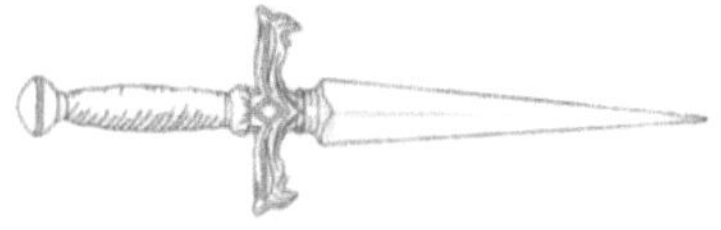

1014 A.E.C.

Tears streamed down Emeryn's face. She wiped them away, cursing at herself for even reminiscing over such things. Emeryn ran her fingers over her lips, remembering Aiden's kiss from the other night, a pang of guilt filling her chest. Why did she feel guilty? Why did she feel as though her heart still did not belong to her? She could see the way Aiden looked at her. He had even been picking bouquets of flowers every morning and setting them outside her door. Aiden claimed they were to brighten up their dreary room, but they left Emeryn with a sense of shame. And she often wondered if he ever grew tired of her lies.

Emeryn glanced over at her son. He was sound asleep on a cot beside her with his arms sprawled above his head. Sunlight peeked through their balcony window, streams of light shining across his small body. His dark hair was ruffled, sticking up in several unusual ways from his restless sleep. He was so young, barely of age to even begin school.

If Aiden knew the entire truth, what would become of her son? All she wanted was to be a good mother and give him a normal life, but she could hardly keep afloat.

Nightmares tormented her, each one a disturbing tapestry of death, blood-soaked seas, and the agonizing rivers of her own suffering. Twisted, disfigured faces jeered at her in the depths of her subconscious, amplifying her despair.

For Emeryn, these haunting dreams held a familiar grip. She was no stranger to fleeing, to concealing her anguish behind a mask of smiles. However, this time was different. This time, she had something precious to safeguard, a responsibility that filled her with fear more potent than any she had ever known. The weight of the secrets she bore in solitude grew heavier with each passing day.

The truth she had kept hidden from the boy's father had been exposed by Aiden, intensifying Emeryn's desperation to protect the other truth she held close—one that held the power to shape her son's entire future. Two distinct secrets, capable of altering her son's life, weighed heavily on her conscience.

And she couldn't deny the truth. She missed his father terribly. It was a horrific ache in her heart. Emeryn wanted nothing more than to be by his side. She was daydreaming of the day they had met like a lovesick child.

Leaning down to kiss her son's forehead, Emeryn lingered over his face. The face of his father. She swore to do everything in her power to protect him, even if it meant lying to him for the rest of his life.

FIVE

"He, the Devil, was born from the malice of mankind. A creation more bitter than the fruit of the forbidden tree."

—Chronicles of the Gods

1025 A.E.C.

Seren's eyes met Kamilah's icy gaze, and the tip of an opalescent dagger pressed against his throat. His heart raced as he realized his hands were securely bound. Kamilah's warm breath brushed against his face as she leaned closer.

"Where is Jude?" she demanded, her tone filled with venom.

A mixture of confusion and fear clouded Seren's thoughts as he struggled to form a coherent response.

"Did you seriously tie me up?" Seren said in disbelief.

She clenched her teeth, her grip tightening on her weapon.

"Answer my question," she hissed.

"I don't know," Seren admitted, his voice strained. "He told me to find Mila before we were separated. Can you just untie me?"

Kamilah released the pressure on the dagger, its glow briefly captivating Seren's attention.

"You came out of the back room. I saw you. I want to know why," she pressed. "Tell me now."

"Untie me first," Seren growled.

"No."

Who did she think she was? If she had taken the time to restrain him, then she would've seen that he was unarmed.

"Fine," he breathed. "If I tell you, will you let me go?"

"Maybe."

Seren released a slow breath, focusing on the empty wall behind Kamilah. Memories of his amnesic awakening resurfaced, filling him with vulnerability. He didn't know who he was, and admitting it made him feel exposed. Despite the uncertainty, he maintained a steady voice. What if she decided to return him to the Obsidian? The thought sent a shiver down his spine.

As Seren concluded his recollection, a heavy silence fell between them. Kamilah continued to pace the room, her brows knitting together. While watching her, Seren couldn't help but notice the change in her appearance. She was now wearing black pants and a long-sleeved shirt, no longer donning her dress.

He anxiously awaited her response, fidgeting against the restraints as his fingers grew numb.

"All you know...is your name?" she uttered.

Seren nodded firmly. "And my age." He sighed. "I remember...most things. I just don't remember...*me*. Not my past. Not where I came from. Nothing."

"Strange," Kamilah admitted. "And to think there's an entire lab hidden beneath the Obsidian, the place where the rich throw their endless parties. No wonder Jude has been so secretive about the job he took." She massaged her temples, frustration etching lines upon her face. "That idiot! Always getting into trouble. Infiltrating a Novem laboratory? Has he lost his mind?"

Seren sputtered in disbelief, his jaw clenched. "That was a Novem lab?"

Kamilah turned to him. "Lumen is on the Council," she said. "I wonder if the Auguries know about this." Her hands ran through her hair. "Oh wow, this is much deeper than I imagined."

"What would they want me for?" Seren asked in confusion.

"That's a great question," Kamilah said. Her eyes narrowed in Seren's direction. "You're telling me you don't remember anything at all?"

Seren squeezed his eyes shut. "I already told you. Trust me, I wish I did."

There had been no time to process anything. The one thing he knew for certain was that he wasn't from the Godless City. There was no way to explain it. He had this deep, unsettling feeling that he couldn't have ended up here on his own. There was just no way.

It was common knowledge that the technology and innovations of Vavilon contradicted the principles of the Gods. Magic was considered a divine gift granted to worthy Priests and Saints, yet the Godless City produced creations resembling magical abilities. Not everyone was deemed deserving of such powers. There was a reason for balance, and this city was trying to destroy that.

The Godless City of Vavilon remained the sole place in Aerithium untouched by theocracy. At its heart, the Council of Novem reigned supreme, nine enigmatic figures responsible for dictating laws and governing the city. Each of the three sectors had a head of security overseeing untouchable armed forces, while a head scientist managed technological advancements within each sector. Yet, above all, loomed the enigmatic presence of the three Auguries.

The identity of the Auguries remained a mystery, concealed from the prying eyes of the public. Rumors suggested they had achieved immortality through a merging of flesh and technology, but such tales were considered blasphemous across the entire continent. The Auguries inspired fear, even in a city that had openly rejected the Gods.

Seren hated to admit it, but he was afraid. What had he done to pique the Novem's interest? What troubled him even more was his strange familiarity with the Godless City—how long had he been here?

"Untie me now," Seren insisted. "I need to go."

Kamilah's demeanor seemed to shift as she broke into a warm, almost jovial smile. "Like that?" She gestured toward his tightly bound wrists. She leaned down and cut the coarse rope. "I'm sorry for the rude awakening," Kamilah apologized. "My trust in people is limited."

"You're telling me," Seren mumbled. "And besides...you shouldn't trust anyone in this place."

Kamilah's arms crossed over her chest. "Why? You're here in the Godless City, too, aren't you?"

Seren gulped. He couldn't argue with that.

"Where do you plan on going if you don't even know where you're from?" Kamilah scoffed.

"I'll figure it out."

Seren pushed himself to his feet, but the room spun, dark spots clouding his vision. He stumbled backward, and Kamilah was there in an instant, her hand steadying him as she helped him sit back down.

"You need to rest before you go anywhere," Kamilah insisted, her hand brushing gently over his forehead. "You have a fever. You won't make it half a block if you leave now."

He shook his head. "I need to leave before I drag you into this. Who knows what became of Jude, and it's all my fault." He met her eyes. "Thank you for your help, Kamilah, but I should go."

All this information had left Seren's head spinning. What on earth was going on? Lumen had even referred to him as his "rat" in the lab. The unsettling images of syringes flashed through his mind. He felt a wave of nausea wash over him.

"Hey." Kamilah set a hand on his shoulder. "It's alright. Jude is clever, and he entrusted you to me. I'm sure he had a backup plan if things went badly. And please, call me Mila, okay?"

"Yeah," Seren managed.

Lumen's sick smile flashed through his head. Seren couldn't stop the sudden shaking of his hands.

"What's your name?" Mila asked gently.

"Seren," he answered, his voice quivering.

"Stay put, Seren. I'm going to get you something to drink."

Seren's eyes darted to the door as Mila approached the small sink in her kitchen nook. He could make a run for it. Seren attempted to stand, but the world immediately warped.

Damn it.

Mila bustled about, the sounds of cabinets and drawers clanging in the room. Seren, defeated, observed her sparse living area—a worn-out couch, scattered books, and simple floral paintings on the wall. A luminous blue Holospectra box, reminiscent of the technology beneath the Obsidian, hung on the wall. Across from it, a closet overflowed with clothes.

Mila returned, offering Seren a glass of water, which he gratefully accepted and emptied in one gulp.

"Let's wait a little longer," she suggested, her voice calm. "If Jude hasn't returned by sundown, I'll start worrying. I don't think you should leave yet. I'm sure he will be of help to you."

"Sundown?" he echoed. "How long was I asleep?"

An ear-splitting alarm blared, shattering the silence within the building. Simultaneously, the Holospectra on Mila's wall flickered to life, projecting an illuminated image onto the wall. The room bathed in the sudden glow as a poised woman materialized before them, her expression eerily indifferent.

"Attention residents of Sector 3. A dangerous criminal has escaped from Lazarek High-Security Prison. This fugitive is armed and dangerous. Residents are warned not to approach the target. If he is seen, please contact the Vavilon Public Security immediately. Any citizen who aids the fugitive will be fined and imprisoned without trial."

A picture was showcased, and within it, Seren's own emerald eyes stared back at him from the holographic display. His raven-black hair was untamed and falling into his eyes. The image lingered for a moment before vanishing.

"Oh wow," Mila whispered. "That's impossible. Lazarek is in Sector 1. That's several miles from here and the Obsidian. Why would they lie?"

Seren clenched his fists. "I'm leaving now."

Mila crossed her arms over her chest. "And where will you go? The city will be crawling with security. Besides, you still need to rest and wait for Jude. You're as white as a winter fox. Here." She walked into her kitchen, grabbing something from the cabinet. Mila sat next to him and forced grainy bread into his hands. "This is bioengineered to give you enough nutrients equivalent to a balanced meal in just a few bites. Eat some."

He hesitantly took a bite from the grainy bread and then pushed it back into her hands.

"Alright," Seren agreed. He had a feeling she wasn't going to give him much of a choice at this point. "I'll stay for a bit, but if Jude doesn't show up anytime soon, I'm leaving. Are you always this bossy?"

Mila smirked. "Jude will be back. I know it. Just try to get some rest. I'm sure he can explain everything."

Seren knew Mila was right. Where would he go? He wanted to scream. He had his name and his age. And...what else? Where was his home? His family?

Seren couldn't help but have a flicker of doubt. What if she turned him in the second he fell asleep? Would he go back to being strapped to a table and mocked by that deranged scientist? Would Seren forget he had even met her? The thoughts made him shudder.

Who was he kidding, anyway? He probably wouldn't get far before collapsing. And he didn't know how to leave the Godless City. It wasn't as if he knew where he would be heading.

He slumped onto Mila's couch, his body instantly surrendering to comfort. Just a few minutes of rest. It was all he needed. Seren closed his eyes and drifted into a dreamless sleep.

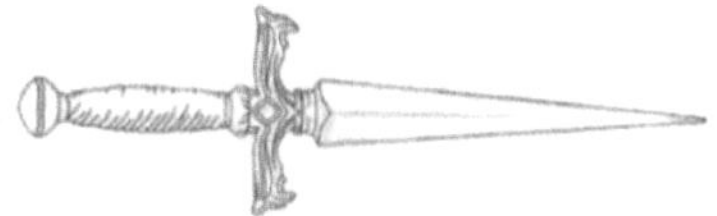

A thundering knock jolted Seren awake. The pounding on the door shook the pictures hanging on the walls. Mila stood over him with her fingers pressed against her lips, signaling him to stay quiet. She gestured toward the closet and silently mouthed, "Hide."

"Open up!" an infuriated man shouted from outside the door. "You are under the orders of the Novem. We know you're in there."

"Just a minute!" Mila snapped. "I'm not decent, jerk!"

"You have two minutes, or we break the door down!"

Seren buried himself deep within the recesses of the closet, desperately covering himself with Mila's garments. It was a less-than-ideal hiding spot, but he had no other choice. Through the slender slits of the closet door, he was able to peer out.

Mila stood in front of the door for a brief period, her movements slightly hesitant. Seren watched as she adjusted the long black sleeves of her top as if trying to ensure they covered all of her skin. Then, with a deep breath, she opened the door.

Three men and two women stood at the entrance. Two of the men donned the traditional armor of the Godless Enforcers, both their faces hidden behind distinctive golden helms fashioned in the likeness of eagles. Large chrome pauldrons protruded from their broad shoulders, gleaming brightly with copper and golden feathers.

Seren immediately recognized the symbol of the Godless City: the chained sun. They were boldly emblazoned on each breast of their robust cuirass.

Both Enforcers were armed with a handgun and an Arc-Caster, a famed weapon only they could acquire. The copper rods of their weapons crackled with unleashed energy even while strapped to their hips. Arc-Casters were known for unleashing arcs of lighting from the barrels—a remarkable feat that granted them limited control over devastating blasts. The blasts had various levels of potency, the most destructive being able to disintegrate flesh instantly.

Seren was unfamiliar with the armor that the other three individuals wore but assumed it was from Lazarek prison. Unlike the Enforcers, their attire was much simpler. The armor they wore was stark black, accompanied by a blood-red cape draping from their shoulders marked by an ominous emblem of a crucifix. Their helmets and gauntlets were trimmed with unforgiving spikes.

The male in the Lazarek armor loomed over Mila, radiating a presence of dominance. Though his face remained obscured, he still sent a shiver through Seren.

"There's been a rumor that you were seen last night with the fugitive after leaving the Obsidian, Kamilah." He said her name with relish, savoring it on his tongue. Seren immediately recognized his heavy Oneriosan accent. "We looked at your records upon our arrival, and there seemed to be some concerns. You have no familial ties to anyone across the nearby countries. You wouldn't happen to be a little Sanguine sadist, would you?"

Mila flinched. "I don't know what you're talking about."

"I think you do."

"Let's not waste any time," interrupted one of the Lazarek women. "If you are harboring a fugitive, you will be detained and brought to Lazarek. I suggest you cooperate so that we can be on our way."

To Seren's horror, Mila smirked. "Do you think that such a threat scares me?" she said.

The male Lazarek Guard laughed viciously. "A fiery little thing, aren't you? But you forgot one thing, foolish girl." He leaned toward Mila. "I'll throw you straight to the Pits. We'll let the demons have their way with you. A shame, really, for such a lovely girl..." He held a tress of her hair between his fingers.

Mila recoiled, the color draining from her face. "I am not harboring a fugitive," she quickly spat. She balled up her fists. "I helped a young man at the Obsidian last night who was clearly intoxicated, and we went our separate ways."

The man roughly grabbed Mila's arm, forcing her inches from his face. "I don't believe you," the man hissed. "A lie lingers on your breath. Why would I trust a monstrous girl like you?"

As Mila tried to wriggle away from his grasp, he gripped her tighter. The spikes of his gauntlets pressed into her flesh, causing her skin to tear. Seren clenched his jaw, silently seething.

Let go of her, you pig.

"You're testing my patience," he said angrily.

"Get your filthy hands off of me," Mila retorted.

A growl escaped the man as he raised his hand, preparing to strike Mila. Seren clutched the handle of the closet.

"Don't you think that is enough, Yakov?"

One of the Enforcers stepped forward, extending a hand to release Mila from his grasp. She rubbed her arm with a scowl, muttering curses under her breath.

"She's clearly lying!" Yakov roared. "The pompous city soldier believes he's all-knowing. Me? I slave day and night in that damned prison. I know a criminal when I see one."

The woman at his side cleared her throat. "He is a Lieutenant, directly under the Novem, so I would be more careful with your words, Yakov. However, the landlord witnessed her bringing the fugitive here. She is lying."

"I never said she wasn't," the Enforcer said. "But, instead of empty threats, we can search the residence instead."

The two Lazarek women maintained silence, mirroring the composure of the Enforcers.

"Well, what are you standing around for? Search the damn building now!" demanded Yakov. "Useless."

Seren's breath caught in his throat as the two women thrashed around Mila's apartment without hesitation. It would be a short amount of time before he was discovered. There was no use even planning an escape, considering the guards were all heavily armed.

"Last place," said Yakov. He pointed to the closet with a sneer. "Will you do the honors, Lieutenant Rome?"

The Enforcer's nod was resolute as he cautiously approached the door, his hand gripping the Arc-Caster. His companion copied his actions, placing a firm hand on his weapon.

"I had hoped I was wrong," Rome sighed. With annoyance, he extended his hand into the closet, gripping Seren's shoulder and yanking him out. The room fell silent as he secured Seren's hands behind his back with steel cuffs.

"This again?" Seren muttered under his breath.

"He is to be delivered straight to the Novem Hall," said the other Enforcer.

Yakov scoffed. "Something is very fishy about this. The Novem Hall? Since when do prisoners of Lazarek go there?" He paced around Lieutenant Rome. "Tell me why I have heard of every criminal to set foot in my prison, but he was kept secret even from me? And look at him! He is nothing but a scrawny little brat," Yakov said. The guard pulled a curved knife out, running his fingers softly down the blade. He reached out, grabbed Seren's shirt, and pulled him to his feet. "Try anything, and I will dig this deep into your gut."

Seren's heart dropped.

"Enough, Yakov!" one of the women shouted. "We were told that he was to return unscathed. We are here to aid the Enforcers in retrieving the target and were instructed to take any conspirators to Lazarek. The rest is not our concern."

Yakov released Seren, nearly causing him to fall over. He snorted. "Fine, but I still think something strange is happening here." He looked Mila up and down. "The little princess is mine. We'll have fun, *krysa*."

Mila winced as he grabbed her, snapping cuffs around her wrists. "Courtesy of the enforcers," Yakov told her. "Try to escape from these cuffs, and you will be electrocuted into unconsciousness. Time to go to Lazarek, pretty girl."

Seren balled his fists.

"No," Lieutenant Rome blurted. He cleared his throat. "I am under new orders to take any conspirators to the Novem Hall as well."

His companion shifted uncomfortably. "Lieutenant, forgive me, sir, but we were told that Lazarek would handle any offenders that assisted the culprit. Isn't that why they accompanied us in the first place?"

Yakov chuckled, spinning his knife in his hand. "I know it is true that Enforcers have powerful weapons and armor. I've heard the armor is as light as a feather but impenetrable. But do you know who I am?" He pointed his knife at Rome. "I have killed demons beyond your imagination. I am sure I can take a snobby soldier like you."

Lieutenant Rome's hand traveled to the Arc-Caster.

"Do you know how I knew something was off about you from the beginning?" Yakov asked.

Rome remained silent.

"I have heard stories of the infamous, *ruthless* Lieutenant Rome." Yakov shrugged. "Sure, I have heard that he is a drunk, but that he is deserving of his title. And you..."

Rome walked backward, away from the group, not removing his hand from his weapon.

"I don't think you are who you say you are..." Yakov said. "I think that you are an *imposter*."

A flash of blue lightning cascaded across the room, cracking with pure energy. It hit Yakov square in the chest, propelling him back into the adjacent wall. He crumpled to the floor in a heap, sparks of electricity dancing off his armor. Rome stood tall with the Arc-Caster steady in his hand. The weapon emanated residual energy, sparks still crackling at its tip.

"I'll bring them to the Novem myself," he confidently announced. "Unless anyone wishes to question my authority and *ruthlessness*." He stomped his armored foot onto the ground. "Anyone?!" he bellowed.

All three of them cowed their heads in silence.

"Wake him up," Rome commanded. "Meet me downstairs afterward. I will get these two loaded into the mechamobile."

The Lieutenant reached out and grabbed Mila by her hair. She cried out as he dragged her out the front door.

"If you run, I will do to you what I just did to my friend back there," he warned her. The Lieutenant turned to Seren. "I suggest you follow and do the same."

Seren followed him down the stairs, fully aware escape wasn't possible. Still wielding his weapon, the Lieutenant strode quickly.

"Pick up the pace," Rome insisted.

As Mila and Seren descended the steps and reached the bottom, the Enforcer grabbed their elbows. He made a sharp left turn, guiding them swiftly into the concealing depths of the shadows. On their right side, a group of Enforcers remained stationed, but none of them noticed their discreet entry into the back alleyway behind the building.

"Stay quiet and follow me."

Mila flashed Seren a curious look as they obeyed. Rome beckoned them down the alley, motioning them to remain as quiet as possible. They obediently trailed behind him as he steered them away from the prying eyes of the crowd. Once they took another sharp turn, Rome ushered them behind the concealment of a large dumpster. He unlatched the keys from his hip and unlocked the handcuffs that bound their wrists. To their surprise, the Lieutenant released an exasperated sigh and removed his helmet.

"I don't know how they wear these all the time."

He smiled, his eyes shimmering gleefully.

"Jude!" Mila exclaimed.

He bowed with an impish smile on his face. "Your savior returns."

Seren couldn't help but laugh. And as his laugh faded, he wondered how long it had been since he'd done such a thing. "William, Rome, and Jude. How many people are you?" he asked.

Jude beamed from ear to ear. "As many as I need to be."

"The Enforcers are everywhere," Mila hissed. "How are we supposed to get out of here without getting caught?"

Jude grimaced. "I'm sorry, Mila. It looks like you're caught up in this too. That was never my intention. It seems this was even bigger than I imagined."

Seren felt his shoulders sink with guilt.

Mila's eyes widened. "Who *are* you?" she asked Seren.

"If I don't find out soon, I'm going to lose it," Seren answered.

"We have no choice," Jude said, interrupting their conversation. His eyes bore into Seren's. "I am to take you out of the Godless City, and there is only one way left. We must go through the Underbelly and into the Behethium Forest."

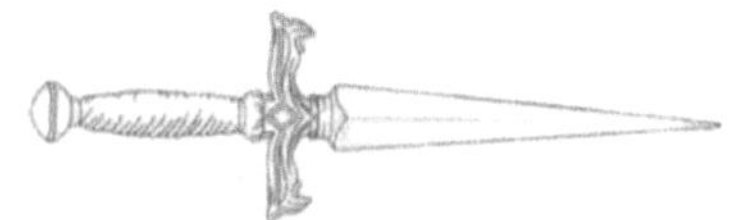

As Jude guided them to an entrance, Mila briefed Seren with details of the Underbelly. Enforcers held little to no power underground and avoided the area altogether. It was infested with the criminals, derelicts, and vagabonds of Vavilon who kept themselves hidden to avoid the dreaded fate of Lazarek.

Their first task would be finding their way through the winding underground sewers. Jude assured them that once they did that, it wouldn't be long before they arrived at the "slums" of the chasms beneath the city.

Jude removed his armor, leaving the essential weapons strapped to his body—the Arc-Caster and one of the pistols on his hip. He handed Seren a shiny, chrome-polished handgun, but Seren hesitated, unsure of his ability to use it. Before he could protest, Mila snatched the gun from Jude and handed Seren her burnished dagger.

"Do not lose it," she demanded. "It was my brother's."

"Thank you," Seren said awkwardly.

The sheathed dagger rested in his grip, bringing an inexplicable warmth that filled his chest. He tentatively explored its surface, fingers sliding over the shimmering opals embedded into the hilt. They sparkled like an ocean beneath a starlit sky, more beautiful than anything he'd ever seen. Before his fingertips could fully encircle the hilt, Mila's hand descended upon his.

"Only use it if necessary," she said warningly. "It isn't an ordinary blade."

He nodded, tucking it into his waistband.

Jude brushed the golden hair out of his eyes. "Let's pray luck stays on our side, and you won't have to."

With urgency, Mila and Seren trailed behind him. They pressed against the alley walls as Jude stuck his head around corners to ensure they kept out of sight while he led the way toward a maintenance hole. Mila and Seren watched as Jude descended a rusted ladder into darkness.

"This was not on my list of things to do today," Mila said with a grimace. She looked down into the hole with dismay.

"After you," Seren told her with raised eyebrows.

"Scared?" Mila teased.

Seren frowned. "No."

Mila tentatively lowered herself into the hole. "Are you sure this is safe?" Mila shouted down to Jude. No response. She groaned and continued down the shaky ladder.

Seren took a deep breath and eased his way down the hole. The ladder creaked underneath his feet as he lowered himself. Upon reaching the bottom, liquid squelched under his shoe. He held back the bile rising in his throat as the stench reached his nose.

"Oh god," Mila groaned. "I'm going to be sick. And I can't see a thing. How are we supposed to know where we're going?"

Somewhere in the darkness, Jude called out to them. "Give me a moment. I'll go turn the lights on from the control panel!"

Mila chuckled dryly. "Of course, only Jude would miraculously know where a control panel is."

Dim lights revealed the concrete tunnels stretching ahead. It appeared as if it had been years since anyone had been in the tunnels. Layers of grime covered the walls, and sewage coated the floors. Greasy rats scurried through the tunnels, not paying any attention to their presence while they skittered through the shallow waters.

Jude sauntered in their direction, his hands now covered in a layer of dust. With an aloof smile, he wiped his hands on his pants.

"And the Gods said, 'let the light guide the way across the umbra of infernal sins and bless those who wield it.'" he declared. He scratched his head. "At least that's what I think they said. I wasn't a very good student as a child."

Mila rolled her eyes. "You still make jokes even now that we're wanted criminals?"

Jude's smile faded. "I am sorry again, Mila. You were the only one I could trust with Seren. I know the Godless City was the safest place for you. I hope you can forgive me."

Mila teasingly bopped the top of Jude's head with her closed fist. "Wipe that look off your face. It doesn't suit you, Jude. You're always getting yourself into trouble." She motioned in Seren's direction. "But you better tell me what's going on."

"Well, luckily, we have quite a scenic walk ahead of us and plenty of time to talk," Jude replied. "And I can tell you how I became your knight in shining armor."

Six

"The Mother, the Father, and the Creator fabricated the Garden of Aetheria. It was meant to be a place of peace and harmony. But there is only dissonance in a creature of war."

—the Seer Diaries of Felix Amos

1025 A.E.C.

Lumen cursed loudly, sucking the blood from the tip of his finger. He angrily swept the chipped glass off the counter, letting it shatter onto the floor. A metallic taste filled his mouth as he bit the inside of his cheek, savoring the pain. With a mutter, he reached for another beaker, gently swirling the magenta liquid inside with the flick of his wrist.

It had only taken Lumen a couple of weeks to perfect the serum. In the beaker, he held a cure for the plague that had befallen Wreiss mere months ago. Hundreds of people had died, and it was only a matter of time until the virus spread over the entire continent of Aerithium.

Of course, Lumen stood as the preeminent scientist of Vavilon, his renown echoing far beyond the city's borders, even reaching distant corners of the continent. And his brilliance went beyond the realm of science alone, encompassing the roles of both doctor and inventor. Still, why should he willingly hand over the cure to the world? What had they ever done for him? He should let them perish and beg their Gods for salvation. Perhaps then they would realize the waste of their devotion. The Gods did not genuinely care for humans. Lumen found his fellow humans to be repulsive and weak. Their blind loyalty to their Gods, and the acceptance of the supposed truths, infuriated him.

Preparing for his journey across Lumina, Lumen poured his antidote into small vials. He had enough wisdom to recognize the importance of bringing it with him. However, he refused to leave a single drop behind. Lumen basked in the idea of the other doctors struggling to cure the plague, a subtle reminder that he surpassed them all. And even if they tried to replicate his cure, it would be much too late.

The Holographus on the table illuminated, casting a bright blue light that reflected off Lumen's skin. A mechanical voice echoed throughout the chamber.

"Doctor Lumen, an intruder has been detected attempting to enter Facility 1-13. Would you like to initiate the lockdown sequence?"

He chuckled, finding amusement in the image displayed on the Holographus. Faith Claramond, a fellow Novem peer, appeared on the screen, her anxious gaze captured by the camera lenses. With a noticeable tension in her jaw, she forcefully cleared her throat, attempting to regain composure.

"Doctor Lumen, I pardon the intrusion. I must speak with you," she announced.

Lumen smirked. Her dedication, having followed him to his private lab in Sector 1, was admirable. Lumen could not deny that he was mildly impressed by the act of boldness.

"Let her in," Lumen commanded.

He reached across the table surreptitiously, slipping a compact device into his pocket. Turning his chair around, Lumen positioned himself to confront her.

Faith held her head high as she stepped through the doors that had opened at his command. Her hair was disheveled, with loose coils poking out her neatly braided locks.

"Hello, Faith. This is my private lab," Lumen said. "What is so detrimental that you decided to follow me?"

Faith's upper lip twitched. "Nobody has heard from you since the Obsidian Lab was compromised. Monsters under your watch infiltrated the city and wreaked havoc. Where were you?"

Lumen scoffed. "I don't care about that. Let Lazarek deal with it. Unless you have news about the boy, get out of my sight."

Faith furrowed her brows. "This has gone too far, Lumen. You were indoctrinated into the Novem for your intelligence and talents for the sake of the people. From where I am standing, you have no care for anyone except yourself and have endangered our community. I pray you never find the boy again. How long did he endure you, Lumen?" she replied cryptically. Faith's ebony skin sheened with sweat as she reached under her coat. "I know what he is."

Lumen clicked his tongue. "Do you know what he is, Faith?" he mocked snidely. "Because I don't think you have the slightest idea."

"I know what you did," Faith whispered. "Your sins are unforgivable."

Lumen held his device behind his back, his fingers brushing the buttons. "My birth was already unforgivable," he laughed. "Do you think you had me fooled? What will happen when the rest of the Novem finds out who you are, Faith? A traitor. A terrorist. A double-crosser. The leader of the Helios Legion has played her cards straight into the Council." Lumen grinned devilishly as a look of devastation befell Faith. "Oh yes, I have known for a very long time, dear Faith. Even so, I think I know your next plan as well."

Faith withdrew her gun, her hands unsteady as she pointed it at Lumen. "You and I know you will not stop until you find him. I don't know what you plan on doing with him, but you will kill us all. You are lucky Vavilon still stands after what you have done!" Faith shouted.

Lumen pushed his chair toward her, his forehead contacting the cold metal of Faith's gun's barrel. She froze in place, her finger hovering above the trigger.

"Look me in the eyes when you kill me," Lumen hissed. "Although, how would your Gods feel about your cold-blooded murder? You'd be falling straight into the Devil's hands."

Faith flinched. "You have no right to judge me," she spat. "I have never met a person as cruel as you."

"Humans are only as cruel as the Gods that created them."

Faith's hand trembled. "You're wrong. The Gods would not stand for this."

"Yet, here you are," Lumen replied calmly. He pressed his forehead harder against the gun. "In the Godless City."

"You and I both know Vavilon is not as godless as it claims to be."

"Perhaps. But that is enough banter. Aren't you going to kill me?" Lumen taunted. "I'm not a patient man."

In her moment of hesitation, Lumen firmly pressed the button his thumb had been hovering above. Faith's firearm flew upwards, sticking to the ceiling in a fluid motion. Startled, she stumbled backward with a gasp. Her finger bore the traces of blood, where her wedding ring had been forcibly torn away, ripping a fragment of her flesh along with it.

"You're in *my* lab," Lumen growled. "You didn't think I would let you march in here and kill me, did you?"

Faith squinted upwards in confusion, finding her gun now pinned to the ceiling. She gaped in awe at the strange contraption.

"It's a magnet," Lumen told her. "You're lucky you don't have any rods in your limbs. I was almost hoping you did."

Faith stepped backward, instinctively edging toward the door, only to discover it was locked behind her.

"I'm assuming you didn't tell anyone you followed me," Lumen said. Rising to his feet, he opened a drawer on his desk and slid latex gloves onto his hands. He retrieved a syringe, holding it carefully in his grasp. "I'm sure you wouldn't have compromised the Helios Legion by doing so. You are quite an intelligent woman, after all. It was clever of you to bring that young mercenary into the Obsidian under a guise. He even had me fooled. He infiltrated my system right under my nose at the most convenient time. I even believed it was the storm. Of course, someone caused that storm." He took a step forward. "And that someone was you."

Faith pushed her back against the door. Lumen couldn't deny the satisfaction rising inside of him at her terror.

"How inconvenient. They'll have to rename themselves the Council Septem," Lumen sneered. "After two of their beloved members are gone." His smile widened. "And what will the three Auguries of the Novem do when they find out the virus in the west has reached through the walls of Vavilon? When it somehow kills the ones who could've found a cure?"

He approached Faith, giddiness bubbling inside of him as she threw herself against the door. "Besides me, of course. But I will be long gone. And then they'll realize how valuable I am. The people will realize that their Gods can't save them, but I can. Only then will I have mercy." And then he lunged forward, plunging the syringe deep into Faith's neck. She let out a terrified scream and threw Lumen off her, his back slamming against the wall.

Lumen rose to his feet, brushing broken glass from his coat. He frowned at the tiny cuts in his hands.

"You're free to leave if you wish," he murmured. "But I advise against it."

Faith shakily pulled the empty syringe from her skin, grasping the punctured area. "What did you do to me?" she cried.

"In less than a couple hours, you will be a contagious cesspool of disease. If you leave, you will be risking the entire city, including all those you love, who will then share your fate. I'll leave the choice to you," he said coldly.

Faith fell to her knees, her hands trembling before her. "No," she whispered. "How could you? Why...why would you do this?"

Why? Lumen wanted to laugh. *Because fate is not resolute.*

"It's just a little experiment I am doing, is all," Lumen chuckled. "Be grateful I gave you a potent version of the virus. You will die quickly."

Unmoved by Faith's anguished cries, Lumen resumed his task. He tucked the vials of the antidote into a bandolier and slung it over his shoulder. It was almost time for him to leave.

Lumen's thin fingers danced across the interface of his Holographus, inputting a command. With determined focus, he finished one final task before erasing any trace of his data from the base server.

Faith trembled on the floor; her knees pulled into her chest. She sobbed as tears streamed down her face. No one had managed to survive the devastating plague that had originated in Wreiss. Lumen knew of Faith's unwavering commitment to the safety of the city. She wouldn't put the entire population at risk, even if she suspected he was bluffing. Unbeknownst to her, even when the fever washed over her, it wouldn't matter. Lumen had sent infected rats across the city. He would not be staying to watch her die. His job was done.

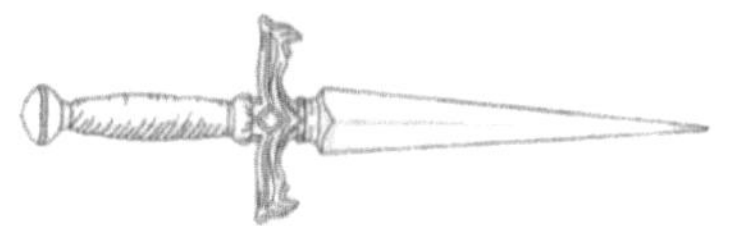

The cybernetic raven tilted its head slightly, watching its master inquisitively. Its singular bionic eye homed in, capturing the subtle nuances of Lumen's biometrics—heightened heart rate and elevated blood pressure. Extending its magnificent black wings, it savored the warmth of the sunlight upon its feathers. It had been months since the two of them had traveled anywhere, and it longed to fly but stayed perched upon Lumen's shoulder.

"Are you reading me again?" Lumen simpered. He stroked the top of the bird's head. The raven leaned into his touch, blissfully enjoying the affection. "We are leaving Vavilon, Grimm," he said. "The time has come."

The raven blinked its organic eye. Its metal claws clenched into Lumen's skin.

"Oh, don't be angry, Grimm," Lumen told him. "We always knew we would leave Vavilon someday. We belong to something much bigger." He stroked the bird's back gently, pondering the long journey ahead.

The Wastelands were believed to be cursed. If it weren't for the weather simulator within the walls of Vavilon, the sun would bore down upon the city. The vast, desolate outskirts stretched before Lumen as if to mock him. The land was barren, miles long of arid terrain, solely occupied by fissured earth and dust. Skeletons of petrified trees, stuck in time, still stood somehow rooted deep into the layers of the earth. Sunlight beat painfully against Lumen's chalky skin, even through his newly acquired clothing.

Lumen understood there were more practical options for escaping the city, yet the blue moon was only a day away. The Behethium Forest posed an impossible route with the Veil growing thin. It carried a curse of its own. During the thinning of the Veil, the forest often became infested with demons. And without a doubt, Seren would be searching for remnants of his past, inevitably leading him to Lumina.

Other matters called Lumen elsewhere as well. In truth, he had always expected that Seren would eventually break free, whether on his own or with outside help. Despite Lumen's fervent desire to believe that he could keep Seren under control, it wasn't necessary anymore.

The Auguries had become aware of Lumen's secrecy. They didn't know why Seren was of importance, and Lumen intended to keep it that way. He had made sure to dispose of any trace of Seren's existence from the Obsidian Lab. It was just another good reason for Lumen to leave Vavilon.

Upon discovering that Seren had managed to escape alongside the daughter of Queen Omaira, Lumen's apprehension had grown. It was certainly a waiting game now. The Sanguine Sisters were sure to catch wind of their princess's presence and track her down. Lumen was not easily frightened, sometimes to a fault. However, the Sanguine Sisters sent a shiver down his spine. It was highly likely Seren's life would be in danger if caught by the Sisters.

"Why are we leaving Vavilon?" Grimm squawked.

The scientist ignored his avian companion, wiping sweat off his upper lip. He glanced behind him, the walls bordering the city still barely in his view. Rain clouds rolled in the distance, heading toward the forest.

"We should have stolen a mechamobile," the bird said. "You're weak."

No, the less attention they brought to themselves, the better. And Lumen did not want to be followed. And he would have to abandon it before entering the borders of any country.

The raven took his master's silence as his cue. He stretched his wings and launched from Lumen's shoulder into the sky. He would serve as Lumen's guide for the following days, monitoring the Wastelands. Before they could reach Lumina, they would have to pass through Kogarashi, his mother's homeland. A knot twisted inside Lumen's stomach at the thought.

Grimm swooped back down, perching back on Lumen's shoulder. "Why are we not going after your subject?" he asked.

"No point for now," Lumen replied curtly. "He will be determined to unravel the mysteries of his past, but he will bring danger upon himself and those around him. The boy's mind is fragile, and I have no doubt that he will eventually come seeking me out, whether by choice or circumstance."

"And will you tell him the truth?" asked the raven.

Lumen smiled sinisterly. "Ah, the truth, my feathered friend, is a weapon all on its own."

SEVEN

"Of the sun and mind, from stars and flesh, with moon and soul. Light will guide the way through the umbra of eternal sins."

—Book One of Metanoia

1025 A.E.C.

As the three of them entered the dimly lit passageway, Jude commanded silence, his gaze fixed on a hand-drawn map. Seren's heart raced with anticipation, eager for answers to his long-standing questions.

"Ah, yes," Jude finally murmured. "I thought this tunnel looked familiar."

Seren and Mila exchanged glances, unsure if he was joking, considering all the tunnels looked painstakingly similar.

Jude lowered the map, the brown paper crumpling in his hands. "Well, it shouldn't be long from this direction. And thankfully, the sewers are usually quiet besides the rats." Jude plugged his nose dramatically. "I'm sure you can tell why."

Mila cleared her throat, putting a hand on her hip. "I'm sure Seren wants to know even more than I do, so are you ready to explain why the entire city is hunting us? There better be a good reason I just lost my apartment."

"You can't go back?" Seren asked.

Mila shook her head. "Not a chance. They had my name. And they had said that conspirators would go straight to Lazarek. Nobody survives the Pits."

"What are the Pits?" Seren said. He recalled the fear on Mila's face when Yakov had mentioned it.

"When Exorcists capture a demon instead of killing it, it's where they take them. Not even the Lazarek guards dare to enter. If a human is placed into the Pits, it's a death sentence."

Seren shuddered. "This city truly *is* godless." He shot an apologetic look at Mila. "You should have let me go in the beginning."

Mila shrugged her shoulders. "Someone once saved me when I was on the run, and I've got to pay it back somehow."

Jude beckoned them forward, and the three continued their trek down the narrow tunnel. Seren carefully navigated the uneven terrain, attempting to sidestep the looming pools of murky sludge water that occupied the tunnel's recesses. However, with each step, the unavoidable became inevitable. It wouldn't be long until Seren's suit from the Obsidian was unrecognizable.

Mila walked past Seren, effortlessly dodging the puddles that threatened to mar her attire. She positioned herself alongside Jude, stealing a quick glance at the map in his hands.

"You both seem oddly comfortable with the idea of being fugitives because of me," Seren said slowly, his voice tinged with suspicion.

Seren was taken aback when Mila let out a laugh. "I guess that's why I was so quick to help you. I have a bit of a fugitive history myself, but it's far from simple."

Jude turned toward him. "I know you're probably wondering if you can trust us, Seren," he said with a wry smile. "But would you believe me if I said that getting into trouble isn't exactly a rare occurrence for me? Call it my 'curse-breaking' hobby."

"So, what happens now?" Seren asked. "We go through the forest and go our separate ways?"

And go...where?

"Well, not exactly. My mission is far from complete," Jude said with a chuckle. "One way or another, I was going to leave the Godless City with you. Although...it seems things got messy." He faced Seren with a reassuring smile. "I'm to take you home to Lumina. And it seems like Mila is now tagging along."

Seren's head spun. "That's where I'm from?" he uttered. "Lumina." It felt familiar to say it. It *felt* like home. "The land of the light." Yes, Seren remembered this. Though when he squeezed his eyes shut and tried to picture what home looked like, it was a blurry landscape of green and blue.

The three of them turned left into another tunnel, identical to the last. A giant rat brushed against Seren's leg and then disappeared back into the lurking shadows. The faint dripping of water echoed in the distance along with their footsteps.

"Jude," Seren said, desperation creeping into his voice. He stopped abruptly, his head hanging low and his eyes fixed on the ground. "How do you know this? Please, tell me what's going on."

Seren couldn't bear the uncertainty any longer. His amnesic state had left him adrift in a sea of confusion. Hearing where he was from only raised more questions.

Jude inhaled deeply. He stopped, walking over to Seren. He looked up into Jude's eyes, feeling a lump in his throat. He wanted to be angry. To demand Jude to tell him what was going on. But instead, Seren felt like a lost child, waiting for an adult to guide him through the muddled uncertainty. And it was closing in on him, almost suffocating.

"Alright," Jude said in a hushed tone. "I'm sorry. I've made you wait long enough. But let's keep walking, okay?"

Seren nodded stiffly and dragged his feet forward.

"I take up a lot of random job offers, and you could say I'm a mercenary of sorts. I was hired by the Helios Legion about a month ago," Jude began.

An audible gasp escaped Mila. "I've heard they've killed innocent people, Jude."

In response, Jude let out an exasperated sigh. "I was hesitant at first, too. The Novem has its way of twisting things and has portrayed them to be a radical religious group of terrorists that follow the Sun God. However, the truth is far more intricate. The Legion owns knowledge of the Godless City that nobody else has. They've been working toward a goal for years." He gulped. "I'm afraid I made an unbreakable oath and cannot speak of it unless the circumstances allow it."

"You idiot!" Mila shrieked. "Why would you do that?"

"I didn't think it would matter. I was told it was dangerous knowledge the world is not ready for, and I am afraid they were right. Besides, there's nothing I can do about it." Jude's eyes hardened. "And as for Seren." He watched him intently. "Faith Claramond is the leader of the Helios Legion, and she is the one who tasked me with rescuing you and bringing you to Lumina."

Mila's eyes widened at his words.

"Do you recall the Council of Novem, Seren?" Jude asked.

"Yes," Seren replied. "The nine."

"You see, Faith is also a member of the Council. She serves as one of the head scientists and works closely with Lumen. While Lumen oversees Sector 1, Faith reigns over Sector 3. It just so happens that Lumen kept his secret lab hidden beneath the Obsidian in her Sector. Lumen has more jurisdiction than any other scientist on the Council, so he can do as he pleases, and the Auguries don't blink an eye. But Faith cares deeply about what goes on in her Sector, so she inserted herself where she wasn't welcome."

Confused, Seren pressed further. "The Helios Legion? They're followers of the Sun God, then?"

Jude cursed as he stepped into a deep puddle, his pants soaked in sludge. He shook off his foot before continuing.

"Yes. Like many others, the Helios Legion believes Vavilon's technological strides will exceed the realms of faith and thaumaturge, and in doing so, cause catastrophe. However, they have vital knowledge about Vavilon that would change everything. Let me just say they know why the land surrounding the Godless City is deemed cursed."

A sudden shiver coursed through Seren. "Why would they concern themselves with me?" he stammered. "I don't understand any of this."

Jude's voice lowered, a solemn undertone echoing from his words. "Faith didn't give me many details about you specifically. She told me the true goal of the Helios Legion after I gave my oath. She told me that history could not afford to repeat itself and that your freedom was crucial. Faith said that the Novem had gotten their hands on something that should not be tampered with. Something dangerous. And by *something*, she meant you."

Seren's breath caught in his throat.

"She was unaware of how you ended up in their facility or how long you'd been there," Jude explained. "Your discovery was made by Lumen, but how he acquired you remained a mystery. As a scientist and not part of the Novem Auguries, Faith had limited access to information. Even she was unsure if the Auguries themselves knew the complete truth. And despite Lumen's twisted and demented nature, he is hailed by his peers in the Novem as the most brilliant scientist in all Vavilon. Some even liken him to Abjiviya the Technophage, the founder of the Godless City."

A blend of dread and unease welled up within Seren as he absorbed Jude's words. Lumen's power and influence within the Council only intensified the enigma shrouding his existence. What if Seren had been asking the wrong questions? Not *who* he was but *what* he was.

Jude continued, "Faith genuinely cared about the well-being of those affected by Lumen's experiments and the secrets hidden beneath the Obsidian. And she was adamant that you were more important than anything else."

Sweat trickled down Seren's neck.

"And that's when I discovered the truth," Jude murmured. "Of course, I couldn't deny the amount of money she was offering. I hate to admit it, but I do have a taste for the finer things in life. But still, I was hesitant about the entire thing. I wasn't sure I was even going to go through with it. Then I found out that everything was happening right where Mila had been working as a server, the Obsidian. At that point, I wanted to know what was going on. So, I became William and did everything Faith told me to do."

They stopped at an intersection of three tunnels. Jude yanked his map up to his nose, whispering to himself. He strained in the dim lighting before pointing to the left one.

"I didn't know what to expect. Then I saw you, and I knew I had to do something. What he was doing to you wasn't right. Someone needed to stop it." Jude's face had paled. "Though the fake identity Helios gave me offered some level of authority, it was severely limited. I'm also not a scientist or a doctor, so it was tricky not to draw attention to myself. Lumen thought I was just an idiot intern. And it was hard to get any information. It didn't help that the staff remained ignorant of Lumen's specific intentions with you. He masterminded the whole operation. And everyone knew better than to vocalize any concerns, given the stringent confidentiality clauses they had signed. If not, Lazarek would be their fate."

Mila watched Seren curiously as if trying to discern why Lumen had been so interested in him.

"There were all kinds of strange things happening in that facility," Jude said. "The scientists spent their days doing unorthodox experiments involving demons at Lumen's command. We were all tasked with separate projects. Lumen isolated you. None of us knew why you were special."

Seren gulped. "I don't think there is anything special about me," he said. "Maybe I hurt someone. What if I deserved to be there?"

Lumen's words rang in Seren's head once again. *Judgment.*

Jude shook his head in disagreement. "No, Seren. There's something significant happening, and you're undoubtedly involved." He clenched his teeth. "While they were preoccupied, I attempted to skim through their documents. Although I'm adept at hacking into tech systems, I could not extract any information about you. If Lumen had recorded anything about you, he kept it well hidden. Once out of curiosity, I questioned Lumen, asking if you were a demon, just to see his reaction, and all he did was laugh. 'Something more' were his words."

Seren's stomach churned. Mila set a hand gently on his shoulder, her eyes softening. "Hey," she said. "Don't worry. We'll figure this out. We're in this together now, like it or not. Jude is going to get you home."

"How long was I there?" Seren whispered.

Jude's expression tightened. "I don't know. From what I heard, you had already tried escaping multiple times. A facility-wide directive was issued, ensuring you were always heavily sedated."

Seren sucked in a breath. "Is this why I don't remember anything?"

"Somnia is a hell of a drug," Jude admitted. "If I'm honest, it's a miracle that you're still *sane*. Besides, maybe some things are better left forgotten."

"Sure," Seren mumbled.

Jude continued. "I could tell Lumen was worried he was killing you. When I helped you escape, it was the first time you had been lucid in a long time. And Lumen did other things to keep you at bay, but I... I didn't do anything." Jude clenched his fists. "I'm sorry."

"You saved me," Seren interrupted. "You could have left me there. I don't know why you're apologizing."

Jude's eyes darted to the ground.

"How long were you undercover for?" Mila asked. "I feel like I've hardly seen you for weeks."

Jude rubbed the back of his neck, and a nervous laugh escaped his lips. "A few days, maybe. I've been busy, is all." He avoided direct eye contact, pulling the map back up to his face.

"So, am I not...human?" Seren asked, his voice trembling. The words caught in his throat, a heavy weight bearing down on his chest. Not human, but not demon? It didn't make sense. His mind raced with conflicting thoughts, and his blood roared in his ears, drowning out everything else.

It was silent for several agonizing minutes. Mila's eyes grazed over Seren again as she walked alongside him.

"I've never been a skeptic, Seren," Jude admitted, breaking the silence. "But Faith was right about one thing. Prophecies are unfolding, and even those that claim to be godless can feel it. Andanova was just the beginning. Veil openings are happening more often, especially during the shifting moon cycles. And though no one says it out loud, we're all afraid that what happened to Andanova might soon befall us all. And my best guess is Faith and maybe even Lumen think you tie into this somehow."

Seren noticed Mila's hands clench at Jude's words.

"The Sundering," Seren said. He remembered that clearly, too. "Hell on earth. How could I possibly have anything to do with any of that?"

Seren came to a sudden halt, his feet splashing dirty water forward.

"What's the matter?" Mila asked. "Did you remember something else?"

"No," Seren whispered. "Do you feel that?"

The once audible scurrying of rats had vanished. An eerie silence dominated the tunnels, absorbing even the faintest echo of their footfalls against the concrete. An icy shiver traced an unsettling path down his spine.

Without warning, a piercing pain exploded behind Seren's eyes. He staggered backward, almost toppling Mila in the process. Darkness fell around him, a cloud of black vapor flooding his lungs and fully enveloping him.

"Seren, what's wrong?" Jude asked.

Seren frantically batted the darkness away as it twined around him in a suffocating embrace.

Could they not see it?

"Fallen lord, take us! We've been searching for you."

Like splintering bones erupting from flesh, the voice was cruel. It burrowed into Seren's chest, freezing him into place.

"Consume us! We offer ourselves to you. Give us flesh. We beg of you."

Mila extended her hand toward him, her fingers grazing the shadows. She pulled her hand back, her mouth agape.

"Seren!"

It coiled around her wrist, winding its way up her arm.

"Let us crawl inside your mouth and live inside your bones. An honor it would be. We beg. We plead. You are different from the others."

Seren covered his ears, falling to his knees.

"We can make you strong again. We'll kill the others and consume them all. Together!"

He could no longer see Jude or Mila as the darkness drowned him.

"Go away!" Seren cried.

"We can help you remember. Take us."

He wanted to remember. He did.

"Wait—" Seren choked.

Regret filled Seren's senses as his lips parted. He frantically clawed at his throat, attempting to ward off the surge of shadows cascading between his lips. The sickening taste of rot and decay filled his mouth, causing him to gag. Overwhelmed by the feeling, Seren collapsed onto his side, writhing as more searing pain erupted behind his skull. He strained to hear the distant screams of Mila. And then, it was gone as quickly as it had come.

The warm sun beat down on his face. A beautiful woman stood before Seren, her arms outstretched. Her fiery red hair blew in the soft breeze, carrying with it the scent of the wildflowers. Seren ran toward her like a moth to a flame, stumbling through the blades of tall grass. She beckoned Seren to her as he neared, her ivory skin glistening in the sun.

"My little star," she whispered.

Her voice was like a lullaby, a familiar song that eased his soul and cradled him in warmth. Yes, he knew her—a memory. A fleeting connection sparked as his hand finally reached hers, but she quickly recoiled her touch and collapsed into the grass behind her.

"Wait!" he cried.

Seren fell to the ground, crying out in pain. Swiftly, he scrambled back to his feet. But as he stared at his own hands, a wave of horror washed over him.

A chilling scream tore through him, belonging not to the present but to the past. It was the anguished scream of a child. And there was blood. So much of it. It stained his small hands and flowed down to his elbows.

Before Seren, the woman lay sprawled on the ground, her body contorted and her crimson-streaked hair fanning out beneath her. Along her lifeless face, blood trickled into her vacant eyes. The scent of iron overwhelmed his senses. He gagged as the blood flowed around his feet. And simultaneously, a haunting melody unfurled, intensifying with each note—a harp's mournful song.

"No! Make it stop!" Seren screamed.

Billows of dark smoke seeped from underneath her body, swirling into the air and taking form. A strand of smoke curled around his ankle, pulling him into the blood-soaked ground.

"You know what you did."

Seren dug his hands into the grass, trying to claw away. He sobbed as he was dragged across the warm, sticky blood. It filled his mouth and covered his body.

"Stop, please!"

A woman's voice, the same voice that had woken him from the darkness in the lab, collided with his thoughts.

"Calm yourself, Seren. It is not real. I will lend you my light."

Seren felt an electrifying crackle go down his spine, and instantly, his fear disappeared. He felt nothing, all his emotions dissolving into a void of emptiness. He closed his eyes tightly and screamed at the top of his lungs. The scream ripped through his throat, its pitch oscillating between the high-pitched wail of a child and a grown young man.

Seren's eyes flashed open. He doubled over, his body convulsing with dry heaves. Inky black smoke spilled out of him, its screeches echoing through the tunnels as it reluctantly left. Then, an overwhelming radiance bathed the entire space, streaming through every crack and crevice, forming a luminous shroud of pure white. The surrounding darkness recoiled as if desperately trying to retreat. It screamed as the light dissolved it, banishing it into oblivion. The brilliance vanished, leaving Seren leaning against the wall, his breaths ragged and labored.

He saw Mila sprawled across the dirty floor, her gaze fixed on the ceiling while she took shallow, rapid breaths. Jude pressed himself against the dirty walls, his hands trembling at his sides, his face devoid of expression. However, as his eyes landed on Mila, he quickly regained his composure. He rushed toward her, crouching to help her sit up.

"It's alright, Kamilah," Jude whispered, gently cradling her face. Mila remained motionless, her chest heaving with each breath. "It wasn't real, Mila. Just an illusion."

Mila clutched her chest, her voice barely above a whisper. "They... looked like corrupted wisps."

Jude nodded in agreement. "Yes, but far too powerful."

Her eyes locked onto Jude's. "Did *you* get rid of them?"

Jude smiled and glanced at Seren before responding. "You give me too much credit, Mila. I believe he did."

Mila took another shaky breath, her voice filled with gratitude. "I don't care how you did it. Thank you, Seren."

Seren remained silent.

"Are you alright?" Jude asked.

"Let's keep moving," Seren said dryly.

Without another word, Seren trudged forward. Was he alright? What kind of question was that? He continued down the tunnel, leaving Jude and Mila several steps behind. Of course, he wasn't alright. If anything, he was going to be sick. He was going to scream. He was going to run until he couldn't run anymore.

"I need to know," Seren heard Mila say. "What did you see?"

"A memory I would've chosen to forget," Jude replied coldly.

"Yeah," Mila responded quietly. "Me too."

Seren's heart ached, but he shoved it away. No, he couldn't think about it. Not now. He needed to reach the forest. Get out of this city. That's what he wished for. And most of all, he desperately wanted to erase the image of his lifeless mother's face from his mind.

Eight

"The thorns of ruin and twisting roots of despair. From the earth, we are born in. It is the birth of err."

—Book One of Metanoia

1025 A.E.C.

Seren spent the rest of the journey to the Underbelly in silence, feeling no desire to speak. Jude and Mila stayed on high alert, walking several feet behind him. They were conversing quietly, most likely discussing what they had just witnessed. Neither of them had asked questions and had thankfully let Seren be.

As they ventured down the tunnel, Jude assured them they had entered the final passage leading to the entrance of the Underbelly slums. It was obvious that he'd been there before, but Seren didn't bother to ask him about it. They pressed on, wading through the filth of the sewers, the minutes stretching on forever. Seren did his best not to think about what he'd seen. For all he knew, forgetting his life was the best thing that had happened to him.

The tunnel gradually widened, branching off in various directions, revealing a disconcerting sight ahead: the passage ended with a concrete wall and a makeshift door. It was an ugly sight, constructed from decaying wood and held together by corroded nails. A large, rusted chain, secured in the middle by a lock, prevented entry beyond. Two imposing figures stood at the entrance, arms crossed over their chests.

One of the men had a sole eye and wore a yellowed eye patch over his left side. The rest of his sallow face was warped with a scar as if an animal had disfigured him. The other man was of a more formidable build, his corkscrew coils of hair tinted red, matching the gleaming crimson weaponry at his side.

Seren slowed his steps, walking alongside Jude and Mila. As they approached, Jude waved at them with a broad smile.

"Good…evening?" Jude said awkwardly. "I can't really tell the time of day down here. Although, buying a pocket-watch wasn't the first thing on my mind while escaping my near death." Neither of the men moved a muscle. "Right then. We are trying to pass through the Underbelly City if possible."

The tall, onyx-skinned man glared at them, his nostrils flaring. "And what business do you have here?" he boomed. His eyes went to the Arc-Caster on Jude's hip.

Jude nervously scratched his neck. "I'm not an Enforcer, if you're wondering. I stole this."

The man loomed over them, and his eyes narrowed. "I will ask again. What business do you have here?"

Mila stepped between Jude and him.

"Enough," she declared, her voice emanating a sense of authority. "I am a Sanguine Sister, and this route through the Behethium Forest is our best chance to evade the radicals who discovered me in the city. We are fugitives seeking safe passage. Please, let us continue, or I will use force."

A newfound confidence emanated from Mila, catching Jude and Seren by surprise. Concern etched across Jude's face as if her revelation unveiled a secret she had struggled to conceal.

The one-eyed man sneered in response, his mocking tone casting doubt upon her claim. "Prove it then. Should you be lying, we'll kill the three of you. Though you are certainly attractive enough to pass as a Sister."

His eyes shamelessly undressed Mila, meticulously tracing every contour of her form. The repulsive aura exuding from the man churned Seren's stomach. Mila's flushed cheeks served as undeniable evidence of his unwelcome gaze, amplifying the discomfort they all felt.

Jude's hands instinctively gravitated toward his Arc-Caster, but Mila reached out and rested her hands upon his.

"If I prove it to you, may we pass?" Mila asked evenly. "Please."

The man licked his lips perversely and looked her up and down, taking extra care to trace over her curves again. "Sure thing, doll. It's your funeral."

Unfazed by his comment, Mila grabbed the soiled hem of her shirt, slowly lifting it over the top of her head. Seren's face burned. He wanted to be respectful and tear his gaze away from her, but he could not. There on her chest and trailing down her midsection, a red-inked tattoo of a serpent adorned her skin. However, the tattoo wasn't what held his attention.

A tormenting array of scars marred Kamilah's back. Against her velvety-brown complexion, the stark whiteness of each past wound stood out prominently. Somehow, Seren recognized the contorted patterns, bearing some sort of ancient demonic script that had been viciously carved into her flesh. Longer, jagged scars marred her underarm region and traced down the contours of her ribs.

The one-eyed man gaped, his jaw hanging open. He clamped it shut, clearing his throat.

"Such a shame someone ruined your pretty skin," he murmured. He reached toward her, trying to graze her skin with his fingers.

Seren stepped between them. This has gone far enough. He glowered at the man menacingly. "I think it's time you let us pass," he growled. "You've had your little show. Now put your shirt back on, Mila."

The one-eyed man lunged at Seren with his crooked teeth bared. The other man held out his thick arm, stopping him instantly.

"Leave them be," he commanded. "We will let them pass. We would be foolish not to accommodate a Sister." An elusive emotion flickered in his dark eyes. His large hand came down onto Seren's shoulder, gripping it firmly.

"Calm down, friend. It is time for you to go."

"It appears so," Seren replied bitterly.

The two men unlocked the massive chain, pulling the door open together.

"I hardly see why that's necessary. Do you see the state of that door?" Jude whispered.

Mila swiftly elbowed him in the ribs. Seren could feel her eyes on him after she pulled her shirt back on.

The three of them stepped inside, the door shutting behind them.

The Underbelly slums were exactly how Seren imagined. He remembered that the city's waste was channeled through colossal underground chutes. It resulted in an abundance of discarded items for the citizens of the Underbelly to scavenge through. Unappealing structures crafted from mismatched scrap littered the subterranean landscape, their neon signs casting an unconventional glow amid the chaos. Rusted spotlights shined above in the cracked cement, adding low light across the city.

Thankfully, the slums were free from the slew of sewage waters, but piles of debris and garbage littered the haphazard streets. The children, clad in ragged clothing, caught Seren's attention the most, running through the rubble barefoot. He even noticed a couple of scruffy tomcats lurking in the shadows.

Their arrival demanded little attention from the desolate crowd. The walls of the cavern were lined with dirty men and women, their weary expressions reflecting the harshness of their lives. Many seemed incoherent, their vacant eyes staring out into the void. Seren wanted to ask what was wrong with them, but somehow, he knew. The way some of them were slumped together, fast asleep. His heart pounded. *Somnia.*

"What now?" Mila asked. "Straight to the forest and then to Lumina?" She crossed her arms over her chest.

"Well, sadly I don't think it'll be that simple—" Jude was cut off as someone shouldered him.

"Move out of the way," the man hissed.

"Sorry," Jude grumbled. The three of them slowly began walking down the streets. "You're not going to be very happy with my plan."

"And why is that?" Mila said with raised eyebrows.

Jude cleared his throat anxiously. "Tomorrow night, there will be a full moon. A blue moon, to be exact. And it's risky because the Veil's barriers will be at its thinnest, but...I think it's our best option. Once the city is in lockdown, we can make our getaway."

Mila clenched her fists. "Are you stupid?" she asked him. "We might as well off ourselves here and now."

Jude winced at her sharp words. "It's our best chance, Mila. They want Seren back. And don't you think the Enforcers expect us to go through the Underbelly and into the forest? I have plenty of money, and I'll be able to supply us accordingly. We need to get out of Vavilon as soon as we can."

Mila frowned. "Jude, do you even know how to get to the forest from here?"

"It's been a long time since I've been here," Jude admitted. "The Underbelly is half the size of Vavilon. It's huge."

Seren surveyed the makeshift city as they walked. The single-story dwellings were packed together like an intricate puzzle of disorderly engineering. A broken bottle crunched underneath Seren's foot.

"What are we supposed to do? Ask someone?" he scoffed. He glanced at a group of scraggly men eyeing them hungrily and grimaced.

"I have a feeling it'll work itself out," Jude said. "I have my ways." He grinned. "You're walking alongside a pillar of luck."

Mila groaned. "Great," she whispered fiercely. "I told that man I'm a Sanguine Sister, and now we're stuck here until we kill ourselves in the Veil."

"At least it might give them a small safety blanket down here," Jude offered. "It wouldn't be the worst thing if that news starts to spread."

Seren shifted uncomfortably. "Mila, what's a Sanguine Sister?"

An old woman coughed from beside them, flashing them a dirty look. She bared her yellowed teeth at Mila before plowing through.

"I'm not a Sister," Mila murmured. "Not anymore. I can't tell you right now."

The tension in the air was palpable as they walked through the littered streets of the Underbelly. Seren couldn't help but notice the curious gazes and whispered conversations that followed them like a shadow. Mila's presence certainly did appear to have stirred something within the community of derelicts.

As they continued, the atmosphere grew increasingly charged with curiosity. Strangers attempted to halt their progress, each offering something strange and mysterious for sale. The first woman, her voice laced with desperation, insisted they buy her homemade moonshine. She claimed it was her most potent and coveted batch yet. Seren could smell the strong scent of alcohol wafting from the bottle, but Mila dismissed her with a shake of her head.

Then came the man with a crooked smile, trying to sell them the bones of a creature, claiming they had healing abilities when crushed to dust. He spoke passionately, declaring the profound significance of these bones. Mila's glare cut through his bravado, briefly freezing him in place before he hurried away.

"Jude," Seren said. "If you've been here before, isn't there anyone you can ask to help us?"

Jude shrugged. "It was a long time ago," he answered. "I'll figure it out. I always finish a job that I start. Don't worry, Seren."

Jude stopped at a few merchants to gather supplies for the upcoming journey through the treacherous woods. To Seren's astonishment, no one dared to deny him service, regardless of their intimidating appearances. His handfuls of golden coins seemed to open doors effortlessly, like a silent language of power. Mila and Seren exchanged cautious glances, concerned that such conspicuous spending could attract unwanted attention.

Jude seemed unconcerned, continuing his purchases with a smile on his face. It was clear that he had a knack for navigating the shady Underbelly. Seren couldn't help but admire his skill, even as a sense of unease lingered in the back of his mind.

"I'll buy us all a change of clothes," Jude announced, breaking their silent musings. "You'd be surprised at the quality you can find down here. Some of the finest fabrics are smuggled into this place. I'll make sure to get you black, Seren."

Seren furrowed his brow, genuinely puzzled. "Why?"

Jude smiled, almost looking nervous. "It seems to be fitting on you, that's all."

Seren's eyes lingered on Jude for a moment before he nodded slowly. "Yeah, okay. But wouldn't blending in with the general population make more sense? Everyone we've seen has been dressed in tattered rags."

Mila wrinkled her nose, clearly unimpressed by the suggestion. "I, for one, refuse to wear anything that reeks of sewage or looks like it's been dragged through the dirt."

Seren couldn't help but smile at her sudden display of vanity. Even in her worn-out attire, she garnered the attention of the men they passed.

"That smile suits you," Mila said.

Seren felt his face warm at her compliment but didn't say a word in return.

After another series of stops, Jude obtained three complete sets of clothing and a pair of sturdy leather boots for each of them. He neatly folded the garments and placed them into individual knapsacks. They discarded their soggy and worn-out shoes, leaving them among the heaps of refuse scattered throughout the streets. Seren eagerly anticipated shedding the suit he had been wearing since his escape.

"I think we should find somewhere to rest," Jude said. "Let's look around, but keep your guard up. I may have brought too much attention to us with my spending." His gaze shifted behind Seren. Seren quickly glanced over his shoulder, catching sight of a small figure lurking in the shadows. "It seems someone has been following us for some time now, so let's stay vigilant."

As they meandered through the labyrinthine paths, Seren kept glancing over his shoulder, but it appeared that whoever it was had slipped out of sight. The three of them walked past a shack, a sickly sweet smell wafting from the entrance that made Seren's head spin.

Mila plugged her nose. "Is that what I think it is?" she said with disgust.

Seren's knees trembled underneath him as if the ground itself had transformed into quicksand. His heart, like a startled bird, fluttered wildly in his chest. He held his breath, desperately wishing the overpowering smell would go away.

"Yep," Jude answered. "Somnia. The most addicting and sought-after drug there is."

Seren blinked through the sudden pounding of his head.

"Seren, are you alright?" Mila asked.

"Let's just get away from this place," he managed, walking at a faster pace. He breathed a sigh of relief as the smell of the Somnia faded.

"You know..." Jude said with a grin. He motioned toward a large neon sign that hung over the entrance of a tall, sideways building that nearly touched the Underbelly ceiling. "This is a fantastic place to gamble."

"Oh, don't you even think about it," Mila scolded. "You'll get us killed."

Jude whined. "Only if I play against sore losers."

As if on cue, a crowd of unruly men burst through the corroded door, their shouts echoing in the air. A burly man forcefully shoved a smaller figure to the ground, showering him with a torrent of profanities. Swiftly regaining his footing, the smaller man retaliated by thrusting a rusted knife into the assailant's abdomen. The large man crumpled, blood pooling on the ground. The surrounding onlookers remained indifferent as the man bled to death before them.

Seren's heart pounded furiously at the sight of the pooling blood. He turned away, trying not to look. His eyes traveled to Mila, who stood frozen, watching the blood pool on the ground, a blank expression on her face.

"Oh Gods, they killed him," Seren breathed.

"Try not to make eye contact," Jude whispered. "Let's just get out of here."

As they turned to leave, the lingering gaze of the men bore into Seren. They sneered and jeered, hurling lewd gestures and inappropriate comments toward Mila. Ignoring their vile advances, she pressed herself against Seren's arm. With every disgusting word they threw toward her, Seren felt his heart race even faster. Jude stayed close behind the two of them.

But it seemed that they weren't going to get off that easy. One of the men stumbled forward, blocking their path, and he brazenly pointed a finger at Mila.

"Don't ignore me, bitch!"

Seren's fists clenched at his sides in response to the insult. Who did the sorry drunk think he was? He took a step forward, feeling Mila's hand reach out and grab his shirt. But before he could get a word in, Jude stepped in front of them, placing himself as a barrier.

"She's not interested in filth like you," Jude spat. "Why don't you move along?"

The man laughed, clutching the sides of his stomach. "What? Is she your whore?" he asked. "There's plenty to go around. Don't be a selfish little brat." He pushed Jude aside, reaching for Mila.

"You bastard," Seren growled.

He felt Mila's breath quicken beside him, her eyes ablaze with fury. In a split second, she forcefully separated herself from his side and positioned herself in front of Jude as a shield. With lightning speed, she drew her pistol, her aim directed straight at the man's chest.

"It seems nobody bats an eye when it comes to murder, so leave me and my friends alone, or you can join yours." She tilted her head toward the dead body and smiled sweetly. "I truly have no problem putting a hole in your stomach if you'd prefer."

The man held his hands up in defeat with a nasty smirk. "I was only messing around. You should be careful where you point that thing, sweetheart."

Mila kept her gun firm in her hand as the man stumbled backward and belched, a bit of drool dribbling down his chin. "Whatever. You aren't worth my time, streetwalker."

Seren released the breath he didn't realize he was holding as Mila lowered the gun. The three of them hurried away, leaving the crowd of men behind. Mila securely concealed her weapon after they had put a considerable distance between them and the chaos.

"Pigs," she scoffed with disdain.

"Were you really going to kill him?" Seren asked hesitantly.

"If it came down to it, I would have."

Jude placed a reassuring hand on Mila's shoulder. "Sorry, Mila. I'll try to get us out of here as soon as possible. Wait here. I'm going to see if I can find us a place to sleep until the blue moon."

Seren, relieved to have a moment of rest, sank wearily against a nearby wall. His back ached furiously, the muscles between his shoulders burning like fire. He took a deep breath to steady himself and wiped his clammy hands on his clothes. Beside him, Mila leaned against the wall, keeping a watchful eye on Jude's every move.

"Are you alright?" she whispered. "You look a bit pale."

"Oh yeah," he lied. "I'm fine."

His eyes squeezed shut. The memory flashed before him once more. Lifeless eyes. Blood. So much blood. In an instant, he snapped his eyes open.

"You don't look fine," Mila muttered.

Ignoring her, Seren watched as Jude stood conversing with a man stationed in front of a rundown building.

"So, Jude's a mercenary," Seren said slowly. "Does he work within a branch of the city?"

Mila let out a soft laugh. "He's more of a solo operator. He trained to be an Enforcer for a while but didn't like it. Rules don't seem to be his thing. The funny thing is that's how we met. He was supposed to arrest me, but instead, he ended up saving me."

Seren didn't bother to ask why she was being arrested; it wasn't his place. Besides...Seren cast his eyes down to his feet. He wasn't sure he was a good person. He wasn't sure of much of anything.

"So, he's in it for the money?" Seren raised an eyebrow.

Mila shook her head profusely. "Jude is different. He's all about helping people, not just money. He's a good person. I honestly don't know much about him."

"And you still trust him?" Seren sputtered. "How long have you known each other?"

"Less than a year," Mila said. "But yes, I trust him. Don't you?" Her eyes met with Seren's. Before he could answer, she tensed suddenly. "Seren, look."

Standing a few steps away, a lanky woman with a shaved head closely watched Jude and his interaction. Her eyes remained fixated on him as he handed over a handful of coins to the man. Seren noticed her hand subtly inching toward the knife secured at her hip. He took a step forward, preparing to warn him.

Without missing a beat, Jude calmly cautioned, "I wouldn't do that if I were you."

And in one fluid motion, Jude drew the Arc-Caster from its holster, the blue sparks at its tip crackling. The woman's eyes widened in response, and she instinctively released her hand from the dagger. Their surroundings fell into a heavy silence as all eyes became fixed upon Jude.

"Where did you get that?" the woman hissed. "Only Enforcer pigs have those."

A sly smile tugged at the corners of his mouth. "I don't see how that is any of your concern. Move along before I make a spectacle out of you."

The woman bowed her head and hurried off like a dog with its tail between its legs.

Mila and Seren approached Jude quickly. "Put that away," Mila said urgently. "Everyone's looking."

"I think that would be foolish," Seren admitted. He looked over his shoulder, seeing the eyes of the slum citizens on them. "We've brought a lot of attention to ourselves. Let's head inside."

"Sanguine witch!"

The elderly woman, who had overheard them upon their initial arrival, hobbled across the street. Her wrinkled face twisted in anger and her bony finger trembled as she pointed first to Mila and then to Jude.

"Enforcer swine!" she shrieked.

Jude's knuckles whitened as he clutched the Arc-Caster, and a fierce determination blazed in his eyes. The hum of the weapon grew louder, its blue sparks dancing. The onlookers, wide-eyed and wary, took a collective step back as the crackling power of the Arc-Caster made the air tingle with tension, effectively warding off anyone daring to approach.

"Damn it," Jude muttered through gritted teeth.

Without warning, a small body collided with Seren's back, a jolt of unexpected weight that nearly sent him stumbling forward. He quickly pivoted to regain his balance and found himself locking eyes with a child. Her pupils were as round as saucers.

"I'm sorry," she stammered. Her small hand gripped the frayed edge of her tattered cloak.

Before Seren could react, the child turned and vanished into the sea of people.

"Seren," Jude warned. "Check if you're missing anything."

Seren patted around his waistband. "All I have is Mila's dagger, which should be—" He stopped. "It's gone."

Without hesitation, Mila sprinted toward the direction the girl had disappeared in. Jude and Seren followed Mila closely, racing down the street. Mila's agility allowed her to close the gap between herself and the young girl in just a matter of moments.

However, the small, fleet-footed child skillfully navigated the maze-like alleyways, knowing every twist and turn like the back of her hand. She slipped through a narrow opening between two decaying pieces of wood, preventing any of them from following.

Mila grasped the child's ragged cloak, causing her to fall backward. But, to their surprise, she recovered, jumping back onto her feet. The child spun around momentarily, revealing her round face, and flashed an impish smile at Mila. She was no older than twelve, grime covering freckled cheeks and dark honeyed skin.

"Give it back!" Mila fumed.

She stretched her arms through the narrow gap, desperately trying to grasp the girl.

The young girl deftly leaped with a nimble maneuver, elevating herself out of their reach. Her eyes gleamed with mischief as she proudly brandished the stolen dagger.

"It looks quite expensive," she said slyly. "Maybe... I'll keep it."

Seren stepped forward. "Just give it back," he said with a scowl.

"I'd be willing to trade," the small girl chimed. "I'll give it back for that." She pointed at the Arc-Caster, still clenched in Jude's hand.

"And what use would a child get out of this?" Jude asked her.

The young girl stuck her tongue out. "Madame Kitsune gets what she wants, and she wants that. She's quite the collector. And who knows, she's in a rather good mood today. Maybe she'll even tell you how to get to the forest."

Mila scoffed. "So, you're an eavesdropper and a thief?"

The girl grinned and spun around. "You know what else the Madame wants?" she asked. "To meet the Princess of the Sanguine Sisters."

Seren stiffened. A princess?

"The slumlord herself wants to see us?" Jude asked with raised eyebrows. "There's no getting out of that one." He lowered his voice and looked between Seren and Mila. "The Madame has complete control of the slums."

The child snickered. "Certainly not. At least you're smart enough to see that. Besides…you've made quite a fool of out of yourselves flashing all your money around. There are hungry eyes everywhere."

"Just give me my damn knife back," Mila demanded.

"I think we both know what needs to happen first," said the girl as she extended her hand.

Jude sighed. "I'm not giving you the Arc-Caster. I'll give it to the Madame once we see her."

The girl pursed her lips. "Well, I want *something*."

Within seconds, a small sack of coins landed at the girl's feet.

"Don't pay her!" Mila sputtered. "She's conning us."

"You don't understand, Mila," Jude said calmly. "If the Madame wants to see us, we have no option. We'll be dragged there, or we'll go on our own free will. It's how it is down here."

"Got that right! You three won't last down here long anyway," the child chortled. She leaned down eagerly to collect the money. Mila caught the dagger by the hilt as it was thrown her way. "You can call me Quinny." She jumped down from her perch in front of them. Quinny smiled at Mila and pointed to her hip. "I want that since I can't have your precious dagger."

"Are you serious?" Mila said.

"Madame will take it anyway," Quinny said with a smirk. "I'm not going to *use* it. Besides, I would cooperate if I were you. Madame has eyes everywhere. Give me the gun."

With an exasperated sigh, Mila reluctantly passed her pistol to the girl. Grumbling under her breath, she securely fastened the dagger to her hip.

"Follow me."

They followed Quinny down the main street, where the narrow alleys and dimly lit walls seemed to close in around them. Seren couldn't help but notice the shift in people's attitudes toward them. The burning glares that had once pierced their backs had now vanished, replaced by averted glances.

It became evident that Quinny held a certain level of respect within the community. Whispers of her name and hushed conversations about the trio's arrival rippled through the crowd. Seren couldn't fathom how such a small child could wield any authority here, but it was clear that harming her would provoke the wrath of the Madame, a name that seemed to instill fear.

Despite the Enforcers' well-founded apprehension of entering this underground city and Jude's nonresistance, Seren was unafraid. If any-thing, his curiosity had replaced his fear.

Quinny had led them away and back to the familiar winding tunnels, much like the sewers. As they rounded the corner, Seren noticed an old man leaning against the wall. He held a tarnished tin in one hand while he flipped a silver coin with the other. A soft hum escaped his lips, gradually transforming into a song:

"A tainted man's dream,
A place so serene,
The Underbelly of the Godless City,

Where the scums of the city prowl,

Above, they show us no pity,

They'll trade you a scowl,

Fugitives and foes,

A pretty penny for your head,

A piece of silver for your woes,

Not worth a breath if you are dead,

This the Godless knows."

The coin slipped from the old man's grasp, its metallic glimmer catching in a sliver of light as it danced across the floor. It came to a halt at Seren's feet, resting amidst a sea of dust and debris. Bending down, he retrieved the coin, the cool metal pressing against his skin. His fingers instinctively brushed away the dirt, smearing its residue onto the fabric of his pants. He hesitantly approached the man, the coin resting in his palm.

"You dropped this, sir."

Shrouded in darkness, the man stood motionless, remaining rooted in the shadows surrounding him. Seren took a step forward, releasing the coin from his grasp, its metallic clink resonating as it fell into the tin can at the man's side.

With a sudden motion, the man's blistered hand shot out and seized Seren by the wrist. His frenzied eyes met with Seren's, a glassy, faraway look inside of them. Etched in his forehead were the chilling words, 'The End is Near.' Blackened, dried blood crusted over his wounds.

"I feel him here. He's in the Heart. He'll scorch the land to dust. Even our bones won't remain," the old man croaked. "The Mother has returned. She's spoken!"

He was insane. Seren tried to pry the man's mangled hands off him, but the man clenched harder.

"You must stop it. It's already begun."

Mila launched herself toward them, a vicious snarl painted on her face. With a forceful shove, she separated the man's clutching grasp from Seren's wrist.

"Crazy old man, keep your hands to yourself," she seethed. "He's crazed from Somnia. Ignore him, Seren."

Casting a lingering gaze at the man, Seren noticed his lips moving, the haunting melody escaping once more from his cracked voice. As if trapped within his own twisted performance, he tossed the coin into the air in the same repetitive motion.

Mila wrapped her fingers around Seren's wrists, urging him forward. "Forget him. Let's go."

They continued to trail Quinny down the deserted tunnel. Eventually, they reached a strange set of doors placed in the concrete wall. They were large, golden, and etched with lovely engravings. A peacock stood amongst a splendor of fauna on each door. Tiny blue and green gemstones sat embedded neatly in the outlines of their feathers. The doors were impeccably polished, bearing no resemblance to anything they had seen thus far. The handles, resembling the pointed faces of foxes, featured vivid red rubies in the placement of their eyes.

Quinny set her small hands on the doors. "You will wait here. The doors will open when Madame Kitsune wishes to see you. And don't you dare try to make a run for it unless you want to be killed."

She used all her strength to crack one of the doors and slipped inside. The door closed noisily. The three waited in awkward silence, not moving a muscle. And it was only a matter of seconds before the doors inwardly opened.

"Please, come in."

A man dressed in shimmering golden attire ushered them inside. As they stepped into the room, their eyes widened in awe. It was a truly magnificent place; nothing compared to the bleakness of the outside. A golden fountain stood at the center, its clear water cascading downwards into a serene pool. Beautiful fish, their scales a blend of orange and white, swam in circles.

Despite the absence of natural light, lush trees and flowers flourished in decorated pots. The vibrant leaves brought a sense of life and freshness to the air. The walls surrounding them were painted a bold red and were decorated with murals painted in gold.

Several people were present and absorbed in conversation. Their attire was extravagant. Rich fabrics draped their figures, blanketing them in vibrant colors. Seren felt a sense of unease, seeing that each of them was carrying formidable weapons. Gleaming knives and guns were holstered at their sides.

It was obvious that within these walls existed an entirely different world, a society of elite criminals detached from the harsh realities endured by those in the slums.

Beyond the fountain sat an imposing chair reminiscent of a throne. Appearing from behind it, an undressed woman took her seat. With a dominant demeanor, she cleared her throat. The chatter instantly quieted, all eyes turning toward her.

Madame Kitsune crossed her slender legs and leisurely reclined against the chair, an amused smile on her blood-red lips. Long, raven-black hair covered her exposed chest. Kitsune was undeniably beautiful, and she delighted in the knowledge.

To further accentuate her allure, she had covered herself in exquisite jewelry. It was not difficult to guess her favorite color. Her necklace shimmered with red diamonds, matching her earrings and bracelets. Kitsune's ostentatious display just further served to illustrate her nature.

"Welcome," Kitsune purred. "I've been waiting for you."

Her voice was nearly intoxicating, as if casting those around her into captivation.

Kitsune rose gracefully, and from behind her emerged a female servant. The woman draped a silken scarlet robe with gold trim over her arms. Accepting the offering, Kitsune enveloped herself in the garment before descending to greet them.

"It is a pleasure," Jude said. "Thank you for having us, Madame."

Jude respectfully bowed to her while shooting a warning look at Seren and Mila. The two of them followed suit.

Kitsune simply smiled, taking another step closer. She surveyed Jude with her dark eyes narrowed. The woman lazily held out her hand.

"Give me the weapon."

Without a word, Jude obediently set the Arc-Caster in her palm. She stroked her slender fingers down its length, testing its feel in her hand.

"What a clever boy. How did you get a hold of this?" she asked him. "These are not easy to come by."

Jude gulped. "If I'm honest with you, it was pure luck."

"Hmm," she mused.

Kitsune seized Jude's wrist. She guided his hand to her lips and grazed the tips of his fingers across her mouth. Jude's face paled. Mila stiffened.

"You speak the truth," Kitsune said. "Interesting. You reek of my kin, little human." She grinned devilishly. "Has someone been making deals with demons?" She dropped his hand.

Jude looked like he was going to vomit.

Kitsune turned to Mila. "What an honor to meet you, your Highness."

Seren held his breath. Mila's eyes burned, and her jaw tightened, but she didn't say a word.

"What an interesting trio you are," she purred. "All of you have a *secret*." Her eyes grazed the three of them and landed on Seren. "And you are truly the most interesting of all."

Jude had been rendered mute, his face still pale. Seren felt his heart pounding in his chest. But he stood up straighter and cleared his throat. "Madame, could you tell us how to get to the forest?"

"The forest?" Kitsune uttered, swiveling toward him. "An interesting request. If you plan on going anytime soon, I suppose you'll be dead in no time." She ran a finger down the porcelain skin between her breasts, letting the robe open slightly. "I am feeling generous. Besides..." She grabbed

Seren's face, squishing his cheeks like a child. "How can I say no to that *delicious* face?"

Mila coughed, but Kitsune ignored the gesture.

"Just follow the rats," she said.

Mila gritted her teeth. "Helpful," she said sarcastically.

In an instant, Kitsune's eyes transformed from deep brown to a piercing yellow. Her teeth sharpened into horrific fangs, and claws erupted at the ends of her fingernails. Seren's eyes widened in surprise. Sensing his shock, Kitsune's facial features softened immediately, returning to normal. Jude and Mila remained unfazed by her transformation, but Seren took a startled step back.

"You see past my Aura?" she asked, looking in Seren's direction. Kitsune stepped behind him, her hands brushing at the nape of his neck.

Mila and Jude exchanged worried glances as she pressed herself into him.

"I knew there was something strange about you. I could *smell* you the second you entered the Underbelly," Kitsune breathed in his ear. "Your Aura is very different. You aren't even aware of it, are you?"

Seren froze.

"What do you mean?" he managed.

She circled around him, her dusky fox-like tails brushing against his skin.

"Tell me, handsome boy," the Madame whispered. "Why do you smell like a human but also reek of immortality?"

Seren's heart skipped a beat. Kitsune laughed and pressed herself into his chest. The tails wrapped around him in a constricting embrace, holding the two of them together.

"In all my years, I've never met a Half-Light. I thought they were a myth. But there's something else. It's as if something has tainted you, something that holds you back. I can feel it, like a darkness radiating from within," she hissed, her voice laced with curiosity. "And there's another unfamiliar scent too, something I can't quite place."

"Half-Light?" Seren whispered shakily. "What does that even mean?"

She ignored his question. "You haven't told your little friends, have you?" she murmured. "You're hiding something."

Seren avoided Kitsune's gaze.

"I can smell your fear," she giggled. "What a delicious smell." Her lips brushed his ear. "Tell me, do they know what you've done?"

Seren felt his stomach plummet. Could she see inside his mind?

"Because I smell that too, young one. Your *guilt*."

The thought crept into Seren's mind, uninvited and unwelcome: *You know what you did*. But he didn't. Though why was Kitsune right? Why was there this horrible, nagging feeling inside of him? What if he was a murderer? Or, even worse, a monster? What if his existence posed a danger to those around him, especially to Mila and Jude, who had risked everything without any inkling of his identity?

Seren stole a quick glance—his friends appearing as though time had frozen around them. The turmoil within him churned. Should he tell them what he had seen? His mother and her blood on his hands. His only memory. What if...what if he'd done something horrible?

Kitsune interrupted his thoughts, placing her hands under his chin. "This Aura is impressive. It must be exhausting. Surely someone taught you to maintain it at a young age."

"I don't know," Seren said flatly. "I don't remember who I am."

These words caused curves to lift on the Madame's lips. "How interesting. I can't tell who your father is, but I know what he is," Kitsune said. "He possesses formidable power, that's without question. I can't help but wonder what might happen if I were to devour all your endless fear." She brushed her tails across Seren's neck. "Do you think I could steal that dormant power from you?"

Seren dug his fingernails into his palms. "What the hell are you talking about? I am sick of this," he snarled. "Unless you can tell me who or what I am, leave me be."

"I sensed that too," Kitsune purred. "The buried anger. But you keep pushing it away. It must be very lonesome to not know who you are."

Seren felt his hands trembling at his sides.

Jude took a step forward. "Please, leave him alone. He's been through enough."

Kitsune turned toward Jude, her lower lip curled, exposing sharp teeth. Before she could react further, Mila pivoted, her blade held steady against the woman's exposed throat in an instant. To Seren's astonishment, not a hint of fear emanated from her. The Madame appeared undeniably amused by the audacious act.

"Do you know what kind of blade this is?" Mila asked her. She pressed it further into the soft skin of Kitsune. When she didn't answer immediately, Mila continued. "This is a holy weapon. I will kill you where you stand, *demon*."

Kitsune smiled wickedly. "You possess a certain level of cleverness yourself. Though, I'm afraid you lack the courage, lost Princess. You have your mother's beauty, but it's a pity. Why do you persist in keeping your powers suppressed? You have the potential to instill fear in others at your disposal. It's even possible you could surpass the Queen herself. So, why, little Princess, do you choose to live in the shadows?"

Mila did not say a word, her hand still on the hilt of her dagger. "My mother will kill you if you touch me. And I will not leave without a fight if you touch my friends."

With a sigh, Kitsune pushed the dagger away with the tips of her fingers.

"Yes, indeed she will. I have been very rude, haven't I?" Kitsune said. The tone in her voice changed, and she seemed calmer. "I'm almost intoxicated by the despair the Underbelly brings today." She licked her lips hungrily. "However, I do not intend on making any enemies this day. In fact, I was hoping to do the opposite. If you are to die here, the Queen would be sure to take it out on someone, most likely me."

Kitsune looked at Mila and let out another deep sigh. "You would be surprised to know even us demons can have mercy. Your human mother is far more wicked than I could ever be. Be careful, Princess. I can feel the hatred pulsating through you like poison."

Kitsune snapped her fingers three times, the sound loud and piercing. "I am aware of your presence, child," she declared with certainty.

Hiding behind Kitsune's chair, Quinny appeared hesitantly. Her head bowed in shame.

"I'm sorry, Madame."

Kitsune exhaled softly. "Curiosity is purely natural for a child," she said. "I've decided that you three will be staying here for now. I can't guarantee your safety outside of these walls, and I know of your intention to cross during the thinning of the Veil. After that, you are no concern of mine."

"What?" Mila sputtered. "Stay here with you? A demon? Why not kill us now?"

Kitsune growled, letting her Aura dissolve slightly to reveal her unsightly fangs.

"Do not disrespect me again, girl. You are dead the moment you cross the forest on the blue moon. Let someone else have the blood of a Sanguine Princess and a Half-Light on their hands. I have enough enemies." She flicked her robe shut with a quick, angry motion. "Quinny will guide you down a safe passage once you wake. Perhaps you should be more grateful for my kindness."

Kitsune turned toward Seren with her foxlike eyes narrowed. "Lucky for you, I am not foolish enough to kill the son of a God."

NINE

"Cunning is the fox, that ensnares the hare, to make through winter's affair. Vile is the man to kill something fair, only to smell blood in the air."

—Book Two of Metanoia

1025 A.E.C.

Seren gazed up at the ornate ceiling in Madame Kitsune's den, watching the shadows cast by the flickering candlelight. By his side, Jude lay sprawled out, his blonde hair in disarray and his once-bright eyes hidden beneath heavy lids. The room had been filled with Jude's laughter and jovial banter earlier, but now, the silence was broken only by his rhythmic, deep breathing. Seren took notice of the dark rings that underlined Jude's eyes and wondered how long it'd been since he had slept.

Even in a demon's den, Jude had been unfazed. In fact, he had claimed that he'd slept in much worse places. And truthfully, Kitsune had been surprisingly accommodating.

Seren looked over at Mila, who lay on a separate bed. Her long hair spilled across the citrine blankets.

A princess.

If Mila hadn't been with them, Seren wondered if Kitsune would have killed them all.

The room was not only luxurious but also spacious. The ceiling was a masterpiece. Golden foxes chased purple peacocks across a red field while magenta cherry blossoms filled a burnt sky. A massive tree lay in the middle of the field, with gold flakes painted into the winding roots that stretched under the vermillion grass. Under it sat a large black fox with nine tails, holding a bouquet of indigo feathers within its jaw.

Seren sighed, rolling over in the silken blankets. Kitsune had insisted they bathe before they "soiled" her sheets with their filth. They had each taken turns in a warm tub, wiping the grime from their bodies. Seren had wished he could stay in the hot water forever.

After Seren bathed, he found Jude had selected a simple yet elegant outfit for him. A sleek black shirt, perfectly matching trousers, and a button-up jacket. It was a stark contrast to the filthy suit he'd been wearing from the Obsidian.

After each of them had cleaned up, Kitsune had food brought to them by her servants. Seren couldn't believe his eyes when he saw fresh fruits and vegetables, along with tender meat. Jude and Seren devoured their meal voraciously, while Mila refused to eat a single bite. Instead, she sipped on wine in silence.

Though even with the comfort of the bed and a full stomach, Seren couldn't sleep. Half-Light? Son of a God? Impossible. Madame Kitsune had to be lying. It was forbidden for a God to have a child with a human. It was unheard of. And which God? Weren't they all of equal power?

He groaned in frustration, slapping his hand on his forehead. He had knowledge within him; he could feel it, but it seemed even that was foggy.

Seren extended his hand in front of him, using his fingers to count all the names of the Gods that he could remember. His brow furrowed in concentration as he silently listed them one by one. *Helios. Servius. Illenia...* And then his mind went blank.

Why was it he could remember all this useless information about the Godless City, but couldn't even name all the Gods?

"Damn it!"

Mila sat up in bed. "Can't sleep?"

"Sorry," Seren mumbled.

"I can't sleep either."

Mila stood, tiptoeing over Jude. She settled next to Seren on the floor, pulling her knees to her chin. Even though she'd scowled at Kitsune's hospitality, Mila hadn't turned down a bath or the chance to change her clothes. She was now wearing a forest-green blouse that covered all her skin and a pair of well-fitted black pants.

Seren sighed. "I just wish I could remember everything. All I have is bits and pieces. It's driving me crazy."

Mila nodded. "I can imagine. I can't sleep knowing I'm in a demon's room," she said, shuddering slightly. "I don't know how Jude is sleeping so soundly."

"Do you think she was right?" Seren asked. He watched the flame of a candle for a moment before continuing. "Could my father really be a God?"

Gods were the ones who answered prayers, shaped the world, and bestowed magic upon the Priests and the Saints. In contrast, Seren felt like he was nothing. He hadn't even found the strength to stand up for Mila when Yakov was hurting her or when that drunken man had berated her. He struggled with a gnawing sense of helplessness. In the grand scheme of things, he felt like a pathetic nobody.

"I'm not sure," Mila replied honestly. "I didn't have a typical upbringing, so my knowledge of the Gods is limited. Recognizing Kitsune was easy; I can usually see through a demon's facade. But those wisps in the sewers were unusual. I didn't recognize them. It was impressive how you drove them away."

Mila locked eyes with Seren, searching for his reaction. "Do you remember anything about the Sanguine Sisters, Seren? It's common knowledge, and people have their reasons for their feelings toward me. You might hate me someday, too."

Seren frowned. "Why would I hate you? If anything, you should hate me for dragging you into all this."

Mila smiled. "Well, technically, *he* dragged me into this." She motioned toward Jude's sleeping form. "But I'd rather help Jude get you home than go back to my life. I was already running. Although..." She crossed her arms over her chest. "At this point, I think I should get half his pay for your return."

Seren let out a soft laugh at her joke.

"Really, Seren," she continued. "And besides, I'd follow Jude anywhere if he let me." Mila's cheeks filled with color. "He's the first real friend I've ever had."

"Yeah," Seren muttered.

"You know it's more than just a job to him. Saving you," Mila said quietly. "He is compassionate. Jude has always accepted me without judgment."

Guilt gnawed at him. He considered that, despite Jude's motives being tied to a job, he had already found himself in a great deal of trouble because of Seren. Jude had even mentioned that the Godless City had been the safest place for Kamilah. Seren had ruined that, too.

"Do people truly hate you for being a Sister? Even if you're a princess?"

Mila wrapped her arms around her legs. "Being a princess makes it worse," she uttered. "I've kept my identity secret for lots of reasons. Once we leave Vavilon, it'll be different. Nobody can know. There are radicals that would kill me."

Seren sat upright in bed, the blankets billowing at his sudden movement.

"Kill you?" he sputtered, his eyes wide. "Why would they do such a thing? Is that who you're running from?"

Mila sighed. "No, not them. It's...complicated."

"I'm more confused," Seren said honestly.

"Sisters are murderers," Mila said as she traced the patterns on the bedspread with her fingertips. "We are no better than the demons of the Veil, and in many ways, we're worse because we're still human."

The silence was deafening.

"Mila," Seren said finally. "Have you ever tried praying to the Gods?"

She let out a laugh. "Why would I do such a thing?"

Seren felt his face flush, suddenly feeling stupid. "If you actually believe that...Why not ask the Gods for guidance? It's just..." He shifted uncomfortably. "Maybe they would forgive you."

He regretted the words the moment they came out of his mouth.

Mila's lips twisted into a frown. "What about you?" she asked coldly. "Have *you* tried praying to the Gods? Maybe your daddy will answer you."

Jude sat up abruptly from his spot on the floor, his hair ruffled. "Okay, listen. I'll give you the short and sweet version, Seren. The Sisters sacrifice men and boys they deem worthy for their own personal gain. It's how they use their blood magic. It's a dark, ancient magic that they have learned and siphoned from powerful demons, similar to how the Priests and Saints siphon magic from the Gods."

Mila pulled her knees in tighter.

"Do you want me to stop?" Jude asked gently.

"No, you can tell him."

Jude took a deep breath before continuing. "The Sisters passionately believe that the Devil is superior to all the Gods, and they await the day when his reign will come, marked by the complete merging of the Veil. As you said before, the Sundering. Through his worship, they hail a demon that claims to be the first love of the Devil himself: Lilith." Jude rubbed his eyes sleepily. "It's a sensitive topic for Mila, as you can imagine, especially considering her mother is feared across Aerithium. And I'm not sure what Lilith has against men, but clearly, she's got some issues."

He yawned, stretching his arms over his head. "Now that I'm done with my theology lesson, you both should really try to get some rest. We have a long journey ahead of us. I'm a light sleeper, so I beg you to keep the conversation to a minimum. I've been awake for three days straight, and I need my beauty sleep." Jude rolled over, tossing the blankets over his head.

"I didn't mean it like that," Seren said. "I'm sorry. It's just..." Gods, he wanted to smack his head against the wall.

"It's okay," Mila answered as she watched Seren fumbling with his words. "You were probably raised that way. I shouldn't have taken it personally."

"Yeah," he murmured.

Idiot.

Mila awkwardly blinked at Seren before standing. "Sleep well." She stepped back over to her bed, turning her back to him.

"You too."

Seren closed his eyes and prayed for sleep to come.

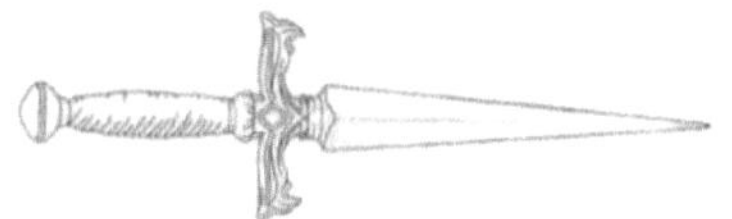

Spring had brought the arrival of sunshine and the melting of the snow. From his window, Seren watched children in the courtyard, their playful laughter filling him with spite. At times, they would point in his direction, and he would instinctively shrink against the wall, hoping they hadn't noticed him. After all, he was just the strange boy in the tower that never left.

He had been waiting for his mom all evening. He had even watched the sunrise and then watched the sunset. Orange and pink filled the sky like watercolors. He watched until the sun was gone, and darkness seeped into the sky. Enid visited, bringing dinner that she set by the door. He ignored it, even when his stomach began to growl. Instead, he traced the images on the stained-glass window, admiring the detail on the dark blue feathers of the fallen angels.

When Seren woke in the morning, his mother still hadn't returned. He was angry that she was allowed to leave whenever she wanted, and he couldn't. Why should he have to stay locked up like a prisoner? It was boring. It wasn't fair. He always did everything she asked him to do. Why should he listen? And besides, what if something bad had happened to her? He didn't trust that strange Priest. He always looked at him oddly and looked at his mom like he was a starved animal, and she was his next meal. He stuck his tongue out in disgust at the thought.

Seren peered under his bed, pulling out his shoes. He put them on, feeling excitement burn through him. He was sure he wouldn't get caught. Besides, he didn't care if he did. His mom hardly punished him because he always listened. One time couldn't hurt. Seren opened the door, peering down the left and right hallway. He smirked. Perfect.

He slipped out of the room and dashed down the hall. It led to a flight of stairs that spiraled down. He giggled to himself, rushing down the steps as quickly as he could. Seren turned the corner and—collided with someone with a yelp. He felt his foot slip off the step. A hand reached out and grabbed him by the collar.

"Be careful. That would have been quite a fall."

Dark eyes peered at him curiously through strands of stringy black hair as the man stood before him. He was clad in his customary navy-colored robe adorned with designs of a golden sun, moon, and stars—a symbol of his esteemed position as a High Priest.

"Hello, Seren," he greeted. "I was coming to greet your mother on this lovely morning."

Seren frowned. "She's not here."

It was the first time he had ever spoken to the Priest. He couldn't remember his name but didn't care to ask.

"Strange," the man commented. "I haven't seen her since last evening." He tilted his head. "And where are you going?"

Seren stuck his tongue out at him. "Wherever I feel like."

A subtle smirk tugged at the corners of the man's lips, his eyes glinting with a spark of amusement. "I could show you around if you would like. There's no reason for you to be sneaking around. It can't be any fun being holed up on this beautiful day."

Seren's heart leaped, and an uncontrollable grin spread across his face as he bounced on the balls of his feet. "Really? But what about my mom?" He leaned toward the man with a whisper. "You could get in trouble."

"Oh, I am sure it will be alright," the High Priest chuckled. "We can wait together until she returns."

"Okay," Seren agreed. "What should I call you? Do I have to call you Father since you're a priest?" He wrinkled his nose.

The man laughed. "No, I would prefer it if you called me Aiden."

Seren followed him down the stairs, studying his features. Aiden wasn't an ugly man, though he looked almost sickly. Despite his youth, his skin bore a pallor that hinted at more than just a lack of sunlight, and dark rings underscored his eyes, suggesting nights haunted by restless sleep. Sensing Seren's lingering gaze, Aiden turned to him.

"So, how old are you, Seren?" Aiden asked.

"I'm almost seven," he piped proudly.

"You should be in school," Aiden responded. "We have a school on the estate grounds. There are plenty of young children that you could get well acquainted with."

Seren's shoulders sagged with disappointment at the mention. "Mom says I can go soon, but she says that all the time."

"I have a feeling things will change for you," Aiden assured. "Don't fret too much about the future. It is a waste of time and energy to do such things. Let's take advantage of this beautiful day we have together instead. Would you like to see the gardens? I've seen you looking out the window often."

"Yes!" he exclaimed. "Are there birds? I like to watch them fly around."

Aiden nodded as they maintained their pace down the spiraled staircase.

"All kinds. Do you like birds?"

Seren smiled widely. "Oh yes, I think they like me too. I see a lot of them outside my window. Sometimes, they'll sit on the ledge. I talk to them, and sometimes they talk back. I wish I could fly." He imitated a bird, flapping his arms.

Aiden paused on the stairs and gave him a beaming smile. "How I envy the aspirations of a child," he said fondly.

They continued down the stairs, the stone echoing beneath their feet.

"These stairs go forever," Seren moaned.

"Your mother requested the highest point in the church with the best view. I think she did it for you."

"Yeah," Seren mumbled. "Maybe."

Aiden could see the change in his attitude and changed the subject. "I need to stop by my study, and then we'll be on our way. Does that sound alright?"

Seren nodded.

"You know," Aiden continued as they stepped into the chamber. "There is a dove's nest on the south side of the church. I can take you there tomorrow if you'd like."

Seren tried to contain his excitement, his mind already envisioning the fluttering wings and cooing sounds. "Yes!" He followed Aiden happily, skipping across the shiny marble floors. As they approached the study doors, memories of their first night in the church flashed in Seren's mind. Aiden had him wait outside, closing the oak doors behind him.

Seren twirled on the tips of his toes, looking up at the vaulted ceiling. A magnificent tree was painted across the expanse. It was the most beautiful painting he had ever seen. The trunk of the tree was golden, twisting and stretching upwards to the heavens, while the leaves displayed an array of rich colors: oranges, reds, and the deepest shades of green. Within the branches, doves perched, looking minuscule in comparison to the rest of the tree. Yet, it was the giant black serpent that captivated most of his attention. Coiling itself around the trunk, its amber eyes emitted a vibrant glow. An unclothed woman stood at the foot of the tree, fixated upon the serpent as she cradled an apple in her open palm.

"Wow," Seren whispered, his mouth hanging open. "That snake is huge!"

"It's actually a wyrm."

Seren's body twitched in surprise. Aiden, appearing beside him almost out of nowhere, held a crumpled note in his hand. Aiden pointed upwards. "It is sucking the essence out of the Tree of Life, also known as the Mother Tree. First, it deceived the mother of all, Eden. Such a wretched beast."

Seren cocked his head to the side. "Will I learn about it if I go to school?"

Aiden smiled. "Oh yes, I could teach you of the Holy Trinity. And Iro is a wonderful teacher. He would be honored to have you join the other children."

"Will I learn about the Veil too?" Seren asked, suddenly feeling small. "I heard a kid outside say that someday the world will be just like Andanova."

Concerned, Aiden clutched the note in his hand tighter. "Yes, you will."

"Mom said that it's another world and that sometimes it collides with ours." He held out his small fists in front of him. "She said that this is us." He raised his right fist. "And that this is the Veil." He raised his left. "And she said sometimes this happens." He slammed his fists together.

Aiden grabbed his fists, separating them gently. "It is the world between," he said softly. "And yes, it does collide with ours in small bursts."

"But Andanova is gone," Seren said. "That wasn't small."

"No, it was not," Aiden agreed.

"Mom said it is a part of the Veil now."

"Unfortunately, yes. The Veil merged with Andanova."

"Will that happen to all of us?" Seren whispered.

Aiden stiffened, and the paper crumpled further under his grasp. "No," he said, though uncertainty lingered in his voice. "We are waiting for someone. Someone very special." He leaned down, adjusting to Seren's height, their eyes meeting. "She will save us."

"Who?" Seren asked curiously.

"The Mother Goddess, Alernaea. She is to be reborn again and cleanse the Veil once more."

"Reborn?" Seren echoed.

Aiden nodded firmly. "Yes, it will be as the Seers have predicted for centuries. When she sacrificed herself for the Veil, fragments of her being were thrown into the ether. And someday, she will return to us."

Seren again peered at the note in Aiden's hand. "What is that?"

Aiden grimaced. "It appears your mother has left for a bit. She asked me to watch over you until her return."

Seren took a step backward. She had left him? With the Priest? He clenched his fists at his side, feeling his eyes well up with tears. An aching, hollow pang began to fill his small chest.

"What do you mean?" he asked. "Where did she go?"

Aiden took a step toward Seren. "I am unsure. It seems she has some personal business to attend to. She felt you would be safer if you stayed here with me. I promise it'll be okay."

"You're lying," Seren said. "I thought Priests don't lie."

"I'm not lying," Aiden argued.

"Yes, you are. You know why she left. Don't you?" He rubbed his head anxiously. "You never come up to my room. Why did you come today?"

Aiden's face paled at the sudden accusation, a flicker of guilt crossing his features. He had known. He had known she had left.

"Seren," he said carefully. "Everything your mother does is to protect you. I promise it will be alright. We can spend some time getting to know one another."

"She wouldn't leave me with you!" Seren shouted fiercely. "I don't even know you, and I don't want to. I don't even want to be here in this stupid church!" Tears began to spill down his cheeks.

That same familiar voice crept into his consciousness.

"Collect yourself, Seren."

Seren ignored her and ripped the note out of Aiden's hands. Tears streamed down his face as he raced down the halls. He could hear Aiden chasing after him, but he didn't stop. He was scared, but he was not alone. He didn't know who she was—perhaps his guardian angel, a Goddess listening to his prayers? When she spoke, an unexplainable connection enveloped him as if she had always been with him, shielding him from within.

So, Seren ran and ran until he found a door that led outside, bursting through it. He tore through a maze of yellow rose bushes, thorns ripping into his skin as he stumbled and cried. Seren ran until he collapsed. He curled into a ball under the roses, heaving and sobbing, holding the note close to his chest. And around him, the delicate blossoms began to wither, the stems blackening as all the life was sucked from them.

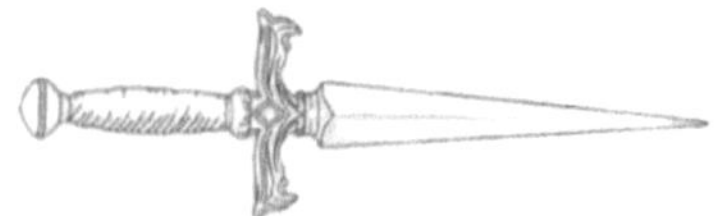

Seren awoke to the loud announcement reverberating throughout Vavilon, even reaching beneath the city's surface.

"Attention residents of Vavilon, the blue moon will rise within the hour, and the Veil's barriers will thin. All civilians are strongly encouraged to stay indoors and seek shelter. The Enforcers have taken all necessary precautions to ward demons away from the city's walls. The Quantum Electron Destabilizer will be activated in thirty minutes."

The doors of the room flung open with a dramatic sweep. In the entrance stood Kitsune with Quinny at her waist. The small girl, dressed in cleaner clothing than before, now sported a decent pair of leather boots.

The Madame smiled, revealing her sharp canines. "It is time for your death," she announced. "Although, a part of me thinks you may live to see another day. You are the son of a God, after all." Her eyes bore into Seren's. "You must hurry before they activate the shielding technology. Leaving or entering the city is impossible once the barrier is up."

Jude jumped out of bed, wearing nothing but his underwear.

"Jude, what's that?"

Seren pointed to his right leg. Jude's leg was made entirely of metal. It had been impossible to tell underneath his clothes, and he had never seen it exposed. It was perfectly built and in pristine condition. The cybernetic limb was undeniably crafted by a highly skilled Mechamagus in Vavilon, evident in the flawless fluidity and seamless movements that mimicked that of an actual appendage. It gleamed a brilliant copper color with swirling designs engraved into the calf and thigh.

"Well, that's obviously my leg, Seren," Jude teased. "Such a silly question."

Kitsune growled. "We don't have time for this. You." She pointed at Seren. "Take off your shirt."

"W-what?" he stammered.

Jude burst out laughing. "That's a strange request before our departure. I mean, I get it, he's devilishly handsome, but this isn't the time for—"

"Believe it or not," Kitsune interrupted coldly. "I am trying to help you, Half-Light. Take it off."

Seren hesitated for a moment, then obeyed, peeling the shirt off over his head. He felt the cool air on his skin as he exposed his back.

Kitsune's long finger twirled in front of him. "Turn around."

Mila went rigid. Jude turned away, and Seren sensed an unease in their reactions.

"I noticed it when you were bathing."

"You pervert!" Mila yelled. "I should've known those mirrors were enchanted."

"Just look," Kitsune growled. She motioned to a hanging mirror on the wall.

As Seren approached the mirror, dread welled up within him as he turned to examine his back. Deeply engraved into the middle of his back were grotesque and twisted scars. Sinister black veins crept beneath the scars like gnarled trees, abruptly halting their course just before they reached his shoulder blades. A strange marking was situated in the center of his lower back: five circular burns seared onto his skin, creating an unsettling, inverted "Y" shape.

"I recognize those markings," Kitsune murmured. "Soul-sealing magic. It's commonly used on demons to keep them at bay. Only someone with powerful thaumaturgic abilities can do that. Usually, a High Priest or a Saint. It was likely meant to suppress your strong emotions and abilities. It needs to be reversed for you to access your full potential. Unfortunately, I can't be of help. But this..." Kitsune's hand reached toward him but quickly faltered. "Is this what I smelled?"

"What could those scars be from?" Mila asked, her voice sounding small.

"I am unsure. I've never seen anything like it," Kitsune answered. "Yet..." She sniffed the air, her nose wrinkling. "The taint is undeniable."

Jude turned to Seren, his fists clenched. "We'll take care of the seal after we leave the city. We will figure out everything."

Kitsune backed up toward the door as if afraid to be near him.

"Put your shirt back on."

Seren happily obeyed, pulling his shirt back over his head.

"How do I get rid of the seal?" Seren asked frantically. "Could it be what's causing my memory loss?"

"It's possible, but I don't know," Kitsune said blankly. "That is all I have to offer you. It is time for you to leave. Now."

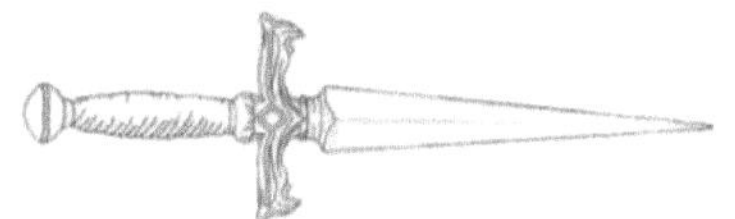

Kitsune's words about following the rats had been true. The rodents, darting dexterously between Seren's feet, were all heading in the same direction they traveled. Quinny informed them of a beast lurking within the Underbelly's deep tunnels, feeding on both man and animals. Kitsune had limited control over the creature, so it was best for them to avoid it.

Seren wondered if it was some sort of abomination, a creature created from underground experiments in a lab like the one he was in. The rats seemed to sense it, whatever it was, and ran toward the forest to escape it.

Quinny skipped ahead of Seren. She dodged the rodents on the trail while humming a cheerful tune. Distant and mute, Mila trailed behind, seemingly nervous about entering the forest. The thinness of the Veil's barriers would leave them vulnerable, susceptible to unwittingly stepping through it and falling prey to the lurking demons that awaited on the other side. The demons desired to cross into their realm, preying on humans to steal their souls.

Seren may have been struggling to remember all the Gods' names, but he remembered the Veil clearly. It was ever-present, the world between their realm and one beyond. There were those foolish enough to intentionally venture into the Veil, driven by the misguided desire for power. After Andanova, anyone could wander into the Veil. It was an unseen force, discernible only to those with the ability to perceive Aura. When the Veil's barriers were thin and collided with theirs, it was as if their worlds suddenly existed as one.

The demons in the Veil came in various forms. And many demons enjoyed making pacts with humans. Such acts were considered the gravest of taboos. When a human made a deal with a demon and died, their soul would be traded off in exchange for the demon's presence in the human realm. It was much easier than consuming hundreds of unwilling souls. One willing soul could make all the difference. Seren couldn't help but wonder how many souls Kitsune could have devoured to secure her position in the realm of humanity.

After leaving Kitsune's den, Seren felt the weight of Jude's watchful eyes. The knapsack he carried on his back, a gift from Jude before their departure, rubbed between his shoulder blades, causing him to grimace.

Since the revelation of the markings on Seren's back, it almost felt as if the pain had intensified.

"I had a memory," Seren announced, breaking the silence. Mila and Jude both perked up and drew their full attention to him. "About...a High Priest named Aiden."

Jude looked like he had seen a ghost. "That's wonderful that your memory is coming back," he offered, his breath visible in the cool air.

"Is that where you're taking me?" Seren asked, cutting into Jude with a glare. "To Aiden?"

"Yes," Jude admitted. "I was told to take you to the High Priest of Stellaris."

"And you didn't just tell me?" Seren's fists balled up at his sides. "You left me in the dark?"

Jude was taken aback by his sudden hostility, a grimace etched on his face. "I was trying to let you remember on your own. It felt like the right thing to do," he said. Jude gave him a hesitant smile. "I'm your knight in shining armor. Remember?"

"I'm not a damsel in distress," Seren snapped. "And you're a mercenary, not a knight."

"Ah, I was wondering if you were mad about that," Jude said with a nervous laugh, the sound bouncing off the tunnel walls. "Are you alright? Was it a...good memory?"

"It was fine," Seren lied.

Jude stopped in his tracks. "Seren, I may be doing my job, but...I'd like to think we're friends."

"Whatever."

Jude frowned. "What? You don't like my company?" He placed a hand over his heart in mock pain. "I am truly hurt, Seren. We've been through so much together in this short time."

Seren rolled his eyes at his teasing tone, feeling the tiniest hint of a smile tugging at the corners of his lips.

"I really meant no harm, Seren. I'm sorry."

"It's fine. I guess I should be thankful I remember something."

A wide smile graced Jude's face but quickly faltered, his eyes clouded with concern. "Seren, I don't know what you expect when you get back home, and I don't know if things will be how you remember."

Seren gave him a mock annoyed look. "Jude," he said with a raised eyebrow. "There is far more that I don't remember compared to what I do."

"It'll come back." Jude searched Seren's face, his features seeming to tighten. "But...I just want you to be prepared. Even Lumina...has seen changes. People are dying, Seren. There's been talk of war brewing between the eastern and western hemispheres. An incurable plague has fallen over Wreiss, and rumors of a mad king ruling Oneriosa have spread. There are even rumors that Vavilon will soon seek to eradicate enough people, driving them to desperation and forcing them to abandon their Gods forever in some sick attempt to reshape allegiance. Yet, what future lies within such a path? And why? The Veil is a growing threat, yet humanity continues to drive further apart."

Jude's words weighed heavily in the air for a moment. "The point is," he continued, "I don't know what you remember, but things aren't good.

And I just want you to be prepared for that. I know I've kept you in the dark, but...I'm sorry. I hope you can still trust me to take you home."

Mila cleared her throat, drawing their attention. She twirled a strand of hair between her fingers before speaking up. "And hopefully, you don't mind me tagging along. Where Jude goes, I go."

Jude couldn't resist a playful smirk, his eyes twinkling with amusement. "Ah, you see, Seren? Mila keeps me around for good luck, or maybe she enjoys my company too much," he said.

Mila's cheeks flushed, and she quickly averted her gaze. "It's not like that," she mumbled.

Seren owed them; that much was certain.

"Let's just focus on getting you home," Jude said. "Okay?" He shot Seren an impish grin. "Besides, the Priest is supposed to give me the final half of my payment."

Looking between his two new allies, Seren felt almost a sense of relief. He believed he could trust Jude to a certain extent, and perhaps that's why it had upset him so much that Jude had kept Aiden from him.

Quinny skipped ahead, her light melody humming through the air. The vibrant notes abruptly ceased, leaving an echo in the quiet surroundings. Before them, the path came to an unexpected halt, marked by a weathered wall. Cracks resembling spiderwebs covered the wall, with overgrown ivy growing out of the fissures. The ivy formed a thick cover on the wall, a wild growth that concealed most of its surface. Tendrils snaked across the worn surface, creating a tangled, mysterious pattern. A large rat darted between Quinny's legs, disappearing effortlessly into the foliage.

"This is it," she said. Quinny pointed to the leftmost side where the ivy was the thickest, and the wall was no longer visible. "There's an opening here if you push yourselves through."

Seren watched the ivy rustle from a rush of wind.

"Thank you," he told the small girl. Seren forced a smile. "Give Kitsune my thanks as well."

Quinny put her hands behind her back, fidgeting in place. "Are you really the son of a God?" she blurted.

Seren laughed nervously. "I don't know."

She lifted her head. "Please, take me with you," Quinny said desperately. Her brown eyes were pleading. She pressed her clenched hands against her chest. "I'm an orphan. Nobody would miss me. Kitsune will get rid of me once I am no longer of use. Please."

The young girl looked at Seren as if he could be her savior, a light at the end of a tunnel of never-ending darkness. She had acted fearlessly and determinedly, but now Seren could see who she truly was—a child. Quinny followed a demon's orders yet was still innocent and untainted. She wanted to be free.

Seren's mouth felt dry. "Quinny..."

It was Mila who answered her without blinking an eye. "Absolutely not. Once we step out of the city into the Behethium Forest, we cannot guarantee your safety. You'll be a burden we cannot carry. I'm sorry."

Quinny shuffled her feet. "If you ever come back here, would you let me come with you?"

The unexpected question startled both Seren's friends and him. Their shocked expressions mirrored his own inner turmoil. But something within Seren, an echo of compassion and understanding, compelled him. He grabbed Quinny's small hand, enveloping it within his.

"Yes," he replied firmly. "I swear it. If fate brings me back here, I will return for you, Quinny." He offered her another smile, but this one was genuine. "And if I unlock the truth that I am indeed a son of a God, I promise to return and share that knowledge with you."

It became unmistakably clear to Seren that he had failed to reciprocate Jude's sacrifice and dedication. Looking into Quinny's eyes, he saw the yearning for something beyond the suffocating grasp of the Underbelly. And he understood her pain.

"Promise?" she squeaked.

"I promise."

Quinny said her goodbyes and the three of them watched her disappear down the tunnels.

"I almost hope we do cross paths again," Jude said fondly. "The little thief was starting to grow on me."

Mila smirked. "Does she remind you of someone?

"You know me too well," Jude laughed. He took a step toward Seren. "I have something for you."

Jude removed his knapsack, carefully lowering it to the ground. From his back, he extracted a sheath, unnoticed by Seren until now. With a deliberate motion, Jude extended the sheathed weapon toward Seren. Accepting the offering, Seren felt the weight in his hands. Gripping the hilt, he drew the weapon from its protective covering. Seren looked at his reflection in the gleaming silver short sword.

"I asked Quinny to buy it for me before we left. I didn't think a gun suited you," Jude told him. "It isn't anything special, but I think it'll do for now."

Mila peered over Seren's shoulder to examine the blade.

"I don't know how to use this thing," Seren argued.

"Hopefully, you don't have to use it then," Jude replied.

Jude delved into his bag, rummaging through its contents. He produced three identical beaded bracelets. Each was crafted with smooth purple stones and detailed with tiny golden sunbursts.

"I was also gifted these. These bracelets are blessed and designed to conceal our Auras. They bear the sigil of the Sun God. And as Seren probably noticed," Jude explained. "Demons have a distaste for intense light. These should deter smaller, weaker demons but won't protect us from everything."

"This is a suicide mission," Mila whispered.

"We might get lucky," Jude said optimistically. "We may avoid the Veil."

"Doubtful," Mila whispered. "A blue moon and the Behethium Forest? The Veil almost always merges here on a full moon."

"We can still go back," Seren offered.

"No," Jude said. "This is our best chance to get out of Vavilon while we can."

The decision was made. Jude took the lead, with Mila positioned behind Seren as they maneuvered through the overgrowth. And they all felt it the second they stepped into the moonlight. The barriers were open, and they had walked directly into the Veil.

TEN

"Before the corruption of the Veil, priests and saints wielded unimaginable power. They painted the skies in celebration, bestowing good health and fortune upon children, and effortlessly healing the sick. However, even I can perceive the burden it places upon them, as only traces of purity remain."

—Exorcist Damian Silver

1025 A.E.C.

Beneath a sky unclouded and serene, the moon shone, casting its bluish glow upon the entire expanse of the forest floor. The sweet scent of petrichor, a lingering reminder of recent rain, wafted through the air and filled Seren's senses.

But there was an undeniable heaviness in the air. It weighed down on them as if pressing down upon their souls. Instinctively, the three of them drew closer as a dense fog began to gather, its chilling touch biting at their ankles.

Within Seren, he felt an unsettling familiarity reminiscent of the stifling sensation that had washed over him when they'd encountered the corrupted wisps. Bile surged in his throat, threatening to choke him. Seren swallowed it, refusing to succumb to the terrible feeling.

Jude retched beside him, emptying the contents of his stomach at his feet. The foul smell wafted up from the floor.

"Oh, it feels awful," Jude moaned as he wiped his mouth on his white sleeve. "It's like there's a weight of ice on my chest." His face had lost color, and sweat pooled on his upper lip.

"Get it together," Mila whispered, her dagger tight in hand, eyes nervously scanning the surroundings. "I don't know how, but we entered it. Instantly. Why did that happen so easily?" And then Mila also vomited, groaning in agony.

"Are you okay?" Seren asked with concern.

Jude and Mila appeared less composed than Seren. In fact, they didn't even seem to hear him. The two of them vacantly stared past the ridgeline of trees. Something was very wrong.

Seren scanned the forest for any movement. They were far too exposed. "We need to get out of the open," he urged. "Can you guys walk?"

If they were in the Veil...the demons were here too. Seren's hand gravitated toward the bracelet on his wrist. They needed to move. Now. Seren frantically grabbed Mila's wrist, her skin feeling like ice against his. "Mila?"

A gust of wind blew through them, nearly knocking them down. Without a moment to brace themselves, another gust followed, carrying a horrific chill that masked the spring air. Delicate frost began to adorn Mila's long eyelashes as she trembled behind Seren.

A ghostly wail resounded in the wind, and it came again, louder. A chill prickled down Seren's spine. Something was coming. "Jude. Mila. We need to go," he said, his breath escaping from his lips in a frosty cloud.

The harrowing wails grew in intensity, and their source drew nearer. And whatever it was, there was more than one. Mila shut her eyes. "We're going to die," she whispered, her lips trembling.

"Damn it!" Seren shouted.

He grabbed Jude's hand, trying to pull his arm.

"It's fine," Jude croaked. "We'll be fine."

Seren swore he could hear Jude's heart pounding.

High above, the treetops trembled, and the branches swayed with an eerie dance. The earth began to rumble beneath their feet. A surge of instinctual dread came over Seren as he felt the unseen force hurtling toward them, drawing nearer with each moment.

The air echoed with the cacophony of breaking sticks and snapping branches as a nightmarish horde burst from the trees. Unnaturally elongated arms propelled them forward, their spindly legs mirroring the haunting rhythm of their movements. Translucent skin stretched over malformed bodies, revealing misshapen humanoid bones and grotesque organs. Within their sunken sockets rested glassy eyes that betrayed no trace of humanity. And then, a horrible cry pierced the air from their repulsive, salivating mouths, each row of teeth gleaming with fresh blood.

Seren's hand clenched around the hilt of his sword, the cold metal biting into his palm. His heart raced. Jude remained immobile, as did Mila. She kept her dagger in hand and stood frozen, a statue of terror.

The creatures snarled, circling in on the three of them. Seren's bones ached as the temperature plummeted even further, and Mila's teeth began to chatter furiously.

And then the frontmost creature lunged toward them, its mouth agape as it let out a guttural scream. Seren swung his weapon, cleaving through the creature's limb. A deluge of black ichor rained upon them, and the demon unleashed a powerful howl.

"Run!" Seren shouted.

Finally breaking free from their paralysis, Jude and Mila seemed to come to their senses.

The three of them took off sprinting, their feet pounding against the ground as they raced away from the horde of demons with all their might. Mila matched Seren's pace, her breaths syncing with his. Jude, trailing closely behind, unleashed a string of curses between gasps.

"What happened back there?" Mila yelled over her shoulder.

"Hell, if I know!" Jude shouted.

They darted through the trees, desperately trying to keep together. Branches, armed with needle-like ends, whipped at Seren's face, leaving a fiery trail of stinging marks in their wake.

The creatures were not far behind. They crashed through the forest after them, trampling everything in their path. Guttural snarls and repulsive sounds filled the night as they rampaged, sending waves of fear coursing through Seren's veins. They were running blindly, only guided by the muted moonlight. But the creatures were fast. Too fast. Seren dared to steal a glance over his shoulder, the blood roaring in his ears.

Their lithe, loping gaits granted them a distinct advantage, propelling them effortlessly. There were at least a dozen of them. Seren caught sight of Jude stumbling behind him, struggling to traverse the undergrowth.

"Shit!"

Jude's swift stride was interrupted as his cybernetic leg unexpectedly plunged through a decaying stump. As gravity mercilessly pulled him downwards, he reacted quickly, relying on his hands to break his fall. Seren's own movement came to an immediate halt. The group of monsters had closed in, preparing to devour Jude. One of them revealed its teeth and was poised to ruthlessly puncture the flesh of Jude's vulnerable neck.

Mila was a blur as she lunged at the demon. As they collided, she expertly rolled on top of the creature, her knife digging into its side. A tortured scream pierced the air, and the demon erupted into a shower of guts and gore.

Mila's dagger shone brilliantly, untouched by any of the ichor that now stained the forest floor. Another creature hurled toward them, but Mila swiftly sliced the dagger straight through its neck. A second torrent of blood followed as the monster burst into visceral matter, spattering nearby trees. The dagger's power had undoubtedly allowed her to accomplish such a feat.

Seren dashed over to Jude and began prying loose the rotting fragments of wood. Splinters dug into Seren's skin as he tried to dig his leg out. He cursed as he peeled the splintering wood apart, warm blood running down his palms.

Meanwhile, Mila deftly swung left and right, fending off monsters as they launched themselves at her. Seren's muscles strained as he yanked

Jude's arm, finally freeing him. Jude stumbled to his feet, rapidly drawing his pistol.

Mila's scream echoed through the chaos as the demon slammed into her side, sending her sprawling to the ground. The creature pinned her shoulders, its viscous saliva dripping onto her face. Seren raced toward it, wielding his sword in one hand. With a powerful swing, he sliced into the creature's back, its spine crunching under his blade. It reared back with a cry, clotted blood oozing from its wounds. Mila jumped to her feet and ran forward, plunging her dagger into its chest.

Bullets erupted from Jude's weapon, each shot precisely felling one creature after another. His marksmanship was flawless, the fatal blows finding their mark between their eyes. Although they were quick, the monsters lacked the strength to match their speed. Seren continued to wield his sword, dark droplets splattering upon him as his strikes landed. The symbol on his back seared with a fiery intensity, paining him with every swing. He killed one. And then another. Side by side, they relentlessly exterminated the horde until none remained standing.

Seren breathed heavily and wiped some of the blood from his face. Jude kicked one of the demons he had shot with the tip of his foot. Its head flopped, and a translucent tongue dangled from its mouth.

"A face that only a mother could love," Jude remarked. Then he grinned. "We make a fantastic team. Looks like you do know how to use that sword, Seren. Lucky guess on my part."

Seren looked at the filthy blade in his hand. It was another reminder that he had no idea who he was.

"I was sure we were going to die," Mila confessed.

"Yeah," Seren commented. "I guess we got lucky."

"Well, you'll never be as lucky as—" Jude was quickly cut off as his metal knee buckled beneath him. He steadied himself against a tree. "I'm long overdue for routine maintenance. I think one of my connectors is loose."

"Let's just get out of here," Seren said. "It's only a matter of time before something else comes along."

A new wave of wailing pierced the air. The ground rumbled beneath his feet again. And this time, he could make a very distinct difference—there was a greater number of them.

"You've got to be kidding," Mila gasped.

Jude willed himself upright, his body quivering on his unsteady appendage. Seren extended a helping hand, but Jude waved him off, a grimace of discomfort contorting his face.

"Yeah, right," Seren retorted. Against Jude's protest, he sheathed his sword and offered a supportive arm. "Quickly."

"This somehow feels familiar," Jude joked.

Seren gritted his teeth as Jude hung onto him. Mila crept forward quickly, keeping a close distance between them. Glowing eyes peered at them in the brush, but they dispersed quickly. Even the other monsters lurking in the forest seemed to be hiding from the stampede.

Mila came to an abrupt halt. "Listen," she demanded, whipping around in a panic. "Turn around! They're coming from this way!"

A pale beast appeared from the verdure and galloped toward Mila's exposed backside. Jude had his gun aimed and fired at lightning speed while leaning against Seren for support. The creature collapsed into a lifeless heap. Another burst into the opening, and Jude shot it perfectly again. Yet, it didn't matter how well he was shooting. They were overpowered. There were too many of them.

"Run, Mila!" Jude shouted.

Just then, a stray cloud encompassed the moon, shrouding the forest in a blanket of impenetrable darkness. They ran blindly in the opposite direction, but Jude began to falter, unable to carry his weight. His knee buckled, and he collapsed.

"Jude!" Seren yelled frantically, fumbling in the darkness to find him, his hands brushing over the ground. He froze. Hot breath ran down his neck, and all the hairs stood on his arms. No. A low growl rumbled next to his ear. He was going to die.

Boom. Boom.

The fleeting glimmer of light emitted by Jude's gun caught their attention. In that split second, the surrounding creatures were briefly unveiled by the mesmerizing strobe effect, their monstrous mouths left wide open. An involuntary gasp escaped Seren's lips as a bullet whizzed past him, piercing through the very demon that had been moments away from snatching him as its meal.

At the perfect moment, the moonlight returned and lit the terrain again. Jude knelt on the ground, his gun steady in his hand as he fired. He shot once. Twice. And on the third shot, his gun clicked silently.

Near the forest's edge, two savage monsters slammed Mila into the ground. With precision, she thrust the dagger into one of them while the other sank its teeth deep into her left arm. Emitting a feral cry, she fought to pull her arm away from the beast.

Seren slammed himself into the monster, using his weight to thrust it off her, but he collided into them with too much force. The three of them hurtled downwards, their limbs entangling painfully. He cried out as they crashed and fell through the dense thicket, offshoots of trees slapping roughly against his face. The vile creature met a jarring halt against a large rock, the sickening sound of its demise echoing through the night, its blood smearing on him as he tumbled past the broken body.

Seren's face slammed into the ground, dirt filling his mouth. Blood flowed down his face swiftly from the gashes on his cheek. Mila's body fell on top of his, knocking the wind out of him. He groaned, heaving her off him.

Despite some bruised ribs, it seemed his body was intact. Mila breathed rapidly, her face covered in small welts and cuts. She moaned in pain, forcing herself shakily to her feet. Seren's heart plummeted when he saw her left wrist's unnatural angle and the bite wound on her arm.

"Mila, you're hurt..."

"We have to go back!" she shouted at Seren. "Jude!"

Seren looked up from where they had fallen, a sinking feeling settling in his stomach. It was a miracle they hadn't been severely injured or killed.

"Mila," Seren said levelly. "I don't think we can safely climb this. I saw Jude run out of ammunition at the worst time, and he could hardly stand on his own."

Mila turned to Seren, her face beet-red. "What're you saying?" she spat. "Jude is *alive*. I'm going whether you're coming or not."

With her intact wrist, she grabbed thick roots sticking out of the ground and attempted to pull herself up the sheer incline. But the roots gave way under Mila's weight, sending her sliding downward.

"Damn it!"

She made another attempt, grabbing a sturdy rock with both hands and hoisting herself upwards. A sharp cry sounded from her, the broken wrist proving unable to bear any strain. Mila persisted, tears flowing down her cheeks. But the ground was still wet from the recent rainfall, causing her to lose footing again.

"Let's find a way around," Seren offered. "We'll waste our time trying to climb."

Without warning, Mila grabbed the loose rock, lobbing it in Seren's direction. It whizzed past the top of Seren's head, grazing his hair.

"What the hell?" he sputtered.

Mila slammed her foot into the ground. "Why do you act so emotionless about everything?!" she shouted at him. She chucked another small rock at him. This time, it bounced off his shin. "Jude could be dead, Seren! Those things were everywhere. Why do you just stand there like an idiot? It's your fault he's here in the first place!" More tears streaked her cheeks as her lips trembled. "I don't know why he's even still helping you. What have you ever done for him?"

"I don't know," Seren whispered. "I'm sorry."

Unhappy with Seren's answer, she rolled her eyes in disgust.

"Let's walk around, Mila. We'll find him."

"Fine," Mila mustered. "Let's go around." Her piercing gaze met with Seren's. "I'll *never* forgive you if he's dead."

Seren didn't deserve forgiveness if Jude was dead. It would be his fault, and he knew it.

"Do you still have your dagger?" Seren asked her, changing the subject.

"Yes. I somehow managed to hold onto it without stabbing myself. What about you? Where is your sword?"

Seren had released it from his grip while tumbling down. It could be anywhere. With a sigh, he looked up at the treacherous slope and scanned the area. Then, perhaps through sheer luck or divine intervention, a glimmer of metal caught his eye amidst the foliage several feet away. He navigated the slippery terrain, reaching out and successfully retrieving his sword.

"That was lucky," Seren said with a breath of relief.

Mila scoffed dismissively, turning her back to Seren. She pointed to a patch of trees that curved around the slope. "We can go that way."

Seren nodded firmly and followed Mila as she took the lead. The forest was denser than earlier and wouldn't be easy to navigate if he had to run. He prowled through the trees, aware of the deafening volume of his breath. Every step he took felt much too loud. Seren winced as a branch snapped under his foot. Mila glared at him from over her shoulder. Taking a deep breath, he crept after her, carefully avoiding any more branches.

The absence of any noise created a growing unease inside Seren. He had expected to see even more demons, but the forest felt too quiet. He kept his hand firmly gripped on the handle of his sword. It was obvious they were still inside the Veil. The heaviness was still weighing upon his chest. It was a nasty feeling, as if he could sense the evil that lurked within the dimension.

Seren stepped over mossy logs, maintaining a respectable distance behind Mila. She had wiped away all her tears, confidently holding her head up. Despite the broken wrist dangling at her side, she gripped her weapon firmly in her other hand. The bite on her arm looked excruciating, with inflamed skin running up to her elbow.

Seren knew Mila had every reason to hate him. And a secret part of him wished she would drive her dagger straight into him to rid him of his pathetic existence. They were in the Veil because of him. Seren wished Jude had left him underground, sparing them both from the disastrous circumstances.

It all came down to him, and for what? A son of a God? How did he even know that was true? Did it even make a difference? He was weaker than both Mila and Jude. He was pitiful. And if Jude's life was lost, he could only blame himself and yet another life would be burdened by his tainted hands.

Jude had already endangered himself multiple times for Seren's sake, and payment meant nothing if he was dead. Deep down, Seren knew that chances were slim that Jude was alive. His leg hadn't been functioning properly, and he could barely stand on his own.

Seren swallowed hard, knowing that Mila's words held some truth. Something was wrong with him, whether it was the result of the seal on his back or something else. While he cared deeply for Jude, a part of him remained detached. He wondered if he was even capable of shedding a tear if he was dead. Or was he truly a monster?

"I'll go to Lumina on my own," Seren whispered, fully aware Mila couldn't hear him. "Once this is over, I'll leave both of you. I promise."

He would find Aiden on his own, demanding answers to the questions that plagued his mind. He needed to understand who he was, why he found himself in the Godless City, and the identity of his father. No longer would he be a burden.

In the distance, the sharp echoes of gunshots pierced the air—one, two, three. Then, an eerie silence settled, broken by Mila and Seren's hurried footsteps.

It had to be Jude, relentlessly reloading his weapon to stay alive.

Mila and Seren raced through the woods, abandoning caution as they sprinted toward the source of the gunfire. They dodged through the trees, the sound of branches loud underneath their rushed footsteps.

"We're coming, Jude!" Mila shouted.

Seren trailed Mila as he maneuvered through the trees. Another shot echoed through the air, this one sounding much closer. He could see a clearing ahead of them, only seconds away. And even through the sound of their trampling footfalls, he heard it. He skidded to a stop. Mila followed suit, her face dripping with sweat.

"Seren, what the hell are you doing?" she asked angrily.

"Do you hear that?" Seren asked breathlessly. "It sounds like a woman singing."

"I don't hear anything, idiot. Let's just get out of here. The forest is playing tricks on you. Jude needs us now."

But Seren knew that voice, and he knew that song.

"Go without me," he breathed. "I'm no help anyway."

Jude could wait. Everything else could wait.

"Are you stupid?" Mila groaned.

"My little star
Even if you wander far
I am where you are
A dream within a dream
Is where you will find me
For I am one with the Mother Tree."

It was a lullaby she had sung to him many times. Ignoring Mila's pleas, Seren walked toward the sound.

She was here.

His mother stood gracefully between two weeping willows. Her ethereal voice filled the air, every note filling him with warmth. Her presence illuminated the night, casting a gentle glow upon the surrounding foliage. She looked like he remembered, with a tender smile and eyes full of love.

"Mother," Seren whispered.

He stumbled toward her without thought. She had come back to him. It was exactly as she'd promised. He felt a hand reach out and grab onto the collar of his shirt.

"Seren, stop!" Mila demanded.

He pried her fingers from him, turning his attention back to his mother. He approached her with open arms, eager to fall into her embrace like a lost child.

Nothing else mattered.

Seren clutched the green silk of her dress, relishing the velvety touch between his fingers, reassuring him that she was real.

A flood of memories washed over him as he rested his head against his mother's chest. The sensation of her once stroking his hair as she had done when he was a child brought a comforting familiarity. He took in her scent—flowers, honey, and home.

Seren's mother gently resumed the lullaby, its cadence filling the air again. He didn't fight the drowsiness that overtook him as his body relaxed. And when Mila let out a bloodcurdling scream from behind him, he let the sleep take him.

Eleven

"Demons live among us in human flesh, and humans walk among us with the heart of a demon. My fingers are blackening, and my soul is crumbling. Soon, the dark magic will take hold of me, and my soul will belong to the Veil. Is this the fate the priests speak of?"

—Exorcist Damian Silver

1025 A.E.C.

Seren couldn't help but blush as Kamilah sprawled across mauve sheets, her arms positioned gracefully above her head. Her luscious hair spilled across the bed like running water. Despite her weary gaze, she stayed transfixed on the radiant stars that twinkled across the ceiling in shimmering hues of blue and purple. The room seemed cloaked in enchantment, creating a mesmerizing illusion of a nocturnal sky. Momentarily, her hand reached upward as if reaching out to touch a star, but it faltered, her fingers falling limp.

Draped in a sheer, black negligee that left little to the imagination, every contour and curve of her body was exposed as she stretched like a rousing tomcat. Embarrassment flushed Seren's cheeks more aggressively this time. He turned away with a subtle gasp.

"Mila, why... why aren't you wearing any clothes?" he stammered.

But she remained unresponsive. The awkward silence hung heavy in the air. Slowly, Seren turned to face her once more.

"Mila?"

She sat up, gingerly swinging her slender legs over the edge of the extravagant bed. She reached beneath the bed and retrieved a medium-sized box. A subtle smile twinkled on her lips as she carefully opened the ebony box. Intrigued, Seren leaned in closer, recognizing the gleaming dagger instantly. It lay on a plush azure velvet sheet, its blade shimmering like clear water.

"Mila, where are we?" he asked her. "You're...healed?"

She looked up from the box with a deep sigh, no recognition that he'd spoken to her written in her expression. Seren positioned himself in front of her, kneeling beside the bed. Furrowing his brows, he waved his hand in front of her face, hoping for even the smallest flicker of acknowledgment. Yet, there was nothing, not even a hint of awareness. Confusion washed over Seren, and he took a step back. Were they under some sort of spell?

The last thing Seren remembered was sprinting through the Behethium Forest, desperately searching for Jude. But then, everything turned hazy and fragmented, like a dream slipping through his fingers. When did they leave the forest? The room before him was entirely unfamiliar and unlike anything he'd seen.

The bed in the room was a masterpiece on its own. It reached towering heights, occupying a sizable portion of the space. The headboard stood as a remarkable piece of art—colossal and adorned with painstakingly crafted details. Every aspect of the room was extravagant, leaving no corner untouched by its grandeur.

Splayed across the floor was the eburnean skin of a bearlike creature. Spanning an impressive ten-foot length, it served as nothing more than a decorative piece in the center of the room. With its jaw agape and reflective glass eyes, it appeared stuck in a frozen state of rage. Each tooth had been meticulously replaced with fang-shaped quartz, glistening in pristine alignment. Seren shuddered, wondering if it had been some sort of demon.

The sound of approaching footsteps jolted him back to reality. Mila rushed to conceal the box beneath her bed. The doors flew open without warning, revealing a beautiful woman striding in. Mirroring the radiant beauty of Mila herself, the woman had the same luminous brown skin and dark hair. She wore a sleek, form-fitting crimson gown that accentuated her every curve. The dress plunged between her breasts and trailed down to her belly button. Sinuously interwoven, black-plated metallic snakes held the dress together across her ribs, accentuating her figure. The woman's chest also bore the same red- tattoos that marked Mila's skin. The intricate ink continued down the woman's arms, depicting snakes wrapping around her arms.

Taking a commanding stance in the room's center, the woman firmly planted her hands on her hips. She took no notice of Seren as her eyes grazed across the room.

"How long will you hide in your room, Kamilah?"

She strode across the room, fixated on a small table at Mila's bedside. A noticeable disdain etched her face as she gazed upon a vase overflowing with a bundle of bluebells and asters, the colors standing out against the room's somber atmosphere. With a forceful motion, the woman swept the vase off the table, its crash resonating through the air. The once beautiful flowers were crushed underneath the weight of the fractured glass. Despite the woman's intense reaction, Mila remained unmoved.

"Insolent child," she scoffed. "Don't you dare ignore your mother."

Seren inhaled sharply. *Mother?* Was this...a memory?

"You really should be more careful wandering the sides of the mountain. There's no reason for you to go out there," Mila's mother snapped. "If you want flowers, simply ask."

Mila turned her head away. With a snarl, her mother grabbed her face, her nails digging into her skin, forcing Mila to make eye contact.

"My perfect daughter," she sighed, her voice holding a hint of affection this time. Her mother released her grip. "I am sorry for my outburst. I worry about you. You know that this is the way things must be. When you take my place as Queen, you will understand. Lilith wants to restore what is rightfully ours, and once you finally meet her, you will see." She brushed Mila's hair back. "You were chosen, my dearest. And tonight, you must prove that you are capable. It is a sacrifice that will not be made in vain."

Mila ignored her, her jaw muscles flexing—the singular sign of her vexation. The Queen furrowed her dark brows at her silent response, her mouth in a tight line of discontent.

Seren shrank back against the wall. Kamilah was supposed to be a...queen? He felt his head spin. It was making more and more sense why she had run away.

"You can't ignore me forever," the Queen growled.

Without a care, Mila crossed her arms against her chest.

"I feel I have been very patient with you," her mother said dryly. "Yet, this is how you repay me? So be it."

The Queen strode purposefully across the room in a visible display of frustration. Without a word, she forcefully pushed open the grand doors. She exited, leaving a lingering sense of unease in her wake.

Mila released a weary sigh, rubbing her temples. But there was no time for her to decompress. The doors flung open once again, and her mother stormed back in. The Queen tugged on a chain in her right hand, and behind her stumbled a cloaked figure. Cloaked in obscurity, not a single inch of their form was visible beneath the trailing expanse of pale fabric. The figure stood motionless at the Queen's side as her hand tightened on the chain.

"Is this what you want instead, Kamilah?" she spat. "I could have you create a Hollow for your first task instead. It is a much more grueling experience for someone as weak-willed as you."

Her mother deftly flicked the hood, causing the cloak to cascade down, revealing a grotesque sight that sent Seren reeling backward. Nausea washed over him.

The man before him was a patchwork of scars, his skin twisted into hideous layers of disfigurement. Every inch of his body was marred, the discolored remnants of wounds dominating every inch of him. Vacant, hollow sockets remained where his eyes had once been. His hands, twisted and gnarled, were shrouded in bandages, fresh blood tracing an unsettling path down his malformed torso. The tattered remnants of his lips were crudely sewn together with crimson string, leaving him unable to speak even if he dared to try. If there had ever been traces of his human existence, it had long been extinguished.

Mila's hands shook at the sight, but she remained silent, not daring to give her mother any satisfaction.

"Someday, you'll be creating Hollows," her mother said. "But for now, I am giving you an easy, painless task. A small sacrifice is a blessing for your coronation as the true heir. Perhaps I erred in my judgment. A little pain might be good for you."

Mila turned to her mother. "A small sacrifice? A blessing?" she spat. "Is that what you call murder?"

As their eyes met, Mila's mother looked disappointed.

"I often wonder why Lilith chose you," the Queen murmured. "You have resisted your fate long enough. It is time to succumb to your true potential. Quit sulking. Even I knew better than to appear this pitiful before my coronation."

The Queen tugged on the chain, motioning the tormented man to follow her. She stopped at the doors briefly before exiting.

"I hope you can make the right decision on your own, and I will not have to intervene."

This time, Mila flinched as her mother forcefully slammed the doors behind her, causing the walls to tremble. After a moment of silence, Mila rose from her seat, taking in a deep, shuddering breath as her hands clenched into tight fists at her sides. Within seconds, a resounding knock echoed through the chamber, signaling someone's presence at her door.

"Go away!" Mila shouted. She threw her hands up in exasperation. "Just leave me alone!"

Reluctantly, the doors creaked open, revealing a small woman who cautiously poked her head into the narrow opening.

"I'm deeply sorry, your Highness," she said softly. "I am bound to follow Queen Omaira's orders."

With a hesitant step, she entered the room, accompanied by another woman who bore a remarkable resemblance. Though their beauty couldn't compare to Mila and her mother's, both women radiated their own captivating charm. Matching golden braids trailed down their backs, their similar features indicating they were sisters. In their fair hands, they carried an assortment of garments, eliciting a groan from Mila as she collapsed onto the bed.

"Please, leave," Mila sighed. She flung her arm over her face, muffling her speech. "I want to be alone."

"Princess," the woman stammered, her voice quivering. "Queen Omaira has requested that we prepare you for the ceremony tonight. It is customary for the true heir to be appropriately attired for their coronation."

"I don't see why it matters. It isn't as if I am becoming the queen just yet," Mila muttered.

"Without being properly coronated as the true heir, you cannot assume the role of queen," the other woman interjected. "Please, the Queen will be furious if we do not oblige her wishes."

Mila removed her arm and sat up from the bed. "Make it quick," she sighed. "I have somewhere to be before tonight."

The women nodded in sync.

Mila stayed still, allowing them to carefully remove her robe.

Seren reverted his gaze out of respect, waiting until they had dressed her. When he finally looked back, Seren couldn't help but gasp in awe.

Mila stood before him in a striking red dress that clung to her every curve. The gown flowed down to the floor, resembling a pool of freshly spilled blood against the marble surface. The women dusted golden make-up on Mila's eyelids and reddened her lips. With seamless coordination, they gathered Mila's hair atop her head, allowing a select few strands to elegantly fall around the contours of her face.

Until then, Seren hadn't fully grasped that Mila was a princess. But as he saw her now, it became undeniably clear. It wasn't just her new attire but how she carried herself with elegance and poise.

"You look stunning, your Highness."

The two women stood before her and bowed together, presenting Mila with a piece of jewelry resting on her forehead.

"Blood rubies," Mila uttered. "How fitting."

Nervously, Mila fidgeted with her hands as the women did their finishing touches. They thanked Mila for allowing them to do as they were told and then hurried out of the room, leaving the two of them alone. She looked beautiful. Seren looked away from her, feeling his heart racing.

When Seren turned back around, he watched Mila approach a gilded mirror hanging on the wall. As she grimaced at her reflection, he wondered what Mila was thinking. He reached out to touch Mila's hand but went straight through her as if he was nothing but air, untouchable and unseen.

"One life," Mila whispered to herself. "For my own."

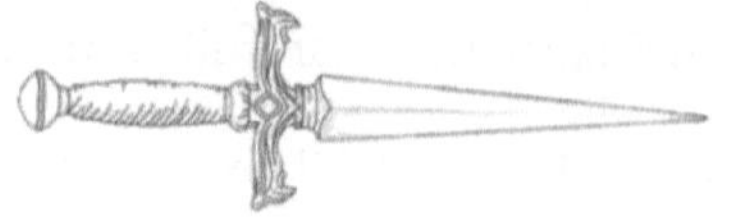

Seren's breath quickened as he descended the spiraling granite stairs. The walls, hewn from shadowy rock, seemed to close in on him as he realized the Sanguine Kingdom existed entirely underground. He couldn't explain the feeling building up inside him, but he had an urgent desire to...*run*. Though he tried to shake the feeling and continued to trail Mila.

They entered a narrow corridor as they reached the bottom of the stairs. The sconces flickered light from red candles across the stone walls. Dust settled on the fixtures, and cobwebs lined the walls. The candles emitted an everlasting flame, never dimming.

Mila abruptly pivoted, guiding them toward a petite door nestled amidst the weathered stone. From the folds of her dress, she produced a small bronze key, skillfully unlocking the door. As it swung open, a spiraling staircase revealed itself below.

Seren groaned. *More stairs?*

The two of them began to descend the staircase, reaching the bottom to find a set of doors resembling those of Mila's own bedroom. What was she doing here?

Mila rapped gently, and as the door slowly creaked open, Seren caught sight of a male face peering out from within.

"Let me in," she whispered. "I'm not supposed to be here."

Seren slipped behind her as she entered the room, utterly stunned. The young man, a perfect likeness to Kamilah, echoed her in every way —

from his facial features to the way he carried himself. Before Mila, he stood with a paintbrush in hand, blue streaks marking his cheek.

"What are you doing here?" he asked, concern evident in his voice. "Mother will be furious."

Mila rushed past him, shutting the door behind her. She reached out and wiped the paint from his cheek with her thumb.

"I should've demanded a blue dress," Mila said softly.

He smiled. "Red suits you."

Mila sighed, settling on his bed. Her dress draped across the turquoise blankets. The room felt cozy but cluttered, with a desk in one corner laden with paints and brushes. Beautiful canvases adorned the walls, each painted in various shades of blue. Seren approached one painting, slowly realizing it depicted the sky. Soft hues of blue seamlessly blended with delicate strokes of pink, stretching across the canvas like dawn's first light.

"I fear Mother is onto us, Kamil," Mila whispered.

"What do you mean?" he asked, sitting next to her on the bed.

Standing, Mila ran her fingers through her hair anxiously, her once neat updo now unraveling, strands escaping as she paced the room.

"We were supposed to have more time," she explained desperately. "Before my first sacrifice. But it's happening tonight." Frustration overwhelmed her, and she forcefully struck the wall. "That wretched *witch*!"

Seren was feeling more and more uneasy. What did the sacrifice even mean? His thoughts wandered back to the words Jude had told him in the Underbelly. Was Mila going to... *kill* someone?

Kamil's hand tightened on the paintbrush, his knuckles blanching. "Tonight?" he stammered. "It wasn't supposed to be until next month."

"I know," Mila replied, biting her lip. "And I have no choice, Kamil. If we try to leave now, it will expose us. I'm certain Mother is testing me, suspecting my true intentions. She must've known that I was planning to leave before the coronation. And that vile Iris likely provided her with information, always prying with her nonsensical questions."

Mila sat on the bed again, her face falling into her hands. "And tonight, I'll be no better than any of them," she choked. "A monster."

Seren's heart skipped a beat at her words.

"You're wrong," Kamil said with determination. "You're different, Mila. Even when we were kids. You're the only one who has ever had the capability to deny the teachings of Lilith. I've seen it myself. You're no monster."

Mila lifted her head, her tear-filled eyes meeting her brother's. "Mother sees right through me," she whispered, her voice trembling. "What if she takes it away? It's all I have left." Fear etched across her face, raw and palpable.

Seren's mind churned, contemplating the weight of Mila's words. *What is it that she fears losing?*

"She won't," Kamil insisted. "If you go through with the sacrifice, she'll overlook your doubts, and you'll be able to keep it until you're the queen. And besides..." Her brother smiled. "You have me."

"What makes you think she won't take it anyway?" Mila asked. "She took yours away."

Kamil's expression saddened Seren. He'd never seen someone look so defeated. "What good is a true name when you don't have freedom anyway?" Kamil said somberly. "It makes no difference for me."

A true name. What does that mean? Seren wondered.

Anger replaced Mila's despair. "It's cruel," she spat. "I can't stay here with these brainwashed fools."

Kamil sighed and stared off into the distance. "They'll come after us, Mila. You're the heir to the throne. Lilith has chosen you as the next successor. We both know that nothing can change that. Do you think leaving will guarantee us a chance?"

"Then I'll find a way to free us," Mila said, exasperated. "Even if I must travel to the ends of the world. I'll do anything."

Somewhere in the distance, a clock chimed, grabbing the attention of both siblings. Mila looked at Kamil's paintings, taking a step forward. Her finger grazed the brushstrokes.

"I promise someday I will show you the sky."

Then Mila pulled the dagger out from under her dress, replacing it with the paintbrush she took from his hand. That's right... Mila had said the blade belonged to her brother. Seren was certain now; this was a memory. But... why was he here?

Kamil's jaw dropped. "Mila," he whispered. "Is this a Seraph blade? It looks just like the pictures. How did you get it?"

"Does it matter?"

"Do you think it could kill Lilith?"

"I think so," Mila said. "But I want you to have it. You must promise me that you'll protect yourself, okay? I will do my best to protect you, but if I ever fail, use it. Even if you must use it on Mother."

"I can't," he began. "If she senses my intentions and uses my name, it won't matter..."

"Listen to me," Mila interrupted. "After the ceremony, I'll come for you. We'll leave and go to the Godless City. I'll find a way to free us forever, Prince Atsu. I will show you a sunset and sunrise. I will show you the stars and the lights of the city. And we will find a way to be free. I swear it."

A small smile settled upon her brother, not reaching his eyes. "Okay, Princess Ata," Kamil answered. "I'll be waiting."

As Mila exited, Seren's gaze lingered on her brother, his attention still fixated on the dagger clutched in his hands. His expression betrayed a profound sadness. Seren found himself momentarily unable to tear himself away.

Why would the Queen, who was rumored to offer sacrifices to Lilith using men, have a son? Mila was desperate to leave with her brother, paranoia consuming her. And although warped beliefs surrounded her, Mila was clearly much different than her mother. The thought of having to kill someone had driven her to tears. But still...she was willing to do it if it meant freeing her brother.

Seren caught up with Mila as she ascended the stairs. Her hurried footsteps echoed through the empty hallways. As she approached the corridor leading to her room, she turned a corner, nearly colliding with a young woman. She smirked at Mila, throwing yellow hair over her shoulder.

"Why are you in such a hurry, Princess?" she sneered. "Shouldn't you be preparing for the ceremony?"

Mila clenched the fabric of her dress. "The ceremony isn't until Devil's Hour," she snapped. "Shouldn't you mind your own business, Iris? After all, you're only the Queen's servant."

Iris flinched. "My apologies, your Highness," she said bitterly. She bowed her head, although it was obvious she was fuming.

"And if you must know, I planned to visit the library before the ceremony. I still have a little bit of time," Mila said. "So, please do get out of my way."

Iris nodded mechanically, taking a step to the right. "I will inform the Queen so she doesn't worry," she said, forcing a smile.

As the two of them walked away, Seren could've sworn he heard Iris curse Mila under her breath.

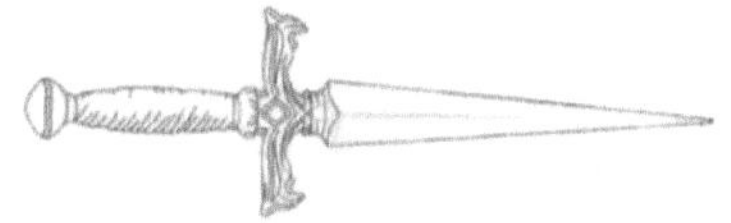

It had been nearly an hour of Mila frantically flipping through books. Seren watched as she flung book after book into a growing pile, grumbling to herself.

Feeling powerless and bored, Seren decided to aimlessly wander through the library. The towering bookshelves loomed above him. Leather-bound volumes with weathered spines and golden inscriptions lined the shelves in an orderly fashion. Memories of the grand library within the Caelestis Church flickered in his mind, where the books had seemed endless. The Sanguine Royal Library, though still vast, seemed almost petite in comparison. A hazy recollection surfaced of Aiden spending countless hours in the library with his nose between pages.

Much like the library in Caelestis, the Sanguine Royal Library also had murals painted across the ceiling. This one depicted the Sisters' story of Lilith. As Seren followed the mural, he was able to understand their portrayal.

In the Garden of Aetheria, the three primordial Gods chose the most beautiful flower to shape the first woman. Together, they finally settled on a rose, the fairest blossom in the entire garden. Infusing life into the rose, they created Lilith, tailored perfectly for Adamus.

The Gods marveled at their creation. Lilith was beautiful, her hair shimmering with a vibrant crimson hue akin to the resplendent rose petals. However, just like the thorns that once encircled her, chains tightly confined her to Adamus. He gripped them firmly, embracing them as a display of the Gods' longing for her subjugation.

Adamus was portrayed as a cruel and twisted figure. The story continued, showing Lilith fighting against the chains of submission, desiring a will of her own. Adamus' desire for her dwindled as she resisted him. He eventually called upon the Gods and was gifted Eden, who became known as the first mother.

Lilith faced exile, cast out from the sacred Garden of Aetheria. The accusatory fingers of the Gods were directed at her, for she had rejected the predetermined destiny they had intended. Yet, as she ventured toward the gates of her banishment, her steps ground to a halt before the Mother Tree. It was painted exactly as the one Seren had seen on the grand ceiling of the Church of Caelestis.

Beneath the Tree, a handsome man offered solace to Lilith. Witnessing this scene, Adamus was consumed by both rage and fury, sprinting to inform the outraged Gods. As the images unfurled, a forbidden love story was unveiled—a clandestine affair between Lilith and none other than the Devil himself. Despite the divine rules and strictures, they defiantly embraced their passionate connection, transcending the boundaries set by the heavens.

But it appeared that the Devil was still not satisfied. In a cunning ruse, he assumed the deceptive guise of a wyrm to trick Adamus into partaking in the forbidden Mother Tree. Once Adamus had consumed its forbidden fruit, he convinced Eden to partake with him. When the Gods appeared to confront him, he pointed a finger accusingly at Eden. Adamus appeared as the true instigator of sin, demanding the Gods to curse both Eden and Lilith for his perceived shame.

Seren froze upon reaching the end of the mural. The Devil and Lilith stood with their hands tightly entwined, resolute before an imposing gate that offered a glimpse into the stygian depths of Hell itself. An insidious darkness crept forth from the ominous void, threatening to seep into the world.

This was the fate the Sanguine Sisters hoped for— Hell on Earth and the fall of humankind. It wasn't a story that Seren ever remembered being told; it served as a grim reminder of the dark forces at play.

Mila slammed a book shut, jolting Seren back to his senses. He watched her stuff a piece of paper into her pocket. It was a map she had evidently ripped out of one of the books. Rising to her feet, Mila took a deep breath.

Seren heard it again—the thundering chime of a clock.

It was time for her coronation.

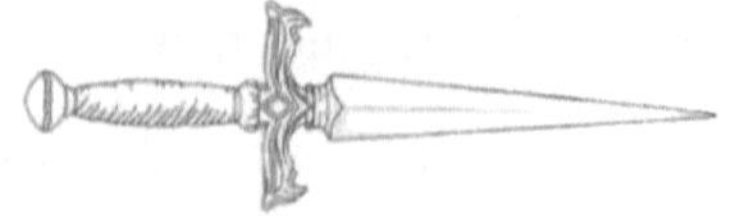

The giant black doors stood ominously before the two of them, their presence casting a dreadful shadow upon Mila's face. Stepping through those doors meant she would be bound to the forthcoming ceremony. As for Seren, he didn't know what to expect, but he knew it wasn't good.

Summoning her courage, Mila drew a deep breath and, with trembling hands, pushed open the colossal doors.

Immediately, they found themselves bathed in the glow emanating from numerous candles that filled the room, casting silhouettes that danced upon the walls. Arrayed in neat rows that spanned the room, the Sanguine Sisters assembled. Draped in translucent veils, each woman clutched a crimson candle, perfectly matching the fabric draping their forms.

Above them all, Queen Omaira stood on an altar crafted from jagged stones, demonic sigils etched into its warped surface, hinting at past dark rituals. At the very center of the altar lay Kamil, bound and gagged. His eyes widened with fear, breath quick and frantic as he strained against the ropes that restrained him. Mila's face blanched at the horrific sight.

No. Seren's breath caught in his throat.

"Kamil," she choked.

"Welcome, my Sisters," Omaira announced, noticing Mila's entry.

The Queen bowed to the silent congregation before her; all the women bowed their heads respectfully in return.

"Tonight, there will be a sacrifice unlike any other. As many of the elder sisters are aware, my two children were born on the eve of a blood moon. My dearest Ata and my son Atsu." She gestured toward her son struggling on the cold slab of stone.

Mila was frozen in place, her lower lip quivering.

"We have anxiously awaited this moment, knowing it carries immense significance. The princess's affection for her brother surpasses all limits, transcending the boundaries of ordinary love. Her devotion is profound and selfless and represents the purest form of affection that can exist between siblings. My daughter's unwavering dedication is such that she would willingly sacrifice her own life to preserve that of her brother."

In a sudden surge, Mila propelled herself forward, but before she could continue any further, strong arms seized her, wrenching her back. The grip of a woman behind her held firm, and Mila writhed and thrashed relentlessly. Her mother remained unfazed by Mila, keeping her composed demeanor without the slightest pause or acknowledgment.

"As my Sisters are aware," Queen Omaira proclaimed, "There is no greater sacrifice than that which is made out of love. Our beloved prince stands as the ultimate testament to this truth, an offering unlike any seen in centuries. Though my heart aches for my dear son, I have always known that this day would inevitably arrive."

"Liar!" Mila's piercing cry erupted through the air.

Seren instinctively reached for the woman, hoping to pry her arms off Mila. But he went through her like smoke.

Mila's mother ignored her outburst and continued. "Lilith will bathe in his blood, and in turn, we will bathe in power. The eternal gift of youth and beauty shall continue to be ours so that we may continue our purpose." Twisted laughter escaped her lips as Mila's screams of anguish grew louder.

With her elbow, Mila bashed the woman's face. Blood spewed from her nose as Mila ripped free from her grasp. Screaming, Mila thrashed toward her mother through a sea of veiled women.

The Queen's words dripped with false sentiment as she spoke. "It pained me greatly to deceive you, my dear," she said. "When you were a child, I tried to paint a picture of your brother being extraordinary. A harbinger of a new era, the genesis of a bloodline destined for greatness! I promised to protect him, to ensure his safety. But deep down, we all knew this fateful day would arrive. All the men in this world are tainted; it is the doing of Adamus. He is the one who cursed humankind."

Mila's desperate attempt to break free was met with the grasp of two other women who held her firmly in place. Despite her struggles, her cries were drowned out by the Queen's relentless narrative.

"This is for you, Princess. For our shared future," the Queen said. "Through this ultimate sacrifice, we shall reap the bountiful rewards that await us. Together, we will reclaim what is rightfully ours." She paused, her gaze intense and fervent. "Can't you see, my dear daughter? This is the purpose Lilith has chosen for you, *Princess Ata*."

Seren watched as Mila's body suddenly went limp, her face falling to the ground, obscured by her hair.

"She calls upon us to pave the path to a new world, one cloaked in renewal. These sacrifices, painful as they may be, shall not persist much longer. Soon, Lucifer will rend the barriers of Veil completely, and only the strongest among us will remain."

Why had Mila stopped fighting? Seren raced toward her, running through the veiled women. Kneeling beside her, he searched her face. Mila's expression was blank, her eyes glassy.

"Kamilah..." he whispered.

He clenched his fists, his eyes traveling up to the Queen. Why did she look so... amused? The Queen reached out her hand, brushing her son's hair back as though he were a small child.

"All of humanity belongs in the Kingdom of Hell, where the strong shall rise, and the weak shall fall," the Queen said, her voice booming through the chamber. "Lilith chose you for a reason. She saw in you the potential to become our future queen, to lead us toward our inevitable destiny. Can't you understand? By embracing this path, you will surpass us all in power. You will be revered, feared, and adored. A throne beside the King of Demons could be yours, Ata. This is what truly matters to you, isn't it? Power. Immortality. The fulfillment of your deepest desires. Imagine it, my daughter, all your dreams coming true."

"No, Mila," Seren said desperately. He reached for her face, cursing as his fingers disappeared into her skin. "Don't listen to her."

"I understand you more than anyone. I know your true nature. You have an insatiable bloodlust that burns within you. You were born with it, Ata. It is the desire to be free from the chains that have held us down for many years. Do not disappoint us, for you are the key to the future." With a nod, the Queen commanded, "Release her. Now, come here, Ata."

Mila took hesitant steps toward her mother, tears pooling in her eyes. To Seren's astonishment, she briefly embraced her daughter.

"Mila!" Seren shouted. "Don't!"

But it was no use. Nobody could hear him.

"It is a heavy burden to carry, Princess Ata. But the pain shall fade as all things do. Now, let us begin."

All the women bowed their heads in perfect unison, their voices intertwining in a bone-chilling chant. The words flowed in an ancient language that Seren couldn't recognize, sending shivers down his spine.

Queen Omaira set a gleaming dagger in Mila's hand. The Seraph blade intended for Kamil. A sinister smile briefly curved at the corners of the Queen's lips. Trembling, Mila stared at the blade in her hands, tears falling upon it, evaporating instantly.

Mila timidly approached her brother. Kamil thrashed against his restraints, his protests muffled. Fear engulfed his trembling form as Mila raised the dagger high above her head, her fingers clinging tightly to its handle. His eyes begged, pleaded.

No. Seren raced toward them. *Stop.*

"I don't want to," Mila quivered.

"Take your sacrifice, Ata."

And Seren watched in horror as the dagger plummeted into her brother's heart.

Twelve

"The Unveiling of Andanova leaves me weary. I traveled to the borders, past the mountains, and waited with the others. We fought with all our might, defeating the demons that escaped. But I cannot shake this feeling that this is just the beginning."

—Exorcist Damian Silver

1025 A.E.C.

With a serpent-like torso of intertwining centipede legs, the demon coiled itself around Seren, ensnaring him within its grotesque embrace. It was undeniably a female creature, with five feminine masked faces, each exhibiting a different emotion. She replicated agony, fear, despair, disgust, and anger among them.

Mila recognized the demon. The sketches she had come across in the archives of the Sanguine Royal Library suddenly flooded her mind. How had she been so stupid and not realized? She should've recognized the Pale Lopers. It was now clear to Mila that the Shademother was responsible for everything.

The Shademother, an immensely formidable and tumultuous demon, had roamed the Veil for centuries, harboring an insatiable longing to breach into the realm of humanity. It was widely known that the more powerful the demon, the greater number of human souls they required to sustain their manifestation in the mortal realm. And it seemed she still hadn't had her fill.

"Sweet dreams, little prince," hissed the demon.

The Shademother cradled Seren like a child, holding him close to her chest. A spell kept him in an induced illusion, leaving him in a fitful sleep. The demon took one of her many arms and touched his hair gently. Mila's heart thumped as the raven color appeared to melt away, changing to a brilliant silvery-white. The creature reached over with another arm to remove the bracelet from Seren's wrist. All her masks turned into grotesque gestures of laughter as she held the bracelet between two spindly fingers.

"The Sun God?" the demon jeered. "Oh, you foolish humans are always blind to the truths of this world. Soon, he will be reduced to a mere mortal. These trinkets are useless."

The bracelet disintegrated in her blackened palm.

"Let him go," Mila said boldly. "You'd be a fool to kill him."

The she-demon chittered, its repulsive form scuttling at Mila with alarming speed. A disturbing smile contorted her wretched masks as if filled with sadistic delight. "And why, little witch? Do you think he is worth more to me alive? I wonder if he will taste as exquisite as your dear friend."

Mila's hands began to shake. "You're lying," she seethed.

"Am I? Or should I show you?"

Images invaded Mila's mind. Jude's lifeless eyes stared into the sky as blood pooled around him. Lopers stalked around his fresh corpse and prepared to devour him.

"Stop!"

This demon was an expert manipulator of perception, capable of delving into one's memories. This Mila remembered clearly. She couldn't trust anything the Shademother showed her. The corrupted wisps had caught her off-guard in the sewers, and she'd acted helpless as they bombarded her with the same nightmare that haunted her. This time, she knew what she was up against.

Mila held her dagger out, the light gleaming proudly under the light of the moon.

"Let him go, or I'll kill you."

"Don't make me laugh, Princess," the Shademother sneered. "That feeble weapon cannot harm me. You are weak, afraid to tap into your gifts, and unwilling to do whatever it takes to save those you hold dear."

At the demon's words, Jude's face involuntarily flashed in Mila's mind once more. The Shademother slithered around the princess, using her arms to contort her body while clutching Seren closely.

"You could have saved him. And you could have saved your brother. And now, you won't save this little prince either."

Mila covered her ears, her broken wrist screaming in pain. "Shut up!"

"What I don't understand," the demon continued, ignoring her demands. "Is why you would want to save him? Isn't he the real enemy? The real monster? Don't you want to see what he's done?"

The images intruded on Mila's thoughts. She tried to force them out but couldn't. She watched Seren standing over a woman, blood covering his palms as he stared at her limp body. Thoughts that were not her own invaded their way into her consciousness.

"You *see*? He is a danger to others and himself. He is not worth saving."

In an instant, a sinister blade of shadow erupted from the ground, impaling itself mercilessly through Mila's left shoulder. An agonized cry escaped her lips as searing pain ripped through her flesh. Mila stumbled backward and leaned into a nearby tree, desperately clutching her wound as blood flooded between her fingers.

"So, will you save him?" laughed the demon. "Or will you die beside him?"

Mila growled ferociously, lunging at the demon with her blade in her unencumbered hand.

Without warning, another blade of shadow lashed out, slicing through her calf with precision and forcefully propelled her backward, slamming her body harshly against the ground. The force knocked the wind from her lungs, leaving her momentarily winded.

At this rate...Mila was going to die. The Loper's bite had already drained most of her strength, causing angry red streaks to crawl up her skin where the wound started. On top of that, her left wrist was completely broken, and the pain was undeniable. Now, Mila was bleeding profusely from her two new wounds, her head starting to spin.

The porcelain masks of the Shademother shifted into despair, their cavernous mouths hanging open.

"This is dreadfully dull," she sighed. "I had hoped for some amusement. Oh, well. You'll be dead soon enough."

The monster sent a hurtling piece of shadow at Mila. This time, Mila ducked, the blade barely missing her head as it shallowly sliced her forehead. A small trickle of blood ran down the bridge of her nose.

She breathed rapidly, clutching onto her bleeding shoulder. It had sliced entirely through her body, the blood flowing too fast. It was only a matter of time before she lost consciousness from the blood loss. She had let the damn demon get to her.

Mila blinked through the fog, willing herself to stand steadily. She stepped through the pool of her own blood, her feet leaving splashes in their wake.

"I think I'll eat him before your demise," declared the Shademother. "In due time, he will merge with me and grant me unparalleled demonic power. His soul is worth thousands! And *why* is that? Tell me before you die, Princess."

Mila breathed heavily. "I don't know," she said.

The Shademother growled. "No matter. I will finally be able to cross into the human realm and devour as many souls as I desire. That is all that truly matters. I wish you to bear witness to your failure." Amidst her maniacal laughter, her masks rotated to the back of her head. A colossal void expanded, poised to engulf Seren.

No.

Mila sensed the tremor building inside of her. Her blood boiled. She didn't want to. But she had to. She would lose them if she didn't act, regardless of Seren's wrongdoings. She refused to have any more blood on her hands. Mila commanded her wounds to ripple shut, coagulating her blood instantaneously. A hum resonated within Mila. She extended her arm forward, willing the pool of blood to ascend from the ground.

"I can do tricks similar to yours," Mila huffed with a smirk.

She sent a spear of blood hurting toward the creature, which was much too fast for the Shademother to dodge. She shrieked as it impaled her torso, prompting a vicious black sludge to spill from her.

"Impossible," the Shademother fumed, looking down at her wound.

Mila laughed as she swayed on her feet. "Oh, very possible."

She delivered another powerful strike to the demon with a single fluid motion. The Shademother screamed in fury as she harnessed the shadows beneath the trees, converging them toward Mila. In her blind rage, the Shademother released Seren from her grasp, her sole goal to eliminate Mila.

Unrestrained, Mila channeled another ounce of her strength. And with a blade forged from her own blood, she shattered one of the porcelain masks, throwing the demon into another fit of wrath.

"Do you think you can defeat me?" she howled. "I called my children back, and they will eat you alive!"

As expected, the Pale Lopers were gathering around Mila in the dark. Their ravenous growls vibrated in their throats, anticipating the taste of flesh. Mila would need more blood to even begin to injure the Shademother enough for her to flee. But Mila had lost far too much and couldn't sacrifice anymore. She could hardly remain balanced, and casting her magic was draining her energy.

Only one choice remained. Mila breathed rapidly, her head feeling too heavy. The shadows had begun to surround her, and the Pale Lopers had brought themselves into the moonlight, merely seconds away from pouncing. With all her remaining strength, Mila dashed toward Seren's limp form. His hair was already fading back into its familiar color.

Mila stood over him, the dagger ready to fall. He began to stir, his eyelids fluttering open, revealing a brilliant amethyst color. She only needed enough to send the Shademother back into the forest depths. She aimed it for his flesh and raised the dagger higher above her head, ready to strike.

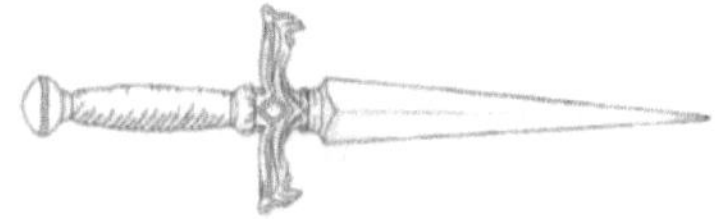

As Seren's eyes flashed open, Mila kneeled over him, clutching her dagger above her head. Her eyes were filled with a frenzy, untamed and wild.

Seren forcefully shoved her off him, sending her tumbling into the dirt. But, without a moment to spare, Mila pummeled back into him, frantically slashing with her dagger. His blade was missing; he was defenseless.

"Mila—stop!" Seren sputtered as he dodged an attack.

"*Die!*"

A disgusting creature slithered in their direction, physical shadows materializing behind it. Its grotesque body bore five masked faces, each painted with a loathsome visage. And trailing behind it was the horde they'd encountered earlier.

Seren's moment of shock gave Mila the opportunity she needed. She dug her dagger into his side, causing him to cry out. Blood gushed from the wound as she roughly pulled it from his flesh. Mila flexed her hand, and the blood spilled into the air, forming into sharp points. She thrust her arm forward, sending five perfectly pointed arrows of blood at the monster.

A resounding crack reverberated through the forest as every arrow found its intended target. The porcelain masks shattered into a million shards, and the creature let out an otherworldly scream that pierced the air. It hastily withdrew, causing the horde of monsters to writhe in pain. Their clawed hands clutched at their faces as if they were also experiencing pain. They vanished into the depths of the forest, leaving no trace of their presence behind.

Mila's strength gave away, and she crumpled to her knees. Her dagger dropped from her bloodstained grip, thudding next to Seren on the forest floor.

"Jude..." she whispered. "I'm sorry."

Seren grasped his side, blood escaping through his fingers. "You..." he whispered. "You stabbed me."

"And I'll do it again," Mila snarled.

Seren flinched at her hostility. "Will you kill me?" he asked, his voice coming out colder than expected. "Like you killed your brother?"

Mila looked at him with a menacing glare. Then she slammed into him, her eyes blazing furiously. Her knees dug into Seren's chest as she snatched the dagger from the ground. The cold tip pressed near Seren's throat, dangerously close, just like the day they met.

"Shut up," she seethed. "I *should* kill you. This is all your fault."

Seren found himself leaning into the dagger, feeling warm blood dribble down his neck. "Do it. Who knows what you could gain from killing me? More power? Isn't that why you killed your own brother?"

Mila recoiled as though he had struck her.

"You don't know anything about me, Seren." Her head drooped, her hair brushing against his cheeks. "I should kill you," Mila repeated. Blood dribbled onto his shirt, leaking from a wound on her forehead. "You're not even human. You're dangerous. I saw what you did. You're a *murderer*."

Seren's throat tightened. "Okay. Go ahead and kill me," he said flatly. "It's what I deserve. But how are you any better than me? Aren't we both monsters?"

And even as he said the words, he didn't believe them. He just wanted, so badly, to feel like he wasn't alone. That maybe...they shared the same burden and pain.

Mila's head fell onto his chest, her hair spilling over him. Her scent washed over him as her hand gripped his shirt, knuckles blanching. "I tried to stop it," she breathed. "It wasn't my fault."

Seren froze. Somewhere in the back of his mind, he could hear his own voice crying out to him. The voice of a child trapped in a world of pain and suffering.

It wasn't my fault.

It echoed over and over again within him like a bad dream. The sorrow welled up like a cup overflowing from the brim, threatening to spill out of him.

Seren forcefully pushed Mila away, and she crumpled effortlessly onto the ground. He did what he knew best. Seren ran. He left Mila behind and ran into the forest's depths without looking back.

Thirteen

"The Mother crafted three precious gifts for her beloved children: a harp bestowed upon Kallista, a crown for Helios, and a mighty sword entrusted to Caelum. After the Great War, they were lost, disappearing into the annals of time, their whereabouts unknown."

—Chronicles of the Gods

1025 A.E.C.

Seren's sides heaved as he collapsed, his back sliding against a tree trunk. He curled into a ball, bloodied hands shielding his head. It was his fault. Entirely his fault. Mila was suffering, her pain a consequence of his actions. Jude was dead. He should have been the one to suffer, not them.

"Stop," he pleaded, voice strained. "I'm sorry."

"You are going to bring all the beasts of the forest straight to you, Half-Light."

Seren's breath caught in his throat as the creature's voice erupted from the darkness. He looked around in the dark but could see nothing.

"It is no wonder you were tampered with. A necessary evil to control those disgusting human emotions."

"Who's there?" Seren demanded, standing up and scanning the forest.

"*Behind you...*" it hissed.

Seren's heart leaped as he turned around to face it. A massive serpent coiled around the tree slowly, its flaming eyes meeting with Seren's.

"*Are you afraid, child?*"

"No," he breathed shakily.

"*But you are afraid of something, are you not? I smell it.*"

Its forked tongue flickered across Seren's skin. He took a step back.

"What do you want?"

Seren felt for his sword, only to find it was gone.

"*I am not going to hurt you. I am not a fool,*" the serpent hissed. "*I merely wanted to meet the Prince myself. I can feel it. Don't you?*"

"What?" he whispered.

"*The Veil calls to you.*" The monster began to twist its body, coiling its thick neck around Seren's arm. "*You are no ordinary Half-Light. You are different. Special.*" Seren saw the gleam of the creature's fangs as it smiled. "*You were never meant to exist.*"

Suddenly, a searing pain pulsed from his wound, intensifying with each beat of his heart. Seren's vision blurred, and a strange sensation enveloped him, sending him into an agonizing cry. His head spun as if caught in a dizzying whirlwind, and his body was flooded with unfamiliar and overwhelming sensations.

"*A paradox.*"

Images flashed before Seren's eyes—ethereal landscapes, ancient battles, fragments of memories, and experiences he wasn't even sure were his own. He struggled to understand everything, trying to grasp any semblance of reality. His limbs trembled as unprecedented emotions coursed through his veins—joy, sorrow, love, and fury tangled together like threads woven in time.

"It will be your downfall. It will be your rising. It is your birth, and it is your death."

With a desperate cry, Seren released the pent-up sorrow inside him, the anguish echoing into the dark void surrounding him. As his voice passed through the air, a seismic tremor rumbled beneath him, causing the ground to quake in response as if the earth acknowledged and mirrored his anguish.

In a breathtaking instant, a brilliant burst of light pierced through the consuming darkness, illuminating the world around him, if only fleetingly.

Seren's heavy breathing filled the air as he stared into the now vacant space where the serpent had coiled moments ago. The eerily silent forest betrayed no signs of the creature's existence. A shiver ran down his spine.

Seren's hand instinctively gravitated toward the wound inflicted by Mila. A gasp escaped his lips as his fingers traced the path of the injury. The wound had vanished without a trace, leaving a mere silvery line.

Gathering his scattered thoughts, Seren shook his head to regain focus. Closing his eyes, he was overwhelmed by the chaos within him. He couldn't do this, not now. He needed to get himself together. There was no time to dwell on the cryptic words of another demon; he needed to get back to Mila. Leaving her alone and wounded in the forest had been a mistake.

Cursing himself under his breath, Seren acknowledged that he had acted like a child, fleeing into the woods. He stood up, casting one last glance back at the tree behind him, but the demon was surely gone. Without wasting another second, Seren sprinted back toward Mila.

Stupid, he thought. *It seems I am always running.*

Seren burst into the clearing, but Mila was gone. The sole evidence of her existence lay in the fresh blood staining the forest floor.

"Mila!" His voice echoed into the night, swallowed by the silence. He called for her again. And again. "Damn it!"

A sudden rustle erupted from the bushes behind Seren, jolting him into a sharp, backward leap. His heart raced in his chest. Panic gripped him as he desperately scanned the ground for his sword, his fingers grazing the cold earth in a frantic search. The snapping of branches intensified. A glint of light caught his eye—a reflection on the blade of his sword. He bolted toward it and swung it toward the source of the noise.

"Wait— Seren!"

He released his grip on the sword.

"You're...alive?" Seren said in disbelief.

Jude limped toward him, his bionic leg barely able to carry any weight. Blood spattered his face and shirt, but he seemed surprisingly unharmed.

"Yes, but not for long if you keep yelling into the forest like that," he grumbled.

"How did you manage to get away?" Seren asked, bewildered.

"Sheer luck and willpower," Jude replied with a chuckle. "I was only moments away from becoming a meal before they withdrew. It seems something else got their attention."

Seren exhaled. "I'm happy to see you." And he truly meant it.

Jude's smile broadened. "You as well," he replied while looking over Seren's shoulder. "Where's Mila?"

Seren hesitated, carefully choosing his words. "We were attacked by a demon and ended up getting separated." It was a partial lie, but Seren was ashamed that he had left her alone.

Jude reached toward Seren's bloodied hands, his eyes wide. "Are you alright? Were you bitten?"

"No... Mila stabbed me. And then used my blood to fight the demon."

Seren had never seen anything like the magic Mila possessed. There was no denying her raw power. She had managed to stay alive while he was ensnared in its spell and single-handedly forced the demon to retreat. Despite her true feelings, Mila had willingly put her life on the line to protect him. The guilt gnawed at him.

"She won't be in the forest then," Jude murmured. He leaned against a tree, wincing. "She rarely uses her magic due to the danger it brings, but one of the gravest risks is attracting the attention of the Sanguine Sisters. They've been searching for their princess for a long time."

"What do you mean?" Seren managed.

"Mila once told me that she doesn't use her magic because of the shared connection she has with her mother. She can track her if she uses it."

Seren's heart skipped a beat. It hadn't occurred to him that the Queen could be powerful enough to traverse in and out of the Veil.

"Do you think...?" Seren trailed off.

"There's nothing we can do now," Jude said. "Right now, all we can do is pray we make it out of the Veil alive." He grimaced as a horrifying screech echoed in the trees ahead of them. "And I'm starting to believe that isn't going to happen."

Seren reached down to retrieve his sword and tightened his grip on the hilt. He refused to let Jude die. Failure had haunted him too often; he wouldn't allow it this time. He glanced at Jude and the gun in his grasp, his brows furrowed.

"Bullets?"

Jude shook his head with a frown.

Shit.

The screech intensified. Seren turned sharply toward Jude.

"I can't run, Seren," he whispered. "Go without me. It's your only chance."

"No." Seren clasped onto Jude's arm, propelling him forward. "I'm not letting you die."

Seren lifted his chin to the starry night sky, choosing one particularly brilliant star as his beacon of hope. Closing his eyes, he flexed his hand, feeling a small glimmer of power course through his veins.

The demonic sounds closed in behind them—a cacophony of monstrous roars. Jude trembled behind him. He knew what Jude was thinking; they were both resigned to death. There seemed to be no way out.

But if Mila was right...

"You're not even human."

If Kitsune was right...

"Son of a God."

The serpent.

"You were never meant to exist."

Then maybe… just maybe…

Seren didn't contemplate it further. He forced Jude's arm around him, carrying most of his weight, and started to run. His lungs burned; Jude grunted and groaned in pain, his cybernetic leg dragging across the ground.

They weren't going to die, not like this.

And that strange yet familiar woman's voice flooded his brain.

"Seren, in time, you will learn, but I will guide you."

Seren recognized the jolt of power coursing down his spine. Somehow, he could see it—the thin barriers lining the edge of the forest, the way out.

"Come on, Jude," Seren urged. "We're so close."

Jude cried out in pain as Seren forced his legs forward. The screams of demons and their thundering footfalls grew louder… and louder… Seren stole a glance over his shoulder, catching a glimpse of the gaping, twisted mouths only feet away. Seren's heart thundered in his chest. The barriers began to fade from his vision as the power he felt started to disperse.

So close… and…

Jude gasped for air, falling to his knees. Seren also crumpled, taking deep breaths of air. The weight upon them had lifted. The moon suddenly seemed brighter.

"We're… out of the Veil," Jude gasped. "And I thought my luck had finally run out."

Seren looked toward Jude, sweat pasted to his forehead. Seren flashed the widest smile he'd had since he could remember, and then the two of them burst into laughter. Perhaps it was the fact they had barely escaped death or the adrenaline pounding in their veins. It felt so good. Laughter bubbled up inside Seren, warm and inviting. He wished it would last forever. Their laughter soon faded, leaving the two of them motionless under the starry sky.

"Mila could still be in there," Seren uttered. He looked behind him, but he couldn't see the barriers anymore. If the Veil was still anywhere near the forest, he could no longer tell.

"No, I guarantee she was taken to the Sanguine Kingdom," Jude said, sitting upright. "Mila is the heir after all."

Images of Mila, her hand poised with a dagger above her brother, flashed through Seren's mind. He shook his head vehemently, refusing to believe it. There had to be more to her story, a missing piece he had overlooked in her troubled past. She had willingly left even though she was heir to the Sanguine throne. He couldn't believe that Mila was as cruel as her mother.

"We have to help her," Seren said.

"Nobody knows where the Sanguine Kingdom is." Jude rubbed the back of his neck.

Seren reeled toward Jude. "I won't go back," he said confidently. "To Lumina. Not without Mila." It was Seren's fault she had been involved. If it weren't for him, she would be safe in the Godless City. He bit the inside of his cheek. Mila had seen the memory of his mother and maybe saw even more than he had. He was a hypocrite. *Monster.*

Jude stood up with a grin, his knee wobbling beneath him. "I didn't say I didn't want to. Nobody knows where the kingdom is, but if anyone can figure it out...it's me." He smirked. "Let's go save a princess."

FOURTEEN

"The sun will burn out, and the moon will crumble. And the stars will rain down upon the heavens. I have seen the beginning of the end."

—the Seer Diaries of Felix Amos

1025 A.E.C.

It didn't take long for Seren and Jude to find the road. The dirt path wound through the forest, the light of the moon casting them enough light to find their way. The two of them kept their eyes glued to the outskirts of the forest as if at any moment, they would find themselves in the Veil again.

"If my memory serves me right, this road leads straight to Durcova. It's under the rule of the Disciples of Servius," Jude said with a sour face. "They're quite arrogant, very strict in their ways, but their borders are open to outsiders. It'll be a long journey."

"How long?" Seren asked. He didn't want to admit that he was exhausted. Jude was incapable of walking on his own, and Seren was starting to feel the consequences.

Jude absentmindedly rubbed the back of his neck—it seemed to be his nervous habit.

"At this rate, with my leg in its condition, it could be several days, and I had to abandon my things. And it looks like you lost your things as well, besides the sword. We're in a bad spot."

Seren patted his back, realizing he was right.

"Well, I think it would be wise of us to stay awake until daylight. The Veil's barriers are still thin, and it's a miracle we found our way out," Seren said. "We can rest in the morning."

Jude's strained breath ran across Seren's neck. "Yeah," he agreed with a soft grunt. "You're right." He chuckled. "Look at you; you'd think you were the mercenary at this point."

"Are you in pain?"

"Only a bit."

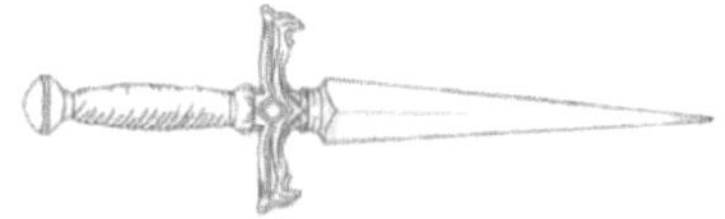

After two hours of walking, their progress was disappointingly slow. Seren's muscles ached with each step, and Jude was starting to feel heavier by the second. He could tell that Jude was struggling more than he would've liked to admit, so he let him hold onto his pride.

Eventually, an opening in the forest revealed a stream meandering through the trees. The two of them were beyond relieved as the clean water beckoned to them. As they hastened its edge, the sound of the running water made Seren realize how thirsty he was.

Jude collapsed on the mossy floor without hesitating. Cupping his hands, Seren scooped up the refreshing water, gulping it down with gratitude. He dipped his fingers into the stream, rubbing away the dried blood that clung to his skin. The water turned a faint pink as it carried the remnants downstream.

Jude, too, took the time to cleanse himself, the rivulets of water clinging to his curls.

Seren watched his reflection in the rippling water, the moonlight glowing on his skin. He reached toward an unusual strand of hair that stood out amidst his dark locks, its color mimicking that of the moon. He briefly held it between his fingers.

"Looks like the trials of our journey have gotten to you," Jude said, noticing Seren's confusion. "You're going white." He gave Seren a weak smile.

"I guess so," Seren mumbled.

After they finished cleaning up, Seren helped Jude to his feet. The morning was still hours away, and they were still far from safe. As they continued walking down the path, Jude grunted with every step, his pain evident.

"Are you from Durcova?" Seren asked, hoping to distract him.

Jude laughed. "No. Rules aren't really my thing."

Mila had said that too when mentioning Jude's past in the Godless City.

"Then where are you from?"

"I'll tell you later, Seren. I'm tired."

There was a somber tone in Jude's voice that Seren didn't understand. A gloom seemed to obscure his bright eyes like an overcast morning. Seren didn't ask him any other questions after that.

Another hour passed, wearing them down until they couldn't go any further. The two of them collapsed on the roadside. Jude groaned as he rested his body against a tree, his eyes tightly shut. The rising sun cast a soft pink hue in the distance, and birds began to sing in the treetops.

"Let me rest for a few minutes," Jude begged. "My nerves feel like they're on fire."

The two of them propped against the tree, their shoulders touching as they basked in the morning sun. Jude nestled his head on Seren's shoulder, his hair ticking Seren's chin. Above them, the birds sang sweet melodies. Seren smiled at the beautiful sound. His eyelids grew heavy, and he surrendered himself to sleep.

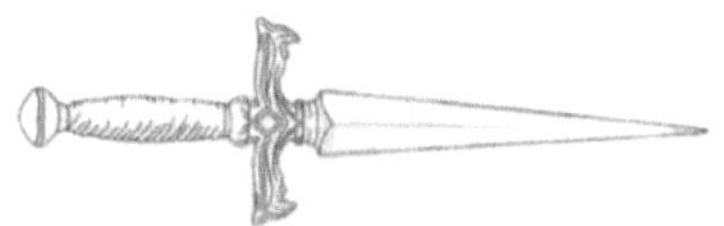

"Promise me, Seren, that you'll always find your way back to me." Her voice echoed from the radiant glow that surrounded her, and Seren struggled to see her face amidst the blinding brilliance that enveloped him.

She had guided him out of the Veil and rescued him from the abyss of darkness. Who was she?

"Seren," she called to him, her plea reaching deep into his soul.

He needed to reach out, to hold onto her, but it was too much. The light burned. He wanted to escape it.

"Stay with me, Seren," her words floated softly, an ethereal whisper. "Even when the darkness calls your name. Stay. Stay. Stay."

Across time and space, an unbreakable bond connected them. It was clear now. He had to find his way back to her, no matter what it took. He reached for her, but it hurt. It hurt so badly. And as their fingertips grazed, he recoiled. He cried out as darkness wrapped around him, ripping him further away from her.

"I can't stay."

And yet...

He sank deep into the darkness, watching the light fade. Isn't this...where...he was supposed to be?

"Rise and shine, Seren!" Jude chimed.

Seren grunted in disapproval as he forced his eyes open. Squinting against the blinding sun, he found himself face-to-face with a chestnut horse, its tawny eyes watching him curiously. It let out a soft whinny before drawing closer and licking his face. Seren sputtered in disgust as he wiped the thick saliva off his cheeks.

"Well, would ya look at that? Seems here like Leilani and Clover have taken a liking to the two of you. Old girls insisted I pull over to check on you two worn-out strangers."

A weathered old man greeted him from a worn wagon with a comforting smile. Attached to the wagon were his two horses. Jude leaned against the dappled horse on the left and gently caressed her head with a loving touch.

"These horses are truly lovely, sir," Jude complimented. He glanced at Seren with a hint of delight. "This kind gentleman has generously offered us a ride to Durcova as he passes through."

The old man nodded, his smile accentuating the lines etched into his tanned skin. "My girls here..." He gestured toward the horses. "They have an uncanny sense when it comes to people. They don't warm up to just anyone, so I reckon I can trust you kids. You can settle in the back of the wagon with the bags of grain and rice. We may be able to reach the nearest town tomorrow by nightfall if we leave now."

He paused, seeming to drift off momentarily before refocusing. "Just come from Lumina, I have," the man continued. "Bless the Caelestis and their acts of kindness. They've been distributing rations to Wreiss, you see. The plague has ravaged us, and now the fish have vanished, too. There simply ain't enough food for everyone." The old man wiped the sweat from his brow with a dirty cloth. "Please pardon my ramblings. My companionship has been sparse."

Expressing their gratitude, Jude and Seren climbed into the back of the wagon as instructed. The old man insisted that they take the opportunity to rest.

Finding a comfortable spot, Seren rested his head against one of the bags of grain, and Jude followed suit, closing his eyes. Seren was unsure if he was asleep, but he seemed at peace.

Releasing a sigh, Seren gazed into the distance.

Who was the mysterious voice that guided him, revealing the barriers of the Veil? How had such a thing been possible? Nevertheless, there was something more—a lingering feeling. Doubts seeped in, causing him to question his own sanity. He remained uncertain about the experiments Lumen had conducted on him and its exacting toll on his mind and body.

As the horses trotted forward, the cart jostled about, and Seren watched the scenery unfold. Without the Veil, the forest revealed a whole new beauty—nature flourishing in undisturbed glory. Birds fluttered in the air, and playful gray squirrels zipped up and down the trees. The two horses appeared content, their strides rhythmic and effortless as they journeyed along the path. The dangers that once plagued the forest had vanished as if they had never existed.

Seren wondered if the Veil had merged elsewhere on the blue moon. Fragments of the history that Aiden had taught him about the Veil lingered in his mind, though the memories remained somewhat dull. The Veil, to him, almost seemed alive in the way it reacted to the moon and fed off negative emotions. During times of war, when the lands were ravaged, the Veil's barriers were likely to open, intertwining with worlds. There was a prevailing belief that the Devil was responsible—that suffering only strengthened him and the taint in the Veil.

Despite overwhelming exhaustion, Seren's mind wouldn't stop spinning. Thoughts of Mila weighed heavily on his conscience. He had been cruel, but he knew what he had seen. Yet, what about what she had seen? Didn't they both have blood on their hands? His stomach churned, twisting into a painful knot. He hadn't meant a single word he said. Mila needed to know that, even if it meant putting his own life at risk. He couldn't bear living with the regret of not telling Mila how he truly felt, whether or not she forgave him. She didn't deserve his judgment. As much as he wanted to find his way home, it would have to wait.

"Havin' a hard time sleeping, are you?"

The old man peered over his shoulder at Seren. He popped something in his mouth and chewed on it with his lower lip. As the old man chewed, the sound blended with the creaking of the wagon.

"Yeah," Seren uttered. "It was a long night."

"I can imagine. I stayed in a small town on the outskirts of the forest last night and could hear the horses whining all night. Thank the Gods, the Veil didn't open where I was. But enough about me, where are you two coming from?" the man asked.

"Lumina," Seren lied.

"Oh, thank heavens," the man exclaimed in relief. "I was worried you were from the Godless City. I mean, I would've still helped you, but... I have my own beliefs. It's an atrocity, really. You'd have to be a fool to submit to no God with the Veil and all. Remember the Andanovans? Their entire country and everyone in it were swallowed by the Veil. To think it never closed there..." He shuddered. "Worshiping a false God like that, I'd say they got what they deserved, and I think the same will come to the Godless. It's a disgrace to us all."

Curiously, Seren asked, "Which God do you follow then?"

The man groomed his patchy gray beard, an eyebrow slightly raised in Seren's direction. "I follow the Goddess Illenia. I mean, how can I not? The sea is the lifeblood of us all. The Six Saints were blessed by her! You've heard of them, right?"

"Refresh my memory," Seren said dully.

The man's face lit up. "The Six Saints, one for each of the six seas, can you believe that? I met Saint Ceraphine for the first time when I was but a lad first acquiring my sea legs." He paused, and a shudder ran through him. "A sea demon had escaped the Veil. I'll never forget it. It was as if I'd looked into the eyes of the Devil himself. I'd never been more afraid in my life. And that's when I saw her. She was like an angel. By the Gods, it was a miracle. The way she controlled the waves and swept the beast out to sea, I'll never forget it."

Suddenly, Jude, who had been silent, sat up and interjected. "If these Saints are so powerful, why don't they bring your fish back and cure the virus?" he spat. Seren was taken aback by Jude's harsh tone; he'd never seen him react in such a way.

The man's knuckles whitened as he gripped the reins. "I wondered the same thing for a bit, but they are Saints, not Gods. All I can do is have faith in my heart." He stared into the distance, not turning to face Jude. "So, how did you lose your leg?"

The question was offhanded and so sudden. But, of course, he would've noticed Jude's limp, and if he were observant, he would've seen the rips revealing the metal hiding underneath.

"I made a deal with a demon," Jude said without missing a beat. "Should I hop off your cart now? I'm not quite sure I've received the full punishment for my sins yet."

Seren couldn't believe Jude's reaction. He coughed, shooting Jude a warning glance. "He's joking, don't mind him."

The old man nervously chuckled, attempting to lighten the mood. "Well, you certainly have an interesting sense of humor," he muttered, clearly unsettled. Silence settled between them, and Jude retreated into himself, curling up and closing his eyes.

Seren could tell that something had triggered him, but he couldn't discern what it was.

"Get some rest, Seren," Jude whispered, his eyes still shut. "You look dreadful."

"Speak for yourself."

The corner of Jude's lips twitched.

Fifteen

"Servius, the God of Obedience, and his brother, Ryuama, God of Wisdom, rarely did agree. To be wise is not always obedient, and to be obedient is not always wise."

—Chronicles of the Gods

1025 A.E.C.

Three days had passed unnoticed, with Jude mostly sound asleep, only interrupted by occasional meager meals generously provided to them. The old man, Ambrose, took brief rests, determined to return to his homeland.

Due to Seren's restlessness, he spent most of his time listening to Ambrose's ramblings. He told Seren about his late wife and son, that both had been lost to the plague. It had been named the Blue Inferno. The infected were killed within a matter of days, with few surviving longer than a week. The longer one survived, the heavier the toll on its victims' minds and spirits, often driving them into the clutches of madness. Even the magic of the Saints, High Priests, and Priestesses proved futile in finding a cure. Whispers circulated that this disease had originated from a demon that had crossed into the human realm, making even the most potent magic ineffective against it. At best, their powers could grant someone an extra day or two before facing death.

Ambrose said that many had come to the belief that those consumed by this sickness would have their souls trapped within the Veil, much like those who bargained with demons. But he refused to believe it. He declared that only the unfaithful would face such a fate, adamantly denying that his family lacked faith. However, Seren could see the hint of doubt in his weary features.

Seren avoided talking about himself and instead turned all the conversations toward Ambrose. He asked him his reasons for traveling on his own. Ambrose explained he had traveled to Lumina for his eldest niece. She had lost her husband to the plague and could not afford to feed her children. The churches had gathered to aid Wreiss for those willing to make the journey. Seren couldn't help but wonder if Aiden was amongst those extending a helping hand.

By the time they reached Durcova, it had grown dark and begun to rain. Unfortunately, the wagon they traveled in didn't have cover, but Ambrose offered to drop them off at the local inn. He claimed he had distant relatives in the town nearby and planned to stay with them for the night.

The town seemed antiquated in comparison to Vavilon. Unlike the towering buildings in the Godless City, small rustic buildings lined the sides of the streets. A road wound through the heart of the town, lit by small lamp posts. Only the sound of the horses' hooves on the cobblestone path could be heard alongside the rain. With a simple gesture, Ambrose directed their attention to one of the buildings. It stood apart, the only one with lights on in the windows.

"There it is," he declared. "However, it is worth noting that the locals here aren't particularly warm toward outsiders. So, be aware. Just be respectful, and everything should go well."

"Jude, we don't have any money," Seren muttered under his breath.

"I know," Jude whispered. "It'll be fine. I always figure it out." As usual, his confidence was unwavering. He took a deep breath. "Do me a favor and don't mention anything about what I said. I'd be mincemeat in a second."

Seren shuddered. "Of course. But, why would you say such a thing?"

"I guess my pain got the best of me, and I lashed out."

Still not understanding, Seren decided to let it go.

As the cart came to a halt in front of the inn doors, the man glanced over his shoulder. "Well, here you are. I wish you good health throughout your journey," he said. "May the Goddess of the Sea bless you."

In response, Seren humbly inclined his head, expressing sincere gratitude. "Thank you for extending your assistance," he softly replied. "We will not forget your kindness. I'm afraid we are unable to offer anything in return."

A warm smile graced the man, reflecting contentment. "Just having some company has been a pleasant reward in itself."

Jude, who had not engaged with the man much since his earlier outburst, unexpectedly spoke up. "I wish you safety in the rest of your travels," he said.

The man nodded stiffly at Jude, clearly trying to hide his true contempt. And just like that, the man and his horses disappeared into the night.

Arm in arm, Seren and Jude walked toward the inn doors. The two of them shivered as the rain began to soak into their already torn clothes. As they entered, the light from a flickering candle barely illuminated the entrance. Their eyes landed on a slouched man in a chair against the wall, his face hidden beneath a worn farmer's hat. Lost in a deep slumber, he seemed oblivious to their presence, undisturbed in the hushed stillness of the room.

Jude cleared his throat to catch the man's attention. But the man barely lifted his chin, keeping his eyes concealed beneath the brim of his hat.

"We deeply apologize for intruding upon this hour," Jude began. "But do you happen to have any rooms available for the night?"

Letting out a long sigh, the man rose from his seat and scrutinized them, briefly scanning over Jude and Seren.

"A couple of outsiders," he grumbled.

"Just passing through," Jude assured.

"And do you happen to have money for a room?" the man asked, tipping his hat above his eyebrows.

Jude's smile faltered, and he scratched his head. "It's quite an amusing story, but I must admit, we find ourselves in a bit of a financial predicament. However, we are willing to work in exchange for a place to spend the night."

The wind sent rain pelting the window. Their situation suddenly felt more desperate. The man was unimpressed by their offers. "We have employees to manage those tasks. Jobs are already scarce enough, especially with traitors abandoning their morals for the Godless City."

"I promise you, sir, our morals are of the highest," Jude said. As he stepped forward, his knee betrayed him, a brief falter that forced him to lean against the nearby wall. The man's gaze homed in on Jude's struggling leg, and disdain twisted his features.

"You're one of them, from the Godless City, aren't you?" the man said. He slammed his large fist into the wall. "I should've known the second you walked in those doors. Only someone from the Godless City would have something like *that*. Leave my establishment immediately, or I'll make a mess of you both." He wrinkled his face and then proceeded to spit directly at Jude's feet.

Seren lunged forward, fingers coiling around the man's shirt. To their mutual surprise, the man stumbled forward, overpowered by Seren's unexpected strength.

How dare he treat Jude this way? The man had cast judgment without a second thought. Seren's grip tightened on the man's shirt, fueled by a surge of indignation.

"*Apologize*," Seren said coldly.

"Seren..." Jude leaned against the wall, shock written across his face.

"Get your hands off me!" the man roared.

He shoved Seren away, causing him to collide with a nearby window. The glass trembled. Seren quickly regained his balance and slammed a fist onto the table.

"Seren, let's just go. We'll figure this out."

"No," Seren seethed. "Not until he apologizes."

"Get. Out. This is your last warning, boy," the man said, his face flushed with fury.

Jude took a tentative step toward Seren, his hand resting on Seren's shoulder. "Let's not make trouble for ourselves here," he whispered. He looked up at the man, nodding. "We sincerely apologize for any inconvenience we may have caused. We'll leave right away and not trouble you any further."

The man remained silent, his eyes glued to Jude, a lingering hostility in his gaze. After a tense pause, Jude broke eye contact and turned back to Seren. "Come on," he urged, tugging on Seren's arm as he led him out the door. The rain pelted their skin as they stood on the empty streets.

Seren's frustration boiled over as he used his foot to kick a nearby rock. "He shouldn't have treated you like that," he said through gritted teeth. "The bastard." The rain streamed down his face, each droplet tracing a path over his skin.

"It's alright." Jude leaned against Seren, his cheek resting on his shoulder. "I suppose I pushed my luck this time. I'm sorry."

Seren stood there, staring at a distant silhouette through the pouring rain. "We can sleep there," he suggested, pointing toward the horse stables nearby. "At the very least, we'll be warm and dry."

Jude's face lit up with a fond smile. "I remember napping in horse stables as a silly child," he chuckled, wrinkling his nose at the memory. "My dear mother always complained about the awful stench I brought back with me. I always got in trouble. Apparently, noble families prefer their heirs to attend grand balls, not equestrian sleepovers."

As Jude spoke about his family, Seren couldn't help but pause. Jude always seemed reluctant to delve into personal stories. Seren wondered if there were hidden layers beneath the casual banter and playful anecdotes, secrets kept close to Jude's heart.

Jude let out a groan as he slipped a bit from Seren's shoulder, his knee trembling beneath him.

"Hold on," Seren said, steadying Jude. "One step at a time, okay?"

The silence of the slumbering town allowed them to move without caution, and even the horses, dormant in their peaceful rest, paid no attention to their arrival. Jude and Seren settled alongside each other, grateful for the warm hay being cleaner than expected.

Jude's stomach growled loudly beside Seren. He shot them an embarrassed glance before admitting, "I'm starving. We'll have to figure out how to get some money tomorrow."

"Yeah, definitely," Seren mumbled.

"Are you alright?"

"I'm fine."

"You still pissed off?" Jude asked.

"No."

Seren felt an overwhelming desire to pummel that man for insulting Jude in such a manner. He watched as Jude moved uncomfortably, pain written on his face as he adjusted his leg. Despite the burning curiosity about how Jude had lost his limb, Seren hesitated to pry.

The memory of Jude's words echoed in Seren's mind—deals with demons. Even if there was truth to it, Jude had done nothing but perform good deeds since the day they had met. It wasn't his business anyway.

With a sigh, Seren leaned his head against the stable wall, watching the rain flood the streets. It had been a week since Jude saved him, yet it felt like an eternity. So much had happened in such a short time. Still, he had so many unanswered questions.

Should he tell Jude about the voice he'd been hearing? *No.* Could Seren trust him, though? *No.* His shoulders tensed. *Maybe. I don't know.* Could Seren trust anyone?

He thought of Aiden. His mother. They were still strangers to him. Seren closed his eyes, picturing the syringes full of Somnia. His hands began to shake, the thought of the sickly smell flooding his nose. Seren's eyes shot open, refocusing on the rain.

No.

He didn't want to remember those things. Regardless, Seren couldn't escape the truth. Something was different about him. Lumen had wanted him for a reason. Seren had done something in the forest. He'd been connected to the Veil somehow.

"In the forest," Seren said. "Something happened."

In the darkness, Jude's eyes flickered toward him. The weight of his gaze compelled him to share more, to relieve the burden that threatened to consume him entirely. The words of the serpent haunted him. Was he truly never meant to exist?

"I didn't feel...myself," Seren admitted. The weight of his words was heavy in the air. "And knowing I'm not...human. I hate it. But what if

Kitsune was mistaken about what I truly am?" His hands tightened into fists, nails digging into his palms. "Gods are meant to embody goodness, strength, and virtue. But what if, deep inside, I am nothing more than a monster?"

In response, Jude chuckled softly. "Humans aren't all they're made out to be. We just have the luxury of hiding that we are monsters. I have met beautiful people with wicked hearts, and I have met demons that granted mercy. There is darkness in all of us."

"Even in the Gods?"

"I have always believed that one cannot understand the power of light if they have never faced the darkness."

His words comforted Seren briefly. Yet, there was another worry, and he couldn't help but wonder if Jude felt the same.

"I'm also worried about Mila," Seren confessed. "She thinks you're dead."

Jude was quiet for a few moments and then finally spoke. "She's tough, and we'll find a way to get her back." Then he smirked at Seren. "You've sure been thinking about her a lot."

Heat filled Seren's cheeks. "I've just been worried."

Jude chuckled. "Mila is a big girl. She'll be alright until we get to her."

"Jude," Seren hesitated. "What did Mila mean when she said you saved her?"

Jude sighed, his voice carrying a solemn weight. "She gives me too much credit. I merely helped her find her place in Vavilon. When I first met her, she was grieving her brother and running from her mother. Mila believed she could never lead a life outside. But I became her first friend, someone who held no judgment for her past. And in return, she has never judged me either. We're both lonely people, simply trying to find our place in this world…" Jude paused. "But isn't it better to be lonely than to truly be alone?"

Even in the warm embrace of his mother during his childhood, a sense of distance always lingered. A memory of Seren's loneliness remained etched in his mind. He had Aiden by his side, but he questioned his true significance in his life. And even now, the waters of his past remained murky, and he had only glimpsed at the surface.

"I'm not sure," he murmured. "I think I've always been lonely."

"Not anymore," Jude said. "We'll have each other."

The words struck a chord, and a strange sensation washed over Seren.

"Jude, have we met before?" he blurted.

Jude laughed. "Why would you ask that? You really do have a lot on your mind."

"I don't know. Perhaps I'm remembering what it feels like to have a friend."

Jude's response was rushed as he tried to quell his anxieties. "You're overthinking. It can't be easy not knowing who you are, Seren, but don't let it consume you. Let's try to get some sleep. We'll need our strength for the days ahead."

"Yeah, you're right."

Jude turned away, and soon, the gentle rise and fall of his breath signaled that he had drifted off to sleep.

Seren was fed up with the never-ending stream of unanswered questions. Frustration gnawed at him, provoking him to clench his fists with determination. There was no doubt in his mind—he solemnly swore that once he successfully saved Mila, he would uncover the truth. He would find his way back home.

"You must learn to control yourself, Seren," Aiden told him. He looked at Seren with aggravation, his brows furrowed. With a grumble, he pressed a cool rag to Seren's bloodied knuckles. Seren turned away from him, gritting his teeth loud enough for Aiden to hear.

"Why did you do it?" Aiden asked him.

"Does it matter?" Seren growled.

Fatigue carried on Aiden's breath as he exhaled. "She'll be back soon, Seren. You'll be alright."

Seren shrugged Aiden's comforting hand off his shoulder and turned to him angrily. "I'd be alright if she would let me leave this damn church. I wish she would just let me go with her."

Seren flinched as Aiden pressed the rag roughly into his raw skin. "She believes your studies are more important than tagging along on her trips. You should be old enough to know this by now." Aiden smiled ever so slightly. "We've known each other for five years now, haven't we? You can usually tell when I'm lying."

Seren gritted his teeth again. "Whatever."

"I hope you have a good excuse for harming that boy. You can't always have the High Priest getting you out of trouble, you know. And I can only keep so many secrets from your mother. I know you would hate to disappoint her."

Seren's heart sank. He didn't want his mother to know he'd been picking fights. Aiden's comment held some truth; he knew her reaction would be negative. But he'd had a hard time containing his anger. Rumors about Aiden and his mother had been spreading all over the estate. Seren had heard women gossiping in the hallways, claiming his mother was charming the High Priest for selfish purposes. Whispers of Aiden's newfound paramour had traveled, and his respect was dwindling within the church.

The other children Seren's age claimed he was Aiden's favorite, and it bothered them all. Half the kids hated him. Why was the bastard child so favored by the High Priest? Was it because the Priest felt sorry for him? Or was it because he was having an affair with his mother?

It didn't matter what they said because, truthfully, Seren hated himself too. Aiden wasn't his father, but he was the closest thing he had to one. He had allowed himself to care about his opinion of him, and it made him feel pathetic. How many days on end had he spent trying to please him? How many times had he been the first person Seren had run to when something excited him or brought him joy? And countless times, it seemed Seren disappointed him. Over and over again. At first, it hurt. It had left Seren with a hollow, empty feeling. But then it changed to anger and soon molded into self-disgust.

"Are you going to answer me, Seren?"

Seren surrendered to defeat. The lifeless form was nestled in his pocket, its body still emitting a remnant of warmth. "It was the birds," he muttered.

"Can you elaborate?" Aiden said, annoyance coating his tone.

Seren reached out and pulled out the dove. He had already yanked the bolt out of its chest but hadn't known his actions would quicken its death. The alabaster chest of the bird was stained as if a red rose had bloomed from its breast.

"He was shooting at the birds for fun," Seren explained bitterly. "But justice is a foreign concept in this place. Forgiveness is handed out so freely." His anger boiled over, and he slammed his fist on the table. "What was the point of speaking up? So you could get a meaningless confession out of him?" Seren faced Aiden. "What's the point?"

Aiden reached toward the bird, taking it from Seren. He gingerly cradled the lifeless bird in his cupped hands. "It still has life," he said. "Not much, but perhaps just enough."

He waved a hand over it, murmuring a prayer. Its eyes shot open. In a panic, it flapped its wings in one last attempt at survival before crashing onto the floor.

"You could've saved it," Seren said, staring at its limp form.

He wanted to blame Aiden. Truthfully, he wished to blame him for many things.

"Perhaps, but maybe this is a good lesson for you."

"A lesson?" Seren scoffed. "What about the jerk who killed it?"

"Its fate was sealed. That is the way of life. It is not my place to bend the laws of nature to seek a future that I see fit."

"Fate," Seren mocked.

What a load of garbage. Fate this. Fate that. It was always about his fate. Aiden was wrong, and Seren intended to demonstrate just how wrong he was. Seren stared at his bloodied knuckles and couldn't deny the satisfaction he had felt pounding the boy's face. He had tormented innocent birds for weeks, treating it as some twisted game.

Seren thought of the bloodied white feathers that had littered the cobblestone. The monster had been smiling. Seren didn't hesitate. He hit him again and again. He didn't stop until Enid pulled him off the boy, sobbing as she did. The boy had held his crooked nose and cried for his mother.

"I did what I felt needed to be done. I'm sure he'll think about it twice now," Seren said. He stood up and reached down to pick up the bird, the body now cold. "Nobody was going to punish him. He got what he deserved."

Seren's face burned with the sting of Aiden's sudden slap as he stood over him.

"It is not our place to cast judgment upon others, Seren. It is that of the Trinity. Are you learning nothing in your classes?" Aiden said sharply. "It is essential for you to understand the significance of refraining from making judgments and taking matters into your own hands."

"I have learned," Seren replied harshly. "The Sacred Trinity of Light. The sun, the moon, and the stars."

What kind of question was that? It was all he learned. It was his entire life. Seren had been promised friends and connections outside of his miserable room. Instead, he was spending hours upon hours reciting sacred laws that Saints and Priests learned. He wasn't going to be a Priest or a Saint, so why did it matter? The knowledge he was instructed to study was far more tedious than that of the other children. Seren was exhausted.

"It is more than who they are, Seren. Light is what guides us. When you do these things, you surrender to humanity's darkness," Aiden said coldly.

"I don't see why what I do matters so much to you," Seren mumbled. "You're not my father."

Aiden's jaw tightened. "You must come to understand the importance of forgiveness. You cannot afford to harbor even a trace of hatred in your heart."

"I don't understand," Seren said with disgust. "You told me that the Gods created us in their image. So, why do people go out of their way to kill? You can't simply blame it on the Devil. The Gods granted us free will. You told me that."

"You're too young to understand," Aiden said.

That was always his response when Seren questioned anything. He was too naive. Someday, he would understand. Seren was expected to keep his mouth shut and believe every word that he was taught. He was never to question anything.

"And what if you're wrong," Seren whispered. "And I am not special?"

Aiden was taken aback, confusion written on his face. He opened his mouth to respond, but Seren didn't let him speak.

"And all this talk of forgiveness is getting old. You can't even forgive my mother. She's kept secrets from the both of us, and you know it. Where does she even go?" Seren asked. "Do you even know?"

"I forgave her long ago," Aiden replied. "I trust her completely."

But they both knew the truth. Even for the purist he was, Aiden would always lie for her. She was the only one who could bring him knee-deep, bathing in his sins. Did he think Seren was blind to it all?

"Seren," Aiden murmured, reaching for Seren's hands. "You have no choice. It is your destiny. You cannot fall victim to the flaws of humankind. Failing is not a luxury you are permitted."

Seren shrank from his touch. That's all it had ever been from him and his mother. They demanded perfection. But he couldn't give it to them.

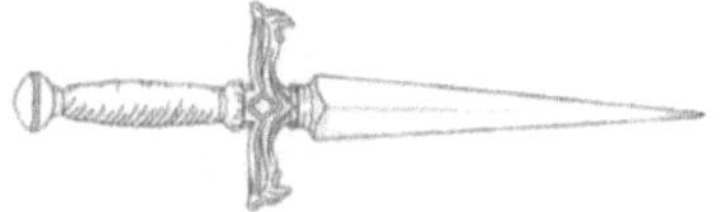

Seren awoke abruptly, feeling a sharp jab against his side. Startled, he found himself face-to-face with a young, scrawny girl, her curly hair and sienna skin dirtied. She appeared no older than fourteen.

"You can't sleep here," she declared. The girl withdrew her pitchfork and planted it firmly into the hay by Seren's side. "My daddy won't be happy to find two outsiders snoozing alongside the horses. It'd be best to leave before he catches sight of you."

Jude stirred beside Seren, his tousled hair full of pieces of hay.

"Sorry," Seren apologized. "We'll leave right away."

He gently guided Jude upright, but Jude stumbled. His leg appeared to be in even worse condition than before. The girl's eyes widened with fascination.

"Wow," she breathed, hardly able to hide her awe. "That's exquisite craftsmanship. May I...?" The girl's hand reached tentatively toward Jude's leg.

"Be my guest," Jude responded, awkwardly adjusting his stance. "Unfortunately, it's not functioning properly at the moment."

She delicately traced the exposed metal with a look of wonder. She glanced over her shoulder. "Come with me," she urged. "I can help you."

Jude and Seren exchanged glances, unsure what to make of the situation. Yet something in the girl's demeanor compelled them to follow her. Guiding them around the stables, the girl led them down a path where the scent of manure lingered in the air. As they followed her, they arrived at a rustic farmhouse, its worn-out appearance a testament to years of use and weathering.

Chickens greeted them as they arrived, their heads turning to acknowledge their intrusion. The girl explained that her father was currently away, motioning for them to follow her toward the house. They stepped inside, and chaos greeted them. Dirty bowls cluttered the sink, and the floor bore the marks of muddy footprints. Guiding them through the house, the girl finally halted near a narrow staircase that descended into darkness.

"Be careful on the steps," she warned.

Jude and Seren cautiously walked down the stairs, accompanied by the faint clicking noise of Jude's leg. The girl reached into her dress pocket, revealing a key that she inserted into the door at the bottom of the steps. She swung the door open with a quick twist, unveiling a room bathed in a soft glow.

The room was a sight to behold, filled with an assortment of tech pieces scattered about. A worn desk, covered in tangled cables and wires, dominated the center. Resting atop the desk was a cracked Holographus, appearing like nothing more than a blank slate of glass. On the shelves, meticulously drawn diagrams of exclusive mechamobiles found only in the Godless City were displayed.

The girl motioned to a worn wooden chair. "If you'd like to take a seat, I can help mend your leg."

Jude did as he was told, sitting down while the girl swept the table clean. He watched her with curiosity as she pulled out various tools from under the desk.

"So, kid, why do you have all this stuff?" Jude asked.

"My name is Anna," the girl corrected him. She paused as she lifted Jude's leg to study it. "And my dad brings it home from his travels. He does it because he knows I want to be a Technophage someday."

"They're the ones who cast false magic, aren't they?" Seren asked.

Anna slammed her fist on the table. "Why does it matter where the magic comes from? Isn't it better than selling your soul to a demon? At this rate, a Technophage is more likely to find a way to prevent the Veil from continuing to open than a Priest or a Saint."

Jude's eyebrows furrowed. "You both could get in a lot of trouble for this," he mentioned, his voice filled with caution. "The Disciples of Servius hate the Godless City."

Anna paused, her grip tightening on the tool in her hand. "You think we don't know that?" she snapped. "Once we have enough money, we're leaving Durcova for good. Curse this country and its ridiculous laws."

Seren leaned against the wall. "I don't blame you," he said softly. "My mother was from here. It's a hard place for a woman to have freedom."

When Jude's curious eyes locked with Seren's, he could sense the unspoken question dancing on his face. It betrayed his deep curiosity about how much of Seren's memory had returned.

Anna focused for a brief period, removing Jude's leg just below the knee. He winced as she set it on the table. "Yes," Anna replied, grabbing another tool. "Women here are blamed for the sins of Eden and must be obedient and subservient. Disciples believe that in doing so, we seek redemption for the sins of the past. Besides, it's believed that human sin is one of the reasons the Veil became tainted, and the first sin happened to be by a woman."

Jude chuckled sadly. "Humans always find someone to blame. It is the way of our species."

Seren couldn't help but scoff at his words. Jude raised his eyebrows in surprise.

"You don't deserve their judgment," Seren muttered.

Anna bowed her head, her voice barely above a whisper. "Thank you." Her unwavering brown eyes burned into his. "They killed my mother. My father wasn't her husband..." Her words trailed off, a mixture of grief and anger clinging to each syllable. "Her husband was cruel and unkind. But she loved my father despite it all. And when I was born... it was clear that I wasn't his. They publicly executed her and left me as an abandoned infant on my father's doorstep." She clenched her fists, the fury within her rising. "I refuse to be a part of this place."

Jude reached across the table, his hand gently settling upon hers. "The world can be a cruel place," he murmured. "May your mother rest in peace."

Turning away, Seren struggled to steady the shake in his hands. "Everyone believes that what they're doing is right, but how can we ever truly know?" he asked bitterly.

The sound of metal grinding together broke the heavy silence. Anna resumed her work on Jude's leg with renewed determination. "We don't," she replied coldly. "Across the continent, there are different versions of the Adamus and Eden story and beliefs about the Veil. Honestly, I don't think anyone knows the whole truth, not even when everyone followed all the Gods equally. But I can feel the difference between good and evil in my heart. And what they did to my mother was evil. I don't care if they claim it was done in the name of Servius. He can go to Hell for all I care. That's why I'm going to the Godless City. I choose to follow no God."

No God.

When Seren woke in the Godless City, he was confident that he did not belong there. *Why?* Had Seren once believed he was better than those who had turned their backs on the Gods? What about Disciples of Servius? Why were they permitted to murder someone and take judgment into their own hands? Aiden's words rang in his head, "It is not our place to cast judgment upon others, Seren."

Anna was silent after that, giving all her attention to Jude's limb. Her nimble hands adjusted and tweaked, her fingers working carefully. Jude and Seren dared not interrupt.

As time passed, Anna couldn't help but taunt Jude, a smirk tugging at the corners of her lips. "You know," she said. "If you had taken better care of this, it wouldn't have failed you." She continued working, a teasing glint in her eyes.

After an hour of painstaking effort, Anna finally pieced the limb together and reattached it. Jude gingerly rose from his seat, his eyes sparkling with anticipation. Tentatively, he took a step forward, testing the sensation of the reattached limb. A broad grin spread across his face, radiating his joy and relief.

"That's perfect," he exclaimed. "Thank you, Anna."

"The issue was below the knee," she explained. "Luckily, I didn't have to tamper with any nerve wiring. If that had been the problem, you would've been out of luck."

Jude frowned. "Then, why did it hurt?"

"Well, when was the last time you had it looked at by a certified Mechamagus?" Anna asked with a frown.

Jude laughed nervously in response. "Good point."

Anna stretched her arms above her head with a yawn. Her eyes traveled over their dirtied attire.

"You both need a bath and new clothes," she commented.

"And food," Jude moaned.

Anna smiled. "Alright," she said. "I'll cook you a proper meal and allow you to bathe, but there's a catch–you have to work for it. Plus, you owe me one anyway for helping you." Her hands found their place on her hips as she laid out the conditions. "Have either of you ever worked on a farm before?"

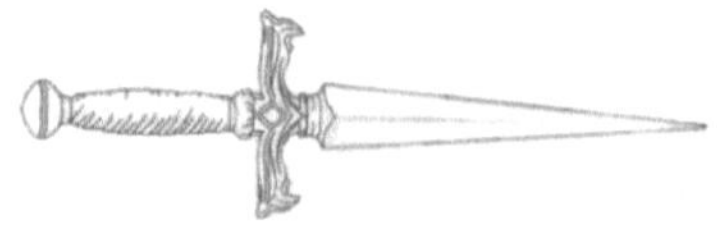

The next several hours tested their endurance as Jude and Seren toiled under the scorching sun. While Jude claimed to have experience in farming, he guided Seren through each task they were assigned. Their responsibilities ranged from cleaning out the stables and tidying up Anna's barn to tackling miscellaneous chores like weeding the vegetable gardens and feeding the animals. As the afternoon progressed, Seren's stomach was also aching with hunger.

Jude's skin was soaked in sweat, causing his golden hair to stick to his forehead. The muscles in his arms rippled as he effortlessly tossed a bag of chicken feed over his shoulder. Seren followed his lead but grabbed two, anticipating the meal they'd been promised.

"Show off," Jude teased.

After they fed the chickens, Seren dusted his hands off on his pants. "We did everything she asked," he said.

Jude smiled, wiping sweat from his brow. "We sure did."

Out of the corner of his eye, Seren saw Anna waving them over. She brought the two of them glasses of water, and they gratefully accepted her offering, gulping it down.

"There's my dad," Anna suddenly exclaimed, pointing past them.

The two of them turned their heads to follow her line of sight down the dusty road.

Approaching on a sand-colored horse was a rugged, middle-aged man. Anna bore a striking resemblance to her father, sharing the same curly hair and complexion. As he drew nearer, a crease formed on his forehead upon seeing two unfamiliar faces standing in front of his home. He brought his horse to a halt and dismounted, eyes sweeping over Jude and Seren.

"Annabeth, who are these strangers?" he asked gruffly. "You two don't look like you're from around here."

Before either of them could muster a response, Anna interjected. "They came desperately, asking for work, Daddy. And we happen to need help around the farm. I promised them a hot meal for their efforts."

Jude and Seren lowered their heads respectfully, acknowledging her kindness.

"We will be leaving after our meal," Jude quickly added. "Your daughter has shown us incredible hospitality."

Anna's father raised his bushy eyebrows in surprise. "Where will you stay?" he inquired.

"We'll see where the road takes us," Jude replied.

The man contemplated his words for a short while. "It's dangerous to wander Durcova without a sure place to go. Many boys your age have gone missing. Rumor has it that the Sanguine Sisters have been all over the countryside."

Jude and Seren exchanged glances.

"Come inside," Anna's father said. "Let's have some dinner and get to know each other."

Anna smiled softly as her dad led the horse to the stables. "Well," she said. "That went better than expected."

Sixteen

"The pedagogue's ignorance. The companion's disloyalty. A downfall of an uprising. Aliferous was he, at the zenith of a perfidious hour."

—the Seer Diaries of Felix Amos

1025 A.E.C.

Lumen's vision blurred as he coughed up blood, the taste coppery and bitter in his mouth. Each blow that landed across his jaw sent waves of agony through his body, leaving him groaning on the ground. Disoriented, he fought to regain focus, blinking away the daze that enveloped his mind. Lumen moaned in pain, his headache intensifying with every passing moment.

Three bandits hovered over him. One figure stood out among the trio, wearing a necklace made from a collection of human and animal teeth. Clearly, he was the group leader, barking commands at the others.

The bandits rummaged through Lumen's belongings, greedily pocketing all his money. One of the men held up two vials, unaware of their contents—one an antidote, the other a dangerous virus.

"Look at this," he said.

The man with the tooth necklace—Bones, they called him—knelt down. He watched as Lumen struggled amidst a coughing fit. He seized the vials from his comrade, holding them up to Lumen's face.

"What is this?" he asked.

Lumen's lips twisted into a painful smile. "Why don't you drink them and find out?" he said.

Bones growled and lashed out with a kick, striking Lumen's ribs.

"Hey, Bones," the bandit said. "This guy's a freak. Take a look."

The man held up several vials of blood, showcasing them to his fellow bandits. Lumen fought to keep his expression neutral, not wanting to reveal the turmoil churning within him.

"I'm a doctor," Lumen coughed, his voice strained. "Nothing more."

Not long before his predicament, Lumen had sent Grimm ahead to scout out Kogarashi. Grimm was meant to return by sunset. The sun was already fading on the horizon, dressing the sky with hues of orange and gold. Where was that hopeless creature now?

"You've taken my money. Just let me go," Lumen said.

Bones smirked, his eyes glinting with malice. "I don't think so," he sneered. His callous hands snatched one of the vials at random. It was the same potent version of the virus Lumen had inflicted on Faith.

Knowing what was coming, Lumen clenched his jaw, his swollen lips making it increasingly difficult to keep them sealed shut. And as he expected, Bones forcefully tilted Lumen's head back, pouring the lethal liquid down his throat with little effort.

As the bandit released his grip, Lumen lunged forward and spat on his face. The other two bandits swooped in an instant, their grip strong and unrestrained. They pinned Lumen to the unforgiving ground as he unleashed a hysterical laugh.

"Now, we'll die together," Lumen jeered.

Bones swiftly unsheathed a jagged knife from his belt. His face flushed a bright red as he took a step forward. "No," he seethed. "You will die right now."

As he lunged at Lumen, a dark figure swooped in between them. The raven's metallic talons raked across the man's eyes, eliciting a horrific scream. Blood gushed down his face and filled his mouth. Bones stumbled and crashed onto the ground, clutching his face.

Lumen was released as the bandits reached for their weapons. His lips curled victoriously, knowing full well that Grimm would be much too fast for them to injure. Like a bolt of shadow, the raven sliced through the air toward them. The bandits stood no chance against Grimm's capabilities, meticulously designed by Lumen.

Even so, time was running out for Lumen as the virus coursed through his veins. Desperately, he scrambled toward the vials, now strewn across the dirt. The piercing screams of the two bandits echoed behind him as Grimm blinded them with his talons.

"I'll kill you!" Bones screamed.

The air was crushed from Lumen's lungs as the bandit crashed into him. He wrestled Lumen in the dirt, pinning him to the ground. His eyes were bleeding profusely, and he was completely blinded but still easily managed to overtake Lumen's small frame.

Lumen's eyes snapped to the disarray of vials strewn across the cracked earth. Among them, another vial of the deadly virus rested within arm's reach. An overwhelming sense of desperation engulfed him as he stretched out his trembling hand. Noticing the bluish tint of his fingernails, a grim realization of his imminent demise consumed him. Without hesitation, he forcefully shattered the vial against Bones' face. A cry of agony erupted from the bandit as slivers of glass and the virus-laden liquid penetrated his fresh wounds. He crumpled to the earth, his chest heaving under the suffocating grip of the virus taking hold.

Lumen attempted to rise to his feet, but his body protested. A grimace of pain contorted his face as blood poured from his nose.

Grimm landed at Lumen's side. "The other two escaped," the bird cawed. "How are you holding up, master?"

"The antidote," Lumen choked.

Grimm quickly retrieved the antidote, grasping it between his claws. Lumen's hands shook as he opened the bottle, pressing it against his lips. He poured the cool liquid down his throat and collapsed.

"Master?" Grimm cawed.

It was too late. Lumen trembled uncontrollably, his body aching with a horrible chill. It was as if his lungs were turning into ice, each breath tight and agonizing. He knew he was going to die, but he didn't care. If the waves of sickness disappeared, then death was welcomed.

The raven hopped on Lumen's chest, digging his claws into his skin, trying to rouse him.

Lumen heaved rapidly. He felt his heartbeat getting weaker with every passing second. Death was only moments away.

"Master, your lips are turning blue. It's not working." Grimm leaped across the dirt, grasping a vial of blood between his talons. He put it in Lumen's purpling hand. "Drink it, master!" the bird demanded, beating his wings frantically.

Lumen's eyes sluggishly moved to the vial in his hand. Why couldn't he die in peace? With quivering fingers, Lumen willed himself to trickle the blood down his throat. Grimm quickly retrieved another vial, setting it in his other palm.

"More," Grimm insisted.

With the rest of his remaining strength, Lumen lifted the second vial, drinking the blood. A faint sense of warmth washed over his chest, and his breath felt easier.

"Bring me another," Lumen said weakly.

After seven vials of blood were emptied, Lumen had the capability to sit upright. By now, his lips should be returning to their pale pink color, and he could see the blue tips of his fingernails starting to fade. Grimm perched on Lumen's shoulder, his cybernetic eye swiveling in its socket.

"Your vitals are returning back to normal," the raven said.

Lumen sighed in relief. "Thank you, Grimm." He looked into the sky, the sun nearly out of sight.

"We are still several miles from Kogarashi," said Grimm. "Let's make camp and rest. I will gather firewood."

With a powerful swoop, the raven soared into the sky. Lumen watched intently as Grimm disappeared beyond his line of sight. Grimm had repaid his debt, saving Lumen's life just as Lumen had saved him, yet the raven had chosen to remain by his side.

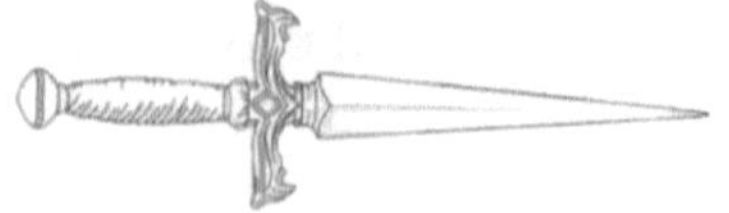

Amidst the Wastelands, the echoes of the crackling fire filled the night. Despite the scorching days, the evenings brought a sharp chill. Lumen sat by the fire, the firelight dancing off his fair skin. The encounter with the robbers had left him contemplative and withdrawn, plagued with a sense of foolishness for being placed in such a vulnerable position. A persisting frustration filled his thoughts, as he had not anticipated encountering anyone in the Wastelands.

The journey had been difficult enough as is. Lumen had hardly been able to sleep at night, and the days felt much too long. He grew sick of eating the bioengineered bread and longed for a warm meal.

Breaking the silence, Grimm squawked, "All your wounds are healed."

Lumen removed his glasses, inspecting them by the fire.

"I expected such," he replied. "I'm grateful these managed to survive. It would be a shame to walk to Kogarashi blind."

Lumen watched the sparkling stars, shining brighter than they ever could within the confines of the city. It had been years since he had left Vavilon. Although Lumen had never had a reason until now.

The Auguries were sure to be furious with his departure. Lumen had made countless promises to them, ensuring he would do everything in his power to help them achieve their goal—immortality. It was true that they had merged themselves with technology, but unbeknownst to others, their bodies could not keep up. Their organic components were slowly deteriorating. Lumen, being the foremost scientist, had spent years doing grueling experiments on demons, promising the Auguries he would find the answer. But when Seren fell into Lumen's hands, he felt compelled to keep it a secret. After years of commitment, Lumen came to the realization that the Auguries were no different from the Gods themselves. What made them believe they were entitled to immortality? Lumen believed nobody deserved such a gift.

"I was foolish not to bring a weapon," Lumen murmured.

"You never did say why you left the sword in the city," Grimm said curiously.

"I surely would've been hunted down if I did such a thing," Lumen said bluntly. "The Auguries would never have let something that significant leave the Reliquerium, let alone the borders of Vavilon."

Lumen's access to the Reliquerium was solely granted based on his high ranking within the Novem. Lie after lie had gotten his hands on that blade. Even holding it with gloved hands had done damage. He looked down at the black veins that spiraled underneath his palms.

"Why did you do it, master?" Grimm asked.

Lumen let out a sigh. "If everything is true, and the boy is exactly what I believe him to be, then I have taken away his fate. I have changed the fate of the entire world." He smirked. "And even the Gods could not stop it."

Grimm cocked his head to the side. "Why didn't you just kill him? Wouldn't that have made fate certain?"

Lumen didn't respond right away. He did have other reasons for wanting to use Seren; the boy was the only one who could get Lumen where he wanted. Seren was a gateway to the realm of the Gods. And not only that, but Seren was his one chance to bring *her* back from the Veil. Once the virus was rampant and faith in the Gods dwindled, the Gods would weaken, and everything would fall into place. But...Lumen could have killed Seren. And Grimm was right. Wouldn't that have set fate in stone? Had he hesitated? *No.* It wasn't that. He still needed him. That was all.

"Something is coming," Grimm said, interrupting Lumen's thoughts. The raven stiffened, raising his wings slightly.

A vast shadow obscured the stars in Lumen's line of sight, sending a chill up his spine and leaving his lungs constricted. The fire grew smaller, faintly emitting light from embers. Grimm shrank behind Lumen, clicking his beak nervously.

A horrifying voice tore through Lumen's mind, a sound like flesh being ripped from the bone.

"Where are you hiding him? I smell him."

Lumen cried out as pain erupted in his skull, the voice piercing him like a thousand stinging needles. A wisp of suffocating darkness coiled like a sinister serpent around his neck, squeezing the air from his lungs. Lumen instinctively gasped for breath, his hands desperately traveling to his throat.

In an instant, blinding fluorescent light flooded his sight. The sudden transition left Lumen disoriented, his vision swirling, and his senses scrambled. Slowly, the disorientation cleared, revealing his surroundings. He found himself standing in his lab, the harsh white light reflecting off the immaculate surfaces. He stared upon his blood-stained hands, watching the tips of his fingers tremble.

On the table, Seren writhed in torment, his body contorting with violent tremors despite the sedatives administered to him. Lumen looked up from his hands, his eyes meeting with Seren's. Seren's gaze, an intense blaze of fiery purple, bore deep into Lumen's core, tearing through every layer of his being. It felt as if Seren's stare had the power to strip away every facade, exposing the raw vulnerability that lay beneath.

Fear surged through Lumen's veins in an electric and paralyzing wave. It was a fear unlike any he had ever experienced, one that gnawed at the edges of his sanity. And another strange sensation surged within Lumen—*guilt*? No. He pushed the feeling away.

Words dripped from Lumen's lips as he hovered above Seren, asking, "Isn't this what you've always wanted? To be *free*?"

Lumen braced himself, his mind racing, anticipating that this could be the catalyst for Seren's freedom. But instead, the boy's body went limp, with mere remnants of hatred and defeat on his visage. Shadows oozed from Seren's fingers, clawing their way into Lumen's consciousness.

"What have you done?" Seren whispered.

And another voice flooded Lumen's mind alongside his. A woman's voice.

"What have you done?"

The raw anguish in their voices echoed continually within Lumen, gradually receding and fading into a distant whisper.

The shadow retreated, leaving Lumen gasping for breath. The fire flared back to life, and the sparkling stars were revealed once more. He wiped the sweat from his forehead, grateful that whatever had invaded him was gone.

From the shadows appeared Grimm, his feathers ruffled. He hesitantly approached Lumen's side.

"What was that?"

Lumen shook his head, his voice filled with uncertainty. "I don't know. But one thing is certain—it was searching for the boy. It must have been drawn to me when I consumed his blood."

"Why would it be looking for him?" Grimm asked in confusion. Even the raven knew that Lumen had been careful with the knowledge of Seren's identity.

Lumen stared up at the stars with a fixed jaw, his mind racing to find answers.

"It appears I am not the only one that has intentions with the boy. Except now, they know what I've done."

SEVENTEEN

"The Mother Goddess loved her first son, Caelum, so deeply that she created Kallista, Goddess of the Moon, and Helios, God of the Sun. For She believed a sky with only stars is much too empty."

—Chronicles of the Gods

1025 A.E.C.

"You're not very talkative, are you?" Anna asked Seren during breakfast.

He shifted uncomfortably in his chair. "I suppose not."

"Why do you have a piece of white hair?"

"I'm not sure," he mumbled. Seren focused on devouring his fluffy pancakes, each bite melting in his mouth. He was aware of Anna's eyes glued to him as he ate his meal, but he did his best to ignore it.

It had been four days since their introduction to Anna. Her father, Andrew, had generously agreed to let them stay on their farm for a few days in exchange for their help.

Jude and Seren decided it was best to keep the details of their journey to themselves.

To explain their presence, Jude created a story, claiming they were brothers, visiting a fictitious relative in Wreiss. He stated that they'd fallen victim to a robbery along the way. Seren was positive Andrew didn't believe their story in the slightest, but he refrained from prying.

It didn't take long to notice that Andrew and Anna were burdened by overwhelming work. Due to Anna's mother's past, finding additional help was challenging.

After finishing their breakfast, Jude and Seren started their daily chores. Seren had been quiet most of the morning, his mind filled with anxious thoughts. Even with the comfort of a bed, he hadn't been able to restfully sleep since they'd arrived in Durcova.

As Seren stroked Fiona, Andrew's horse, she nestled against him, responding warmly to his touch.

"We can't stay here forever," he said, turning to face Jude.

Jude let out a heavy sigh, leaning his shovel against the barn wall. "I know," he replied. "But we have no leads to find Mila. I'm at a loss where to even begin."

"It's been nearly a week," Seren complained. "We have to do something. We can't just wait around as if a Sister will magically appear and lead us to her."

Jude's eyes sparked with excitement. "That's it!"

"What?"

He grabbed onto the collar of Seren's shirt. "Andrew said young men have been going missing around here. This means that the Sisters have focused primarily on men in Durcova."

Seren shrugged. "It makes sense," he said. "The Disciples of Servius blame Eden, and the Sisters blame Adamus."

Jude put his fingers under his chin. "If we manage to get on the Sisters' radar, then we might be able to reach Mila."

Seren pondered his words. "How?"

"Well, we know they're known for seducing men," Jude said. "And wouldn't they opt for easier targets? Like a couple of outsiders whom nobody would miss?"

"It's a ridiculous plan," Seren admitted.

Unfazed, Jude offered him a devilish grin. "True. But it might just be crazy enough to work."

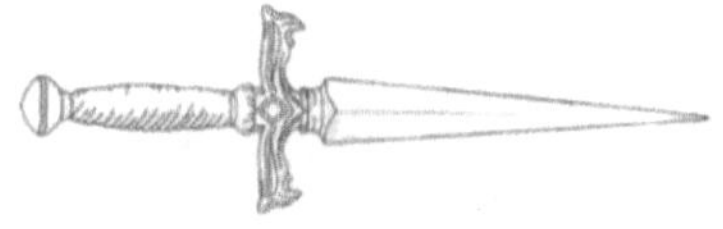

After a tiring day of work followed by a delicious dinner prepared by Anna, Seren ensconced himself next to Jude by the fireplace. Engrossed in a book Anna had lent him, Jude was comfortably seated, his feet poised near the fire.

Seren rubbed between his shoulders with a slight exhale.

"How is your back?" Jude asked, not looking up from his book.

"It's no different," Seren lied.

That morning, he had awoken before the sun had risen. Entering the bathroom, he washed his face with unusual vigor as if trying to cleanse away something unseen. Seren had stared at his reflection for a long while, studying the curve of his mouth and the edges of his cheekbones. The single trace of his mother was the green in his eyes.

But who is the rest?

His finger traced his reflection as if doing so would reveal the truth. Turning, Seren lifted his shirt, inspecting his back as he had done for the last couple of days. The seal was fading, barely visible compared to what it had once been. The twisting black veins pulsed at times but otherwise remained unchanged. He couldn't dismiss the possibility that whatever had overcome him in the Behethium Forest had caused it.

Seren stood there until the sun's rays streamed through the window, accompanied by the music of birds. It usually brought a smile to his face, but not today. He washed his face again. And again. And again. Each time he looked in the mirror, the same face stared back at him, and he couldn't bear it any longer. Suddenly, the glass shattered. The mirror fragments fell to the floor, and warm blood flowed down his knuckles.

Jude had flung the door open, his eyes wide with concern. Though he had not said a word or asked a question, he simply helped Seren pick up the broken glass and told him he would tell Anna it was an accident.

Seren brushed his fingers over his knuckles, seeing the faint traces of what were now scars. If he were normal, it would have taken days to heal.

"Let's give it a shot tonight," Jude proposed, breaking Seren away from his thoughts. He flipped a page of his book. "I'm feeling lucky. Just let me finish this chapter."

Anna appeared from the kitchen and peeked over Jude's shoulder. During their time with Anna, she had grown fond of Jude. Seren had caught her several times admiring him. He couldn't blame her; it seemed he had a certain effect on people.

As she settled next to Jude on the floor, Seren's thoughts involuntarily shifted to Mila. And in that moment, a twinge of annoyance washed over him. Jude didn't seem nearly as concerned as Seren was about Mila's belief that he was dead. In fact, he'd been so nonchalant about everything concerning Mila while Seren found himself thinking about her more than he wanted to admit.

"What are you going to do?" asked Anna curiously.

"We're going to visit the local tavern," answered Jude. "I've heard this town serves the best ale."

Interrupting their conversation with his resonant grunt from the kitchen, Andrew chimed in, "Indeed! The finest ale is available right here in Calarinn!" He tossed a few shiny golden coins in their direction. "Fetch me a pint, won't you?"

After Jude reached the end of his chapter, they both freshened up. The two of them put on clean clothes, wearing the dull, brown colors that most of the townsfolk wore. Jude rolled up his pants slightly, purposefully exposing his leg, a testament that they were outsiders. Jude cautioned Seren when he went to strap his sword on his back.

"It's too obvious," he said. "And if we get lucky, the Sisters will be sure to take it anyways." Jude patted his hip where his gun was concealed. "We always have this if things get out of hand. Andrew happened to have some bullets from Vavilon."

Andrew gave them directions to the tavern; it was only a short walk from their farm. Jude and Seren gave a heartfelt goodbye to Anna, knowing it was possible they wouldn't be returning. They didn't tell her they might not return, but she had thrown her arms around Jude, hugging him tightly. And when they left, she watched from the porch, waving at them until they were out of sight.

The evening was warm, a welcome change after several cold nights. Signs of spring were all around them. Fresh blue and purple flowers lined the dirt path. Along the valley's edge, majestic mountains stood tall, their peaks stretching toward the sky. Side by side, Jude and Seren watched the sun's gradual descent behind the mountain range, painting the horizon with a breathtaking display of colors.

"I love the sky," Seren said, mostly to himself.

Jude grinned. "Would you look at that? I'm finally getting to know the real you."

"I guess," he said flatly.

To his surprise, Jude halted and turned to him. "What do you say we take a detour? I want to show you something."

Seren didn't argue as Jude grabbed his wrist and started running.

The sun had completely set, and the stars had begun to awaken. At first, there were only a few, but as darkness continued to fall, they dusted the sky like diamonds. Seren breathed in the cool air as he lay underneath the vast sky. The long grass tickled his arms as he put his hands underneath his head.

"How long has it been since you last laid beneath the stars?" Jude asked, turning to Seren.

"I don't know," he admitted. "I have this terrible feeling that everything I loved was taken from me. Even the sky."

"Is that why you're so adamant to get Mila?" Jude murmured. "She was taken from you also."

Seren laughed. "No, it's not like that," he said. "But when we were in the forest, the demon pulled me into her memories. I saw her past. And...I just know she doesn't belong with the Sanguine Sisters. She doesn't want to be there. Just like I felt when I was in the Godless City. And it's my fault that she got dragged into this."

"Technically, it's mine," Jude said honestly. "I was worried you were blaming yourself. You never told me you saw her memories."

"I figured it was not my place. But I'm curious, why haven't you been more worried?" Seren asked him.

Jude sighed. "Mila is much more powerful than me. And she'd told me many times that someday her mother would come back for her, so I can't say I am surprised." He smirked. "Regardless, though, I am sure we will see her again."

"Yeah," Seren said. "I just...I can't go to Lumina until we help her."

I won't go to Lumina without her.

Jude chuckled. "You're right about that. I don't think she's been there before, either. You'll have to show her around."

"What about you?" Seren asked. "Are you from Lumina as well?"

There was a brief period of silence.

"No. That isn't where I am from. I'm kind of a wanderer."

"Well, then, where are you from?"

"You wouldn't believe me if I told you," Jude said solemnly. "Nobody ever does. The place I'm from...doesn't exist anymore."

Seren snorted. "Are you sure I wouldn't believe you?"

Jude pointed to the sky. "Look, a shooting star."

Seren looked upwards, watching it graze across the sky, leaving a trail of light behind it.

"I am glad we met, Seren," Jude said suddenly. "Truly."

Seren found himself sitting upright, his fists slamming into the ground. "I still don't get you," he said fiercely. "You never tell me anything about yourself. Yet, you've been so willing to help me and risk your own life for me."

"You forget I'm being paid," Jude said without a hint of emotion.

"So, is that it then? Everything you've done is for money?"

Somehow, Seren doubted that.

Jude's smile faltered. "Do you believe in redemption, Seren?"

"W-what?" he stammered.

Jude sat up, his hands running over the grass. He grabbed a stray flower, plucking it from the ground. He began to tear off the periwinkle petals one by one before continuing.

"I've been trying to redeem myself my entire life," Jude finally said. "Perhaps that's why I'm so desperate to help when I can." His blue eyes met with Seren's. "It's selfish. I'm truly a selfish person, Seren."

"Why would you say that?" he murmured.

"Because I'm trying to save my soul."

Seren's heart skipped a beat. He thought of Jude's words to Ambrose. Had he meant what he said? If that was true, then that meant....

"If you're a monster, then I am too," Jude said.

"No, you're not," Seren argued. He squeezed his eyes shut. "You are nothing like me."

Jude stretched his legs with a deep exhale. "Would you like to know something?" he asked, his voice growing quieter. "I once learned that when a star dies, we can still see its light for nearly a hundred years. The stars we're looking at may have died long ago, but we're still admiring them together. Even if you cannot see it, I can see the light in you. Even if you were to implode into yourself, collapsing into darkness like a star, I would still see it."

"Why?" Seren whispered. "I don't understand."

Jude laughed, and it was as if the stars grew brighter when he did. "I guess that's just the kind of person I am. And it's surely gotten me into a lot of trouble, but it also brought me here with you."

Seren met his gaze, feeling warmth fill his chest.

"I'm glad we met, too."

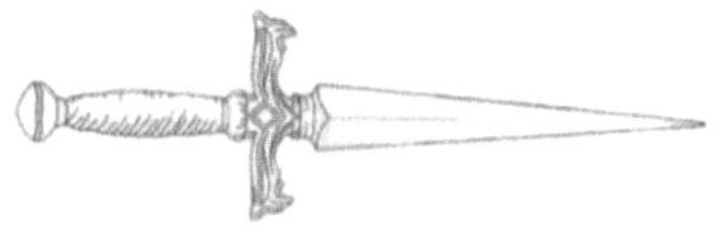

Jude and Seren continued toward town, making their way back onto the dirt road. Seren had been silent since their conversation on the hill.

"Are you alright?" Jude asked, breaking the stillness.

Seren nodded. "Yes, just thinking. I'm surprised they allow a tavern in this town if they're so strict. You'd think even alcohol would be taboo in a land of obedience."

Jude laughed softly. "Would you be even more surprised to know that there are ladies of the night here as well? Of course, they're damaged goods in the eyes of the Disciples. I find it ironic that lords are quick to give in to their desires but punish others who do the same."

"It's no surprise that lords have no magic," Seren scoffed.

"Poor Servius," Jude said with a snicker. "Maybe he isn't as powerful as the other Gods. Perhaps he has no magic to offer."

As their feet hit cobblestones, a distant chorus of laughter filled the air. The shopkeepers shut down their establishments, leaving the tavern the only building to stand out. Light flooded from the open windows into the street.

"Looks like it's quite the happening place tonight. Shall we, my dear friend?" Jude suggested with a mischievous twinkle in his eye.

Together, they approached the tavern. As Jude pushed open the wooden doors, Seren followed closely behind. Inside, the uproarious laughter seemed to defy the constraints of societal norms. The tavern was bustling, and the air was heavy with the scent of aged wood and spiced ale. Only the barkeep noticed their entrance, his eyes narrowing as they slipped through the crowd. Amidst the symphony of clinking glasses and conversations, they were otherwise unnoticed. Jude and Seren approached a table nestled in a secluded corner. Boisterous men propped themselves casually on nearby tables, the amber liquor in their glasses sloshing out the sides.

"Now, we wait," Jude said.

Seren scanned the room. "There's not very many women here," he noted. "And how will we know if any of them are Sisters?"

"I'm assuming they'll pose as ladies of the night," Jude said. "Sisters are clever. I have a feeling we'll know if we come across one." He let out a deep sigh, planting his elbows on the weathered table. Jude watched intently as the barkeep filled a row of frosted mugs. "I wish we had money," he moaned. "Can't we tell Andrew we were robbed and use his money for some ale?"

Seren chuckled. "And then what would you say when he smelled the alcohol on you?"

"Good point."

An hour passed with no obvious signs of a Sister. The few women they had seen appeared to be locals; the gruff barkeep had called them by name. He'd glared at Seren and Jude from behind the bar top for quite some time. It was no surprise when he started to make his way over to the two of them. Seren tugged on Jude's sleeve, bringing his attention to the barkeep.

"Uh oh," Jude murmured.

The barkeep loomed over them, his face flushed bright red. "You two! If you're not laying down any coin, then it's time for you strangers to hit the road."

A hand descended onto his shoulder from behind.

"Nonsense, Maurice! Everyone is a friend tonight."

Seren and Jude turned their attention toward the newcomer, who fixed his piercing gray eyes upon them. "It is my birthday, after all. Actually..." The young man spread his arms wide and elevated them into the air.

"Tonight's drinks are on the house for everyone!" He shot them a friendly smile. "Put it on my uncle's tab, Maurice."

"As you wish. Anything for the nephew of Lord Glynn," the barkeep muttered. Shooting them a begrudging look, he snapped, "You got lucky."

An impish grin spread over Jude's face. "I couldn't agree more, sir. If you wouldn't mind, we'd love a couple of glasses of your finest ale."

The young man who had come to their rescue was already engrossed in conversation elsewhere, leaving the barkeep to huff and move off to fulfill the request.

Moments later, with a loud thud, he deposited two hefty mugs in front of them and departed.

"He probably spit in it," Seren said.

"Probably," Jude agreed as he took a swig. "Oh, this is delightful."

With a hint of hesitation, Seren raised the glass to his lips and took a tentative sip. To his pleasant surprise, the ale greeted his palate with crisp sweetness. He tasted notes of crisp apples and juicy pears.

"This is silly," Seren sighed. "I don't think we're going to find a Sister."

Jude took another drink. "Maybe not, so why not drink to our hearts' content? What do you say?" He raised his cup to toast. "Let's drown our sorrows."

A muscle feathered in Seren's jaw. Noticing his frustration, Jude's expression softened.

"I promise we will find a way to Mila," Jude assured. "I haven't given up. I just know that it will work itself out. Trust me. Why not enjoy this night when we can have as many drinks as we want? You're so pent-up, Seren. Relax."

Jude then chugged the rest of his drink, calling the barkeep over for another round. Seren stared at the now two full cups in front of him.

"Okay," Seren muttered in defeat. "We get Mila, and then we go to Lumina." He grasped the first cup and chugged the liquid down. His stomach churned as he grabbed hold of the second cup.

"You won't regret it," Jude said, lifting his cup in a toast.

They clinked their glasses and proceeded to drink the night away.

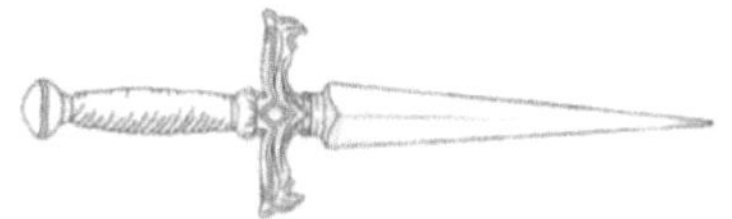

Seren's temples throbbed as he leaned against the wall, and the room started to spin. Nausea gripped him, and he wondered if he'd had one too many drinks. A nauseating blend of bile and ale churned in his stomach. Beside him, Jude giggled childishly, his own judgment impaired.

"Jude," he grumbled. "I'm going to be sick."

"Don't be such a baby, Seren," Jude teased. "Finish your drink."

Shaking off the dizziness, Seren sat up straight. "I'd say you're the baby. If I remember correctly, I outdrank you."

"It would appear so," Jude replied with a grin. "The barkeep can hardly believe you're still breathing."

They both turned to look in the barkeep's direction. As expected, he watched Seren intently, a mix of disbelief and admiration etched across his features. He seemed perplexed, struggling to understand how Seren had managed to consume such an astonishing amount of alcohol. Determined, Seren firmly grasped his cup, staring back at the barkeep.

In one swift motion, he downed the remnants of his drink without taking a breath, the liquid sliding down his throat easily. The room hushed, the air thick with anticipation, as the final drop vanished down Seren's throat. A long silence stretched before the barkeep erupted into applause. A few patrons turned their heads toward them, eyebrows raised.

Seren leaned close to Jude, his voice no more than a whisper. "Did you honestly think you could outdrink the son of a God?" He smirked.

Jude howled with laughter, holding his sides. "You cocky bastard! Where have you been hiding?"

They tried to stifle their laughter as dirty looks were cast in their direction from others.

"You should see how pink your face is," Seren told Jude.

"Oh, really?" he asked playfully. "Tell me, does it take away from my princely features?" Jude leaned in closer, his breath smelling of ale.

"I'd say the rosy cheeks are a nice touch. It's as if the lack of magic from Servius pales in comparison," Seren said with a broad smile.

"Oh, stop, you're making me blush."

The two of them burst into laughter once again. As their laughter died out, Seren thought about how often he'd found himself laughing since he'd been in Jude's presence.

Jude took a sip of his drink, licking his lips. As he set his drink down, he tilted his head, watching Seren's fingers drum on the table.

"Something on your mind?" Jude asked.

"Just the usual," Seren murmured.

"Do you want to talk about it?"

"It's this feeling that I have…" he began. "As if there's something I'm supposed to be doing."

"I think we all feel that way."

"There's something else too. I've been meaning to ask you…" Seren said slowly. "Jude, do you know something that I don't?"

Jude's lips parted, "Seren—"

"Hey, you two!"

The young man who had been buying their drinks hovered over them. With an air of confidence, he settled himself in a chair beside them. "You both appear to be having a good time. It seems we haven't properly introduced ourselves," he greeted. "I am Lord Thomas Glynn." He looked quite young to call himself a lord. He couldn't have been much older than Jude or Seren, perhaps twenty years at most. "I just recently took over my uncle's estate as he's left the country for some time," he said as if sensing their doubt.

Seren inclined his head in a bow. "Thank you for the drinks," he said. "It is truly a pleasure to make your acquaintance."

Thomas responded with a wide smile, his hearty laughter filling the air around them. "No need for such formalities," he said, leaning back in his chair. "I see you've impressed Maurice." He motioned to the empty cups in front of Seren.

"His father is a heavy drinker," Jude said. "He's been drinking since he was only five years old. It's tragic, really."

Seren shot Jude a glare, to which he simply shrugged.

"So, where are you two from?" Thomas asked casually. He propped his boots on the table and ran fingers through auburn hair.

Jude, caught up in his intoxicating haze, answered without hesitation. "We have just arrived from the Godless City," he revealed.

Seren clenched his hand in surprise. He had expected him to go along with a fabricated story, but his inebriation had clouded his judgment.

Thomas' face lit up with a cunning smile as he leaned in, his voice lowered to a whisper. "You won't face any judgment from me," he said. "Between you and me, the lords of Durcova aren't as innocent and obedient as they appear. I mean, honestly, can you blame us?"

"Certainly not," Jude agreed. "If it wasn't for Vavilon's advances, I'm afraid I'd be out of luck."

"Exactly," Thomas said. "I only hope they can advance enough to deal with the wretched Veil. I heard a rumor that it merged on the fringes of the forest during the blue moon and has yet to close. Seems it is there to stay."

Seren's breath caught in his throat.

Suddenly, Thomas changed his tone, his excitement bubbling over. "But, enough of that. Let's share a drink together!"

Before he knew it, Seren found himself downing two more drinks in the company of Thomas and Jude. Despite the continuous dirty looks cast their way, the young lord seemed unaffected, paying no attention to the disapproval they received.

Jude and Thomas hit it off quickly, and a pang of envy washed over Seren. Jude had a certain charm that he did not possess.

"You know what would make this night even more memorable?" Jude slurred. He leaned against Thomas, whose face burned a bright shade of crimson.

"Women?" Thomas interjected. A playful grin stretched across his features.

"Not just any women," Jude said. "*Beautiful* women."

Thomas chuckled and leaned in closer. "You do realize I'm a lord, right?" he slurred. "I can get us whatever we desire. We lords don't have to conform to those insufferable *rules*." His laughter sent a pang of discomfort through Seren.

Thomas wrapped his arms around Seren and Jude, pulling them close to him. His breath, reeking of alcohol, flooded across Seren's face. In a hushed tone, Thomas whispered, "I know of a secret place where you'll find an abundance of beautiful women. I'll take you there."

He raised his arms, commanding the attention of everyone in the bar. "By my decree, this celebration has come to a close!" he declared. "I bid you all a pleasant evening."

Thomas went toward the exit without wasting any time. He beckoned them to follow him, promising to lead them to a clandestine location he called a secret haven.

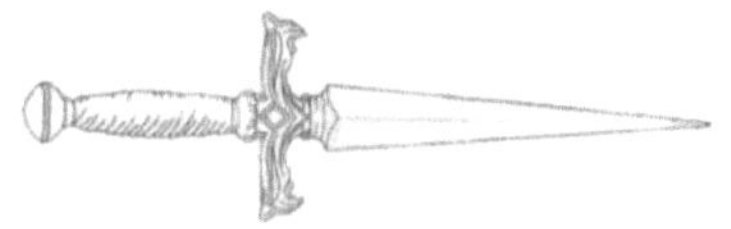

Jude stumbled alongside Thomas, their laughter infiltrating the stillness of the night. Seren couldn't shake off the nagging feeling in his gut as they walked for several more minutes, finally reaching a beautiful, gated entrance.

Thomas unlocked the gate with a flourish, revealing the grandeur beyond. A sense of unease settled in Seren's chest. Should a lord of Durcova lead two outsiders to some so-called 'secret' place on his private estate? Was this truly the conduct befitting a lord meant to represent Servius? Seren's mother had escaped a man who saw her as nothing more than an inadequate wife, yet the men of Durcova were free to engage in all sorts of debauchery with women as they pleased. It was disgusting. And to think that Servius was okay with this. The knot in Seren's stomach tightened.

Thomas beamed with delight at the two of them and said, "Welcome to the Glynn Estate. I'll gladly show you my private afterparty." He raised a finger to his lips. "This stays between us, my new friends."

Seren's feet felt glued beneath him. He thought about Anna and her mother's fate. She had been murdered in cold blood for her apparent "sin," and yet, here they were. His fingers curled in contempt.

"Come on, Seren," Jude said, seeing his hesitance.

Thomas confidently guided them through the darkness that surrounded the vast estate. Jude and Seren followed him as he circled around a garden, their footsteps echoing softly on the cobblestone path. Eventually, he led them to a charming two-story building.

The ivory doors swung open, and a world of decadence unfolded before them. Sparkling chandeliers illuminated the marble floors and gilded walls. The smell of expensive perfume assaulted Seren's senses. Plush, velvet couches invited guests to sit on them. And as their eyes swept across the room, they felt the stares of beautiful women. Their giggles and whispered conversations echoed within the chamber.

"Do as you please," Thomas said slyly. "Just bear in mind the importance of discretion." A woman with curly brown locks enveloped the young Lord from behind. "I intend to revel in the remainder of my birthday." Another woman trailed her fingers down his neck. "If you require my presence, spare yourself the effort of summoning me. I won't answer."

Before either of them could respond, Thomas was swept away by the women who had ensnared his attention. A flicker of unease passed through Seren, and he cast a worried glance in Jude's direction. To his surprise, Jude was remarkably composed, and his demeanor transformed. His voice dropped to a hushed tone. "Try to engage with women who have their chest covered. They may be concealing their Sanguine markings."

Seren clutched onto Jude's shirt, preventing him from leaving. "Is that really why we came?" he whispered in relief.

Jude chuckled dismissively. "Come on, Seren. I may have my faults, but being a lecher is not one of them. Besides, I found Thomas much more charming than any of the women here." He arched an eyebrow. When Seren didn't respond, Jude's features softened. "I know you're upset we're here, but remember we're doing this for Mila."

Jude was right. It was not the time or place to think about his mother's past or think about Anna's mother. Thomas was only a pawn and nothing more. Seren released his grip on Jude. On cue, a hand softly traced his back.

"Are you a friend of Lord Thomas?"

A stunning woman with bronzed skin and curly blonde hair clasped her hand with Seren's. Her round face broke into a sweet smile.

"Y-yes," Seren stammered.

"You seem tense," the woman murmured. She rubbed his shoulders gently. "Why don't you sit down, and I'll help you unwind?"

Seren allowed the woman to lead him to an armchair. As he sank into the cushion, she began to rub his shoulders. He tried not to flinch from her touch, although he desperately wanted to peel her hands away.

"Why don't you take this off?" she suggested while tugging at his shirt.

"No, I'd rather leave it on," Seren said. He glanced over his shoulder, noticing her exposed chest with dismay. "You don't have to be doing this for me."

"Oh, don't be shy," she insisted.

Despite Seren's protest, she grabbed the hem of his shirt, abruptly lifting it over his head. As the fabric slipped away, she gasped in surprise, stumbling backward.

Seren turned around, ripping the shirt out of her hands. "I had said no," he said coldly, pulling the shirt back over his head.

"S-sorry," she fumbled, her face flushing with embarrassment. Quickly retreating, she mumbled another apology as she excused herself.

Seren let out a sigh. This had to be a waste of time. Coming here was a mistake.

Scanning the room, he caught sight of Jude flirting with a red-haired woman several feet away. He seemed to be enjoying himself. Seren watched as Jude leaned toward the woman, whispering something in her ear. She giggled and ran her fingers under his chin, pulling him in for a kiss. Seren gritted his teeth and rolled his eyes, sinking even further into the chair.

Just as Seren was about to stand, long black hair cascaded against his neck. A silky voice whispered in his ear, "A story can be told with scars. I find them to be lovely."

Caught off guard, Seren looked up to face an enchanting woman. Her green eyes fluttered with long, thick lashes.

The woman's hands found their way into Seren's hair, gently massaging his scalp. He immediately noticed the form-fitting gown that covered her entire chest.

"Do you have scars too?" Seren asked.

"Yes," she said with a sigh. "I'm afraid most men don't think I am as beautiful once they find out." She rested her head on his shoulder, silently pleading for sympathy.

Seren smiled forcefully. "I'd be a hypocrite to say it bothered me."

His heart skipped a beat as her soft arms wrapped around him from behind, her hands clutching his chest. With a delicate touch, she pressed her lips against his neck, a subtle warmth against his skin.

"Aren't most men hypocrites?" she murmured, her words laced with a hint of venom. As much as she tried to conceal it, her true emotions seeped through.

The woman circled around the chair, her hand brushing against Seren's leg. As she settled onto his lap, her intoxicating scent washed over him. "But not you. You're different, aren't you?" Her eyes locked onto his. "It seems your friends have gone to have fun of their own."

"It would seem so," Seren replied, noting Jude's absence.

"Would you like to accompany me to a more private setting?" she suggested, her voice a seductive purr. With a coy smile, she gracefully rose from his lap, extending her hand as an invitation. Seren clasped her palm, allowing her to guide him across the grand chamber. They moved together down a candlelit corridor toward a secluded room tucked away in the distance.

The woman closed the door behind them, the soft click of the lock sealing them off from the outside world. Seren decided that if she wasn't a Sister, he would kindly turn her down and find Jude. They would return to the farm and find another way to get to Mila. Even so, he was going to take a chance.

"I don't even know your name," Seren said from behind her.

She turned around to face him and laughed. "Most young men don't care to ask, and I don't usually care to tell. I'll make an exception for you. You may call me Lana."

She settled on the magnificent bed, beckoning Seren to join her. He obliged, his fingers gliding across the silken blankets. He inched closer to her, feeling the heat of her skin as her lips grazed against his neck.

"Don't you want to know my name?" Seren asked.

"It doesn't matter," she answered.

Seren gulped as she ran her fingers down his back. He closed his eyes, pulling his hands to his sides.

Please, stop touching me, he thought.

"What's wrong?" Lana asked.

Seren grasped her hands, pulling them away. "What if I'm not different, Lana? What if I'm like all the other men?" he whispered, a hint of provocation in his voice. He hoped to elicit a reaction, to reveal her true intentions.

"Oh, it wouldn't matter," she said. "I already have you right where I want you. It's always too easy."

A sleek figure emerged from beneath the folds of Lana's clothes—a slender snake coiled around Seren's wrist. Lana's smirk deepened as its fangs punctured his skin. The creature moved swiftly, retracting into her garments, leaving no trace of its presence. She delicately lifted his wrist, her eyes narrowing as she observed the puncture wounds. Already, the skin showed signs of healing.

"Interesting," she said. "I've never seen that before."

"You're a Sister," Seren breathed.

Lana leaned into him with a smile. "Clever boy."

As the snake's venom coursed through Seren's veins, an intense warmth enveloped his chest, setting his heart ablaze with uncontrollable excitement. His knees weakened beneath him. Unable to resist the impulsive urge, he reached out, gingerly brushing a strand of Lana's hair against his face. The desire to be closer to her consumed him, overpowering his senses. Leaning in, he pressed his face against her chest, feeling his heart hammering against his ribcage. Lana reached out a hand and cradled his cheek.

"You smell amazing," he whispered.

"You flatter me, little pet," she said smugly. Her fingers trailed through the hair falling behind his ears. "I might just keep you for a bit."

The sensations became too much to bear. Seren lifted his head from Lana's chest and wrapped his hands around her waist, pulling her into his lap. A surprised gasp escaped her lips as he pressed her against him. He *needed* her. He yearned for her. She was all he wanted.

"You're stronger than I expected," Lana said.

Seren nestled his face into her neck, letting her sweet aroma wash over him. He kissed Lana's neck slowly, feeling her shudder under his touch. She pushed his head away, watching him intently.

"That's enough of that," she demanded. "It's time to go. You will follow me, understand?"

"Not yet."

Before she could utter a word, a surge of raw desire coursed through Seren. With commanding strength, he effortlessly flipped her onto the bed. Positions reversed in an instant, he swiveled to face her, his body hovering over hers. A mixture of shock and desire danced across her face as he suspended himself above her. His lips grazed her ear as he leaned in, releasing a trail of hot breath along her neck. She arched her back slightly, breath ragged. His free hand descended her side, tracing the silk of her dress.

Her voice weighed heavily as she whispered, "How could you resist my command?"

"Because I want you so badly," Seren murmured.

"Stop."

He pulled away from her as the words seared through his heart. "Of course," he said. "If that's truly what you want."

"It is," Lana responded firmly. Sitting up, she appeared flustered, watching him quizzically. "That's never happened before. You shouldn't have been able to defy me." She traced her finger over his wrist where the snake had bitten him. "Leave with me and do not resist. Understand?"

Seren nodded without hesitation. He would follow her anywhere.

EIGHTEEN

"It is a small price to pay to use dark magic to vanquish the demons that escape the Veil. But what else am I to do if the Gods only answer the priests and the saints?"

—Exorcist Damian Silver

1025 A.E.C.

Seren followed Lana closely as she led them through the concealed network of underground tunnels beneath Durcova. Jude discreetly trailed behind, accompanied by another woman. Soon, she matched Lana's pace, and Seren walked side by side with Jude.

The glow of eternal flames from the sconces ignited a strange familiarity as if he had encountered these same red candles before. His mind felt cloudy, with only one prevailing thought...he needed Lana. Her scent, her lips—intense desire consumed him. Whatever he was doing before had slipped from his memory, and he found himself not caring. All that mattered was being with her.

Beside him, Jude released a wistful sigh, his gaze fixated on the other woman with unwavering attention. "Isn't she perfect?" he said. "Her skin is as deep as a midnight sky, and her hair a glorious flame." Jude swooned.

"And she smells like a summer evening on a perfect day. Songs should be sung about her beauty. Don't you agree?"

"Sure," Seren mumbled.

"I think I love her," Jude confidently proclaimed.

The woman abruptly halted, pivoting on her heels to face them directly. "Silence yourselves, or you'll be gagged," she said.

Jude's mouth snapped shut at her command.

"We should have taken that vile Lord with us, don't you think, Lana?"

Lana clicked her tongue disapprovingly. "Such a decision would have been reckless. This was neither the time nor the place to involve a man of significance, Frida. You still have much to understand."

Frida pouted with her arms crossed, glancing back at them. "I suppose you're right. Blondie mentioned that they came from the Godless City. Nobody will notice their absence."

"Exactly," Lana replied. She surveyed Seren, pursing her lips thoughtfully. He felt like his heart would burst in his chest. "And they're quite handsome as well. It's a shame, really."

The air grew colder as they ventured further into the winding tunnels, the soft echo of their footsteps reverberating through the stone. The flickering light of the candles began to grown dimmer.

"Alright, we're almost to the portal," Lana announced. Pausing, she smoothly reached into the folds of her gown, producing two blindfolds. One, she extended to Frida. "Just a precaution." With a commanding gesture, they beckoned Jude and Seren closer, instructing them to bow their heads as the blindfolds were securely fastened.

"Frida," Jude whispered playfully. "Is now really the time for such things?"

Frida scoffed at his teasing remark. "Just follow instructions," she growled.

Lana's arm enveloped Seren, her lips brushing his ear. "Stay close," she said quietly. "We're almost to our destination."

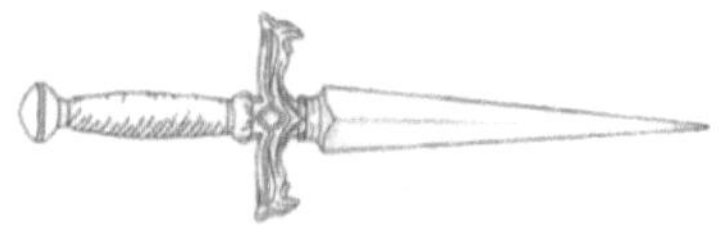

The once comforting warmth in Seren's chest had dissipated, replaced by an empty ache and a nagging headache. With a sense of uncertainty, he blindly followed Lana's guidance toward the supposed portal. A dizzying sensation engulfed him as they stepped through, disorienting his senses. Shortly after, a door swung open with a creak, signaling their arrival at the intended destination.

Through the fog in his brain, he strained to comprehend the women's conversation, their whispered words blending with an unfamiliar voice.

"You know the rules, Lana. You must await proper inspection. They could potentially be excellent progenitors," the unknown voice said.

Lana responded with a defiant huff, "Too bad. I've taken a liking to this one."

Then, in an instant, everything rushed back to him. Memories flooded his mind like an overwhelming wave crashing onto the shore. He and Jude had finally achieved what they had hoped for, to be captured by the

Sanguine Sisters. With each passing minute, they were inching closer to their goal of finding and reaching Mila.

"Throw them into a cell. We'll have them inspected," the woman's voice commanded.

The unmistakable jingle of keys pierced the air. Moments later, the creaking sound of another door echoed through the underground chamber. Lana carefully untied the blindfold, granting him sight once again.

A grim scene lay before him—an expansive underground prison revealed itself. Rows upon rows of cold, iron-barred cells lined the dimly lit stone walls, most eerily unoccupied.

"This is goodbye for now. Be a good boy and get into the cell," she whispered.

Seren scanned the confines of the prison, desperate to gather every detail. At the sole entrance and exit, a lean woman stood guard. Dressed in a sleek black jumpsuit, a leather belt encased with throwing daggers adorned her waist. Even if he made a run for it, he was unarmed, and she would surely strike him with her weapons.

Observing his brief pause, a flicker of confusion crossed Lana's face. The prison guard, too, took note, her hand slowly drifting toward her waistband.

"Anything for you," he said quickly. Without further delay, Seren stepped into the cell. As he followed her orders, the look of uncertainty faded from Lana. Shortly after, Jude joined him. The heavy door swung shut, sealing them in. Jude pressed his forehead against the cell bars while emitting mournful moans.

"Oh, Frida. Please don't leave me," he begged. Desperation compelled Jude to extend his arms through the bars in a futile attempt to reach her. Frida stood near the door, rolling her eyes as she watched the prison guard lock it.

"Are they always that way?" Frida asked in disgust.

"Depends on their personality," said Lana, her attention still lingering on Seren. "The venom can cause different reactions."

The two of them departed without delay. Jude's sorrowful stare followed Frida as she exited. Seren's stare wandered a few cells away, where a thin young man caught his attention. Swaying back and forth, lost in his own rhythm, the young man's face was concealed by his hands as he sobbed uncontrollably. Seren's stomach sank at the sight, but he tore his eyes away, shifting back to Jude.

Seren expected that with the departure of Frida and Lana, Jude would return to his usual demeanor. But to his surprise, instead of bouncing back, Jude visibly faltered. He seemed to lose all his strength and slumped against the wall, eventually sliding into a seated position.

"Seren, how could she abandon me? I feel like I can't possibly breathe without her here," Jude whined. "I don't know if I can go on."

Seren knelt beside him, noticing the sweat running down his forehead. "It's the venom affecting you. You'll be feeling better soon enough. Just try to get some rest for now." He reached out and brushed Jude's hair back, feeling the terrible heat of his skin. Jude reached up and grabbed his hand, squeezing his fingers briefly. Seren pulled away, blush filling his cheeks.

Embarrassment washed over him as Seren recalled his actions when the venom had affected him. The haunting memory of exploiting Lana, looming over her like a predator, filled him with a deep desire to disappear into thin air.

Jude waved his hand in front of Seren's face, jolting him back to the present and redirecting his attention toward him.

"Seren, it's love," he said emphatically.

"Whatever you say. Please tell me, you have your gun at least?" Seren whispered.

"Of course not. My dear Frida asked me to give her any weapons, and of course, I obliged."

With frustration mounting, Seren massaged his temples and couldn't help but let out a defeated groan. Once again, they found themselves in this predicament without a concrete plan—a recurring theme for them. Struggling to recall the kingdom's layout, Seren hoped that if he managed to escape the cell, he might recognize certain corridors and navigate his way to Mila.

Overwhelmed with exhaustion, he slumped against the wall, resting his head on Jude's shoulder. The effects of the venom and ale had worn off quickly, but they had still taken their toll. Seeking a moment of respite, he closed his eyes as Jude continued to whimper, eagerly awaiting Frida's return.

The jingling of keys woke Seren from an uneasy sleep. The sound of the door opening grated against his ears, echoing through the prison cell. He sat up groggily as the door swung open, revealing the prison guard and a woman adorned in emerald robes. He couldn't help but be captivated by her presence as she swept across the room, her garments flowing behind her. Carrying herself with poise, she entered the cell with an enigmatic stride.

"Are these the two you wanted me to look at?" the woman asked, surveying the room and finally landing on Jude, who was sound asleep against the dirty wall.

"Yes, Lana favored the dark-haired one. I think they're worth examining before being turned to Hollows," the guard said. "They should remain docile for now."

The robed woman knelt beside Jude, her dainty hands cupping his face. He barely resisted her touch, still under the influence of the venom. She pried open his jaw, inspecting his mouth, and widened his eyelids to gaze into his eyes. Seren flexed his hands, feeling anger boil inside of him as she put her hands all over Jude.

"Isn't that interesting? If I'm not mistaken, your eyes are Andanovan blue," she said with a hint of surprise. Her examination continued as she lifted his arms. "He appears to be well-built as well." However, disappointment crossed her face as she came across his cybernetic limb. "An unfortunate addition, but not a hereditary trait. He will do nicely, nonetheless."

As the woman looked toward Seren, he couldn't help but tense under her scrutiny. He looked past her. The open door taunted his thoughts. It could be his only chance. But... he couldn't leave Jude.

"I can see why Lana was so reluctant to give you up," the woman said, her voice filled with intrigue. "Something is interesting about you, but I can't pinpoint what it is." With a determined look, she turned to the guard. "Fetch me some restraints. I'll be taking them both."

The guard nodded, acknowledging the woman's orders, and hurried away, leaving Seren alone with her. Sensing her imminent attempt to grab him as she did with Jude, a surge of adrenaline coursed through his veins. Without a second thought, he sprang to his feet and forcefully collided with her, using his body weight to pin her against the wall. Her surprise was unmistakable as she struggled to break free, her arms useless under his firm hold.

"Where is Kamilah?" he demanded.

The woman fought against his grip, writhing and squirming to escape. But he wasn't about to let her go without the answers he sought. Pressing even harder against her, he could feel the air being crushed from her lungs.

"Tell me where Princess Ata is now," he pressed, his voice growing even more forceful.

The woman's eyes widened when he used Mila's true name. Before she could open her mouth to speak, the prison guard interrupted.

"Drop her, now!"

The guard brandished a throwing knife, ready to intervene. Without hesitation, Seren released the woman. She crumpled to the ground with a gasp, taking in much-needed breaths.

"Wait..." the woman choked out, clutching her chest. "Stop."

The guard slowly lowered her knife, all the while keeping Seren in her sight.

"He spoke her true name," the woman finally said, rising to her feet. "There is only one reason he would know it. And it is bound by law that we cannot harm or kill him unless permission is granted under the Covenant." The woman rubbed her chest, her expression grim. "I will personally retrieve the Princess and let her decide what to do with him."

The robed woman swiftly exited the cell, shutting the door behind her. Left alone, the guard leaned against the wall, her gaze now tinged with suspicion as she observed Seren through the bars. Ignoring her watchful eyes, he shifted his attention to Jude, who was starting to regain consciousness. Groaning, Jude rubbed his head as he tried to piece together the events that had led him to this unfamiliar cell.

"I think we might have had one too many drinks, Seren," Jude groaned, leaning his head on Seren's shoulder.

"You'll be okay." He brushed the hair away from Jude's forehead, grimacing at the feverish heat.

"I feel awful," Jude grumbled.

"I know."

This time, Seren reached for Jude's hand, tenderly squeezing it between his fingers. Their eyes locked.

"Why do you look so terribly and painfully handsome even now? Do you enjoy tormenting me?" Jude murmured, his free hand reaching to trace Seren's jawline.

Seren tensed, feeling heat creep into his cheeks. "You really aren't feeling well, are you?"

Footsteps echoed down the corridor, causing them to tear their focus away from each other. Another woman dressed in the same emerald robes as the one before approached the bars. Her gaze fixed directly on Jude. Seren's stomach plummeted; he had hoped they would have a few minutes to talk.

"Is this the progenitor?" she asked the guard.

Jude shot Seren a confused glance. "Progenitor?" he mouthed.

The prison guard, still staring down at Seren, nodded. "Yes, take him. For now, the other one is protected under the Covenant of the Beloved."

As Seren began to rise from his seat, ready to defend Jude, Jude's hand tightened its grip around his, forcing him to remain seated.

"Let them take me," he whispered, his voice barely audible. "I'll be alright. Just worry about Mila. She'll be able to help."

Reluctantly, Seren complied, sliding back on the ground.

A mischievous grin stretched across Jude's face. "Plus, I don't mind being surrounded by beautiful women while I wait," he teased. "I am sure I can make do. Plus, I still have a job to do. Don't I?"

Seren rolled his eyes. "I thought you claimed not to be a lecher?" he retorted, his voice laced with mock disbelief.

Jude smirked.

The guard held her daggers in her hand, a subtle warning not to intervene as the cell door was opened. The robed woman bent down to shackle Jude. The urge to step in and cling to him overwhelmed Seren, yet he stayed in his place, trusting Jude's reassurances.

"I'll see you soon, Seren," Jude promised.

The door shut noisily as Jude allowed himself to be led away. Seren watched as she took Jude away, leaving him in an empty cell.

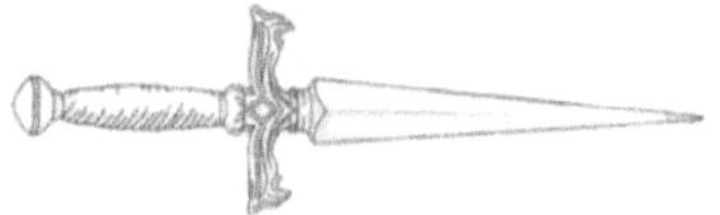

Seren blinked groggily, realizing that he had fallen asleep once again. His eyes fluttered open to the sight of the guard retrieving the man who had been crying in the neighboring cell. The trembling form, now shackled, betrayed the fear that gripped him. Seren couldn't help but empathize, knowing all too well the likely fate that awaited him. He would be changed into a Hollow. Seren felt helpless as he watched two women in red robes escort the man away. He wished he could help or offer him any measure of comfort in his final moments.

The door to the prison let out a creaking groan as it swung open, revealing the woman Seren had previously attacked. She spoke over her shoulder to someone.

"I assure you, he spoke your true name," she said. "If you claim him, he is bound by the Covenant."

The sound of Mila's voice reached Seren's ears. As the door opened fully, she followed closely behind the woman. "There must be a misunderstanding," Mila insisted.

"I assure you, Princess, this is no mistake. His cell is here."

As they approached Seren's cell, he rose from the cold, hard floor, feeling a surge of anticipation as he met Mila's gaze. Recent days had etched their toll on her, evident in the puffiness of her eyes—a testament to countless tears shed. She stood before him, draped in a long, silken nightgown of midnight blue, her hair neatly braided down her back with silver twine woven through it. The sight of her healed wrist, and the demon bite transformed into a scar filled him with relief.

Mila stared at him, her mouth agape. Her hands reached out, gripping tightly onto the bars of his cell.

"What are you doing here?" she gasped.

"Is he yours, Princess?"

"Yes," Mila snapped. "You were correct. Now, I demand you give us a moment alone. I wish to speak with him before deciding what to do."

"Of course, your Majesty," the woman said, bowing slightly before retreating.

Mila turned sharply toward the prison guard, who slouched in a chair by the door. "Go inform my mother that I have claimed a Beloved under the Covenant," she insisted.

The guard nodded stiffly, leaving the two of them alone. With the privacy they had now been granted, Mila wasted no time. She pressed herself against the bars of Seren's cell, her intense stare locked with his own.

"What the hell are you doing here? Are you out of your mind?" Mila growled. "How did you even know about the Covenant?"

"I didn't," Seren confessed. "They acted strange after I called you by the name Ata."

Mila flinched at his words. "You've just committed suicide. I hope you know that."

Seren gritted his teeth. "I came here to say I was sorry and to help you. You could at least say thank you," he said, his frustration rising.

"Thank you?" she scoffed, her knuckles blanching as they gripped the iron bars. "For what? Getting my best friend killed? For being stupid enough to get caught by a demon and forcing me to save you? You're the reason I'm here, Seren."

Seren gripped the bars, his hands near hers. "You think I don't know that?" he told her. "That's why I'm here."

Mila turned abruptly, her braid nearly whipping him. "I won't claim you. I don't care what they do to you."

"Jude's alive," Seren said.

She whipped around frantically. "Where is he?"

"I don't know. They chose him as a progenitor."

Mila's face flushed bright red, followed by a defeated look. They both knew what it meant. The Sisters hoped that Jude would help them carry on their bloodline.

"I can't leave, Seren. Even if I wanted to, you don't understand," Mila whispered. She shook her head with frustration. "You shouldn't have come here."

"So, you've given up?" Seren asked, his tone flat with disappointment.

"It's none of your business," she said with a scowl.

But Seren couldn't let her shut him out. He reached through the gate, determined to make her understand. He clutched her hand, his grip firm.

"Then help me understand, Mila. I know you didn't want to kill your brother, just like I didn't want to kill my mother. I don't know the truth behind either of their deaths, but you aren't a monster. Even if I am, I know you're not."

"What would you know?" Mila spat, wrenching her hand free. She turned her back on Seren again, refusing to meet his gaze.

"Was it Jude's idea for you to come?" she asked.

"I told him I wouldn't go to Lumina without you."

"Oh."

"I saw your memories," Seren said. "He didn't."

The silence hung in the air for several seconds.

Mila finally said, "I can ask them to alter your memories so you're spared. I'll ask them to let Jude go too."

"Fantastic, another round of memory loss," Seren scoffed with a forced laugh, his frustration steadily mounting.

"Oh, shut up," Mila hissed.

Seren slammed his hand into the wall, causing the bars to tremble. "Will they even let you, Mila?" he asked her, his voice raising. "You couldn't save your brother. What makes you think you can save us?"

Mila whirled around to face him, her eyes blazing with rage. "You got yourself into this mess. I didn't ask you to come here. I didn't ask to be rescued."

"You don't want to be here. You and I both know that."

"Just stop."

Seren groaned, rubbing his temples. She was so stubborn. Why was she choosing to be so damn difficult?

"Just tell me what the Covenant is, Mila. Could it help us?"

Mila didn't answer immediately, her expression softening slightly as she pondered her response. "It will keep you safe for a bit. I must claim you as my lover, and you'll have to prove it. It's your only chance." She reached into the cell with those words and grabbed him roughly by the wrist. "If you're the son of a God, now is the time to prove it. Clean up this mess, Seren. I meant what I said in the forest. And if Jude dies, I will kill you."

"I can accept that," Seren said calmly. His heart plummeted at the thought of Jude being harmed. "But you might want to make more of an effort to show our love is realistic when we're in the presence of others. I would refrain from death threats."

Ignoring his comment, Mila warned, "I hope you're ready to face my mother. I'll have the guard bring you the terms of the Covenant."

Then, without another word, Mila exited.

Seren kicked the wall, cursing under his breath. He shouldn't have expected a different reaction from Mila, but for some reason, it had ticked him off. Seren sat down, burying his head in his hands for several minutes until the guard finally returned and slipped a scroll through the bars of the cell.

The law stated as followed:

Article I: The Sanctum of the Beloved

1. Any male lover, chosen by a member of the royal lineage, shall be protected from sacrifice for a predetermined period defined by the Queen's decree.

2. This period of sanctuary shall be a test of devotion and loyalty, during which the male lover must prove his integrity and worthiness to the Sanguine Sisters and their deity.

Article II: Duration of Protection

1. The initial period of sanctuary shall be no less than one year, spanning twelve moon cycles from the moment of the royal pairing.

2. Following the successful completion of the initial period, the male lover's protection can be extended for additional terms, each lasting no longer than three years, upon the Queen's discretion.

Article III: Ritual of Binding

1. To seal the protection afforded to the male lover, a sacred ritual of binding shall be performed by the Queen or Princess herself, invoking the powers of Lilith.

2. The binding ritual serves as a spiritual contract, forging a link between the chosen male and the Sanguine Sisters, ensuring his immunity within the designated period.

Article IV: Failure of the Beloved

1. If the male lover fails to pass the trials set forth by the Sanguine Sisters, his protection shall be revoked at once.

2. Revocation of protection indicates that the male lover is no longer exempt from sacrifice and shall be subject to the customary rituals and traditions of the Sanguine Sisters.

Seren wondered if they could convince the Queen of their love or if she would see through their lie. His fingertips idly traced the mysterious scars etched between his shoulders, a constant reminder of his unexplained origins. He had escaped the Veil and even driven the wisps away—perhaps he did hold the power to save Mila and Jude. He closed his eyes. He didn't know which God he was praying to, but he uttered a prayer and hoped that his father was listening.

Nineteen

"An empty throne for a Queen lost in time. The zephyr carries the burden of a thousand goodbyes."

—Book One of Metanoia

1005 A.E.C.

The familiar memory plagued Emeryn's sleep, dragging her back into the depths of the Veil. Once again, she found herself immersed in its cursed realm, desperately searching for a demon. Each step was burdened as her gown became entangled in the gnarled branches of the haunted forest. Still, she pushed forward, gasping for precious breath as she ran. The heaviness of the Veil made it difficult to go on, but she knew she had no choice. Against all reason, she yearned for one thing, and this was the only way.

Emeryn sensed the presence of the lesser demons drawing near, their screeches echoing behind her. Determination surged within her, compelling her to push beyond her limits. She willed her legs to continue propelling her forward, straining every sinew, fully aware of the risks she faced. Even if it meant her death, even if her body gave out, she refused to stop.

It was as if the demon was calling her. She knew exactly where to go and where to find it. The pull intensified as she neared her destination, right at the base of the mountain. The call seemed to emanate from the cave's depths, its formidable entrance resembling the jagged, gaping mouth of a creature waiting to devour her.

Emeryn cast one final glance over her shoulder, fully aware that this marked a pivotal moment where her life hung in the balance. She cautiously entered the cave, immediately sensing a numbing chill permeating her body, sending shivers coursing through her veins. It was pitch black, the moon's light no longer guiding Emeryn. Her fingers grazed against the cold wall of the cave, feeling her way through the darkness.

"I smell a human. A desperate human..."

The voice that resonated was devoid of warmth, its icy tone sending an instant surge of fear coursing through Emeryn. And then, around her, purple gemstones growing from the rock crevices began to emit a soft glow, illuminating the cave.

A cloaked figure emerged from the darkness, adorned in robes as dark as the vast expanse of the night sky. Antlers twisted atop the creature's head like the branches of dead trees. The mere presence of the demon caused Emeryn's breath to hitch, caught in her throat as a wave of apprehension washed over her. She contemplated turning and running, but she was frozen in place.

"Does he know you're here?" it asked her. *"Does he know what you are planning?"*

Primal fear clutched Emeryn's heart at the demon's words. Of course, he didn't know. And how did the demon know about him in the first place? She collapsed to her knees, trembling.

"You know what he is, don't you, child?"

Emeryn's lower lip quivered, her chest filled with regret. She couldn't be sure, but...still.... Even now, the mere thought of the twisted marks that marred his back churned her stomach, leaving her nauseous.

Emeryn whispered, "It makes no difference."

"Do you know what I am?" it asked.

Emeryn shuddered. "You're one of the seven, aren't you? A Fallen."

"Clever child. I am not like the others. I could not leave the Veil even if I were to consume a million souls. This is my curse. I can beckon, and I can call. And I have sensed you for quite some time."

"What do you want from me?" she managed. She knew the answer. Demons only wanted one thing from humans.

"Your soul holds a peculiar essence," the demon mused. *"I could sense you even beyond the Veil. You're a Reborn. I have never met one that has lived as many lives as you."*

"Reborn?" Emeryn echoed.

"Your soul must be weary. It is a heavy burden to carry the weight of a soul that has never been satisfied. I shall grant your desires, but upon your death, your soul shall be mine. Do you comprehend the weight of this pact?"

"Yes," she choked. "I'll do anything. I need this."

The creature's laughter resonated through the cavern, a repulsive sound that seemed to reverberate off the walls. *"How unfortunate to be burdened with such a desire,"* it sneered. *"I do not envy humans; love is a curse. And you reek of it."*

The demon knelt on the cavern floor with a sinister smile contorting its decayed face, jagged cheekbones scraping against mottled skin.

Emeryn watched as a blackened rose sprouting from the cold, desolate rocks unfolded before her. The demon delicately plucked the rose from the earth with its fleshless hands, bringing it toward its shadowed visage. In a flash, the rose disintegrated within the creature's palm, transforming into a powdery residue that blew into the air.

An indescribable surge consumed Emeryn's being. She felt a searing pain deep within, as if her very core was being reshaped. She keeled over, clutching her stomach with a gasp. Sweat began running down her forehead.

With a wicked laugh, the demon relished the unfolding events. *"How fascinating this shall be,"* it said. *"Now, scurry away, little mouse, and pray you make it out of the Veil alive."*

Emeryn stumbled to her feet, her stomach aching. She took off with one last look at the demon, running back into the forest. She could hear the demon laughing from behind, bouncing off the trees. Tears streamed down her face as she raced beneath the moonlit sky, her chest heaving with each labored breath.

Please, she silently begged. *I can't bear to die, not now.*

But as the pain intensified, coursing through her like fire, it became unbearable. The ache in her new womb grew, weaving a web of torment that drained her. Exhaustion washed over her like a suffocating wave. She was moving slower than before but knew she had to keep running until she was free of the Veil. If she could find her way out.

Caught off guard by a hidden root, her legs tangled underneath her and sent her crashing to the ground. Emeryn moaned, feeling her world fade into darkness.

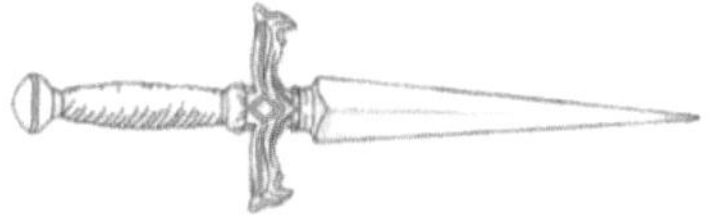

Strong arms lifted her, and for a moment, she was enveloped in the scent of roses after a recent rain. The moonlight bathed them both, revealing the contours of a face she failed to see clearly. Instinctively, she pressed herself into his chest, her fingers tightening around his neck.

"Emeryn," he whispered, brushing away the hair sticking to her face.

"It's you."

No, this had to be a dream. The last time she'd seen Samael, he'd been different—not the kind man she'd met several weeks ago, the one who had kissed her until she was dizzy and breathless. He had been bitter and angry, demanding her to stay away from him.

That's right...

But...

"Why are you here?" she whispered, eyes squeezed shut. Why was he always there when she needed him the most? Appearing out of nowhere as if he knew exactly where to find her?

And yet, had Emeryn really believed that this would change anything? If she could finally do what she was supposed to—be a mother. Could he love her? Would Samael accept her?

"I..." his voice faltered.

Always hiding. Forever hesitating.

"Put me down," Emeryn demanded.

Samael did so without a second to waste.

Emeryn had done it. She had gone into the Veil and made it out alive. Her hands ran over her waist. She had finally gotten what she wanted, but she remembered the creature's words.

Love is a curse, and you reek of it.

"Samael, I'm a woman now," she said confidently. "I'm capable of bearing children." She took a step forward. "Would you...stay by my side now? Is this what you wanted?"

Samael sucked in a sharp breath, and his eyes darkened. "Emeryn, what have you done?" he asked coldly.

She took a step back, her heart pounding in her chest. "It doesn't matter," she said. "Answer my question."

He gripped her by the shoulders too roughly, his eyes boring into hers. "What have you *done*?"

"Can you blame me?" she shouted, her hands pushing him away. "I was worthless to my husband. And even you..." Tears ran down her cheeks. "You left."

"Emeryn, what have you *done*?" he seethed. "It never mattered. You are not lesser than any other woman. Where did you get this delusion that it bothered me?"

"Of course, it matters!" she sobbed. "Why else would you push me away? Everything felt perfect, like a dream, and then you..." Emeryn buried her face into her hands, not wanting Samael to see her cry.

"I try," he said softly. His fingers began to tremble. "I try to stay away from you. To leave you be. To think that maybe if I just stay away it would change, but I *can't*. Don't you see? It's *insufferable*. It's *torture*. And I am absolutely and inevitably selfish. And you are... *everything*. Being denied you is being denied air to breathe and water to drink. And if I am selfish for doing the one thing that helps me to survive, then so be it."

Then, Samael grasped Emeryn's neck and put his lips on hers. He had never kissed her this way before. It was usually gentle, as if she would break under his touch, but this time was different. He kissed her like he was the breath in her lungs, the iron in her blood. He kissed her as if, any second, she would be ripped from his grasp. He kissed with a hungry *need*. His fingers dug into her back, and his breath was uneven against hers.

Samael pulled himself away and held her face between his hands. "Emeryn, in every life, I try to stay away, to give you peace. It seems I am not strong enough."

In every life... is that why she had grown to feel so comfortable with him so quickly? As if she had always known him. The demon had called her Reborn—is this what it had meant?

"Will you stop pushing me away?" she asked. "Will you stay by my side?"

Samael's eyes widened, sparkling like starlight under the moon.

"Oh, Emeryn," he whispered, "You do not understand. I have said a thousand goodbyes, and I have spoken a thousand 'I love yous.' I have beheld every star and explored every corner of the universe, yet nothing can compare to you. I always wait for you, and you always slip away. For you to stay by my side is all I could ever ask for. I would wage a war against the entire world if it meant I could keep you by my side for eternity."

Emeryn kissed him deeply again. As Samael wrapped his arms around her, she felt the happiest she had ever felt in her entire life. And yet, another feeling rose within her, a sensation she couldn't shake as much as she wanted to. It was a strange feeling as if she had altered the course of destiny itself, as if she had been in this moment before but that, this time, it was different. This time, she had done something that defied fate—maybe even defied the Gods themselves.

TWENTY

"Born in blood, from darkness shall rise. The King of chaos and demise. Bathed in light, born from sin. A war that even the Gods cannot win."

—Book Two of Metanoia

1025 A.E.C.

It didn't take long for Queen Omaira to summon Seren to the throne room. The prison guard had relinquished his safekeeping to the Queen's chamberlain. Instantly, he recognized Iris, the woman who had crossed paths with Mila before her brother's death. Iris bound his hands roughly, a smirk playing on her lips as she ensured he couldn't escape. The sense of being restrained was becoming all too familiar.

"Who would have thought that the princess would run away and find herself a lover?" she taunted. With a firm grip on his arm, she led him out of the confines of the cell, warning him against any thoughts of escape if he wanted to see Mila again.

Obediently, he followed. "As long as I know Mila is safe, I won't resist."

Iris cackled. "You should be more worried about your own safety."

"I only care for my princess," he said.

She scoffed at his words, tightening her grip on his arm before leading him into a dimly lit corridor. The stone walls of the passageway were decorated with looming tapestries, their intricate designs woven in rich, somber hues that matched the solemn architecture of the underground castle. Red candles flickered in sconces, casting shadows of their figures upon the walls.

Seren's footsteps echoed on the polished, black marble floor as they walked. He found himself captivated by the various paintings that lined the corridor. Each queen of the past was captured with meticulous detail, their regal countenances frozen in time, immortalized on the castle's walls.

The corridor led them past Queen Omaira's portrait. Seren's gaze lingered on the empty spot beside it, a void awaiting the presence of Mila, the future queen.

"You would never find your way out," Iris taunted, seemingly aware of his thoughts. A cruel smile played on her lips. "You'll die here."

Seren ignored her, keeping his gaze fixed ahead as they ascended a spiraling flight of stairs, each step feeling never-ending. Finally, after what felt like an eternity, they reached the summit of the endless staircase. Before them stood a pair of imposing onyx doors. The polished surface of the doors gleamed ominously against candlelight, their sheer height enough to make his head spin. Intricately carved serpents coiled around the edges of the doors, the ends of their tails meeting in the middle.

With a flick of her hand, Iris swung the doors open. Seren couldn't help but suck in a breath in awe. The grand chamber stretched out before him, adorned with six majestic thrones. It donned the same obsidian and crimson colors that seemed to dominate the entire castle. The central throne stood prominently among them, surpassing the others in height. Behind them, a massive tapestry showcased the intertwined figures of twin serpents—one red, the other black—coiling around each other. Queen Omaira sat gracefully upon her polished onyx throne, her presence commanding and regal. She wore a flowing merlot gown that cascaded elegantly to the floor.

Beside the Queen, Mila sat poised on her own throne, her eyes glued to Seren as he entered the chamber. She was breathtaking as always, adorned in a shimmering gold gown with hair cascading down her shoulders. Flanking Queen Omaira and the Princess were two thrones on each side, each occupied by young women all in modest black gowns. They all bore a striking resemblance to Mila and her mother and were undoubtedly members of the royal court.

As Seren entered, Queen Omaira rose with a visible trace of annoyance on her face. With a commanding gesture, he was guided to the center of the chamber, where he stood before the court. The hushed whispers and exchanged glances among the courtiers made him want to shrink into himself.

"You may unbind him, Iris."

She stiffly proceeded to unbind his hands. Iris noticed Mila's unwavering attention on him and smirked.

"What is your name?" the Queen demanded.

Without hesitating, he bowed to her, falling to his knees upon the marble floor. "Seren," he said.

The Queen squinted at him. "It appears the princess has chosen you as her own under the Covenant, and though I, personally, find such attachments to be distractions," she said bitterly, "it is a law that even I must abide by. However, I ensure you will fail the trials I set before you."

Omaira's fingers glided delicately along the ornate carvings of the throne. "Once, I was foolish enough to surrender my heart to a man, and it nearly razed my very being. Though now, I would not change the past. Sacrifice, you see, is intricately woven into the fabric of love itself. What truly astonishes me is that, in your attempt to evade your own fated destiny, you have brought someone else into it, Princess Ata."

Mila bowed her head, avoiding her mother's threatening stare.

"What a mess," the Queen continued. "And to think the lunar eclipse is only days away." She rubbed her temples dramatically, then stepped down from her throne toward Seren. She stopped in front of him, her head cocked to the side. Her fingers lifted his chin upwards so that their eyes met.

"Have you fully grasped the weight of your destiny? You will sacrifice your life for the sake of the princess. Eventually, you will die by her hand. No amount of love can stop it. Can you accept that?"

Seren nodded firmly. "I already have. I will die happy if granted even one more day at her side."

The Queen raised her hand, appearing displeased with his response. "The Trials will begin at the Devil's Hour. The princess will always accompany you. Make sure neither of you leave the kingdom, Princess Ata. Your every move will be constantly monitored. I have more important things to attend to." She smiled sweetly at Seren. "Enjoy your short time with your beloved while it lasts."

Without wasting another minute, she dismissed the entire chamber, signaling everyone to leave.

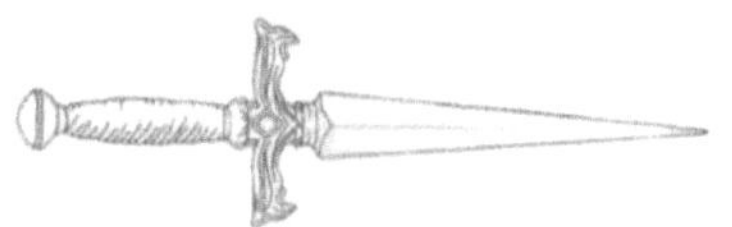

Mila sat on the edge of her bed, her hair obscuring her face. Seren remained in silence, the weight of it stretching the seconds into what felt like an eternity. Both were acutely aware of the guards stationed outside the door. She had taken Seren's hand and led him to her room as if he were her true lover, but the moment those doors closed, she hadn't brought herself to meet his eyes.

Seren hadn't anticipated the Queen allowing him to move freely with Mila, but then again, she believed him to be nothing more than an ordinary human.

"Kamilah," he whispered. "Please, talk to me."

Her face fell into her hands. "I can't save anyone. You're going to die. Jude is going to die. And I'm powerless to change it." Mila's voice cracked, small sobs escaping through her words. "Becoming the queen won't change anything. You don't understand." Her shoulders convulsed with each ragged breath. "Everyone I've ever cared for, and everyone I've ever loved, will be gone. And I doubt you'll even pass the trials. My mother will see right through you, and by tomorrow, you'll be dead."

Seren found himself reaching toward Mila, the thought of comforting her passing through him, but he pulled away. "Mila, is it really so unrealistic that I could care for you?" Seren asked. "I have confidence I can pass the trials."

Mila raised her head, tears streaming down her face. "You have no reason to care."

"I do, though," Seren murmured. "You and Jude are everything I have right now. I don't even know who I am. Don't you see that? And, even after everything I've witnessed, I've been desperate to get you out of this place since you were taken. I can't go home until I know you're free." He raked his fingers through his hair with an exasperated sigh. "Besides, you wouldn't be here if it weren't for me. I was foolish in the forest."

Wiping her tears, Mila sighed. "My mother would've found me eventually," she whispered. "Besides, you'd still be trapped in that lab if we had never met."

"You saw my mother," Seren said. "I belonged there. Jude should have left me."

"And you saw my brother. I belong here."

"No, Kamil was right," Seren argued. "You're good. You're not like your mother. You could have left me to die in the Veil, but you saved me."

With nothing but sadness in her features, Mila met his gaze, her room's soft lighting casting a gentle glow. "Even if that is true. It doesn't matter. I don't have control over anything. My true name doesn't belong to me, and it never will."

"What does that even mean, Mila? Kitsune said you had the potential to surpass your mother in power. So, what am I missing?"

Seren didn't want to ask her the real question that was in the back of his mind. Why had she done what her mother asked and killed her brother?

"It is true that there is something different about me," Mila answered. "Magic has always come effortlessly to me, unlike my connection to Lilith. It's as if there's an inexplicable resistance within me, a missing link that sets me apart. I cannot fully explain the reasons behind this, especially when we are all bound to Lilith from birth. But, in the end, none of that matters now." Mila paused, her hand clenching the edge of the bed tightly.

"Once the eclipse occurs, I will come face-to-face with Lilith, and I will take my mother's place as Queen. Any resistance or doubts I have felt will dissolve, and I will fully succumb to the power bestowed upon me. Lilith has chosen me as the heir, breaking the two-hundred-year legacy of ruling queens."

Seren's eyes widened with concern. "But if you feel resistance, can't you stop it? Fight against it?"

Mila shook her head, her expression filled with defeat. "The royal blood that flows within me makes it impossible. The first queen forged a pact with Lilith ages ago, and its terms are unalterable. Once I assume the role of queen, I will be bound just as my mother and the queens before her. My true name will no longer belong to me or my mother; it will belong to Lilith. I will become nothing more than a slave, forever tethered to her will for the rest of my days."

A wave of helplessness washed over Seren, leaving him feeling small and insignificant. Her true name. It was why Mila followed her mother's every command so easily.

"I don't understand the true name," he said. "What does it mean?"

"Royals always have true names," Mila uttered. "As do demons, Priests, and Saints. It is usually given by the Gods, or...given by the Devil." It felt as if someone had clutched Seren's heart. "True names are complicated. A true name can be taken, but only by someone powerful enough to take it."

How could Seren have ever thought that he could stop the inevitable? Who was he, just one person, to believe that he could stand against an entire cult of women who harnessed dark and demonic power? The Sisters, including Mila, were essentially cursed, forever bound to the will of Lilith, and Seren was starting to realize the sheer magnitude of it all. And Mila's true name already belonged to her mother. All Queen Omaira had to do was hand it over to Lilith, and everything was over.

"I'm sorry, Mila," Seren said. "I'll do everything in my power to pass the trials and buy us time."

She grasped the folds of her dress, turning her head away from him. "It should've been Jude, you know," Mila whispered. "He should be here."

"I know."

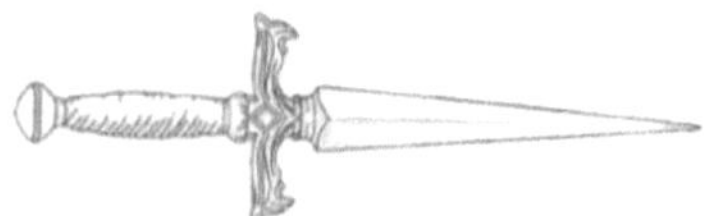

The enthralled audience of Sisters, adorned in matching red robes, fixed their gaze on Mila and Seren as they entered the grand throne room hand in hand. They filled the chamber along the sides in rows, reminiscent of when they had gathered for Kamil's sacrifice.

Seren and Mila wore matching attire, a customary practice for the trials. Mila's servants had bestowed upon them the finest garments Seren had ever worn. He donned a black button-down shirt that shimmered with gilded silver accents, and a row of brilliant, matching snakes elegantly lined the collar. Mila mirrored his style, wearing a form-fitting jumpsuit adorned with identical designs.

Seren's heart hammered in his chest as he caught sight of the Queen. She rose upon their entrance with a wicked smile etched onto her face. "Welcome, Princess and her Beloved," she greeted with a condescending sneer.

Mila and Seren stopped in the center of the room, both bowing respectfully to her.

"The first trial shall begin without any delay. I have chosen the Trial of Resistance."

Seren glanced at Mila, searching her face for a glimmer of emotion, but she remained focused on the Queen.

"As the Beloved of the future queen, it is vital for you to exhibit self-control. And so, for this trial, a potent venom shall be administered to the Beloved," the Queen continued. "This venom shall drive the recipient to the brink of madness. The Princess must determine if the Beloved can be tamed and resist the venom's influence. The Princess shall have the assistance of the Hollows."

The Queen gestured toward the cloaked figures lurking in the shadows along the chamber walls behind them—no doubt the same twisted men Seren had glimpsed before. It wasn't until she pointed them out that he realized they were there.

"Mila," he whispered. "What does she mean?"

"Silence," she hissed.

"By law, it is forbidden for any Sister to intervene. However, I harbor no worries. A mere human male is no match for the heir," Omaira said smugly. "How unfortunate that he will die at her hand on this day."

The Queen's words disgusted Seren. She showed no regard for Mila's feelings, relishing the prospect of her suffering from his demise. He struggled to rein in the anger bubbling within him. Failure to comply would seal his fate—instant death—rendering all their efforts meaningless. While he hadn't been able to resist the venom from Lana fully, the effects had faded quickly. Silently, he pleaded with Mila, hoping she would grant him a chance to resist if he lost control.

Iris stepped forward from beside the Queen, signaling the commencement of the trial. Descending the steps, she approached them, her red robe trailing behind. A pale yellow snake coiled around her neck, its ruby eyes fixed on Seren. As Iris reached him, she extended her hand, commanding him to present his wrist.

"This is madness," Seren protested. "You are willing to put Mila in harm's way for this?"

Iris's laughter echoed through the chamber, and the audience joined in. "Silly boy," she said. "The only one in harm's way here is you."

Seren turned to Mila, their faces mere inches apart. "Should it come to it, do not hesitate to kill me."

Mila's voice lowered, carrying only to his ears. "Trust me, I don't plan on dying today."

Then, aware of the lingering gazes, Seren took hold of Mila's waist and drew her toward him. Although she felt tense in his grasp, he leaned closer, their lips locking in a kiss. As his hand weaved through strands of her hair, she hesitated but soon returned the kiss. He could feel her heart pounding in sync with his as he pressed against her. Gently pulling away, he hoped she understood the purpose of his actions. If he believed death was around the corner, wouldn't he seize a stolen kiss from the one he loved?

"What a tender moment," Iris said with disdain. "Now, the wrist."

Seren clenched his teeth and extended his arm. The snake's fangs sank into his skin, and in an instant, the world dissolved around him.

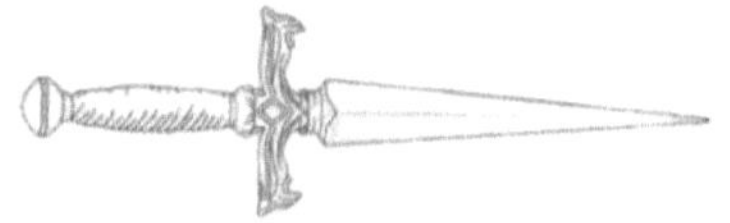

Mila tried to hide her anxiety as the snake slithered away from Seren's body, its head vanishing into the tangle of Iris's curls. Iris directed a triumphant smirk toward Mila from over Seren's shoulder. Leaning in, Iris whispered something into his ear, causing his entire body to tense. She stepped away from him, pleased with Seren's reaction.

"Good luck, little sister," Iris taunted.

Mila disregarded her sister's remark. As Iris ascended the stairs, Mila closed the distance to Seren. His figure remained unmoved, back turned to her. Mila reached for his shoulder, sensing a tremor beneath her fingertips.

"Seren?"

His hand shot out, seizing Mila's with a vice-like grip. She recoiled, gasping as she tore her hand free. Seren whirled around to confront her; his eyes glazed over as if he were in a dream.

"It's your fault," he hissed through clenched teeth. "You should have been the one who died."

Mila stumbled backward, balling her fists. She had held onto the hope that Seren would be resilient enough to overcome the venom's effects entirely. Her only solace lay in the possibility that what Kitsune had said held truth—that he truly was the son of a God. And if that was the case, Mila prayed that the venom's potency would fade away quickly.

Regardless of how much time Mila had, she wanted to convince her mother that she truly loved him. She stared at Seren, searching for a glimmer of recognition in his vacant gaze.

"Seren, remember why you're here," she pleaded. She hoped the desperation in her voice was convincing. However, Seren's features remained cold and distant, as though the person she knew was trapped within a cage of deceit.

"I'm here because of *you*."

Seren stepped closer to her, his unkempt hair falling into his verdant eyes. He lashed out and gripped her arm, the pressure almost unbearable. Mila was taken aback by his strength, feeling her bones groan under his grasp.

"Try to resist it, Seren," she begged, wincing in pain.

Deep within Mila's heart, a confession remained sealed—one she would never dare utter to him. Against all odds, she couldn't bear the thought of killing Seren. It was precisely what her mother desired. It was an obvious manifestation of her deep-rooted hatred toward Mila. Determined to resist the clutches of the same darkness that had poisoned the Queen's soul, Mila refused to succumb to the same evil.

Seren remained an enigma to Mila. She struggled to understand the depths of his intentions. Why would he risk his own safety to aid her in her escape? He reminded Mila of a lost puppy wandering aimlessly. Although she resented him for it, an unexpected pity for Seren grew inside her.

With each passing moment, his grip on Mila grew tighter. She couldn't help but cry out as his fingertips dug into her skin. Desperate to free herself, Mila battled against his grasp, her mind racing for any possible means of escape. Reluctant to resort to using her powers against him, she realized that time was running out, leaving her with limited options.

"Do you know who I am?" Mila cried. "Please, Seren."

But his eyes remained void of recognition. Then, Mila saw them—familiar embers began to glow in his eyes, the same strange color she had witnessed in the forest. Panic flooded Mila, knowing she couldn't let anyone witness the inhuman color.

With a surge of adrenaline, Mila twisted her body, attempting to free herself from Seren's clutch. The sudden movement caught him off guard, and she broke free for a fleeting moment, reeling backward.

However, Seren was quick to react, his movements fueled by rage. He lunged again, faster than she predicted. Mila crashed to the ground before fully comprehending what was happening. The impact knocked the breath from her lungs, leaving her gasping for air. Struggling to regain her composure, Mila found Seren looming over her.

"I was wrong about you," he said coldly.

"Seren, please, snap out of it!"

Mila reached out to him with a shaky hand, but her efforts were in vain. He seized her violently and yanked her to her feet. Their faces were mere inches apart, the intensity of his stare sending a shiver down her spine.

Mila and her brother, Kamil, had sparred countless times, and she'd been in this position before. She kneed Seren in the groin, creating a brief window of opportunity for her to break free. Her eyes wandered up to the Queen, who was watching through slanted eyes, clearly suspicious. Time seemed to stand still as Mila clenched her jaw, contemplating her next move. It became clear that Seren's rampage might not come to an end.

"I'm sorry," Mila said. "I'll try not to kill you."

She closed her eyes, focusing her mind and channeling the dark power within her. With each beat of her heart, she felt the surge of energy coursing through her veins, fueling her connection to the Hollows. The room grew heavy with tension as the air crackled with power. Her hands trembled slightly as she reached out, fingertips brushing against the invisible strings that bound the Hollows to her will. Their bodies, responding to her command, twitched as if sensing her touch.

With a silent incantation, Mila commanded the Hollows to stir, to rise from the depths of their mindless existence. Slowly, they began to writhe, limbs jerking with inhuman movement. But hidden beneath her facade of control, guilt gnawed at Mila's conscience. She knew the Hollows were once living men, forced into this nightmarish existence. Once filled with life, their eyes were now empty, devoid of any semblance of humanity. They were now mere vessels, souls torn asunder and twisted into tools of blood magic. Mila knew the weight of their sacrifice and the price paid for her power, but at that moment, she couldn't afford to dwell on their suffering.

A chilling laugh echoed through the chamber, vibrating through Mila's very bones. The Queen smiled down upon her daughter, impressed by her efforts. Commanding multiple Hollows at once wasn't easy for a Sister, yet Mila hadn't even broken a sweat.

The Hollows encircled Seren, forming a protective barrier between Mila. As the mangled hands reached for him, Seren skillfully maneuvered his body, seizing hold of the nearest Hollow and careening it into another with a resounding crash.

Mila gritted her teeth. She commanded a Hollow to seize Seren, beckoning it to subdue him from behind. To her astonishment, he was lightning-fast. A bone-shattering crack reverberated through the chamber as Seren effortlessly snapped the Hollow's arms like fragile twigs. Fear spiked through Mila's veins, her heart pounding in her chest. Where had he found this newfound strength?

Queen Omaira slowly rose from her seat, all amusement having dissolved from her.

"Has the Princess grown *weaker*?"

Mila refused to acknowledge her mother's words, focusing solely on Seren. Desperation coursed through her as she wracked her brain for a way to break through to him. Her mother was perceptive, always seeing through her lies. Mila knew her mother didn't believe in the supposed romance between her and Seren. Above everything else, she wanted to prove her mother wrong. Just this once.

Besides, what if her mother saw the truth about Seren? Even the Shademother in the forest sensed something extraordinary in him. His soul was worth thousands. Mila knew her mother would sidestep the Covenant if she uncovered his true nature. It couldn't happen.

Queen Omaira wouldn't get the satisfaction of winning this time. Mila decided to stop fighting. Yes, that was the answer. It went against her mother's desires, after all. She wouldn't allow her to have more blood on her hands. Mila's arms fell limply to her side.

The Hollows withdrew, no longer trying to fight Seren. Confidently, Mila strode toward him, feeling the searing gaze of astonishment bore into her back. As she closed the distance, the embers of hatred still smoldered within Seren, but she didn't stop.

"You better wake up soon, Seren," Mila murmured. "Or else I'll have to kill you."

Then, she leaned on her toes and pressed her lips against his. It was a declaration of defiance against her mother's expectations. Even as Seren's hands constricted around her throat, she kept her mouth pressed against his. Mila hoped her mother watched as he slammed her into the ground and squeezed her neck until her head began to spin.

Twenty-One

*"It is love that has cursed us. It is love that drives us to madness.
And it is love that drives us to hate."*

—the Personal Diaries of Felix Amos

1025 A.E.C.

Seren woke up with his hands wrapped around Mila's throat. He released her instantly, his hands shaking. She gasped for air, her neck already beginning to bruise from his grip. The lingering eyes from the audience of Sisters watched the two of them intently.

"Mila," Seren whispered, his voice trembling with remorse. "I'm so sorry I hurt you." He recoiled from his hands, staring at them in disbelief as if they were foreign entities. Seren collapsed to his knees, feeling the weight of the monstrous actions bearing down on him.

Omaira's demand rang in his ears, her cold words slicing through the chamber. "Kill him! Now, Iris!"

Mila managed a barely audible cough. "You can't," she gasped. "He resisted before I killed him. He...passed." Her voice faded, her strength giving way as she attempted to sit up.

Seren rushed to her side. He couldn't control the tremors in his fingers as they brushed against the horrifying marks. "You should've killed me," he growled, surprised by the anger in his own voice. "I could have killed you."

A fragile smile tugged at the corners of Mila's lips, her eyelids fluttering shut. "I wouldn't have let you," she whispered weakly. "You stopped right before I was about to kill you."

The Queen, infuriated, descended from her throne and approached the two of them. "What is the meaning of this, Ata?" she asked. "You allowed him to overpower you."

Mila forced herself to sit up, her eyes meeting her mother's. "I love him, remember?" she responded, her voice raw. "It seems you've forgotten the sacrifices love can bring."

Ignoring the presence of the Queen, Seren scooped Mila into his arms, lifting her from the ground. Nobody stopped them or said a word as he exited the doors, slamming them shut behind him.

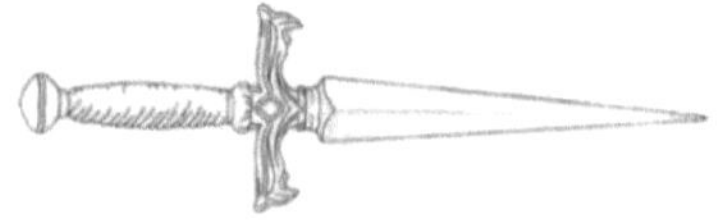

Two more trials. That was what the Queen decreed. Seren had no desire to do any of it, especially as he watched Mila wince in the mirror as she massaged her neck. Her servants had provided her with medicine that alleviated the swelling and restored her voice, but the purple and blue splotches remained.

"Can't we get separate rooms?" Seren asked.

Mila let her hair fall over her neck, covering the marks before turning to Seren. She raised her eyebrows. "No. That would look strange. My mother is already suspicious as is. What's the problem?"

Sighing heavily, Seren lay on the bed with his back turned away from her. "I don't want to look at you."

Mila didn't answer and settled on the bed next to him. "The day after tomorrow, I'll be queen," she finally uttered. "Try to survive till then."

Survive at what cost? He wanted to turn around and tell Mila to let him die now. He wished to confess to the Queen that they were lying. Even looking at Mila filled him with guilt. What if he had killed her? His mouth went dry at the thought. He wouldn't have been able to live with himself if that had happened.

"What about Jude?" Seren asked quietly.

"It's already taken care of."

He turned to Mila. "What do you mean?"

"I managed to bribe Lana, the woman who brought you here. I promised her a position in the Royal Court once I am queen, in exchange for breaking Jude out. I asked her to take him to Lumina. He'll be safer there."

Seren sighed in relief. "Thank the Gods."

"I wouldn't have let you kill me, Seren," Mila said firmly. "I knew you wouldn't."

"Yeah," he murmured.

"You should eat something. You'll need your strength to finish the trials."

"I just want to sleep," Seren said bitterly, turning his back to her again. He clenched the fabric of his shirt, feeling his uneven breath.

"Seren, it isn't your fault," she sighed. "That trial is how my father died. My mother ended up killing him. I was a baby."

So, Mila had been afraid when the trial started. He admired her for not letting the Queen see her falter; she was so much stronger than him.

Seren was thankful when Mila finally drifted off to sleep. However, he knew he wouldn't be able to rest at all. It was impossible for him to tell the time of day in the Sanguine Kingdom, making the hours hard to gauge. He missed the sky. Being confined in the underground kingdom was causing him to grow more and more restless. The castle contained elegance with its stone walls, winding staircases, and luxurious throne room, but the lack of windows made it clear that it was built into the chasms beneath the ground. Seren hated the thought.

The reason behind the kingdom's concealment was clear. Demons were repelled by the sunlight, and somewhere lurking in the kingdom was Lilith. Only Omaira had come face to face with the demon, and tomorrow, Mila would meet her. After that, there was nothing more Seren could do.

Seren stood up, distancing himself from Mila's side. His eyes gently traced over her, lying sprawled across the bed, deeply asleep with her mouth slightly open. Leaning toward the bed, he covered her with the blankets before stepping away.

Sleep was impossible. He walked across the room with a sigh. Mila had left a tray of food for him sitting near the door. As if he could eat. Seren growled, and his arm swept across the food, the tray clattering noisily onto the floor and the food splattering. Mila didn't stir.

"Damn it," he cursed.

He was helpless against the future. He had tried reaching for the voice that had guided him, but she had been silent. It was as if she had left him the moment he had entered the underground depths of the kingdom. He was *alone*.

Seren collapsed onto his knees, fresh berries squishing under his palms. He bowed his head down, biting his lip until it bled.

"Please, father," he whispered. "If you can hear me. Please, listen."

Seren continued his prayers to his father, repeating them in his head until they blurred together. He eventually fell asleep, his stained hands still clasped in prayer.

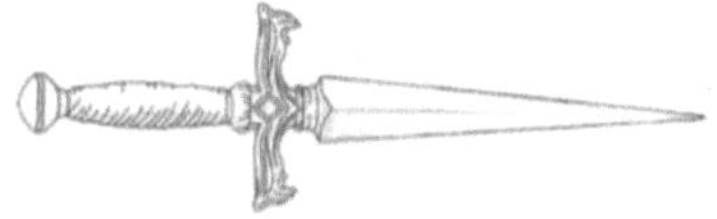

Several hours had passed when Iris's sudden knock startled Mila and Seren awake. Without waiting for a response, Iris barged into the room, making it clear that the time for the second trial had arrived. Mila cast a peculiar look at Seren as he rose from the ground, his hands stained red. As he strode over to her, their hands instinctively reached for each other, fingers intertwining.

"Already?" Mila mumbled.

"You know how Mother is," Iris answered.

"No new matching outfits this time?" Mila asked sourly.

Iris surprisingly smiled. "I think your Beloved may have shocked the Queen. I don't think I have ever seen Mother so furious before."

Mila returned the smile.

Together, they followed Iris as she led them down the spiraled stair-case, their fingers still clasped tightly. With each step, Seren's heart raced as he wondered what trial awaited him this time.

As the grand doors of the throne room swung open, revealing the expectant audience before them, a palpable tension filled the air.

The Queen, her smile retaining its wickedness, welcomed them. This time, she gestured for Mila to sit down beside her. Mila released her hand from Seren's and stepped onto the marble steps, settling beside her mother on her throne.

"I hope you don't mind," Queen Omaira said in a saccharine tone. "We are on a rather tight timeframe due to the impending eclipse. I simply cannot afford to waste any time. For your second trial, I have chosen the Trial of Nightmares."

Mila stiffened in her seat at her words.

"In this trial, you will prove your endurance for the Princess's sake. And it will begin *now*."

As a sudden gale swept through the room, it extinguished the candles, plunging everything into temporary darkness. Seren was encircled by a group of Sanguine Sisters, their crimson candles igniting and casting a feeble glow upon their red robes. Their haunting words echoed through the air, sending a shiver down his spine.

"We bring you the Trial of Nightmares. Prepare to confront your darkest fears and most painful memories, and face the depths of your soul."

And with their final words, the flames abruptly vanished. The world seemed to tilt and twist, warping and contorting, until Seren found himself fully immersed in complete darkness. He trembled against a biting wind, feeling an unmistakable fear course through him. The world was empty and devoid. He was alone. He reached out, desperate to touch something real, but was denied.

"Hello?"

His voice echoed, rattling around in his brain. Was this his fear—to live inside darkness without even a glint of light? To be just as alone as he felt?

Then, within the depths of the profound darkness, a sound appeared, faint and distant, like the delicate strumming of ethereal music. It stirred a spark of recognition within Seren as if he shared an inexplicable connection with that haunting melody.

A strange pull beckoned him forward, drawing him toward the source of the sound. In a stumbling haze, he blindly moved ahead, instinctively following it.

As he ventured closer, a faint light emerged amid the abyss, drawing him nearer. Someone was here.

Seren drew closer and closer until he finally arrived at the source of the melody—an oasis of color in the midst of the surrounding darkness—a harp and its player. The harp's body was a work of art, meticulously carved from bone, radiating a soft, otherworldly glow. Nimble hands danced across the strings, played by a mere child. When he glanced up at Seren, his playing ceased, and the gentle luminance of the harp began to fade away. A boy with silvery-white hair and eyes the color of amethyst.

The boy was Seren.

Seren's knees trembled beneath him as he took a step forward. Moving closer, a figure emerged behind the boy, clasping his shoulder. Seren froze, feeling his breath catch in his throat. It was Aiden. This was a memory. Looking down at the boy, at Seren, Aiden's face was soft and warm.

"Keep playing, Seren."

The boy nodded stiffly and resumed playing, his fingers brushing delicately across the strings. The music was beautiful, almost unbearably so.

Stray tears ran along Aiden's face as he closed his eyes, listening to the melody. "I knew it," he breathed, his eyes flashing open. "I knew it was you all along. You've been reborn, Alernaea."

The harp. Seren remembered now.

He blinked, and there he was, seated in the very spot where the boy had been. Seren's fingers gracefully danced over the strings, playing with effortless skill as if he had honed this craft throughout his entire life. The strings felt natural beneath his fingertips. It felt right. And yet...

Aiden moved in front of him, his eyes narrowed. The melody became louder, too fast, Seren's playing uneven.

"You should have been the one to die."

He couldn't stop. His fingers played on their own accord, and his fingertips were beginning to bleed.

"It's your fault, Seren."

Tears began to stream down Seren's face. He could hardly breathe as his lungs constricted. The melody continued in a tangled mess.

"I didn't..." Seren began, his voice faltering.

Aiden's piercing gaze bore into Seren's as he loomed over him, fingers curled.

"I was wrong about you," he said. "You *failed* me."

Seren released his bloodied hands from the harp and fell to his knees. He yearned for Aiden's forgiveness, a glimmer of mercy. Aiden's hands descended upon his shoulders as Seren knelt before him.

"I'm sorry," Seren whispered. "I don't know how to redeem myself for what I've done. It was an accident."

Even though he had stopped playing the harp, he could still hear it. The sound grew louder and louder, causing his bones to shudder. Seren covered his ears, tears streaming down his face. He hadn't meant to. He didn't mean to kill his mother. It was an accident.

Aiden's hands found his, prying them from his ears. "Cleanse the Veil, Seren," he commanded, his words slicing deep into Seren. "Only you can save us all from the Sundering. Only then will you be forgiven."

Seren couldn't. He didn't know how. But before he could open his mouth and respond, a condescending laugh flooded his ears. He turned his head and saw him. Lumen stood behind him, a crooked smile dancing upon his lips.

"Why don't you enlighten him, boy?" Lumen taunted. "Why don't you share the truth? Or have you conveniently forgotten what happened?"

It felt like a fist had collided with Seren's chest instantly. He was forcibly transported through time and space, abruptly thrust into the clutches of another memory.

He stood frozen, his heart pounding as he looked down at his mother's lifeless form. The weight of the tragedy that had befallen him threatened to suffocate him all over again. *No.* A hushed cry escaped his lips, laden with anguish and disbelief.

"No, not again," he whispered. His hands trembled. Seren began to violently shake her as if the sheer force could jolt her back to life. The vibrant hue of her dress was drowned in a sea of crimson.

"Mom!" he wailed. "Come back. I'm sorry!"

Seren sobbed uncontrollably, burying his head on her cold chest. She was truly gone, and an overwhelming sense of guilt consumed him. And then, he saw them. Other lifeless bodies were strewn across the grass, bleeding into the stems of the hellebores. Enid, her vacant eyes haunting him. It was all his fault. Jude, Mila, and Aiden—all lying motionless.

Stumbling backward, his breathing grew labored as a chorus of denials echoed within him.

No. No. No.

It was his fault. He should've listened to Aiden. And there it was—the harp, every string broken and bloodied by Seren's hands.

It had to be perfect.

The music had to be *pure.*

Just as Seren was supposed to be.

But he had been so alone. So *angry.*

So... *tired.*

Seren had played the harp with pure malice. A holy instrument that only he could play, and he had defied Aiden. And in doing so, he had caused this. He had called the demons, and they had killed everyone.

A hand descended softly upon his quivering shoulder. Looking upward, he found himself staring into Lumen's yellow eyes. Lumen kneeled beside him, fingers brushing across his mother's eyelids to close them. Gently, he wiped away a tear clinging to Seren's cheek.

"I can help you," he said calmly, reaching out his hand.

Seren hesitantly placed his stained hand within Lumen's.

"I... I killed them," Seren said, his voice barely audible. "I didn't mean to."

"Oh, I know. It was not your fault," he replied empathetically. "Come with me, Seren. I will take you far from here."

And so, Seren took Lumen's hand, and the world shifted again, propelling him through time. Lumen's grin greeted Seren from across a table, his kind eyes watching him. "How are you feeling?"

"Better today," Seren replied with a smile.

He trusted Lumen then, for he promised to help him—and he did. Countless days flashed before his eyes, filled with the time they spent together and the trust Seren had developed for Lumen. Until that day. The day he desperately wanted to forget, the day he *had* forgotten. The day Lumen betrayed him.

Vulnerable, broken, and alone, Seren was haunted by nightmares of his mother's death. His dreams became his own personal hell, a torment of Aiden's disgust and his mother's anguish from which there was no escape.

Lumen watched him crumble and took advantage of him. He offered comfort, pretending to be a friend, someone who wanted to help. Through every shred of solace he provided, Lumen weaseled his way into Seren's mind, extracting insecurities from the crevices of his being.

The voice that had guided him for so long had grown quiet. She had always been there, a second mother in the shadows. He could vividly recall her teachings—how to conceal his true self for safety, the shield she provided in a way he struggled to explain. Yet, after his mother's death, when he needed her most, she remained silent. She became a faint whisper, offering warmth sparingly. Despite knowing she was still present, safeguarding their shared secrets, he couldn't shake the feeling of abandonment.

Seren resented her for leaving him unanswered. The questions that were turning him bitter were ignored. He hated her for it. He hated her so much that he did the one thing she had told him never to do.

"You must never resist me, Seren. Do not call to the dark, even if it calls to you. I will shield you always and for eternity if you do not push me away. Remember that there is a time to reveal yourself, and there is a time to keep yourself guarded."

He resisted. He was angry and tired of feeling alone. Lumen made him feel like he was more than just a potential piece of divine intervention. He made him feel *human*. It was all he ever wanted.

Seren remembered it well. While playing the harp alone in the crypt of the church, a transcendent moment unfolded when they suddenly appeared. A tingling sensation enveloped him as if the music had taken physical form, drawing out a thrum within his soul. With an incessant wave, her voice flooded his mind, bombarding him with demands.

"Conceal them."

"Show no one."

"Hide them."

"Tell no one."

Why should he be forced to endure solitude? To never embrace his true self? The burden of concealing his identity, the weight of a hidden truth, had become too heavy. Lumen understood him. It was this realization that prompted Seren to make his decision—to expose his most guarded secret, one he hadn't even shared with Aiden. He solemnly vowed to keep his true form hidden, a pact forged with the guiding voice. Concealing his true self had become second nature with her help, but the weight of the facade had become exhausting. He no longer wanted to hide.

The instant he revealed himself to Lumen, a flicker of something passed across the doctor's face as if he had been expecting this revelation all along.

The voice returned, distant and unreachable, warning him: "*What have you done, Seren?*"

"*Run.*"

"*Run.*"

"*Run.*"

He couldn't.

He screamed.

He thrashed.

Seren lay strapped upon the frigid table, the harsh fluorescent lights cutting into his skin.

"No," he begged. "Please, don't."

Lumen's face came into focus as he smirked. "A pity," he said. "They truly are beautiful."

His hand swung over Seren as he reached out to a tray on his right. The object clanged against the metal tray as he picked it up—a cruel blade crafted from bone, emanating light.

No. No. No.

Seren's eyes followed Lumen's hands until he couldn't see them anymore.

"Stop!" he screamed. "Please!"

"Isn't this what you've always wanted? To be free?" Lumen hissed. "I can give that to you, Seren. Don't you see that? I can take this fate away from you."

Seren was voiceless, screaming silently into a void. It burned—white-hot pain, agony, torture. The tether snapped. It was as if breath was being crushed from his lungs, a hollowness filling his chest. Lumen had taken it. Taken everything from Seren. The sky. He took the sky. The pain was too much, unbearable. It transcended physical pain, surpassed loss, and went beyond it all.

Why.... why? Give them back. Please.

Seren's once white and black feathers now lay in a bloodied cascade on the floor. A solitary white feather, its tip stained with crimson, floated gently into his open palm. As his fingers closed around it, his gaze locked onto Lumen's. It was as if Seren's soul had split in two, a Veil of darkness bleeding between, with his own personal hell begging to be unleashed. Seren envisioned Lumen's bones breaking beneath his grasp, his skin withering, and the life slowly fading from his eyes until he crumpled into a worthless heap. Lumen deserved nothing less. It would be his *judgment.*

And, from the distant depths of my mind, Seren heard her cry:

"What has he done?"

"What have you done?"

"Seren..."

An embrace encircled him from behind, abruptly pulling him away from the vivid memory. The touch was warm and comforting. It was Mila, pressing herself against Seren's back, her hair brushing against his cheek.

"It's over, Seren. You're safe now. Try to take a deep breath," she reassured him, gently wiping a tear from his face. "You're crying."

"Am I?"

How strange. Warm tears were running down Seren's face, falling into his lap. He allowed Mila to wipe them away, feeling too dazed to mind.

"The trial is over," she said.

He surveyed his surroundings, realizing they were in her room. "How...?" Seren whispered.

"Well..." Mila paused, taking a deep breath. "I used my magic," she finally confessed. "I was careful not to let anyone notice. Your eyes began to change, and I was afraid others would notice. If my mother expects you to be more than human, then nothing good could come from it." She bit her lip. "I didn't know what else to do, so I had no choice but to take extreme measures. I stopped your heart long enough for you to lose consciousness. I was able to bring you to my room before you...changed again."

In a quiet, almost defeated tone, he asked, "Does that mean I failed?"

"My mother has granted one last trial," she answered with relief. "You remembered something, didn't you, Seren? You look so broken..."

They faced each other for a moment, her warm brown eyes looking deeply into his. She reached out, her hand brushing the tendrils of his hair.

"Why does your hair change?" Mila murmured. "It looks like starlight."

Seren froze as her other hand found his cheek.

"What's going on, Seren?"

"Don't pretend to care about me now, Mila," he said icily.

She withdrew her hand, looking hurt. "Seren…"

"Just don't," he interrupted her. "There's no audience to deceive here. We don't have to pretend."

Mila remained silent as he turned his back to her. He felt her presence as she settled on the bed beside him. He couldn't bear to look at her and certainly didn't want her to see him cry any longer.

They sat in heavy silence until the gentle rhythm of Mila's breathing indicated that she had fallen asleep. It was clear that harnessing her magic drained her of energy, leaving her exhausted. He turned back toward Mila. Her hair cascaded across her arms, framing her face. Each subtle breath Mila took caused her long lashes to kiss her flushed cheeks. She was beautiful, scars and all.

Why had she protected him? Twice at that. Perhaps it was simply ingrained in her nature, a reflection of the goodness her brother had attested to. Regardless of her true feelings toward him, the fact remained that she had selflessly come to his aid.

He couldn't resist the urge and reached out, his fingertips brushing a stray strand of Mila's hair away from her cheek. As he observed her peaceful expression, he couldn't help but wonder how long she had held him and stayed, attempting to calm him. What had he said?

Seren's fingers traced his lips as he thought of their kiss. His heart skipped a beat in his chest, betraying him. Warmth filled his cheeks at the mere thought. Mila's lips had been so soft, and her breath hot as it coalesced with his. He shook his head, feeling stupid for allowing his mind to wander.

He approached the mirror hanging on her wall and stared back at the stranger in the reflection. Silvery-white hair. Eyes of an inhuman color. His fingers traveled upwards as he touched his hair, feeling its unnatural softness. He took a deep breath, realizing he had let his Aura fall away, exposing his true self to Mila. He had been too vulnerable.

As his fingers touched the surface of the glass, he watched in fascination as the strange violet shade slowly transformed, replaced by the familiar green color of his mother's eyes. His hair faded back into its inky-black color, besides the one stubborn strand that refused to change.

The seal was supposed to control his Aura, but it was fading, and his control was slipping away.

Seren stepped backward, falling into the bed with a loud sigh. His eyes drew upwards to the captivating expanse of stars above. He lifted his hand, his finger hovering underneath the brightest star.

"Is this who I am?" he whispered.

Who was he? He was Seren, the apparent son of a God and a murderer. Wasn't he the one destined to cleanse the Veil, as he had always been told? A reincarnation of a Goddess meant to save the world? He let his hand fall and clutched the blankets tightly, his heart racing in his chest. With his eyes squeezed shut, he tried to calm himself, urging a deep breath. He wanted to scream.

He had seen the truth. He went to the Godless City on his own. He had turned his back on the Gods, hadn't he? He had run. Seren reached under his shirt, feeling the horrific scars beneath his fingertips. Why had he chosen to share his wings with Lumen when he had been too afraid to show even Aiden? He was a fool. Everything that had happened was his fault.

Cleanse the Veil.

Seren couldn't. He didn't know how. He had failed Aiden, and yet, all he longed for was to be with him now. To be... home. But it wasn't home, was it? Not without his mother.

He needed Aiden's guidance, his wisdom, and the unwavering belief Aiden held in his ability to cleanse the Veil. Most of all, he needed Aiden's forgiveness. He had to overcome the final trial set by the Queen, no matter the cost. And perhaps he could uncover a way to free Mila from the binds that held her. When it was all over, he would find his way back home.

And if you fail?

The doubt crept in. Hadn't he always failed?

"I'm sorry," Seren muttered. He clutched his head in his hands. "I can't do it."

Seren was the child who had always cried. Who angered too easily. A boy with a love for the stars and the sky. The one prophesied to stop the Sundering. He was Seren, the *failure*.

"Seren?"

He felt Mila's hands on his back. "I can't," he choked. "I don't know how."

"Seren," Mila whispered again. Her arms wrapped around him just as before. "I know. You can talk to me."

"I can't. I just...can't." He took a gasp of air, his body shuddering. "You wouldn't understand." A sob ripped through him as he tried to fight the agony.

Mila grabbed his face, pressing her forehead against his. Warm tears traced his skin as she held their heads together, his tears pressing against her cheeks.

"Breathe, Seren."

This time when she said his name, a calm overcame him as if she was pulling him out of the deep waters of his sorrow. His shoulders fell limply, and he collapsed into her, their lips grazing.

Mila let go of him, their foreheads separating as they moved apart, but their shoulders remained pressed against each other.

"Did you remember who you are?" she asked softly. "When you did the trial?"

"Yes," he uttered.

"I'm sorry. You shouldn't have had to remember that way."

Seren took a deep breath, finally feeling as though the suffocating weight was being lifted. "I needed to remember sooner or later."

"So..." Mila trailed off. "Was Kitsune right? Are you the son of a God?"

"I wish it were that simple," he said shakily.

"Oh." Sensing that he wouldn't elaborate, Mila turned to face him. "We should talk about what's to come tomorrow. I don't know why my mother is allowing you another trial, but I have a strange feeling. She even said you'll attend the gala before I am crowned queen. I'm not sure what she has planned, but I can't promise that I can keep you alive."

He exhaled and forced a smile. "Your mother is kind of crazy, you know that?"

Mila returned the smile and rolled her eyes. "You think?"

"So, what happened to you killing me?" Seren asked. Their shoulders were still touching, and their legs were pressed against each other.

"I don't think that'll be necessary anymore."

Seren leaned toward Mila, his hand overlapping hers. She tensed as he neared, her brown eyes giving away unease.

"What about kissing you?" he asked.

"W-what?" she stammered.

"Will kissing you be necessary again?"

Mila's face flushed with color. Despite clenching her fist, she didn't withdraw her hand or move away as he inched closer.

"You have a lot of nerve. That trial really did mess with your head," she breathed, her eyes tracing the curve of his mouth.

Seren pulled away seconds before reaching her lips. "I'm only teasing you."

Although, truthfully, he wanted to kiss her again and again until he forgot everything else.

Twenty-Two

"The trinity of items, holy in might, only wielded by the one they call the Half-Light."

—the Seer Diaries of Felix Amos

1025 A.E.C.

The servants dressed Mila in a sheer purple gown that cascaded elegantly down her figure, showcasing her shoulders and back. As she attempted to conceal the scars on her back with her hair, the two Sisters, introduced as Aria and Rhiannon, reassured her that her beauty remained undiminished. Delicate gold snakes were embroidered along the hem of her dress, while matching bracelets adorned her wrists.

Meanwhile, Seren sat awkwardly, a mere observer, as the Sisters applied makeup and fastened exquisite golden pins into Mila's hair. Finally, a small golden crown embedded with black diamonds was carefully placed atop her head.

Aria ran her fingers over the dark circles beneath Mila's tired eyes, her expression filled with concern. She applied a cool rag to them, offering a momentary relief. "You've pushed yourself to the limit, dear Princess," Aria murmured.

Rhiannon quickly interjected, casting a protective glance at her sister. "Nevertheless, you are absolutely radiant," she proclaimed, her voice carrying a subtle warning. "You possess the grace and strength fitting of a queen."

"I don't want to be queen."

The clatter of hairpins falling to the floor jolted Seren's attention toward them. Both women stiffened at her declaration, exchanging anxious glances. A hushed silence fell upon them as they gathered the pins and continued to arrange Mila's hair. Aria's fingertips delicately grazed over the bruises, still marking Mila's neck.

"We understand," Aria murmured. "We have been by your side, dear Kamilah, for countless years. Our duty has always been to care for you since you were a mere child. And your brother, too. His death pained us." She tenderly cupped Mila's face, her touch imbued with nostalgia. "A part of me has always wondered..." But Aria's voice faltered as if the words struggled to reach her lips.

"I don't know how to sever the bonds," Mila said in a monotone. "I'm sorry."

Without a moment's hesitation, Rhiannon slapped her sister. Aria winced and cradled her reddened cheek.

"We are forbidden to discuss such matters," Rhiannon hissed. "I apologize, Princess." She bowed to Mila, sweat forming on her forehead.

"No need to apologize," Mila assured her kindly. "On another note, will Seren also be dressed for the gala?"

The attention of both women shifted toward Seren, causing him to squirm uncomfortably in his seat, feeling a sudden bout of self-consciousness.

"Yes, it does surprise me, to be honest. It's unheard of for a Beloved to attend a gala," Aria mused. "It makes me wonder what plans the Queen has in store."

Rhiannon slammed her foot on the ground. "Quiet down," she growled, shaking her head.

Aria frowned but chose to focus on handing Seren neatly folded clothing, the gesture signaling the end of their interaction. "It seems we're finished here. We wish you the best, Princess. The next time we see you, you will be our queen."

Rhiannon and Aria rose from their seats and made their way to the exit. Aria disappeared behind the door, but Rhiannon paused, her hand lingering above the handle.

"We are not born evil, young Beloved," she whispered. "Nor are we born with a hatred for men. If anything, we are cursed, bound to the will of the Queen, just as she is bound to Lilith. I don't know why, but I felt compelled to tell you." With those cryptic words, she disappeared, closing the door behind her.

Seren stared at the regal attire in his hands, its accents matching Mila's outfit once again. He traced the outline of the golden buttons. Taking a deep breath, he started peeling off his clothing.

"I'm afraid, Seren."

Mila's back was turned to him, and Seren could see the slight tremble of her shoulders. He adjusted the collar of his shirt, his hands slightly unsteady.

"It will be alright, Mila," he said, even though he wasn't sure if he believed his own words. "Even if you become queen, I will find a way to get you out of here. I promise."

Mila turned toward him, her eyes welling up with tears. "Please, don't make a promise you can't keep," she whispered. "You won't be able to forgive yourself if you're unable to follow through."

Her words sent a pang of worry through Seren's heart. He knew that she was right. And he also knew that she was thinking of the promise she had made to her brother. Empty promises couldn't be made when the stakes were so high, and her future hung in the balance.

Taking a deep breath, Seren strode across the room to her, reaching out and grasping Mila's quivering hands. "Mila, I promise you this," he said, his voice steady. "I will do everything in my power to face the last trial, to overcome every obstacle that stands in the way."

He could see Mila searching for the truth in his words. A flicker of hope began to replace the doubt in her gaze. She squeezed his hand, a small smile tugging at the corners of her lips.

"You don't know when to give up, do you?"

Before he could respond, a knock echoed on the door. The doors opened, revealing Iris, dressed in a stunning blue gown that showcased the Sanguine markings on her chest. She respectfully bowed to Mila upon her entrance.

"I will accompany you both to the gala," Iris announced. "Please, follow me."

Mila and Seren followed Iris, staying side by side. Mila seemed tense, her body rigid. He gently placed his hand on her back, feeling her relax slightly at his touch. As they approached the grand doors to the throne room, anxiety began to bubble within him.

Iris pushed open the grand doors, revealing the breathtaking gala before them. The room had transformed beyond recognition, adorned with Sisters dressed in exquisite attire, engaged in lively conversations and graceful dance moves. The sweet melodies of a symphony filled the air. From her throne, the Queen locked eyes with Seren upon their entrance, withholding a greeting as she whispered something to a court member at her side. A vermilion snake rested on her shoulders like a piece of jewelry.

Something about Queen Omaira seemed different. Seren's eyes drew toward the crown perched atop her head. It was a magnificent creation, a striking combination of weaving black snakes and shimmering red rubies. The very symbol of power and authority that would soon be passed on to Mila.

"Do at least pretend to enjoy yourself, Princess," Iris hissed between them. "Mother is watching."

Without waiting for a response, Iris turned and walked purposefully toward the Queen, her graceful figure cutting through the crowd. Left behind, Mila and Seren exchanged worried glances, silently sharing their mutual apprehension.

As he glanced back at Omaira, he couldn't shake the feeling of her pressing gaze upon him. It was obvious he was the sole male presence amidst the splendor of the gala, a rarity amongst the Sisters. Their curious glances and whispers hinted at their unfamiliarity with such an occurrence. He couldn't help but feel the weight of scrutiny settle upon him.

"Shall we, Princess?"

Seren extended his hand toward Mila. She raised her eyebrows in question but, without hesitation, placed her palm in his. They stepped into the center of the grand room as the Sisters parted to create a path for them. He firmly rested his right hand on the small of Mila's back, guiding her. As the melody of the music filled the air, their bodies moved in synchrony.

"You know how to dance?" Mila asked, her voice filled with genuine surprise.

"Apparently so," he chuckled. He pulled Mila in closer and dipped her, their faces momentarily close. "I may have a few hidden talents. I can also play the harp if you'd believe that."

Her lips curved into a delighted smile. "So, you can dance, play the harp, and wield a sword? You're full of surprises, aren't you?"

Unable to contain his smile, he replied, "You have no idea."

"So," Mila whispered, her head leaning against his shoulder. "What is it like to remember who you are?"

Seren's hand tensed, causing Mila to wince. "There simply isn't time to think about it," he said hoarsely.

He twirled Mila across the floor, memories of his mother flooding back. His heart ached as he remembered her touch and patient guidance while teaching him how to dance. It was a bittersweet memory but one that he would hold dear.

"It's almost worse," Seren whispered, "to remember. I would rather only think about being here with you."

He yearned to erase it all from his mind once more, a desperate desire to avoid dwelling on any of it at this moment. The weight was overwhelming—too much for him to bear. The thought alone threatened to unravel his composure; he feared it might unleash a torrent of emotions beyond his control. What if... a part of him had chosen to forget?

Mila pressed herself a little tighter against him. "Tell me something good," she said. "A memory that makes you happy."

"Okay," he said in defeat. "My mother taught me to dance. I remember when she would tease me and show me the proper steps. She had said that someday I would need to know how to share a dance with someone I truly cared for. Although she never spoke about him, I think my father danced with her."

Her hand tightened against his. "She sounds lovely, Seren."

He smiled. "She was."

"I've never seen you smile so much," Mila said in a hushed tone.

"You once told me that smiling suited me," he said. "I guess I figured I should aim to please my princess."

Mila rolled her eyes, but he could see the curves forming at the corners of her lips.

As they moved across the floor, every step held the weight of his mother's teachings. He guided Mila with the same tenderness and care his mother once bestowed upon him. While dancing with Mila, he felt an inexplicable sense of warmth. It was as though his mother's spirit danced alongside them, guiding their steps.

While the two of them continued to dance, twirling and spinning in perfect harmony, he could feel the stares of Sisters upon them. However, Seren paid no attention. The room seemed to fade away. All he could focus on was Mila's presence and the rhythm of their sway.

"Who are you really?" she murmured.

He brought her closer to him, her breath on his face. "I'm afraid to tell you."

"Why?" Mila breathed, her lips dangerously close to his. "Do you not trust me?"

"It isn't that," he said, pulling away. "I can't. Not now."

After what felt like both an eternity and a fleeting second, the song reached its crescendo. Mila nudged him gently, signaling the end of their dance.

"I see Lana," Mila said, her voice filled with urgency.

She grasped Seren's hand, dragging him behind her. They weaved through the Sisters until Mila's hand landed on a woman in a green dress. Lana turned around in surprise to see the princess, her eyes briefly grazing over Seren before she bowed politely, a genuine smile on her face.

"Your Highness," Lana greeted, her voice filled with respect. Her eyes dragged over Seren a second time, almost looking smug. "And the Beloved."

Mila leaned in closer, her voice barely audible. "Did you take care of it?"

Lana quickly glanced around, ensuring no one was listening, before nodding. "Yes, it was quite easy. It seemed he had fallen ill and was no longer suitable as a progenitor. He was due to be disposed of, so I took it upon myself to intervene."

Relief washed over Mila, a smile of gratitude spreading across her face. "Where is he?" she asked anxiously.

"Lumina, as requested. I left him on a church doorstep," Lana replied. "Though I must admit, I'm exhausted. I've never had to use a portal to travel such a distance before."

Mila's shoulders relaxed as she sighed in relief once more. "Thank you, Lana. You will be rewarded generously for this." She turned to Seren, her face beaming. He had never seen her smile so sincerely before. "Jude is safe."

As Mila and Lana exchanged celebratory words, Seren couldn't help but feel a pang of realization. He had been so caught up in their dance and shared connection that he had forgotten Mila's true quest. Jude was the one she longed to be reunited with, not him. He was the one who was supposed to be here with her.

Mila's hand touched his shoulder. "Seren, what's wrong?"

"I'm worried. What do you think your mother is planning?" he said. "Shouldn't the trial have started by now?"

"I've been wondering that myself," she replied softly. "Just be on guard, okay? And if you don't mind..." Mila smirked. "Let's dance again. I enjoy seeing that angry look on her face when we act like we're in love. You're quite the performer. Which reminds me..." Her fingers lightly brushed over her lips.

"I'm sorry," he said with an awkward smile. "I shouldn't have said that last night. I wasn't feeling myself. And I'm sorry for not warning you before the trials. I hadn't planned on kissing you."

"It's alright," Mila said with a grin. "Next time, a warning would be nice."

Next time?

The two of them resumed their dance, twirling and swaying gracefully together. Mila's laughter filled the air, her smiles, and playful gestures suggesting a world where it was just the two of them again. But beneath the facade, Seren's heart weighed heavy with a sorrow threatening to consume him. Even if he passed the trial, he couldn't prevent Lilith from bonding with Mila, leaving him once again as the one who failed those he cared for. He was going to lose her.

"You look like you're in pain," Mila teased, noticing the shift in his demeanor. "What happened to your enjoyment?"

Silence hung between them as he struggled to find the words. Instead, he surprised Mila by pulling her closer, their bodies moving in sync. With a gentle yet firm grip, he dipped her lower than before, their breath intertwining.

"You look beautiful, Mila." And as he looked into her lovely brown eyes, he wished he could kiss her one last time.

Mila's face flushed at the unexpected compliment. Momentarily taken aback, she couldn't find her voice to respond. But he didn't give her a chance anyway. He spun her around, and the Queen's eyes met his. He could see something brewing inside of her. Something dangerous.

Mila clutched his shirt tightly as he pulled her in closer.

"Seren...I...."

But she was quickly cut off. As if the Queen had read his mind, she rose from her seat. She held up her hand, motioning for the music to halt. The hushed whispers and melodic notes ceased.

"The gala has come to an early end," she announced. "According to our customs, only the heir is to meet Lilith."

Iris, who must've slinked behind them, gripped Seren from behind, ready to guide him out of the hall. But the Queen's next words froze them in their tracks.

"Not him," she declared, a malicious smile forming. "He will stay. He still has one more trial to face."

Dread coursed through Seren's veins. His heart hammered in his chest like a drum. Even Iris couldn't hide her surprise as her eyebrows furrowed in confusion. However, she didn't dare to challenge the Queen's orders. She released her grip on him and bowed her head in deference. One by one, everyone in the room followed suit. They filed through the massive doors, leaving Mila and Seren alone with Omaira. She resumed her seat, her velvet dress cascading across the throne.

"The Devil's Hour is near," the Queen said calmly. "Although, we do have a bit of time to spare. Princess Ata, come here."

As Mila heard her true name, she involuntarily stiffened beside him. He could hear her breath quicken as she reluctantly obeyed her mother's command. The Queen drummed her fingers impatiently on her armrest. Every step on the marble echoed ominously through the chamber. Finally, Mila stood before her mother, fear dancing on her features.

"Do you have any idea how long I've reigned?" Queen Omaira asked, her tone dripping with entitlement. The snake on her shoulders slithered off her, wrapping itself around the legs of the throne.

Seren remained silent and unmoved, knowing that any response would only further fuel her anger.

"A long time," the Queen answered on his behalf. "And I had no intention of relinquishing my throne any time soon. But then, fate led me to encounter her father." The Queen's voice turned bitter, her tongue clicking with annoyance. "Of course, I was oblivious at the time. How could I have known? He was a direct descendant of Adamus, the sole reason Kamilah was chosen to be Queen. And why should I be forced to surrender sovereignty to a pathetic little *brat* who doesn't even want it?" With each word, her fury escalated, punctuated by the violent thud of her hand slamming upon the armrest. "She even dared to think she could kill Lilith." The Queen revealed Mila's glimmering dagger, pulling it from her garments. She waved it in front of Mila's face. "And all these years, you dared to defy her? To defy *me*?"

The madness lurking within the Queen's gaze sent a shiver down his spine. She stood up, holding the dagger high into the air.

"Even as your true name escapes my lips, I sense your defiance. It has always been there, lingering beneath the surface. And naturally, Lilith would never allow me to end your life. No, she desires you. But she has bid her time, patiently waiting for this day. The day that you are finally of age to take the throne. It's maddening. She knows my every thought, every move. She predicted that the love you felt for Kamil would be your ultimate downfall. Your weakness. And she was right. I managed to take control, making you plunge that dagger into his heart. Your true name belongs to me, and I must hand it to Lilith. That's her command to me."

A deranged scream erupted from the Queen's lips, followed by chilling laughter. "All I am permitted to do is weaken you, to assist in binding you to her will. What a *waste*." She grasped Mila's shoulder. "Princess Ata, from this moment forward, you will obey every one of my commands. You will kneel before your Queen."

"Mila!" Seren cried out, his voice echoing through the room.

"Stay still!" the Queen bellowed. "Unless you wish to fail your final trial now and meet your demise." She forcefully grasped Mila's hair as she fell to her knees. She thrust the dagger forward, severing a handful of Mila's hair. "Have you ever asked her how she got her scars, Beloved?"

"Please, don't hurt her," Seren begged.

Ignoring his words, the Queen cut another chunk of hair away with a swift swipe of the knife. "Here is an idea: will you still love the princess when she is no longer beautiful?"

Mila remained frozen as her mother relentlessly cut away chunks of her hair, the locks falling to the ground. A sadistic smile played on the Queen's lips as she lightly grazed the knife against the soft skin of Mila's cheek. Blood ran down her chin, flowing down to her collarbone.

Seren balled his fists at his sides. "Please, stop."

"Of course, I would have to rid her of that pretty face, too," the Queen sneered. She sliced deeper into Mila's tender flesh.

"Stop!" he cried.

He lunged forward but quickly froze as the Queen held the dagger menacingly above Mila's eye. Mila trembled as the tip of the dagger hovered dangerously close.

"Now, now," Omaira warned. "Don't you want to pass the final trial?"

"This is wrong," he choked. "Please, stop. I don't care if I fail the trial. Kill me if that is what it takes."

The Queen gritted her teeth, her grip faltering on the dagger. "You would sacrifice yourself for her?" she spat. Seren flinched as she slammed the knife into the marble tile, allowing it to clatter away.

"Yes," he said. "I'll do anything to end this."

The Queen's hands ran across her face as she paced the floor. "Wrong," she argued. "You're selfish. A liar. A coward. You won't!"

"I will."

A bloodcurdling scream suddenly erupted from her lips, an unholy, rage-filled sound that pierced the air. She clawed at her face, writhing hysterically before them. "No!" she shrieked. "No! No!"

Mila stood frozen, her eyes wide with shock and fear, as her mother's torment unfolded before them. And somewhere in the distance, the haunting chime of a clock echoed.

Seren, too, stood frozen in sheer horror as the Queen's legs grotesquely morphed into a monstrous serpentine tail. Her once human eyes rolled back, only to reveal menacing slit pupils. Her flowing hair transformed into a mass of writhing black snakes as if under a spell. Her crown fell from her head with a resonant clatter and tumbled down the stairs. The Queen's deranged screams transformed into maniacal laughter.

Seren took a step backward, cold sweat trickling down his neck. "You're Lilith?" he mustered. "I don't understand."

Disregarding his feeble presence, her scaled fingers glided across the trail of blood staining Mila's face. She brought her fingers to her lips, savoring the taste upon her forked tongue.

"We finally meet, little Princess," she crooned. Her words had an eerie, hypnotic quality that chilled him to the core.

"Stay away from her," Seren warned, his voice barely concealing the fear coursing through him.

Lilith turned sharply toward him. A malevolent smile twisted her features as she slithered closer, the snakes in her hair hissing. "You," she hissed. "Omaira sensed something peculiar about you. So, I had to see for myself. Yet, all I find is a trembling little boy."

He could not deny that he was afraid. Mila was out of his reach, and he was defenseless.

"The Queen isn't Lilith?" he uttered in confusion. His voice came out quiet, certainly comparable to a child's.

Lilith's shrill laughter reverberated through the chamber. "You foolish child, we are forever intertwined. Bound by an unbreakable pact. Omaira reminds me of the original queen, both reeking of desperation. It happened centuries ago, and the memories linger in my mind as vividly as if it were yesterday. Can you imagine it? A queen willingly venturing into the Veil, driven by the betrayal of her unfaithful husband and thirsting for revenge. It was poetic as if the Gods themselves had bestowed her upon me. She begged for power and her own kingdom. And after patiently waiting within the depths of the Veil, the day came when I could finally break free.

Through a fateful pact, she and all who followed her became forever bound to my every command. And soon, your beloved princess will meet the same fate."

Large, multicolored snakes slithered from corners of the room, swarming together across the floor.

"Though the blood of Adamus grants the princess resistance to my influence, it is of no consequence. In the end, she is just a mortal being. Her power is unmatched. And together, we will be great. The blood of corruption runs deep within her, calling the dark forces of magic straight into her very being." A red snake coiled its body possessively around Mila's wrist. "Child, you are aware of it, aren't you? Your very name now belongs to me, Princess Ata. And soon, our souls will become irreversibly intertwined, and the Queen will move on into the Veil."

Tears streamed down Mila's anguished face.

"No!" Seren shouted, desperate to save her. But his attempt to reach her was thwarted as serpents tangled around his ankles, constricting him in their grip. He fought against them as they slithered up his legs. "Set her free!"

Laughter escaped Lilith's lips, echoing throughout the room. "And why would I listen to an insignificant little cockroach like you?" she sneered. "You failed your second trial. You have not been bound by the Covenant since then. So, why don't we play a little game before our official coronation? Princess Ata, I want you to kill your Beloved."

Mila didn't move from her position.

"Oh yes, that's right," Lilith murmured. "You aren't her Beloved because she doesn't *love* you." She smiled in his direction. "Shall I rephrase? Princess Ata, kill that trembling boy."

Mila rose to her feet, tears streaming down her face. Lilith's laughter continued as Mila took hesitant steps toward the gleaming dagger on the floor. Panic surged through Seren as he watched her hand steadily grip the weapon. He tried to fight against the suffocating grip of the writhing snakes, but his efforts seemed useless.

"Mila, please."

It was useless to beg. Mila succumbed to the demon's command and possessed no free will under her control.

She advanced with the dagger poised above her, her eyes clouded with darkness. Seren thrashed against the serpents, yelling with all his might, determined to break free. But all his fighting only seemed to make their hold tighter. Realizing this, he relaxed his body. But it was no use. The snakes tightened further, and the largest launched forward and struck. As the fangs sank into his side, the snake recoiled quickly. Its body went limp, and the others followed suit, falling one by one onto the floor.

"What?" Lilith said, baffled. "Attack him!"

The snakes slithered around Seren, but their intentions were unclear. However, there was no time to ponder their motives.

Mila lunged at Seren, the razor-sharp blade of the knife narrowly missed his neck. Instinct kicked in, and he rolled across the floor, narrowly avoiding the dagger's deadly plunge as it struck the ground with a thud. Fear clenched his chest, but nothing could compare to the shock that pulsed through him when Mila turned the dagger on herself. She sliced a deep, crimson-laden gash down her arm. The sight of her blood seeping onto the floor made his stomach turn.

She flung the dagger aside, her hand tensing with hidden power. In the blink of an eye, blades made of her own blood were launched toward him. One sliced into his thigh, causing searing pain to shoot through his body. He cursed as blood trickled down his leg. There was no time to dwell on his injury. Mila's control over her actions was lost as she unleashed another blade of blood, its sharp edge barely grazing his left shoulder.

"Mila, fight against it!" he shouted. He breathed heavily as blood poured across the marbled floor.

She paid no attention to his pleas as she conjured an arrow of blood, hurtling it straight toward his head with deadly precision. He dodged the projectile, his heart pounding in his chest. The slickness of his blood splashing on the floor nearly caused him to lose his footing. At the perfect moment, she sliced into his arm, blood now trickling down his fingertips.

Determined to break through to Mila, he locked eyes with her, willing her to resist Lilith's influence. Yet, he could see no hint of struggle against the demon's control. She summoned another blade of blood, poised to plunge into his chest. Lifting her hand, she prepared to deliver the blow.

He felt a jolt of electricity go down his spine. With speed he didn't know he had, he rolled out of the way, the blade only scratching his shoulder. He balled up his fists, feeling a strange vibration inside his body. Without thought, he dashed toward Mila, hoping to subdue her. He wasn't fast enough. Mila commanded the blood into a whip, lashing it at him with remarkable speed. The whip coiled around his neck, cutting into his skin. Desperation filled him as he tried to grasp the formless blood, but it slipped through his fingers. He dropped to his knees, feeling the pressure on his throat intensify as Mila crushed his airway.

Instinct compelled him to persist in trying to grasp the whip, even though it proved futile. Blood flowed down his arms as he writhed against the suffocating grip.

"Wait!" Lilith commanded, her voice cutting through the air.

Mila froze at her command. The blood dripped down Seren's neck, then splashed onto the cold floor. Seren gasped for air, his head throbbing. Confusion flickered across Mila's face, a brief glimmer of her true self breaking through the control that consumed her.

Lilith dipped her fingertips in the blood that covered the marble. She brought Seren's blood to her mouth, tasting it.

"What is the meaning of this? What are you?" Lilith hissed, her eyes narrowing. "And why won't they attack you?" She pointed her fingers toward her mass of serpents. "What have you done to them?"

Seren took deep, ragged breaths, sweat pooling on his forehead. "I...don't...know..." he gasped.

"I want your true name," Lilith hissed. "Tell me what it is."

"You already know my name."

The demon slithered in Seren's direction, her eyes darkening. "Tell me your true name, now!" she roared.

And then it dawned on him. He should've known. The true name's power—its ability to bind or break, control or conquer. Lilith wasn't her true name. This revelation explained the unshakeable bond between the Sisters and why attempts to sever it had always failed.

Why would the blood of Adamus be resistant to the demon? It had been Lilith who had been shackled to him, not the other way around. Seren's mind raced, recalling the teachings from the Church of Caelestis, which had always revolved around Adamus and Eden without mentioning Lilith.

It was Eden who was believed to have eaten from the Tree. It was Eden who had been blamed for the original sin. And although Eden was referred to as the mother of all, she was the harbinger of sin in the eyes of humankind.

Seren's thoughts drifted toward the Disciples of Servius and their resentment of women. He couldn't help but see the striking parallel. This demon harbored an all-consuming hatred for men. Her deepest desire was to cleanse the world of their existence. But if the Devil had truly deceived her, why would she willingly assist in opening the Veil? Unless there were grains of truth in each story, distorted to suit their agendas.

"You want my true name?" Seren said, his voice steady. "Why don't you tell me yours first?"

Lilith froze, fear etched into every line on her face. "How dare you?" she seethed.

"I know your name," Seren said. "*Eden.*"

The demon screamed in disbelief, the snakes in her hair mimicking the sound.

And then, as if a shroud had been lifted from Seren's eyes, he saw them—the tethers that bound Mila to the demon. They resembled chains tightly engulfing her being, each pulsating with unsettling, unholy energy, relentlessly binding her to the demon's will.

Determination fueled Seren as he followed the path of the tethers. He reached out to them, feeling the tangible force of the bond that held Mila prisoner. It was evident that she was now resisting, but the grasp of the bond remained unyielding.

"Your eyes," Eden sputtered. "Tell me who you are!"

Seren ignored her, his bloodied fingers brushing against the bonds. Turning to face the demon, he reached for Mila's hand and squeezed it tightly.

"Her name is *mine*."

The tether connecting Mila to the demon snapped in that instant, writhing toward Seren like a snake. It spiraled around his wrist, binding itself tightly to him. The raw power of the bond sent electricity coursing through his veins.

Seren's eyes locked onto Mila, a strange connection forming between them. He could feel the weight of her struggles, the frustrations and pain inflicted upon her. The bond between them was forged.

"Seren," Mila gasped. "What have you done?"

"That is impossible!" Eden shrieked. "You are no king! You are nothing! You cannot take her name for your own!"

But somehow, he had.

Eden recoiled; any trace of fear was quickly overshadowed by her rage. "I'll kill you!" she screeched. "And I will kill her! If I cannot have her, no one can!"

Mila scurried to her feet, eyes fixated on the dagger just within reach. She maneuvered through the advancing serpents. Closing her fingers around the dagger's hilt, her grip tightened. Yet, it didn't matter.

The chamber around them transformed as if driven by Eden's malev-olent will. Words of a dark incantation spilled from the demon's lips, her voice echoing with sinister power. The air thickened with the scent of iron as the chamber filled with blood. The thick liquid surged, pouring in from hidden crevices, rising with relentless force and flooding past their ankles.

"Mila!" Seren cried out.

The weight of the blood slowed Seren's movements as he headed toward her. He watched in horror, unable to intervene, as snakes climbed up Mila's body, their bodies wrapping around her like tendrils. One of the serpents snatched the dagger from Mila's grip in its mouth, leaving her defenseless. His mind raced as he waded through the blood, moving closer to her. But the liquid had already reached his navel.

"First, I want you to watch her die," Eden hissed. "I want you to *feel* it."

Seren could only watch as Mila struggled. Her body contorted in pain as the snakes mercilessly constricted around her. And he *could* feel it—not her pain, but something else. The tethers were stretched too thin, as if fraying and about to snap any second. The sickening sound of bones crunching filled the room as Mila cried out.

"No!"

If he hadn't come back for her. If he'd just left her alone. It was because of him. His mother's fate and the lives of those he cared for echoed through his mind. He couldn't bear to lose Mila, too, not this way.

With a scream, Seren swam toward Mila. Warm blood filled his mouth as he yelled her name. Amidst the chaos, he felt it. The seal on his back was burning with an intensity that threatened to consume him entirely. It was a sensation he had never felt before— overwhelming and unbearable.

He finally heard her again. A distant plea.

"Seren, do not let the darkness consume you."

If he could harness this power, if he could control it, then maybe, just maybe, he could save Mila.

"Seren," she warned.

But he couldn't afford to listen, and he couldn't bear the weight of her words. He shoved her voice forcefully into the recesses of his mind.

"Seren, calm down."

"Shut up!" he cried out. "Unless you're going to save her, shut up!"

He watched as Mila's head fell limply; her lips stained a chilling shade of blue. With a final guttural scream, he unleashed everything threatening to consume him.

Seren felt like something inside of him was being torn, as though a piece of his very being was severed. The pain echoed the memory of when his wings were torn from his back. Tears blurred his vision as he saw the thin barrier separating worlds. Just as he had witnessed the tethers holding Mila, he could now see darkness oozing from the crevices of reality. With every fiber of his being, he willed the barrier to open. And as he screamed, the Veil obeyed his command. It parted, revealing a thin gateway of darkness.

A chorus of demonic screeching sounded behind him. The scent of blood permeated the air, beckoning the demons from the Veil instantly. They flooded in, the sound of their bodies splashing into the blood around him. His heart slammed painfully against his chest as he watched grotesque creatures forming a horde.

Eden's face contorted in shock. "Impossible!" she screamed.

Seren hurried toward Mila, praying that she was still alive. As he neared her, the gleam of the dagger cut through the thick, viscous blood. Taking a mouthful of air, he submerged himself. Blood filled his nose as he reached for the subtle glow of the dagger, grabbing it by the hilt. With a gasp, he pushed himself to the surface, wiping his eyes. Wading toward Mila as quickly as possible, he hoped to reach her in time.

"Get off!" he screamed. He dug the dagger into the bellies of the snakes in a frenzy, watching them explode into oblivion and dissipate into nothingness.

Mila's limp body fell against him. He could feel her faint pulse through her cold skin. He slung her over his shoulder, keeping the dagger in his grip.

"Stop!" Eden's voice pierced through the chaos from behind. "You fools! It is not me you want!"

Eden was fighting off the small demons as they climbed upon her body, confused by the overwhelming scent of blood. Their howls of pain mingled with an otherworldly symphony, a desperate attempt to claim prey.

Seren's eyes wandered to the steps where the thrones sat, slick with blood. The marble above them, however, remained untouched. The dagger in his hand blazed with a brilliant light, its power pulsating with each beat of his heart.

A grotesque creature, baboon-like and deformed, hurtled off the wall. With Mila in his arms, movement was limited. He used his free arm to slash through the demon.

Another demon, similar in form, emerged from the sea of blood and propelled itself at them. With relentless determination, he swung his weapon, cutting into the creature's flesh. Immediately turning his attention to yet another approaching them, he slashed the dagger again and watched it be forcefully expelled from the world.

"Damn it. There's too many of them!"

Mila stirred on his shoulder, her lips returning to color. "Seren," she murmured.

He brushed her bloodied, mangled hair out of her eyes.

"Princess Ata," he whispered. He felt the bonds tighten between them. "Tell me how to get us out of here."

"Portal," she whispered, her eyes still closed. "Behind...the tapestry."

Seren looked toward the colossal tapestry of twin snakes looming behind the assembly of thrones. He quickened his pace and ascended the steps. The blood-soaked stairs were slick, making it even more difficult.

Eden's cries echoed behind him, indicating she was still fighting off the oncoming horde.

As he reached the summit of the stairs, a demon's desperate grip snagged his ankle, sinking its teeth into his flesh. A sharp cry of pain escaped his lips as he fiercely shook off the creature. Undeterred, he sprinted across the expanse of the marble floor, closing in on the tapestry. With a forceful tug, it swung open, revealing a vast, ominous mirror. He secured the dagger on his hip and clutched Mila tightly with both hands.

"I'll find you!" Eden echoed behind him. "And I will learn your true name!"

Without looking back, Seren stepped through the portal. With Mila cradled against his chest, they hurtled into the unknown.

Twenty-Three

"Fate cannot be altered. It is what the Gods say. But I have seen fate, and it can be an ugly thing."

—Exorcist Damian Silver

1025 A.E.C.

Kogarashi had always been known as the land of eternal winter. The peaks of the mountains were adorned with a perpetual blanket of white, starker than even the clouds above. As Lumen passed through the outskirts of the country, his steps left traces in the fresh snow.

Legend had it that the God of Wisdom, Ryuama, wanted to create a land of continuous reflection, untouched by the rapid changes of seasons. Many traveled across the country seeking the guidance of the great God, Ryu. Even those with a dedication to other Gods had climbed the tallest mountain, Kazahana, seeking the great wisdom of the deity.

Passing through Kogarashi stirred bittersweet memories of Lumen's mother. Despite her union with a High Priest of Lumina, her heart had always belonged to her God. He could vividly recall her words, assuring him that he was blessed by the very hands of the God. Despite enduring ridicule for his distinctive appearance, Lumen found comfort when his mother described his skin as reminiscent of snow—untainted and pure. In her eyes, Lumen possessed a different perspective on life, one she believed to be bestowed wisdom. He treasured those moments where her love and acceptance were unwavering. However, the weight of Lumen's lineage loomed heavily upon him. He knew that he was a reflection of his father. Sometimes, it was as if his mother couldn't even bear to look at him.

Lumen's existence was only due to an unspeakable act that the High Priest often mentioned with cruel reminders. He was a product of a sinister violation, his true father leaving an indelible mark on his mother's life. Despite the man he called father vowing to raise him with love and care, Lumen found himself starved of such things.

As he journeyed toward his homeland, memories of his past relentlessly haunted him, refusing to escape. They served as a constant, painful reminder of his festering resentment toward the Gods. Countless times, he had confronted his adopted father about his purpose, desperately questioning why the Gods would bring him into existence as nothing more than a manifestation of an unforgivable sin. Yet, his father could only offer a somber truth in response—the Gods, in their boundless power, had also given birth to the personification of evil itself, the Devil.

As he neared Lumina, weariness seeped into Lumen's very bones, urging him to find respite. Although he had little desire for a detour, he knew there was a task he must fulfill before leaving the borders of Kogarashi. To his relief, he discovered that he still had several vials of the virus, unharmed despite his recent encounter with the bandits. Retrieving a few vials from his belongings, Lumen fastened them securely to Grimm's legs. With a command, he instructed the bird to unleash the contents upon the nearest unsuspecting town. The faster the virus spreads, the quicker people would see that prayer could not save them. It was what needed to be done. They needed to know the truth.

Grimm did not question or hesitate. He launched from Lumen's shoulder into the sky with a powerful thrust. There was no need to wait. Grimm always found his way back to Lumen. He pressed forward and continued to walk until lush grass finally replaced the crunch of snow underneath his feet.

Flowers of various hues danced in the wind across the valley. It was as he remembered. It had been nearly four years since he'd set foot in Lumina. The rolling green hills of the valley were a welcome sight after his tiresome journey through the Wastelands. He longed to collapse into the grass and take an afternoon nap, but he was too close to his destination.

With a deep breath, Lumen followed the dirt path that stretched before him, knowing which direction to go by heart. This road would lead him to the town of Merlock, where he could rest before traveling to Stellaris. Of course, Lumen had his money taken while in the Wastelands, which meant the sooner he was in Stellaris, the better.

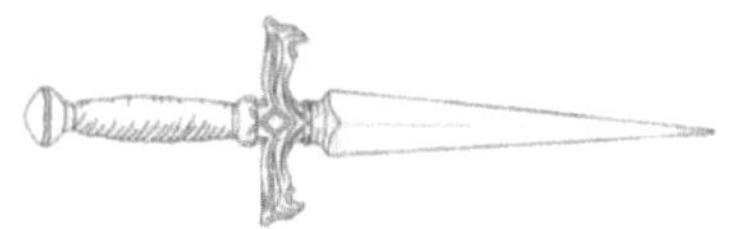

It didn't take very long for Lumen to reach Merlock. The streets were bustling and full of excitement. It appeared the festival for the Spring Equinox was only days away. Children ran through the streets, giggling and laughing, their hair weaved full of flowers.

Carts filled to the brim with flowers lined the sides of the streets as the townsfolk busily prepared for the grand celebration. Each cart showcased an array of blossoms meticulously selected to honor the Gods of the Trinity. Towering sunflowers, for Helios, bathed in golden hues of sunlight. The delicate moonflowers, which only bloomed under a moonlit sky, were included for Kallista. And there, amidst the floral symphony, the starflowers, representing Caelum, twinkled, their petals resembling the very stars that decorated the heavens.

Lumen had never found much joy in these pointless festivals. It bewildered him to see the townsfolk investing their precious time and energy into these events, pretending that the Gods protected them from the Veil.

Lost in his thoughts, Lumen was caught off guard by the sudden impact of a child crashing into him. He found himself thrust into the dirt. He clenched his fist, ready to curse at the child, when a hand reached out to help him to his feet.

"I do apologize," said the woman. "My nephew isn't always very observant."

Lumen accepted her hand, feeling his legs shake beneath him. "It's fine," he replied. "Most children are that way." He dusted his clothes off with a sigh.

The woman's smile revealed lovely laugh lines on her dark skin. "You don't look like you are from around here," she remarked. "Could I offer you any help?"

"I'm afraid not," Lumen answered. "I am headed to Stellaris. I was robbed on my travels here, so I cannot purchase a horse as I hoped." He offered her an innocent smile. "But don't let me dump my troubles on you. I'll be on my way. I have a long walk ahead of me."

As he walked past the woman, her hand reached out, gingerly pulling the fabric of his shirt. "I am headed to Stellaris for my sister this afternoon to get some salves from the apothecary. You're thin enough. It should be no problem fitting on my horse with me."

Lumen was relieved. Although he missed the easy transportation of Vavilon, a horse would hasten his travels. It truly amused him that so many people refused to adapt to the technologies that the Godless City offered, even after all these years. The importance of faith overshadowed all else.

"I would appreciate that. Thank you."

The woman informed him she had a couple of errands to take care of before doing so and suggested he stroll the streets before they left. Lumen thanked her and decided to sit on a nearby bench, resting his tired body. He closed his eyes, feeling the spring breeze ripple through his hair. Even the smell of the air was nostalgic, carrying the aromas of the many flowers of Lumina.

"Excuse me, mister!"

Lumen jolted awake, having faded into sleep without realizing it. The same child who had run into him earlier hovered above him. He shrank back from the child.

"You dropped this earlier."

The boy revealed Lumen's bandolier, which held all his vials, hanging it above Lumen's lap. He quickly snatched it from the child with a scowl.

"You'd do well to keep your hands to yourself," Lumen scolded.

The boy said nothing and hurried away fearfully. Lumen grumbled to himself, slinging it over his shoulder. How had he been so careless not to realize he was missing it? The exhaustion was taking a toll on him.

Within a few minutes, the woman returned with her handsome black stallion. Lumen felt relieved as she waved him over from the side street. He weaved through the citizens, making his way over to her. She climbed upon the horse and extended her hand. Accepting her hand, Lumen pulled himself onto the horse's broad back.

A wave of gratitude washed over Lumen as he realized the woman accompanying him seemed content with silence. He was in no mood for tedious conversations. In fact, his mind was elsewhere. He couldn't stop thinking about Grimm's question several days before. He glanced down at his hands, the black veins throbbing in his palms. If he had killed the boy, his fate would have been sealed. But still. Without his wings— his true form of divinity—Seren could not cleanse the Veil. Yes, Lumen had nothing to worry about. The boy would become desperate and that's exactly what Lumen needed.

A sly smile played across his lips as he envisioned the pieces falling into perfect alignment. The Gods would find themselves vulnerable, and Seren, unwittingly entangled in his scheme, would become a pawn in a deadly game of manipulation.

Godkiller. Lumen shuddered deliciously. That's what they would call him.

Around three miles into their journey, Lumen's keen eyes caught sight of Grimm soaring ahead in the sky. Observant as always, Grimm was intelligent enough to discern that keeping a distance was best for now. The raven would be seen as nothing more than an abomination, a creature that had escaped its *fate*.

After what felt like an arduous two-hour ride, the vibrant town of Stellaris finally came into view. Its streets were abuzz with life, teeming with people. Stellaris, boasting numerous shops, overshadowed Merlock in size. It was a colorful town; the cream buildings sported vibrant red roofs, and portrayals of the Gods were everywhere to be seen. Painted across fences, sides of buildings, and the sidewalk were the unmistakable symbols of the sun, moon, and stars. In the center of the town stood a smooth, white marble fountain portraying the Moon Goddess, holding up a cauldron to the sky.

"Well, I'm off to the apothecary. Is this alright for you?" the woman asked.

"Yes, thank you. I'll be on my way," Lumen said.

As he dismounted from the horse, Lumen swayed on his feet. Once the woman had disappeared, Grimm descended from above, landing carefully on Lumen's shoulder.

"The deed is done," the raven confirmed. "Where to now?"

"You'll see. We are close."

Lumen adjusted the bandolier on his shoulder and had a sudden urge to peer inside. He opened it up and cursed loudly.

"What is it, master?" Grimm asked, peeking into the bag.

"That little brat snatched a vial," Lumen growled.

Despite the setback, he knew turning back around was not an option. Without another word, Lumen closed the bandolier and continued forward. He strode through the busy streets, observing similar festivities around the town—a medley of colors and sounds. Navigating through the crowds was a nuisance, but Lumen pressed on. At last, he managed to break free from the commotion, heading down a cobblestone path bordered by familiar buildings, leading him exactly where he needed to go.

As Lumen rounded a corner, passing the weapons shop, an impressive sight unfolded before him—the Church of Caelestis. In the distance, it sprawled like a castle on the horizon.

"You're not heading there, are you?" An elderly man, leaning against the wall of the weapons shop, scrutinized Lumen. "Haven't you heard? They say the High Priest committed blasphemy, leading to the Unveiling that happened a few years ago. That church is now tainted with a curse if you ask me. If you're in need of assistance or a High Priest, I would head north to Sanctus. It isn't far."

Lumen sighed and rolled his eyes. "Well, I certainly didn't ask you, did I?"

"Don't say I didn't warn you," said the man. He promptly disappeared inside the shop while grumbling under his breath.

Unfazed by the man's warnings, Lumen continued down the path. Even he could not deny that the craftsmanship dedicated to the Church of Caelestis was impeccable. The three spires were each adorned with stained-glass windows made with stunning hues handpicked for each of the stories they told. Ivy crept upwards, embracing the walls and threatening to cover the windows. Even in its state of neglect, it was a masterful piece of architecture.

A sea of hellebores engulfed the grass, their touch tickling Lumen's ankles as he made his way toward the doors. He came to a halt, his gaze fixated on the towering eastern church spire. The once-vibrant stained glass was now covered in cobwebs. The crystalline blues revealed the portrayal of the Fallen—angels who, driven by a zealous pursuit to cleanse the Veil, had themselves succumbed to corruption. Now, the most powerful demons in existence were cursed to wander the Veil for eternity. Pure angels had existed in a time preceding the fracturing of the Gods, when they reigned united, sharing power. Lumen found it difficult to fathom that there was once an era where all the Gods had been followed equally.

In front of the carved doors of the Church of Caelestis, a brief hesitance overcame Lumen. Grimm ruffled his feathers as if sensing his master's unease. Finally, Lumen grasped the heavy doors and slowly pushed them open with a creak, revealing the church's interior.

Dust filled Lumen's lungs, causing him to cough uncontrollably. "Disgusting," he croaked. He wiped his watering eyes with another hack.

The tiles echoed beneath Lumen's footsteps as he walked into the corridor, his eyes intentionally avoiding the painting he had stared at countless times as a child. The depiction of the Tree held no appeal for him, and the story of Adamus and Eden on the walls of the Eastern chamber failed to capture his interest. Yet, inexplicably, the mural of the great Mother Goddess always halted him in his tracks. However, this time, for some reason, he couldn't bring himself to look at her.

Thick layers of dust and cobwebs coated everything in sight. Lumen stopped for a moment, pausing at the portraits of the many generations of High Priests. Just as Lumen remembered, his adopted father was portrayed in the painting. The constant frown lines on his face appeared to be etched permanently into his skin, while his robes remained impeccable, devoid of any wrinkles. With a slight smile, Lumen brushed his fingers across the painting.

"I wonder if you knew that even the Devil has a purpose," Lumen murmured. "For how could light exist without the dark?"

Making his way through the church, Lumen noticed the eerie emptiness that filled the air. It wasn't unexpected, but still strange to witness. Pausing at the doors leading to the garden, he took a minute to absorb the stillness that surrounded him.

With a final deep breath, Lumen pushed the door open, shielding his eyes from the bright rays of sunlight. The yellow rose bushes were in full bloom in the garden, forming a vibrant maze. As Lumen navigated through, he carefully stepped over the entanglements of flowers and thorns, noticing the neglect that had befallen the garden over time. He weaved his way through until, at last, he caught sight of him.

Sitting on a bench in the garden, the High Priest of the church held a yellow rose stem between his slender fingers. Deliberately, he pressed his fingertip onto a thorn, watching the fresh blood trickle down his finger. His ink-black hair was disheveled and unwashed, and even his robes appeared dirty.

As Lumen stepped out into the open, feeling the sun beam upon his head like a halo, the priest's head lifted, and his eyes met Lumen's. The rose slipped from his hand, falling to the ground.

Lumen smiled. "Hello, brother. It's been a long time."

Acknowledgements

I want to start off by thanking both of my parents. Both of you have supported my dream to become an author since I was little. When describing my future as an author, you both always said "when" and never saying "if." Even when I doubted myself many times, neither of you ever doubted me for a second.

A special thanks goes to my little brother, Seth, for taking the time to read my initial draft and provide constructive criticism that greatly improved my book. I knew I could count on you and your blunt honesty. Your support and willingness to listen to my endless story-related rambles meant the world to me. I hope you're prepared to deal with that until the series is over!

To my grandparents, you both have always supported me and my dreams. Grandma Terry, thank you for all the times you supported my book addiction as a child. Many of my fondest memories are spent reading my piles of new books on hot summer days on your porch swing.

I also want to thank the new friends I've met as a debut author. Victor Cabinita, author of the debut *Superstring*, I'm so grateful to call you a friend and I cannot wait to read your novel. Kita Smith, author of the debut *A Mind of Magic.* I adore you so much, and I only wish we lived closer, so we could enjoy Hobbiton together! Thank you to Maressa Voss, author of, *When Shadows Grow Tall*. She was an amazing beta-reader and pushed me in the right direction.

Last but certainly not least, a big thank you to my husband, Dylan. Your patience with my hours spent in front of the laptop and your willingness to hear me out on every nuance of my book lore mean the world to me. As the greatest Dungeon Master and an amazing storyteller, you've helped me so much with this story. You dedicated yourself to my story, and for that I am forever grateful.

Writing a book is no easy task but the support of my family and friends has helped my motivation immensely.

About the Author

K.C Wassem lives in Oregon with her four children and her husband. She is a stay-at-home mom, and often found wrangling children. K.C has dreamt of being an author since she was seven years old and hopes to gain readers that love her characters as much as she does. She is currently working on the second book in the series.